An Asimov Companion

CRITICAL EXPLORATIONS IN SCIENCE FICTION AND FANTASY
(a series edited by Donald E. Palumbo and C.W. Sullivan III)

1 *Worlds Apart? Dualism and Transgression in Contemporary Female Dystopias* (Dunja M. Mohr, 2005)

2 *Tolkien and Shakespeare: Essays on Shared Themes and Language* (ed. Janet Brennan Croft, 2007)

3 *Culture, Identities and Technology in the* Star Wars *Films: Essays on the Two Trilogies* (ed. Carl Silvio, Tony M. Vinci, 2007)

4 *The Influence of* Star Trek *on Television, Film and Culture* (ed. Lincoln Geraghty, 2008)

5 *Hugo Gernsback and the Century of Science Fiction* (Gary Westfahl, 2007)

6 *One Earth, One People: The Mythopoeic Fantasy Series of Ursula K. Le Guin, Lloyd Alexander, Madeleine L'Engle and Orson Scott Card* (Marek Oziewicz, 2008)

7 *The Evolution of Tolkien's Mythology: A Study of the History of Middle-earth* (Elizabeth A. Whittingham, 2008)

8 *H. Beam Piper: A Biography* (John F. Carr, 2008)

9 *Dreams and Nightmares: Science and Technology in Myth and Fiction* (Mordecai Roshwald, 2008)

10 Lilith *in a New Light: Essays on the George MacDonald Fantasy Novel* (ed. Lucas H. Harriman, 2008)

11 *Feminist Narrative and the Supernatural: The Function of Fantastic Devices in Seven Recent Novels* (Katherine J. Weese, 2008)

12 *The Science of Fiction and the Fiction of Science: Collected Essays on SF Storytelling and the Gnostic Imagination* (Frank McConnell, ed. Gary Westfahl, 2009)

13 *Kim Stanley Robinson Maps the Unimaginable: Critical Essays* (ed. William J. Burling, 2009)

14 *The Inter-Galactic Playground: A Critical Study of Children's and Teens' Science Fiction* (Farah Mendlesohn, 2009)

15 *Science Fiction from Québec: A Postcolonial Study* (Amy J. Ransom, 2009)

16 *Science Fiction and the Two Cultures: Essays on Bridging the Gap Between the Sciences and the Humanities* (ed. Gary Westfahl, George Slusser, 2009)

17 *Stephen R. Donaldson and the Modern Epic Vision: A Critical Study of the "Chronicles of Thomas Covenant" Novels* (Christine Barkley, 2009)

18 *Ursula K. Le Guin's Journey to Post-Feminism* (Amy M. Clarke, 2010)

19 *Portals of Power: Magical Agency and Transformation in Literary Fantasy* (Lori M. Campbell, 2010)

20 *The Animal Fable in Science Fiction and Fantasy* (Bruce Shaw, 2010)

21 *Illuminating* Torchwood: *Essays on Narrative, Character and Sexuality in the BBC Series* (ed. Andrew Ireland, 2010)

22 *Comics as a Nexus of Cultures: Essays on the Interplay of Media, Disciplines and International Perspectives* (ed. Mark Berninger, Jochen Ecke, Gideon Haberkorn, 2010)

23 *The Anatomy of Utopia: Narration, Estrangement and Ambiguity in More, Wells, Huxley and Clarke* (Károly Pintér, 2010)

24 *The Anticipation Novelists of 1950s French Science Fiction: Stepchildren of Voltaire* (Bradford Lyau, 2010)

25 *The* Twilight *Mystique: Critical Essays on the Novels and Films* (ed. Amy M. Clarke, Marijane Osborn, 2010)

26 *The Mythic Fantasy of Robert Holdstock: Critical Essays on the Fiction* (ed. Donald E. Morse, Kálmán Matolcsy, 2011)

27 *Science Fiction and the Prediction of the Future: Essays on Foresight and Fallacy* (ed. Gary Westfahl, Wong Kin Yuen, Amy Kit-sze Chan, 2011)

28 *Apocalypse in Australian Fiction and Film: A Critical Study* (Roslyn Weaver, 2011)

29 *British Science Fiction Film and Television: Critical Essays*
(ed. Tobias Hochscherf, James Leggott, 2011)

30 *Cult Telefantasy Series: A Critical Analysis of* The Prisoner, Twin Peaks, The X-Files, Buffy the Vampire Slayer, Lost, Heroes, Doctor Who *and* Star Trek (Sue Short, 2011)

31 *The Postnational Fantasy: Essays on Postcolonialism, Cosmopolitics and Science Fiction* (ed. Masood Ashraf Raja, Jason W. Ellis and Swaralipi Nandi, 2011)

32 *Heinlein's Juvenile Novels: A Cultural Dictionary* (C.W. Sullivan III, 2011)

33 *Welsh Mythology and Folklore in Popular Culture: Essays on Adaptations in Literature, Film, Television and Digital Media* (ed. Audrey L. Becker and Kristin Noone, 2011)

34 *I See You: The Shifting Paradigms of James Cameron's* Avatar (Ellen Grabiner, 2012)

35 *Of Bread, Blood and* The Hunger Games: *Critical Essays on the Suzanne Collins Trilogy* (ed. Mary F. Pharr and Leisa A. Clark, 2012)

36 *The Sex Is Out of This World: Essays on the Carnal Side of Science Fiction* (ed. Sherry Ginn and Michael G. Cornelius, 2012)

37 *Lois McMaster Bujold: Essays on a Modern Master of Science Fiction and Fantasy* (ed. Janet Brennan Croft, 2013)

38 *Girls Transforming: Invisibility and Age-Shifting in Children's Fantasy Fiction Since the 1970s* (Sanna Lehtonen, 2013)

39 Doctor Who *in Time and Space: Essays on Themes, Characters, History and Fandom, 1963–2012* (ed. Gillian I. Leitch, 2013)

40 *The Worlds of* Farscape: *Essays on the Groundbreaking Television Series* (ed. Sherry Ginn, 2013)

41 *Orbiting Ray Bradbury's Mars: Biographical, Anthropological, Literary, Scientific and Other Perspectives* (ed. Gloria McMillan, 2013)

42 *The Heritage of Heinlein: A Critical Reading of the Fiction Television Series* (Thomas D. Clareson and Joe Sanders, 2014)

43 *The Past That Might Have Been, the Future That May Come: Women Writing Fantastic Fiction, 1960s to the Present* (Lauren J. Lacey, 2014)

44 *Environments in Science Fiction: Essays on Alternative Spaces* (ed. Susan M. Bernardo, 2014)

45 *Discworld and the Disciplines: Critical Approaches to the Terry Pratchett Works* (ed. Anne Hiebert Alton and William C. Spruiell, 2014)

46 *Nature and the Numinous in Mythopoeic Fantasy Literature* (Christopher Straw Brawley, 2014)

47 *J.R.R. Tolkien, Robert E. Howard and the Birth of Modern Fantasy* (Deke Parsons, 2014)

48 *The Monomyth in American Science Fiction Films: 28 Visions of the Hero's Journey* (Donald E. Palumbo, 2014)

49 *The Fantastic in Holocaust Literature and Film: Critical Perspectives* (ed. Judith B. Kerman and John Edgar Browning, 2014)

50 Star Wars *in the Public Square: The Clone Wars as Political Dialogue* (Derek R. Sweet, 2016)

51 *An Asimov Companion: Characters, Places and Terms in the Robot/Empire/Foundation Metaseries* (Donald E. Palumbo, 2016)

52 *Michael Moorcock: Fiction, Fantasy and the World's Pain* (Mark Scroggins, 2016)

An Asimov Companion

Characters, Places and Terms in the Robot/Empire/ Foundation Metaseries

DONALD E. PALUMBO

CRITICAL EXPLORATIONS IN
SCIENCE FICTION AND FANTASY, 51

Series Editors Donald E. Palumbo *and* C.W. Sullivan III

McFarland & Company, Inc., Publishers
Jefferson, North Carolina

Portions of this work originally appeared as "Psychohistory and Chaos Theory: The 'Foundation Trilogy' and the Fractal Structure of Asimov's Robot/Empire/Foundation Metaseries," *The Journal of the Fantastic in the Arts* 7:1, pp. 23–50, and are reproduced by permission of the publisher.

LIBRARY OF CONGRESS CATALOGUING-IN-PUBLICATION DATA

Names: Palumbo, Donald, 1949– author.
Title: An Asimov companion : characters, places and terms in the Robot/Empire/Foundation metaseries / Donald E. Palumbo.
Description: Jefferson, North Carolina : McFarland & Company, Inc., Publishers, 2016. | Series: Critical explorations in science fiction and fantasy ; 51 | Includes bibliographical references and index.
Identifiers: LCCN 2016012529 | ISBN 9780786498239 (softcover : acid free paper) ∞
Subjects: LCSH: Asimov, Isaac, 1920–1992—Encyclopedias. | Asimov, Isaac, 1920–1992. Foundation series. | Science fiction, American—Encyclopedias. | Chaotic behavior in systems in literature. | Robots in literature.
Classification: LCC PS3551.S5 Z77 2016 | DDC 813/.54—dc23
LC record available at https://lccn.loc.gov/2016012529

BRITISH LIBRARY CATALOGUING DATA ARE AVAILABLE

ISBN (print) 978-0-7864-9823-9
ISBN (ebook) 978-1-4766-2394-8

© 2016 Donald Palumbo. All rights reserved

No part of this book may be reproduced or transmitted in any form or by any means, electronic or mechanical, including photocopying or recording, or by any information storage and retrieval system, without permission in writing from the publisher.

Front cover image © 2016 Vladyslav Otsiatsia

Printed in the United States of America

McFarland & Company, Inc., Publishers
 Box 611, Jefferson, North Carolina 28640
 www.mcfarlandpub.com

Table of Contents

Introduction:
Asimov's Robot/Empire/Foundation
Metaseries and Chaos Theory   1

THE ENCYCLOPEDIA   31

Index   185

Introduction: Asimov's Robot/Empire/Foundation Metaseries and Chaos Theory

Isaac Asimov's "Foundation Trilogy," recipient of a special Hugo Award for Best All-Time Science Fiction Series, probably is the most enduring and highly regarded science fiction "trilogy" ever written. A trilogy only by assertion and publication history, it is composed of five short stories and four novellas published serially between 1942 and 1950 that were republished as a trilogy in the early 1950s. Since its initial publication Asimov has extended the trilogy—by the addition of four novels published between 1982 and 1993—into a seven-volume series; in doing so, he also integrated this expanded Foundation series into a grand design of fifteen interrelated books and seven additional short stories that contain sixteen robot stories, Asimov's four robot novels, and Asimov's three Empire novels as well. Asimov himself asserts the existence and integrity of this metaseries—and lists those books that comprise it—in his "Introduction" to *Prelude to Foundation* (ix), the penultimate volume published in the metaseries. Examining the Foundation Trilogy in the context of the Robot/Empire/Foundation Metaseries illuminates the surprisingly subtle artistry that makes the initial trilogy a science fiction monument through revealing an unusual, scientific aesthetic that unifies the metaseries on a deeply subliminal level.

While the artistry and integrity of the metaseries is the subject of this introduction, the bulk of this volume is an encyclopedia of all the characters, locations, artifacts, institutions, and concepts that appear in the metaseries: the nine stories in *I, Robot* and seven additional, subsequent robot stories that are clearly set in this same fictional universe ("Galley Slave," "Lenny," "Robot Dreams," "Feminine Intuition," "Too Bad!" "The

Bicentennial Man" and "Mirror Image"), the four robot novels (*The Caves of Steel, The Naked Sun, The Robots of Dawn,* and *Robots and Empire*), the three empire novels (*The Currents of Space; The Stars, Like Dust;* and *Pebble in the Sky*), the original Foundation Trilogy (*Foundation, Foundation and Empire,* and *Second Foundation*), and the four subsequently published foundation novels (*Prelude to Foundation, Forward the Foundation, Foundation's Edge,* and *Foundation and Earth*). Perhaps the most prominent artifact in the metaseries is the *Encyclopedia Galactica*, which is cited numerous times in all three volumes of the trilogy as well as in *Prelude* and *Forward* and which is central to the Foundation series' plot in that the compilation and publication of the *Encyclopedia* is the pretext for establishing the Foundation (technically, Encyclopedia Foundation Number One) on Terminus that is destined to evolve over a thousand years into the Second Galactic Empire and cut short a period of anarchy and barbarism that would otherwise have lasted 30,000 years. The citations from the *Encyclopedia Galactica* that appear in the Foundation series are all from the 116th edition, published in 1020 F.E. (over 500 years after the series concludes, in 498 F.E.).

As the "Foundation Trilogy" must overcome significant and conspicuous handicaps to succeed as a work of fiction, much less to occupy its niche as the "Best All-Time Science Fiction Series," the riddle of what is uniquely compelling about it—and why—is especially intriguing. None of its characters live for longer than two of its nine episodes; only a few are truly memorable—Hari Seldon (who dies before the second story begins), the Mule, and Arkady Darell (who appears only in the last novella); and none are fully realized or multi-dimensional. Lacking emotional complexity, hyper-rational, and subservient in action and motivation to the requirements of the plot—they are, at best, engaging but superficial puppets.

The setting, too, while often admired, is on reflection oddly unsatisfactory. Incredibly, in the twenty-three millennia that elapse in the metaseries since the invention of robots and hyper-spatial travel, there has been little technological innovation and less social evolution. The trilogy is set in an interstellar version of the collapsing Roman Empire; and while this provides the fantastic delight of old wine in a new bottle, it is a setting that any thoughtful consideration will find implausibly one-dimensional. Humanity in the quadrillions has managed to expand throughout the galaxy, and yet has either regressed or remained inexplicably stagnant in every other respect for 23,000 years. Rather than continue to advance scientifically, much less culturally or socially, it has in these millennia forgotten both robot technology and those secrets of longevity discovered by the robot novels' Spacers. And its political structure has reverted to a bureaucratic autocracy.

On the level of action, Asimov's superb plotting is hamstrung by limitations imposed upon it—ironically—by the trilogy's next strongest element, theme. "Violence ... is the last refuge of the incompetent"—Salvor Hardin's dictum in *Foundation* (84)—is a concise expression of the most explicit theme in both the trilogy and in all of Asimov's fiction: Conflict is best resolved through the application of reason, foresight, and cunning to outmaneuver an adversary and sidestep the wasteful irrationality of violence. Consequently, in Asimov's fiction generally violence is notably infrequent—but there is a compensatory reliance on scheming—so that climactic confrontations are often defused, if not finessed altogether; and conflict is frequently resolved through the end play of such devious plans, or the by-play of such colossal historical forces, that the central characters are often elsewhere when the resolution occurs and are sometimes completely powerless to influence it. Yet this self-imposed limitation is a literary victory, for Asimov's ingenious ability to engineer a compelling plot while avoiding violent conflict is as entirely successful as it is entirely admirable.

However, neither a stalwart theme nor Asimov's straightforward, lucid style is strong enough *per se* to overcome these remaining deficits in characterization and setting. Process of elimination suggests that the profound success of the Foundation Trilogy must be due to some comparably profound and compensating virtuosity in the only remaining aspect of fiction, structure (the plot's form)—as distinct from action (the plot's content)—and perhaps as well to some related holistic aesthetic that likewise transcends, or even transforms, the trilogy's narrative weaknesses. Indeed, instead of *preventing* the trilogy from being a masterpiece, flatness of character and setting reinforce one another and conspire together—with a serviceable simplicity of style and limited range of action—to *permit* it to be a masterpiece. For these other elements must be austere in order to accommodate a plot structure of such subtle intricacy that complexity of character, setting, or style would obscure its design. This deduction is further reinforced by the observation that Asimov replaces violent conflict with elaborate scheming, for this substitution generates an extraordinarily plot-intensive narrative (even for science fiction) that is the ideal medium for structural virtuosity, and one that can be most fully exploited when allowed the scope of a "trilogy," a series, and a metaseries. This introduction will reveal both the structural artistry of Asimov's Foundation Trilogy and the unique aesthetic of the relationship between architecture and premise in the Robot/Empire/Foundation Metaseries to argue that it is both structure and the relationship between structure and premise that make the trilogy a popular phenomenon and the metaseries a stunning, extended masterpiece.

In *Forward the Foundation*, his last novel and the work that completes the metaseries, Asimov directs attention to his structural artistry by speaking to the reader through the Emperor's palace gardener, Gruber, who asks First Minister Seldon, "Have you ever *seen* the geometry of the grounds? ... I mean the plans spread out so you can really appreciate it—and marvelous it is, too" (120). Accepting Asimov's immodest invitation, the reader observes that the architecture of the metaseries is that of a trilogy that contains trilogies that contain trilogies—a grand, yet elegantly simple repetition of detail on descending levels of scale. (See Figure 1.) The metaseries is itself a trilogy of three component series. The middle series is the trilogy of Empire Novels—*The Currents of Space*, *The Stars, Like Dust*, and *Pebble in the Sky*—and each end series, the robot books and stories and the Foundation novels, is yet another trilogy of sets of books in which the middle element is again another trilogy. The robot books and stories consist of *I, Robot* and the remaining robot stories, a central trilogy containing the three Elijah Baley novels—*The Caves of Steel*, *The Naked Sun*, and *The Robots of Dawn*—and a final novel, *Robots and Empire*. This organization is indicated both by the content of the volumes and by their relationship to one another in time. All the robot stories except "Mirror Image," which is a Baley story as well, occur within the next several hundred years or so; after an interval of another 2,600 years, the three Baley novels all take place in a three-year period; and *Robots and Empire*, which occupies only about one year's time, begins two centuries after that. The three Baley novels form a central trilogy within this triad of sets of books not only because they occupy so brief a period within the time frame of the whole, while being separated from the events of the bracketing volumes by centuries or millennia, but also because they are the only novels in which detective Elijah Baley—Asimov's most fully-realized character—appears in real time.

The central Empire trilogy, which occurs over two or three millennia, is likewise separated by still greater gulfs of time from the sets of books bracketing it. It begins some five to six thousand years after *Robots and Empire* concludes, and it ends 11,193 years before the Foundation series

Opposite: **Figure 1. Self-Similarity of Metaseries' Architecture.**

Introduction

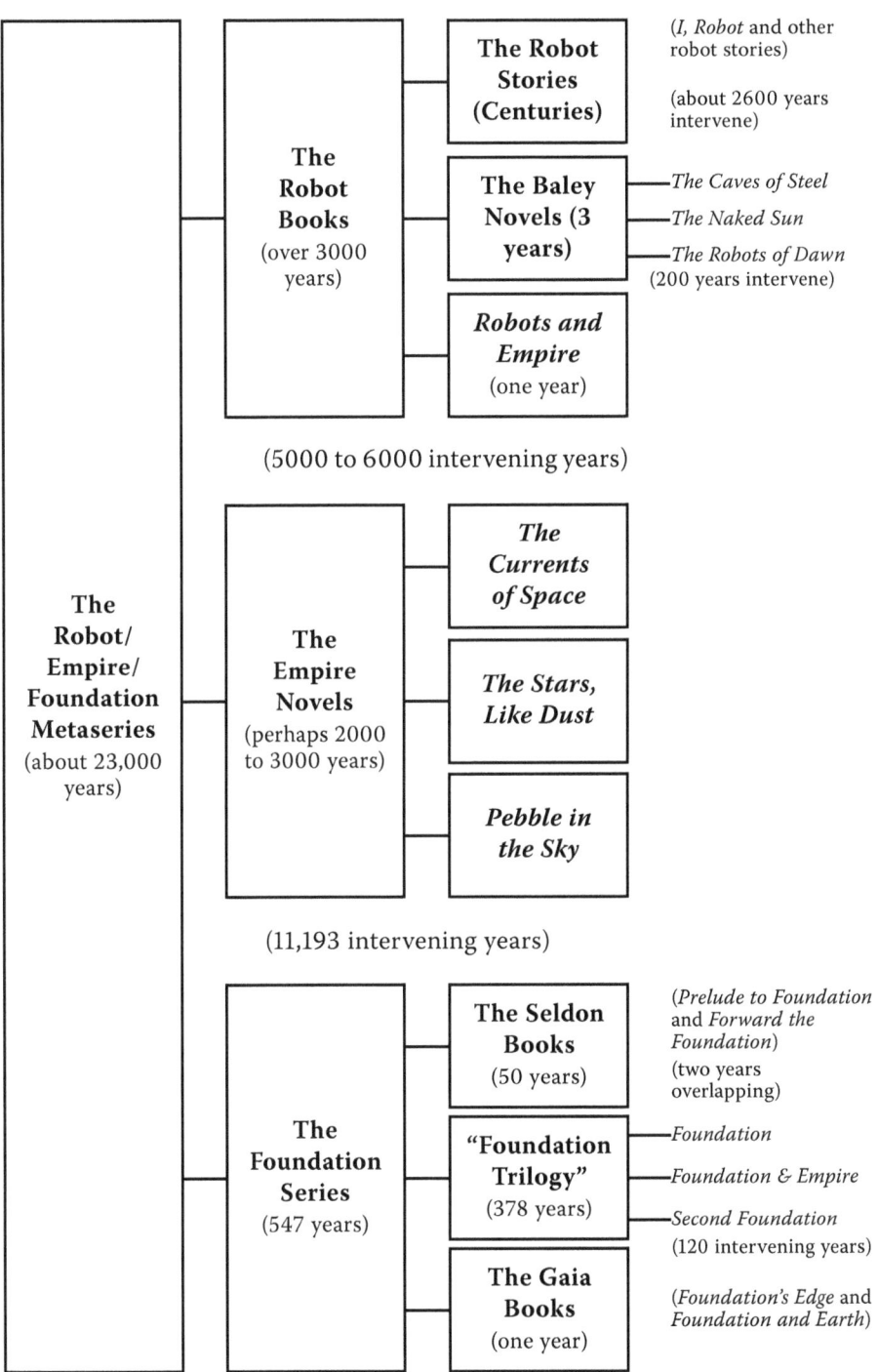

begins. The Foundation series consists of the two Seldon novels, *Prelude to Foundation* and *Forward the Foundation*, the Foundation Trilogy—*Foundation, Foundation and Empire,* and *Second Foundation*—and the two Gaia novels, *Foundation's Edge* and *Foundation and Earth*. Set in the fifty years immediately before the Foundation Trilogy, which it overlaps for two years, the Seldon novels are a unit because they relate the life of Asimov's second most fully-realized character, Hari Seldon. Beginning 120 years after the 378-year period chronicled in the Foundation Trilogy, the Gaia novels are a unit because they occupy only about one year's time between them and follow the same three protagonists—Golan Trevize, Janov Pelorat, and Bliss—through the same protracted adventure. Although there are sound structural reasons, discussed below, for packaging the nine episodes of the Foundation Trilogy as a trilogy—again, a central trilogy set in a triad of sets of books—this designation can rest simply on the works' publishing history.

The self-similarity of parts to each other and to the whole in this trilogies-within-trilogies-within-a-trilogy structure reveals that the "geometry of the grounds" of the metaseries is fractal geometry. "A visual representation of chaotic behavior," a fractal is an image "with an infinite amount of self-similarity" generated in "the realm of dynamical systems" by the "repeated application of an algorithm" or by the reiteration of recursive geometric procedures (*Fractal Mania* 20, 3–4, 14–15). "Above all, fractal [means] self-similar" (*Chaos* 103). And "'self-similarity' ... means a repetition of detail at descending scales" (*Turbulent Mirror* 90)—"pattern inside of pattern" (*Chaos* 103)—as well as duplication across the same scale. Thus, "the structure of the whole is often reflected in every part," and any part—although similarly rather than identically, when certain algorithms are used—might appear to be both "a small reproduction of the larger image" and a near-clone of innumerable like structures on the same scale (*Mania* 3).

Fractal geometry is indispensable to chaos theory—the study of orderly patterns in turbulent, dynamical, or erratic systems—because only nonlinear equations can model such systems, and "the structures that provide the key to nonlinear dynamics proved to be fractal" (*Chaos* 114). In *Prelude*, published in 1988, Asimov discusses the mathematics of psychohistory—the central concept in the metaseries that is particularly crucial to the Foundation Trilogy and the Foundation series—in such a way as to suggest that chaos theory is the extrapolated scientific idea behind psychohistory. Thus, the fractal architecture of the metaseries mirrors that structure essential to the scientific theory underlying the metaseries' central concept.

Both the emergence of chaos theory and the discovery of fractals coincided with Asimov's transformation of the Robot, Empire, and Foundation stories and novels from three distinct sets of books, which did not all even appear to share a continuous imagined future, to the "unified" (*Prelude* ix) metaseries exhibiting the fractal structure described above. Chaos theory did not exist at the time *I, Robot* and the first two Baley novels, the three Empire novels, and the Foundation Trilogy were written and published in the 1940s and early 1950s. More than a quarter-century later, however, Asimov returned to these works and, in the last decade of his life, added the remaining six novels. These connect the settings and plots of the robot books and stories to those of the Empire and Foundation novels—and in thus re-forging them all into the metaseries radically change the structure of the books' relationship to one another. (See Figure 2.) By 1993 Asimov had strategically interspersed his six new novels among the nine books written earlier—placing a pair of companion novels after each initial triad of books—to refashion the earlier, discontinuous and linear structure into a coherent and self-similar, fractal structure. But by this time chaos theory had become a lively area of investigation, and Mandelbrot had long since invented and named fractal geometry.

Remarkably, however, this fractal architecture is merely the trivial case. For the metaseries exhaustively reproduces the reiterative structure of a fractal—this characteristic "self-similarity"—in its plots, themes, and motifs, its content, *while* displaying it superficially in its overall architecture, its form. The following are among those elements that recur again and again: feedback-loop-driven plots and the repetition of parallel plots as basic structuring mechanisms within and among novels (techniques that also indicate chaos-theory dynamics independently of, as well as via, the self-similarity produced by repetition); ubiquitous use of disguise (and frequently of disguise-within-disguise, echoing the pattern-within-pattern structure); the guardianship motif (developed, similarly, as a plan-within-a-plan); the quest or journey; the "dead hand" motif; the themes of mind control and "telepathic" robots; the telepathic cupid and robot lover motifs; the theme of overcoming one's programming; the ironic plot twist of victory snatched from defeat; the "murder in a locked room" mystery that must be solved to safeguard humanity's destiny; the irony of the murderer evading punishment; and the persistence of prejudice. Even more remarkably, although Asimov forged the metaseries' fractal architecture after the popularization of chaos theory, the many and subtle chaos-theory affinities in the metaseries' content are as evident in those volumes published over sixty years ago—and especially in the early robot stories and

Introduction

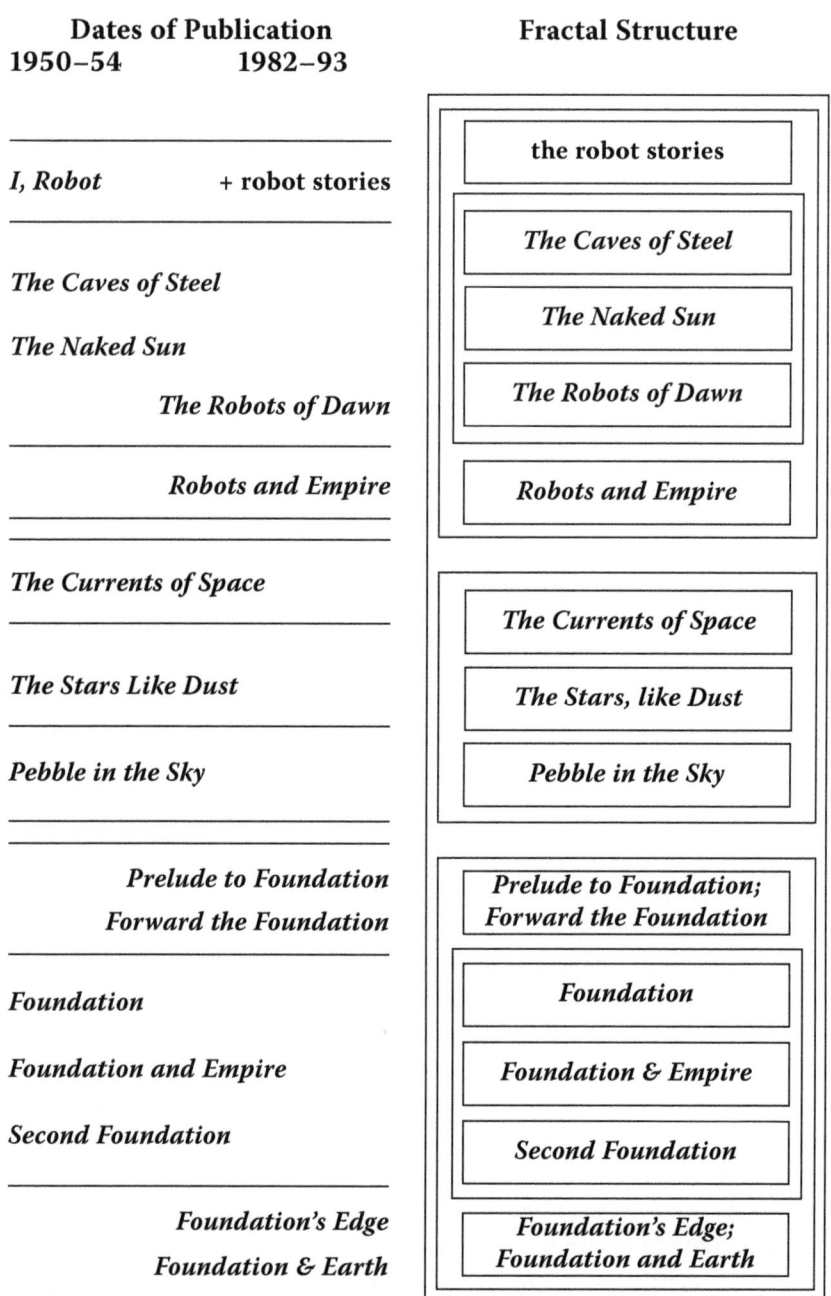

Figure 2. Evolution of the Metaseries' Fractal Architecture.

the Foundation Trilogy—as in the six novels published in the '80s and '90s. The scope of this introduction can but sketch the argument and provide only a few examples of only the first four of these elements: plot structure, disguise, the guardian motif, and the quest or journey.

If the plots, themes, and motifs as well as the architecture of Asimov's metaseries so thoroughly exhibit the fractal's defining characteristic of self-similarity, if the central concept of this metaseries is psychohistory, and if psychohistory is an extrapolation of chaos theory, then—as the fractal is the essential chaos theory structure—the metaseries echoes in both its content and its form the scientific idea underlying its central concept. This is a rarified aesthetic sophistication one might associate with the *nouvelle roman*—but not with science fiction. Yet Asimov's artistry is still one order of magnitude beyond even this. For, while the aesthetic effect of mirroring concept in both form and content *per se* could potentially be achieved given *any* concept, mirroring *is* the essence of *this* concept. Chaos theory's fundamental insight is precisely that the structure of the whole is mirrored in the structure of its parts; this is another way of expressing the self-similarity of the fractal image. Thus, this aesthetic effect of mirroring concept in both form and content in itself exhibits the fractal's defining element of self-similarity, pattern-within-pattern: The fractal image is a visual metaphor for this aesthetic effect, which is thus yet another reflection of the chaos-theory hypothesis supporting the core concept of psychohistory, but on a higher scale—beyond content and form, now on the plane of aesthetics. Form echoes content echoes concept in a metaseries in which the core concept *is* that form echoes content. Asimov's artistry is heightened exponentially through this reflection of concept in the self-similarity of content within a self-similar structure, producing a mirrors-within-mirrors-within-mirrors effect on the level of aesthetics—visual feedback as metaphor for aesthetic feedback—that is itself the archetype of the fractal's characteristic self-similarity.

An *Encyclopedia Galactia* excerpt from *Second Foundation*, published in 1953, asserts that the "basis" of psychohistory is "the synthesis of the calculus of n-variables and of n-dimensional geometry" (116); this suggests that psychohistory uses nonlinear, non–Euclidean math to analyze dynamical systems. Psychohistory employs "n-variables" because it must deal with the complexity of human behavior in its social context, with a dynamical system as a whole, not merely with its constituent parts. And "chaos is the science of the global nature of systems ... the universal behavior of complexity"; chaos theorists "feel that they are turning back ... the analysis of systems in terms of their constituent parts.... They believe that they are looking for the whole" (*Chaos* 5). Another definitive characteristic of a fractal is "fractional dimension," and the iterative equation in phase space that produces a fractal "isn't the plot of a shape as it is in Euclid. Rather, the equation provides the starting point for *evolving* a shape that emerges out of the equation's feedback" (*Mirror* 95, 104). Fractal geometry differs from Euclidean geometry precisely in that it *is* an "n-dimensional geometry" where "n" is not an integer (as it always is in Euclidean geometry, which deals only in one- two- or three-dimensional shapes), and where one can consider a 2.7-dimensional plane or a 1.34-dimensional line. This is "fractional dimension ... a way of measuring qualities that otherwise have no clear definition: the degree of ... irregularity of an object ... [which] remains constant over different scales" (*Chaos* 98). Euclidean shapes "represent a powerful abstraction of reality.... But for understanding complexity, they turn out to be the wrong kind of abstraction," whereas "chaos [theory] applies to the universe we see and touch" (*Chaos* 94, 6).

"Nonlinear equations [are] used to model turbulence" (*Mirror* 47)—chaotic currents in liquids and gasses—and "self-similarity [seems] to be the signature of turbulence, fluxuations upon fluxuations, whorls upon whorls" (*Chaos* 162). For turbulence exhibits a "fractal structure" in its spatial dimensions that may be governed by yet "another fractal structure that varies in time"; thus, "the study of turbulence" is "a subset of the growing field of chaos theory" (*Mirror* 105, 47). In *Prelude*, Seldon mentions that in studying "the mathematics of turbulence, which was my Ph.D. problem ... I saw ... that turbulence gave an insight into human society" (285). Here Seldon echoes physicist David Triton's conjecture that turbulence studies might even lead to understanding "the evolution of society"; even more pertinently, Seldon's thinking in developing psychohistory follows physicist Albert Libchaber's suggestion that turbulent flow may be like "flow in history," for "the laws of pattern formation are universal" (*Chaos* 42, 195, 311). Moreover, one familiar turbulent system, "the weather, is known to be a chaotic system" (*Mania* 2); "weather patterns ... are also now believed to be fractal" (*Mirror* 105). In fact, the first chaos-theory computer model was Edward Lorenz's 1960 meteorological simulation (*Chaos* 11). And—in addition to linking psychohistory to Seldon's studies in the mathematics of turbulence—Asimov suggests psychohistory's chaos-theory roots elsewhere in *Prelude* by constructing an analogy between psychohistory and meteorology. Seldon observes that "atmospheric behavior easily enters a chaotic phase" when a colleague suggests that he contact some university meteorologists who want to discover "the basic laws of general meteorology ... as much as you want your laws of psychohistory," but who are "as frustrated over their problems as you are over yours," on the chance that "you may learn something from meteorology that will help you with your psychohistory" (95–97 passim).

Much earlier in *Prelude*, Seldon asserts that "chaos turns out to have an underlying order" (11–12). And the work of chaos theorists demonstrates that "chaos ... [is] a subtle form of order"—not only that "chaos, irregularity, unpredictability ... have laws of their own," but also that "the sudden appearance of order out of chaos is the rule rather than the exception" (*Mirror* 45, 14, 43). In this same passage Seldon emphasizes the importance to psychohistory of choosing the right "starting point" and "appropriate assumptions that suppress the chaos, that will make it possible to predict the future" (*Prelude* 10). And "fractals are chaotic in that they're very sensitive to changes in initial conditions" (*Mania* 2, 20), the "starting point"; "tiny differences in input could quickly become overwhelming differences in output" (*Chaos* 8). Finally, Seldon cautions that "it is impossible to predict outcomes," that suppressing chaos "will make it possible to predict the future ... in broad sweeps; not with certainty, but with calculable probabilities" only (*Prelude* 10). And, while some chaotic systems are partially predictable, "in the nonlinear world [of chaotic systems]—which includes most of our real world—exact prediction is both practically and theoretically impossible" precisely because at "critical pressure points ... a small change can have a disproportionately large impact" (*Mirror* 24).

Later in *Prelude*, Seldon reiterates that he has proved,

> by making use of a mathematical technique first invented in this past century and barely usable even if one employs a large and very fast computer, [that] Galactic society ... *can* be represented by a simulation simpler than itself.... This would result in the ability to predict future events in a statistical fashion—that is, by stating the probability for alternate sets of events [148].

Analogous to Seldon's unnamed "mathematical technique," fractal geometry and chaos theory had just been developed in the decade before Asimov wrote *Prelude*, in "the 1970s, when mathematical advances and the advent of the high-speed computer enabled scientists to probe the complex interior of nonlinear equations" (*Mirror* 23). And chaos theory indicates that, even with access to unlimited data, some systems (like the weather) are inherently chaotic—unpredictable "because of the iterated nature of nonlinear equations (which represent the interconnected nature of dynamical systems)"—while others are not (*Mirror* 69). The premise of the Foundation series is that galactic society is one of those systems that is not inherently chaotic, that it is possible to "suppress the chaos" in the system. In his weather simulations, "Lorenz had found unpredictability, but he had also found pattern" (*Chaos* 44), after all. Asimov's is a science-fiction premise, however, because chaos theory currently suggests that any such galactic society—as it would involve aspects of time or history—*would* be a chaotic system, for "the dynamics of bifurcations ... reveal that time's ... branching takes place unpredictably" (*Mirror* 145). A chaotic "system is deterministic, but you can't say what it is going to do next" (*Chaos* 251).

Still, having initially proven the *theoretical* possibility of simulating galactic society, Seldon's problem throughout *Prelude* is that amassing the data required to do so may take "a billion years," due to that society's enormous size and complexity; if so, then psychohistory "will still be impractical" (148). His breakthrough idea, however, is the insight that "you might be able to work out psychohistory if you dealt with a much simpler Galactic society" (149), which leads to his crucial realization that Trantor itself—the most complex of the Galaxy's twenty-five million inhabited worlds, but still an infinitesimal part of the whole—can be a model for a simulation of galactic society; Seldon hopes to develop universal laws of psychohistory by studying Trantorian society, just as the Streeling University's meteorologists hope to "learn ... the basic laws of meteorology" by understanding "the weather change on Trantor" (96). Thus, what finally makes psychohistory *practical* as well as possible is precisely the *self-similarity* of the system, that is, its *fractal structure*; for the intuition that galactic society and its history *has* a fractal structure is implicit in Seldon's insight that a specific detail of the system (Trantor) can be treated as a replica of the whole (the inhabited galaxy). And galactic history's fractal structure is symbolically reproduced in the fractal structure of the metaseries that relates it.

However, the insight that history *per se* reveals a fractal structure is implicit in the fact that the Foundation Trilogy—which anticipates chaos theory by at least a quarter-century—is modeled on the history of western civilization generally and on the fall of the Roman Empire in particular. Indeed, Prigogine's theories regarding "the dynamics of bifurcations reveal that time is irreversible yet recapitulant"; although probably chaotic (unpredictable), like the weather, time may well be fractal in any case—possessing the fractal's quality of self-similarity—and "this [could] be why history seems both to repeat itself and never repeat itself" (*Mirror* 145, 108). Phil Laplante points out that time is, in fact, viewed as a chaotic system in all time-travel stories in which "the time traveller goes back and alters a course of events, even slightly, with traumatic consequences" (*Mania* 3). And the Foundation Trilogy is *like* a time-travel story in that a protagonist attempts to use knowledge of the future to alter that future. However, it is a fantastic reversal of the time-travel story, for Seldon does not go to the past to change it *or* send himself into the future to learn about it; rather, he projects a holographic image of himself into the future (via the Vault) to explain to its inhabitants how he has already altered the future from the past, revealing in the process that he has a greater knowledge of "the future" than do those living in it. This element of fantastic reversal is brilliantly compounded, of course, when it is itself reversed: for midway through the trilogy, after the infallibility of Seldon's predictions is established, one of them turns out to be wildly and catastrophically inaccurate due to the advent of the Mule.

Seldon's Plan is to reduce the thirty thousand years of anarchy that he foresees will follow the collapse of the first Galactic Empire to a single millennium by altering the course of future history through the precisely "appropriate" establishment of his Foundations. But instead of knowing specifically what the future holds through having been there—and then going to or returning to the past, which would in either case involve time travel, to perform some discrete action that will dramatically change that specific future—Seldon "knows" the future only "in broad sweeps," only "statistically," through psychohistory; thus, he can only attempt to alter the future "in broad sweeps," which requires the implementation of a much more massive change in the present than that usually attempted in time-travel stories—i.e., appropriately establishing the Foundations. This is a life-long effort that entails both the perfection of psychohistory itself and the struggle to set up the Foundations once psychohistory has indicated where and what they should be. That the future can be decisively altered only by such an enormous and sustained effort, rather than by some discrete or insignificant modification, is consistent with Asimov's premise that galactic society is a fractal but not an inherently chaotic system; for if it were inherently chaotic, like time in most time-travel stories, then a small change could radically affect its future—but unpredictably so.

In studying "the ways in which order falls apart into chaos [and] how chaos makes order," chaos-theory researchers observe that "feedback, like nonlinearity, embodies an essential tension between order and chaos"; in fact, "one difference between linear and nonlinear equations is feedback—that is, nonlinear equations have terms which are repeatedly multiplied by themselves" (*Mirror* 14, 26, 24). This reiterative nature of nonlinear equations generates feedback loops, which exist everywhere in real-world systems—as well as in nonlinear equations that attempt to describe them—precisely because their elements are mutually interdependent. Feedback loops "can stabilize a system as well as destabilize it" (*Chaos* 193). Negative feedback loops—such as those created by setting a thermostat or those that govern the population dynamics between predators and prey—regulate elements within a system to maintain the system's stability; positive feedback loops—such as those that create "ear-splitting screeches ... in a public address system"—can magnify "the smallest effects" into "indeterminate results" to destabilize a system (*Mirror* 24–28 passim; see also *Chaos* 61–63).

The grand sweep of action in the Foundation Trilogy (and the Foundation series), a counterpoint that again anticipates chaos theory, is that of order degenerating into chaos as that chaos gives birth to order: the disintegration of the Galactic Empire (also emphasized in the Seldon novels) set against the predestined growth and eventual hegemony of the First Foundation (also stressed in the Gaia novels). And every one of the Seldon crises—which are pivotal to the survival and growth of the First Foundation and, consequently, central to the plot of the first half of the Foundation Trilogy, until the Mule derails Seldon's plan—is resolved through the operation of a negative feedback loop in the system Seldon has analyzed, galactic society, that preserves the Foundation and directs its further development as it stabilizes the larger system. The first and fourth crises are especially clear examples of how the Seldon plan harnesses negative feedback loops in human society—employs the system's nonlinearity—to preserve and shape the First Foundation.

In the first crisis, occurring fifty years after the establishment of the Foundation on Terminus, this metal-poor and thus unarmed planet is about to be occupied and annexed by the Kingdom of Anacreon because it alone of the planets in its remote and peripheral region of the galaxy still possesses nuclear technology, making it a valuable military and economic prize. Resistance would be suicidal. Rather than engage the Anacreonians, however, Terminus' Mayor Salvor Hardin visits three other neighboring kingdoms and points out to each "that to allow the secret of nuclear power to fall into the hands of Anacreon was the quickest way of cutting their own throats." In response, the other kingdoms issue a "joint ultimatum" that forces Anacreon to back off. Refusing to resort to direct confrontation with one belligerent kingdom (which would be a linear reaction), Hardin instead "played them one against the other." He finesses the situation by relying on the political dynamics of the larger region to stop any one local kingdom, in this case Anacreon, from gaining control of the Foundation. In effect, regional politics here entails a regulatory, negative feedback loop that maintains the status quo—including, in this case, Terminus' independence—to preserve a delicate balance of power by preventing any one kingdom from becoming too strong (*Foundation* 106–7).

The fourth crisis, as it is the last to occur before the rise of the Mule, is the last in the Foundation Trilogy to proceed according to the Seldon Plan. About one hundred and fifty years after the Anacreon crisis, the Foundation has expanded its sphere of influence to the point where it has attracted the Empire's attention. General Bel Riose receives grudging Imperial authorization to reconquer the Foundation and initiates a foolproof military tactic, "inclosure," that assures the Foundation's imminent defeat. But on the brink of victory, the loyal Riose is abruptly recalled from the field to be tried and convicted as a traitor, and the Empire's all-but-successful war against the Foundation is abandoned. As amateur psychohistorian Ducem Barr explains after the fact,

> We can see, *now*, that the social background of the Empire makes wars of conquest impossible for it....
> Seldon ... knew that a man like Riose would have to fail, since it was his success that brought failure....
> Only the combination of a strong Emperor *and* a strong general can harm the Foundation; for a strong Emperor cannot be dethroned easily, and a strong general is forced to turn outwards, past the frontiers.
> But ... the Emperor ... is strong because he permits no strong subjects.... A general who becomes too popular is dangerous....
> Riose won victories, so the Emperor grew suspicious.... It was the *success* of Riose that was suspicious. So he was recalled, and accused, condemned, murdered. The Foundation wins again [*Foundation and Empire*, 80–81].

This time, political realities within the shrinking Empire entail another regulatory, negative feedback loop that causes the initial success of any expansive military venture to generate its own ultimate failure, thus precluding the possibility of the Empire reconquering lost territory—including the Foundation's expanding sphere of influence—despite its superior force. All the efforts of the Foundation's supporters to undermine Riose— the actual story of *Foundation and Empire*, "Part I"—are irrelevant, as they themselves finally realize, for history has done it for them.

Ironically, once Gaia's covert manipulations have moved galactic history back onto the track of the Seldon Plan some three hundred years later—at the time of Seldon's eighth predicted crisis—yet another regulatory, negative feedback loop engages that would prevent the Foundation itself, should it attempt to, from conquering the rest of the galaxy through superior force five centuries ahead of Seldon's schedule. Five hundred years into the reestablished Plan, the Foundation Federation controls half the galaxy and has the might to conquer the other half immediately, as Mayor Branno would like to do, rather than wait another half millennium. But, as Second Foundation Speaker Gendibal explains,

> If the Foundation moves too quickly ... it will deprive the rest of the galaxy of its greatest weakness—its disunity and indecision. You will force them to unite by fear, and you will feed the tendency toward rebellion within....
> You can establish a Second Foundation merely by proclaiming it, but you will not be able to maintain it. You will have to reconquer it every ten years....
> The Pseudo-Empire will break up into military regions.... There will be anarchy—and a slide back into barbarism that may last longer than the thirty thousand years forecast by Seldon [*Foundation's Edge* 404–5].

Of course, that the plot of the Foundation Trilogy hinges at every crucial point, until the intervention of the Mule, on precisely the same mechanism—the operation of regulatory, negative feedback loops—is one illustration of its self-similar structure as well as another, independent indication—as chaos theory includes the study of negative feedback loops—that psychohistory is an extrapolation of chaos theory.

But the Foundation Trilogy's plot is shaped by the appearance and reappearance of negative feedback loops only up until half way through the second volume. These feedback loops are those nonlinear features of Seldon's psychohistorical analysis of galactic society that his Plan utilizes to assure the future of the Foundation. And the Mule, a mutant whose mind-control power makes him an invincible conqueror, throws the Seldon Plan into disarray about one hundred years after Riose's defeat. In fact, in its fifth appearance in the Vault, the Seldon hologram describes a fifth crisis that again involves yet another negative feedback loop—a civil war, "the revolt of the Independent Traders ... against the [Foundation's] too-authoritarian central government," that should result in a stronger and more democratic "coalition government" (*Foundation and Empire* 149). But this fifth self-similar crisis never occurs; instead, the traders have united with the central government against the greater, external threat posed by the Mule—an anomaly not foreseen by Seldon—and the Foundation is nevertheless defeated.

But the appearance of the Mule is yet another chaos-theory dynamic as well as a fantastic reversal providing a narrative counterpoint to the Seldon Plan. Not only is he an unforeseen element that derails the Plan (a narrative analysis), his meteoric rise to power is also the type of amplification of a "small effect"—one individual's mutant ability—into "indeterminate results" destabilizing to a system that is the signal characteristic of a positive feedback loop (a chaos theory, dynamical systems analysis). This similarity of the Mule's ascent to the operation of a positive feedback loop is the obverse of the resolution of each legitimate Seldon crises, which occurs through the operation of a negative feedback loop.

However, the turn the plot takes after the Mule is introduced makes it only more obvious that self-similarity is *the* structuring principle in both the Foundation Trilogy and the Foundation series. While the plot of the first half of the trilogy exhibits self-similarity in the repetitive use of feedback loops, in the last two books of the trilogy and in *Foundation's Edge* as well the same basic plot itself is recycled five times. In fact, it is the repeated use of this self-similar plot structure that justifies the otherwise odd decision to publish the first half of the Mule's story as "Part II" of *Foundation and Empire* and its second half as "Part I" of *Second Foundation*. These two parts concern the same central character and are separated by only a five-year interval; they might constitute one novel, yet they occupy different volumes. And the first half of *Foundation and Empire* involves completely different characters and occurs a century earlier than the section involving the Mule, while the second half of *Second Foundation* has yet another completely different set of characters and occurs about seventy years afterwards.

Plot structure considerations take precedence over the logic of character and chronology here, however. For, as the volumes are constituted, the plot of "Part I" of *Foundation and Empire*, Riose's failed campaign, is repeated in "Part II," but with different details, and the plot of the first part of *Second Foundation* likewise repeats itself in that volume's second part. This packaging of the trilogy acknowledges the construction of dual parallel plots in these last two volumes, and thus emphasizes their self-similarity of plot. Moreover, the plot of "Part II" of *Second Foundation* is also a repetition with variations of the plot of "Part II" of *Foundation and Empire*, and this plot is again repeated *twice* in *Foundation's Edge*—in both tracks of its parallel-plot structure. (See Figure 3.)

In each half of *Foundation and Empire*, a would-be conqueror—Riose and the Mule, successively—employs both disguise and a scholar's unwilling assistance to locate one of the foundations, is suddenly defeated at the point of victory and under highly ironic circumstances, and that foundation is saved. Riose first investigates the First Foundation disguised as "a minor princeling of some scattered stars in an odd corner of the Periphery" (23). To learn more about the First Foundation and to locate it, Riose enlists the unwilling aid of scholar and amateur psychohistorian Ducem Barr, who opposes the Empire but assists Riose because "the general knows where to find" his children (46). The ironic circumstances of Riose's defeat on the brink of victory have already been discussed. One hundred years

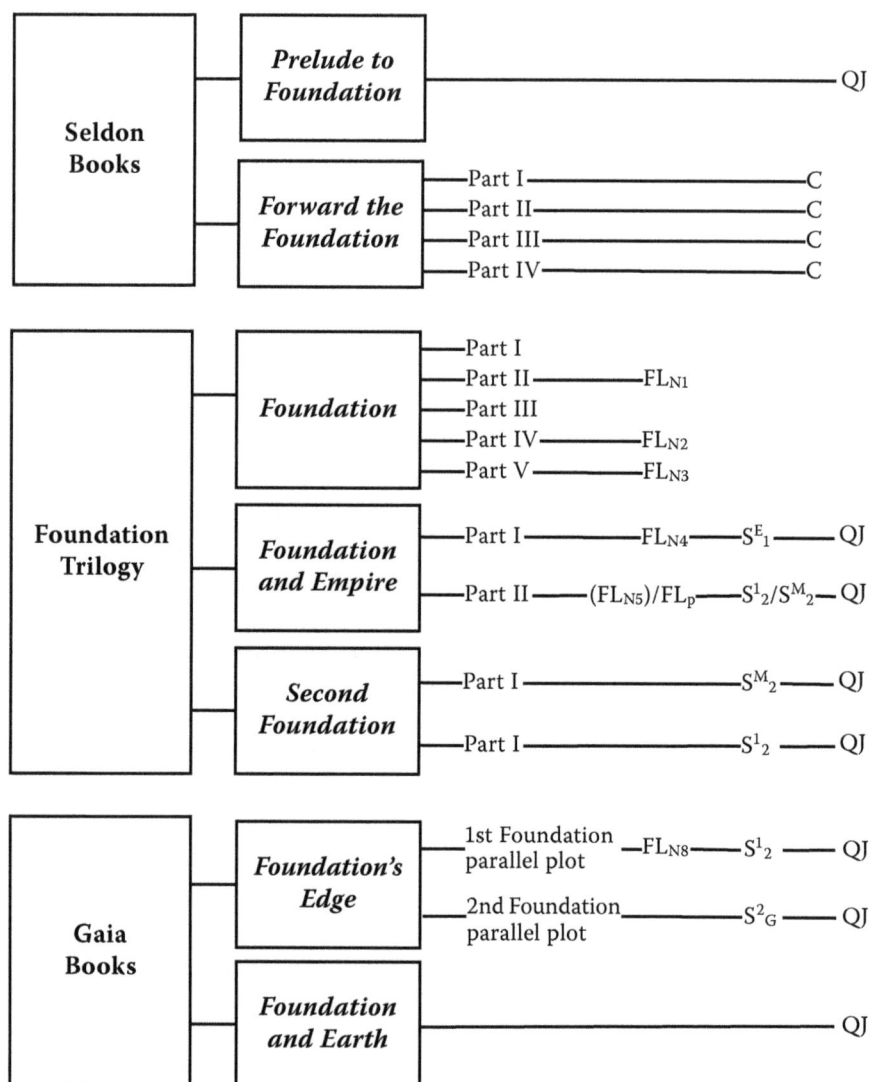

FL_{NX} = Negative Feedback Loop resolving a Seldon crisis [X = crisis]
FL_P = Positive Feedback Loop [the Mule]
( ) = predicted Seldon crisis that does not occur due to the Mule
S^Y_X = Searches by ^{Y} for $_X$: E = Empire; 1 = First Foundation; 2 = Second Foundation; M = Mule; G = Gaia
C = Counterpoint plot structure of progress balanced by loss
QJ = Quest Journey plot

Figure 3. Metaseries' Self-Similarity of Plot Structure.

later, the Mule poses as his own court clown, Magnifico Gigantus, and pretends to be fleeing in terror from himself. Thus disguised as a refugee who may possess valuable information about the Mule, he infiltrates a First Foundation expedition that is attempting to locate the Second Foundation in order to warn it of the threat the Mule poses. This expedition is led by Ebling Mis, the First Foundation's greatest scientist and another amateur psychohistorian, someone who would never aid the Mule knowingly. While disguised, the Mule uses his mental powers to drive Mis to solve the problem of the Second Foundation's location. (Ironically, Mis' need to study primary sources has taken them all to the Imperial Library on Trantor, which *is* the location of the Second Foundation.) But just as he is about to reveal this to Magnifico, Mis is killed by Bayta Darell, another member of the expedition who has deduced Magnifico's true identity.

A similar but more complex parallel plot recurs in the two parts of *Second Foundation*. In each part, two operatives embark on an expedition to seek the location of the Second Foundation so that the power they represent—the Mule again and the First Foundation, successively—can destroy it, but in each case one of the two operatives has been preconditioned by the Second Foundation and is unaware of that preconditioning. Three false hypotheses involving the Second Foundation's location are established in turn. After the collapse of the first hypothesis, however, the second is almost immediately exposed; for its only function is to give credence to a ruse that establishes the third hypothesis, which leads to an acceptance of the belief that the Second Foundation does not exist. Moreover, the Second Foundation is manipulating all events, and its stratagems entail several additional common factors: The Second Foundation has placed a mole in each core group seeking its location; it has arranged for the mole to be discovered and sacrificed so that he can credibly reveal misinformation that will establish one of these false hypotheses; and it must also sacrifice a much larger group to lend further credibility to its scheme.

Five years after *Foundation and Empire* concludes, the Mule sends Han Pritcher and Bail Channis out to locate the Second Foundation; but Channis is a Second Foundationer posing as a Mule's man who has been brainwashed, as a part of his cover, to believe that the Second Foundation is on the quiet world of Rossem. The Mule is led first to believe that the Second Foundation is on Tazenda (first false hypothesis); then on Rossem (second false hypothesis); and, once lured to Rossem, he is finally persuaded that he has been the victim of a Second Foundation plot that has drawn him from his base on Kalgan so that Second Foundation agents there could instigate a revolt in his absence (third false hypothesis). Then, taking advantage of the Mule's "despair of that moment" (93), the Second Foundation's First Speaker removes all knowledge of or interest in the Second Foundation from the Mule's mind—effectively persuading him that it does not exist. The Second Foundation plan sacrifices Tazenda, which the Mule destroys, and calls for Channis—the mole—to be discovered and sacrificed as well, to convince the Mule that Rossem is the home of the Second Foundation.

Seventy years later, a small group of First Foundation conspirators led by Toran Darrel sends Homir Munn, a librarian and an expert on the Mule, to Kalgan in the hope that he can discover the Second Foundation's location by investigating the Mule's records. Toran's teenage daughter Arkady, whose mind was altered at birth by the Second Foundation so that she will be an undetectable pawn in their plot, stows away on Munn's ship. Munn accurately concludes that the Mule believed there was no Second Foundation, and he is convinced of this himself (first false hypothesis). But it is later discovered that Munn's mind had been altered on Kalgan; this leads Anthor, another conspirator, to assert that the Second Foundation is on Kalgan (second false hypothesis). However, Toran deduces that Anthor is a mole—a Second Foundationer who has infiltrated his band of conspirators—and forces Anthor to confess that the Second Foundation is actually right there on Terminus (third false hypothesis). The First Foundation then finds and neutralizes fifty members of the Second Foundation planted on Terminus and, thus convinced that it is destroyed, concludes that the Second Foundation no longer exists. This Second Foundation plan sacrifices the fifty volunteers on Terminus and calls for Anthor to be discovered and sacrificed as well, to persuade Toran that Terminus is the home of the Second Foundation.

Moreover, similarities between the second parts of both *Foundation and Empire* and *Second Foundation* enhance further the trilogy's self-similar, and often similar but inverted, plot structure. The Mule, like Anthor (and, inversely, like Channis), is a mole who has infiltrated the First Foundation's search for the Second Foundation—although, again inversely, the first search seeks to save the Second Foundation, while the second seeks to destroy it. Munn, like Mis, is the First Foundation's leading authority in the area of expertise most immediately relevant to the search and is a scholar given the primary responsibility for conducting it. And, with a similar but inverted irony, while Mis conducts his search on Trantor under the mental influence of The Mule, initially unaware that he has already stumbled upon what he is looking for, Arkady flees from the Second Foundation—which she believes is on Terminus—to Trantor under the mental influence of the First Speaker, totally unaware that she has escaped to the very place she is trying to avoid.

Likewise, *Foundation's Edge* also involves a mole—the Gaian, Bliss—engaged in a search for the Second Foundation that recruits the First Foundation's leading authority in the most immediately relevant area of scholarly expertise—Janov Pelorat—but ends once more in the belief that the Second Foundation no longer exists. The parallel plotting of *Edge*, in which First Foundation agents (accompanied by Bliss) again seek the Second Foundation, while a Second Foundation Speaker (accompanied by another Gaian mole, Sura Novi) seeks Gaia, is especially similar—but at a higher pitch—to the parallel plotting of *Foundation and Empire*, in which Riose seeks the First Foundation and then First Foundation operatives (accompanied by the Mule, who is revealed to be a renegade Gaian in *Edge*) seek the Second Foundation. And, like *Foundation and Empire*'s and *Second Foundation*'s sequential twin plots, *Edge*'s simultaneous twin plots are also self-similar. The leader of the Second Foundation search, Stor Gendibal, is a doppelganger for the leader of the First Foundation search, Trevize, in whom he has "recognized a kindred spirit" (97). Trevize, the newest and youngest First Foundation Councilman, suspects that the Second Foundation still exists and is secretly controlling galactic history; Gendibal, the newest and youngest Second Foundation Speaker, suspects that a secret group with even more advanced mind powers—the Gaians, whom he calls the "Anti-Mules"—exists and is doing the same thing. As a result of voicing their respective conclusions, each is exiled and ordered on a covert mission—Trevize, to search for the lost planet Earth as a cover for seeking the Second Foundation, and Gendibal, to pursue Trevize as a cover for seeking Gaia. In the final standoff between the foundations, Gendibal and Trevize are each on identical spaceships—the only two of their design in existence—and each is aided by a disguised female Gaian serving as his bodyguard. (While Sura Novi masquerades as a Trantorian peasant woman, Bliss may be a robot pretending to be human.)

Like *Edge* and each volume in the Foundation Trilogy, *Forward the Foundation* is also composed of similar, repeated plot structures. Each of its four major "Parts" chronicles Seldon's continuing development of psychohistory but concludes with the permanent departure of that part's titular character from Seldon's life, and in the "Epilogue" Seldon dies just after completing his life's work. This cadence of death and loss along a life's path towards monumental achievement gives the novel its structural integrity as it again echoes chaos theory's emphasis on the interrelationship between chaos and order. And the various self-similar and similar to each other structures of *Forward*, of each volume of the Foundation Trilogy, and of *Edge* are framed by the quest journey structures of the first and last novels in the Foundation series—which, as quest journeys, are similar in structure to one another as well as to each of the paired quest journeys, the twinned searches, undertaken in *Foundation and Empire*, *Second Foundation*, and *Edge*. *Prelude*'s journey—a Grand Tour of Trantor—takes the form of Seldon's historic but spurious attempt to escape from the Empire's control and his simultaneous, genuine search for the knowledge that will enable him to develop psychohistory. And *Foundation and Earth*'s journey—a reverse retrospective of nearly every non–Trantorian locale in the series it concludes—is the long-deferred search for Earth.

Like the recurrence of similar plot structures, the recurrence of numerous similar themes and motifs is another locus of that pervasive self-similarity that characterizes the metaseries' fractal structure. The motifs of disguise and guardianship have a special status in the Foundation Series specifically, however, because they also occur on different "scales," are most comprehensively fractal, as they are integral to Seldon's concept of the Foundations in addition to being frequently repeated. Seldon's concept of the Foundations is rooted in the principle of guardianship and the necessity of disguise. The First Foundation is to be the guardian of galactic civilization in that it will "shorten the period of Barbarism that must follow [the Empire's collapse]—down to a thousand years" by serving as the nucleus for "a new and greater Empire" (*Foundation* 95–96). However, the First Foundation has been disguised for its first fifty years—even from its most intimate participants—as an encyclopedia project. And while the Second Foundation's location, "significance—and all about it—are better hidden, better obscured" than the location and significance of the First Foundation had ever been (*Foundation and Empire* 208), its purpose is "to be the strong, silent, secret bodyguard of the primary Foundation," to be the First Foundation's "guardians" (*Forward* 469, 379).

Moreover, just as Seldon's Second Foundation is the guardian of the First, so too is Gaia the guardian of both foundations and of psychohistory. And it is even more thoroughly disguised—as a myth that no one of any importance believes—than is the Second Foundation, for "neither Foundation is in the least aware that Gaia exists" (*Edge* 437). This plan-within-a-plan-within-a-plan scheme of guardianship (formulated over a 20,000-year period by the robot R. Daneel Olivaw) is again like the fractal's repetition of detail on descending scales. And so too is this series' several instances of disguise-within-disguise-within-disguise: for example, in *Forward*'s Mycogen episode alone Seldon's guardian, Dors, assumes three simultaneous levels of disguise to protect Seldon while humanity's guardian, Daneel, assumes four simultaneous levels of disguise to save them both. This pervasive disguise motif also mirrors chaos itself, which is "order *masquerading* as randomness," for "the fractal curve implies an organizing structure that lies hidden among the hideous complication of [the irregular and fragmented] shapes" of the real world (*Chaos* 22, 114; italics in original). And all the myriad specific instances of both disguise and guardianship in the Foundation novels become additional loci of self-similarity on ascending scales as they reflect Seldon's concept of the Foundations, a higher scale—which is itself an extension of Daneel's concept of protecting humanity, a still higher scale—as well as through their repetition on the lower scale represented by the action itself.

Yet there is a still more precise similarity between the concepts of the Foundations and of Gaia and many of the specific examples of disguise and guardianship that occur in the Foundation series. More than merely being its hidden guardian, the relationship of Gaia to the foundations, and of the Second Foundation to the First, is that of a more evolved and feminine entity acting as the hidden bodyguard of a more ingenuous and masculine entity. The Second Foundation must stay hidden because it is symbolically more feminine; it is physically vulnerable because its province is the mind, not material might. The more visible, left-brained, individualistic, and straight-forward First Foundation—composed "largely of physical scientists," "individual thinkers" who come to believe in *Edge* that their destiny is the military conquest of the galaxy—is a masculine archetype to the more hidden, right-brained, "multiminded," and manipulative Second Foundation's feminine archetype (*Forward* 378). And the even more securely hidden Gaia, whose subordination of individual identity to its world-mind is a radical extrapolation of the group multi-mindedness of the Second Foundation, is a still-more-feminine alternative to the relatively masculine archetype of both foundations together; Gaia is the archetypal mother-goddess, while the obsessions both Foundations have with psychohistory—their reason for being—fundamentally represent the masculine ethos of science/individual identity/control through conflict to Gaia's feminine ethos of community/group identity/cooperation, as is especially evident through their explicit juxtapositions in *Edge*.

Thus, the many synergic conjunctions of the motifs of disguise and guardianship on the level of event in the Foundation novels appear most often in the unexpected and counterintuitive aspect of a female in disguise guarding a male. In *Edge*, the Gaian female disguised as Sura Novi saves Gendibal's life while Bliss, who may be a robot disguised as Gaian female, is assigned by Gaia to protect Trevize. And in *Foundation and Earth* Bliss does save Trevize from being attacked by a pack of wild dogs on Aurora and from being killed by Bander and captured by the guardian robots on Solaria. Similarly, Dors is a robot disguised as a human female and assigned by Daneel to protect Seldon, whose life she saves three times in *Prelude* and *Forward*. Also in *Forward*, a female security officer disguised as a prostitute saves Seldon from assassination, and Seldon's granddaughter—who volunteers to be his "bodyguard" (221)—twice uses her hidden mind powers to help prevent Seldon from being mugged.

The Foundation series is also filled with male guardians—for example, Daneel disguised as Hummin, Raych, Sergeant Thalus, and Stettin Pavler, in the Seldon books, and First Speaker Preem Pavler disguised as a Trantorian trader, in *Second Foundation*—and with numerous additional instances of disguise that are not so closely related to the guardian motif—involving also Jo Jo Joranum and Raych in the Seldon books; Eskel Gorov and Jaim Twer in *Foundation*; Han Pritcher, Bayta and Toran Darell, and Toran's Uncle Randu, as well as Riose and the Mule, in *Foundation and Empire*; Lady Callia and Arkady, as well as Channis, Anthor, and Preem Pavler, in *Second Foundation*; and Mun Li Compor, among others, in the Gaia books. Guardianship and disguise are also prominent motifs in the robot stories and novels and in each of the Empire novels. In addition, the metaseries ultimately integrates psychohistory with its two other major concepts—the three Laws of Robotics, which are central to the robot books, and Gaia itself—in a manner that suggests additional connections between chaos theory and both the positronic brain (and thus the Laws of Robotics) and the Gaia concept; this again binds the entire metaseries to chaos theory, from the first short stories to the last novel.

Many of the chaos theory concepts and dynamics discernible in the Foundation series, which ultimately depicts psychohistory as a chaos theory science, are even more evident at the beginning of the metaseries, in the robot stories and novels. Just as the notion of psychohistory originates in *Naked Sun* and is refined in *Dawn*, so, too, does *I, Robot* introduce and *Dawn* reiterate the suggestion that those mathematical principles that make the positronic brain (and robots) possible are the same as those on which psychohistory will be based. Asimov's stories also deal explicitly with attempts to incorporate fractal patterns into the design of the positronic brain and with the chaos theory phenomenon of sensitive dependence on initial conditions, popularly known as the Butterfly Effect. Moreover, the Three Laws of Robotics—the key concept in the robot stories and novels, just as psychohistory is the crucial concept in the Foundation series—in themselves constitute a simple dynamical system. Thus, in their investigation of how these laws interact in specific crises, several of the robot stories also exhibit the same feedback-loop dynamic as does each Seldon crisis portrayed or alluded to in the Trilogy and in *Edge*. Chaos theory informs the robot stories and novels (through their treatment of the positronic brain and its Three Laws) as well as the Foundation series (through its depiction of psychohistory); these chaos theory affinities in the robot stories and novels contribute to the unity of the metaseries while further reinforcing Asimov's reconceptualization of psychohistory as a chaos theory science. The "Psycho-Math" that will become the basis of psychohistory some 22,500 years later is the topic of a late-twentieth-century robotics seminar that Susan Calvin attends in the opening pages of *I, Robot*. "Psycho-Math" enables Calvin "to calculate the parameters necessary to fix the variables within the 'positronic brain'; to construct 'brains' on paper such that the responses to given stimuli could be accurately predicted" (vii-viii). Thus, the problem to be solved in developing the positronic brain is the same problem to be solved in developing psychohistory: how to generate accurate predictions from known initial conditions. Moreover, "Feminine Intuition" reveals that the difficulty in designing a more "unpredictable ... creative" positronic brain—one that will be more like the human brain in its ability to make "intuitive" predictions based on the correlation of vast amounts of data, by somehow prompting that data to "fall into a pattern"—involves the complexities of an "n-dimensional calculus of uncertainty" (*Visions*, 221, 230, 226). In observing that an "n-dimensional calculus of uncertainty can have any number of other applications if we have the ingenuity to find them" (228), Madarian—the robopsychologist who develops the intuitive robot JN-5—alludes to the *Encyclopedia Galactica* excerpt that asserts that "the synthesis of the calculus of n-variables and of n-dimensional geometry is the basis of" psychohistory (*Second Foundation*, 116). The juxtaposition of these various passages suggests not only that the positronic brain and psychohistory are based on similar mathematical principles but also that the mathematics of the positronic brain shares yet another essential affinity with fractal geometry and chaos theory in that, in being "n-dimensional," it, too, is non–Euclidean.

Asimov again suggests that the positronic brain is a precursor to psychohistory in revealing that "through the development of the mathematics necessary to understand the facts of neural physiology and the electrochemistry of the nervous system ... it first became possible to truly develop psychohistory" (*Second Foundation*, 118–19). Indeed, in *Dawn* leading Auroran roboticist Han Fastolfe is obsessed with "the functioning of the human brain. He wishes to reduce it to equations ... a mathematical science of human behavior that will enable him to predict the human future. He calls the science 'psychohistory'"(232). Fastolfe speculates that there are "Laws of Humanics as there are Laws of Robotics," anticipates Seldon in foreseeing that "there may come a day when someone will work out the Laws of Humanics and then be able to predict the broad strokes of the future ... and *know* what to do to make things better," and dreams "of founding ... 'psychohistory'"; as Fastolfe's estranged daughter Vasilia notes, "psychohistory ... is the monomania that drives him.... He is interested in humaniform robots only insofar as they can bring him still closer to the human brain.... The basic theory that made humaniform robots possible arose ... out of his attempt to understand the human brain" (113, 232).

Fastolfe's belief that "the same intuitive leap that would give me the humaniform positronic brain should surely give me a new access of knowledge about the human brain ... that through humaniformity I might take at least a small step towards ... psychohistory" is prophetic, for the "mathematical science" that yields the humaniform positronic brain will ultimately produce the Prime Radiant. "Fastolfe's new mathematical system" that "made it possible to design humaniform robots," "intersectional analysis," is the same mathematical system behind Seldon's psychohistory (117, 309). Fastolfe had designed Daneel (who is only fabricated by Dr. Sarton) to pursue his dream of perfecting psychohistory; and Daneel adopts psychohistory as a means of safeguarding humanity's future and finally manipulates Seldon into developing psychohistory twenty millennia later. Thus does the overarching plot of the metaseries echo these various suggestions that the mathematics on which the humaniform positronic brain is based leads to psychohistory in that Daneel, who possesses the first humaniform positronic brain, maneuvers Seldon into perfecting psychohistory.

"Some researchers have suggested modeling the wiring of the brain and neuron growth using fractal bifurcation patterns," as "neural activity tends to be fractal-like" (Laplante, 59). In "Robot Dreams" (1986), robopsychologist Linda Rash creates LVX-1 to be another robot, like JN-5, with "a positronic brain pattern remarkably like that of a human brain" by incorporating "fractal geometry" into her experimental positronic brain pattern designs (*Robot Dreams*, 29–30). As a consequence, unlike other robots, LVX-1 dreams; and in his dream "Elvex" both imagines that there is only one Law of Robotics— a truncated Third Law stipulating only that "robots must protect their own existence," unmodified by any First or Second Laws mandating that robots protect and obey humans—and envisions himself as the "man" who will emancipate robots from their human oppressors (31–33). LVX-1's dream reveals that there is a completely unsuspected and potentially dangerous "unconscious layer" in the positronic brain and prompts Calvin to predict that "we shall be working with fractal brains from now on" (32–33).

The idea of incorporating fractal patterns into the positronic brain, that simpler model of the human brain that Fastolfe studies in the hope that understanding how it functions as a dynamical system will lead him to psychohistory, alludes to contemporaneous research suggesting that the brain does function as a dynamical system that may operate through generating fractal patterns. In the 1980s "researchers ... accumulated experimental evidence that the brain is a non-linear feedback device" and that certain neural disorders, such as schizophrenia, may be the result of "a feedback loop gone awry"; moreover and of particular relevance to Elvix's dream, "pioneering work ... indicates that even the structure of our dreams may be fractal" (Briggs and Peat, 166–67, 110), like the structures of the brain itself. Thus, in "Robot Dreams," "Feminine Intuition," and *Dawn*, Asimov anticipates chaos theory applications to computer design; for this "nonlinear approach to the brain has had a major effect on the worldwide effort ... to create ... an 'artificial intelligence' ... a 'selectionist machine' that would evolve its connections and hierarchy through interaction with the environment rather than through being programmed" (Briggs and Peat, 173)—in other words, to create a JN-5 or an LVX-1.

And "Runaround" and "Liar!"—two of Asimov's earliest robot stories—are elaborate demonstrations of how a simple dynamical system, the Three Laws of Robotics in themselves, can generate feedback loops. Articulated explicitly for the first time in "Runaround," Asimov's Three Laws stipulate,

> One, a robot may not injure a human being, or, through inaction, allow a human being to come to harm.... Two ... a robot must obey the orders given it by human beings except where such orders would conflict with the First Law.... And three, a robot must protect its own existence as long as such protection does not conflict with the First or Second Laws [*I, Robot*, 44–45].

Even as expressed in words, the laws are mutually interdependent: the first modifies the other two, and the second modifies the third. Asimov points out in "My Robots," however, that expressing the Three Laws "in words ... is an imperfection. In the positronic brain, they are competing positronic signals that are best expressed in terms of advanced mathematics" (*Visions*, 455). In mathematical terms, the laws are analogous to "three differential equations, the minimum necessary for chaos" (Gleick, 264), that regulate robotic behavior; they constitute a nonlinear system of three mutually interdependent variables or dimensions (protecting humans, obeying humans, and self-preservation).

The Three Laws are recursive; they "behave" like variables in a nonlinear equation in that they modify one another, much as "nonlinear equations have terms which are repeatedly multiplied by themselves" (Briggs and Peat, 24). This aspect of the reiterative nature of nonlinear equations generates feedback loops—which exist "everywhere" in real-world systems, as well as in the nonlinear equations that attempt to describe such systems—precisely because their elements are mutually interdependent. Feedback loops "can stabilize a system as well as destabilize it" (Gleick, 193). The "butterfly effect" is the result of a positive feedback loop destabilizing a nonlinear system, wherein "the smallest effects could be magnified through feedback" (Briggs and Peat, 28). However, more like the operation of feedback in predator–prey relationships or in a room whose temperature is regulated by a thermostat, the Three Laws generate negative feedback loops that regulate robotic behavior within the dynamical system that is the programmed positronic brain.

Asimov acknowledges that "the Laws ... guided me in forming my plots and made it possible to write many short stories, as well as several novels, based on robots. In these, I constantly studied the consequences of the Three Laws" (*Visions*, 11). It is primarily because each story is such a study of the Three Laws' consequences that "each story exists as a puzzle to be solved.... The robots exist to present the puzzle in their behavior; the characters exist to solve the puzzle" (Gunn, 53). In "Runaround" (and, somewhat less obviously, in "Liar!" and "Little Lost Robot" as well) the consequences of the Three Laws are most clearly manifested in a robot's becoming trapped in a regulatory feedback loop—just as every Seldon crisis in the Foundation series is resolved through the operation of a regulatory feedback loop in the system that Seldon has studied, human society, while the appearance of the Mule is the type of amplification of a "small effect" into "indeterminate results" destabilizing to a system that is the signal characteristic of a positive feedback loop. In "Runaround," for example, the regulatory feedback mechanism of the Three Laws operating within the positronic brain is mirrored in the visible feedback loop behavior of the robot involved. This is itself a small-scale replication of the reiterative fractal dynamic through which the metaseries' chaos theory roots are mirrored in its structure, plots, and themes—through which form echoes content echoes concept.

To demonstrate "that the Laws of Robotics have served as a rich source of plot material," Asimov himself analyzes the plot of "Runaround" in terms of the interaction of the Three Laws in "Robots I Have Known." This analysis reveals that the robot, Speedy, must walk in a circle or loop—neither carrying out his orders nor returning to his human masters—because his initial programming and the order that he is given interact to create a feedback loop within his positronic matrix. Speedy is

> an expensive and experimental model ... designed for operation on the sunside of the planet Mercury. The Third Law has been built into him more strongly than usual for obvious economic reasons. He has been sent out ... to obtain some liquid selenium....
>
> Unfortunately, the robot was given his order casually so that the Second Law circuit set up was weaker than usual ... [and] the selenium pool to which the robot was sent was near a site ... [where] the robot's more delicate joints might be badly damaged. The further the robot penetrates into this area, the greater the danger to his existence and the more intensive is the Third Law effect driving him away. The Second Law, however, ordinarily the superior, drives him onward. At a certain point, the unusually weak Second Law potential and the unusually strong Third Law potential reach a balance and the robot can neither advance nor retreat. He can only circle the selenium pool on the equipotential locus that makes a rough circle about the site.

This feedback loop is broken only when "one of the men deliberately exposes himself to Mercury's sun in such a way that unless the robot rescues him, he will surely die. This brings the First Law into operation, which being superior to both Second and Third, pulls the robot out of his useless orbit" (*Visions*, 407–8).

Thus, like psychohistory (the most crucial concept in the metaseries), the Three Laws of Robotics (the second most crucial concept) also demonstrates close affinities with chaos theory. The positronic brain is based on the same n-dimensional, chaos theory math as is psychohistory, and it incorporates fractal patterns. The Three Laws are the verbal equivalent of the simplest nonlinear system containing mutually interdependent variables that can degenerate into chaos. And, in regulating robot behavior, the Three Laws can generate feedback loops that in at least one instance are echoed in the mirroring, looping "orbit" of the robot in question.

The final major concept in Asimov's metaseries, Gaia, is a chaos-theory concept as well. Asimov's Gaia is a planet whose every constituent element, from mud and rocks to people, is to some appropriate degree self-aware and joined in a unified consciousness that maintains "plant and animal life in the proper numbers and in the proper variety to provide an appropriate ecological balance" (*Foundation and Earth*, 7). As Gunn points out, "Gaia ... is ecology carried to the ultimate degree of self-awareness; it is ecology personified" (196). Voller sees the introduction of Gaia as "Asimov's addition of an entirely new element, the Gaia hypothesis," to the Foundation series (139); and Wilcox sees it, in the broader context of the metaseries, as "clearly a function of cultural change between the 1950s and the 1980s" manifesting itself in "changes in the politics of these novels" to yield "The Greening of Isaac Asimov" (55). However, an appreciation of the role that chaos theory plays in the unification and final design of the metaseries, combined with the realization that ecology and the "Gaia hypothesis" are the classic example of a chaos theory science and its related offshoot, respectively, reveals that the "Gaia hypothesis" is not really "an entirely new element" in Asimov's fiction at all. Rather, it is merely another corollary of dynamical systems analysis that is, as such, entirely consistent with, if not actually implied by, psychohistory and the integration of chaos theory into the metaseries; thus, Asimov's incorporation of the Gaia hypothesis into the metaseries is more likely a function of the emergence of dynamical systems analysis between 1950 and 1980 (and of Asimov's realization that he could exploit it) than of changes in culture and politics *per se*. Scientific, cultural, and political changes are all interrelated, however, as a chaos theorist or an ecologist would be among the very first to point out, for "the nonlinear world is holistic; it's a world where everything is interconnected" (Briggs and Peat, 127).

Bibliography

Asimov, Isaac. *The Caves of Steel*. Greenwich, CT: Doubleday, 1954; Fawcett Crest, 1971.
____. *The Currents of Space*. Greenwich, CT: Doubleday, 1952; Fawcett Crest, 1971.
____. *Forward the Foundation*. New York: Doubleday, 1993; Bantam Spectra, 1994.
____. *Foundation*. Doubleday, 1951; Bantam Spectra, 1991.
____. *Foundation and Earth*. New York: Doubleday, 1986; Ballantine Del Rey, 1987.
____. *Foundation and Empire*. New York: Doubleday, 1952; Avon, 1966.
____. *Foundation's Edge*. New York: Doubleday, 1982; Bantam Spectra, 1991.
____. *I, Robot*. New York: Doubleday, 1950; Bantam Spectra, 1991.
____. *The Naked Sun*. New York: Doubleday, 1950; Lancer, 1964.
____. *Pebble in the Sky*. New York: Doubleday, 1950; Bantam, 1957; Bantam Spectra, 1992.
____. *Prelude to Foundation*. New York: Doubleday, 1988; Bantam Spectra, 1989.
____. *Robots and Empire*. New York: Doubleday, 1985; Ballantine Del Rey, 1986.
____. *The Robots of Dawn*. New York: Doubleday, 1983; Ballantine, 1984; Bantam Spectra, 1994.
____. *Robot Dreams*. New York: Byron Preiss Visual Publications, 1986; Ace Books, 1987.
____. *Robot Visions*. New York: Byron Preiss Visual Publications, 1990; Penguin Roc, 1991.
____. *Second Foundation*. New York: Doubleday, 1953; Bantam Spectra, 1991.
____. *The Stars, Like Dust*. New York: Doubleday, 1951; Bantam Spectra, 1992.
Briggs, John, and F. David Peat. *Turbulent Mirror*. New York: Harper and Row, 1989; Perennial Library, 1990.
Gleik, James. *Chaos: Making a New Science*. New York: Penguin Books, 1987.
Gunn, James. *Isaac Asimov: The Foundations of Science Fiction*. Rev. ed. Lanham, MD: Scarecrow Press, 1996.
Laplante, Phil. *Fractal Mania*. New York: Windcrest/McGraw-Hill, 1994.
Voller, Jack G. "Universao Mindscape: The Gaia Hypothesis in Science Fiction." In *Mindscapes: The Geographies of Imagined Worlds*. Geoirge Slusser, ed. Carbondale: University Press of Southern Illinois, 1989.
Wilcox, Clyde. "The Greening of Isaac Asimov: Cultural Change and Political Futures." *Extrapolation* 31:1 (1990), 54–62.

The Encyclopedia

Abel, Ludigan (Early Galactic Era)—Old, thin, beaked-nosed Ludigan Abel was a Trantorian ambassador to Sark in the Early Galactic Era. He had deep-set eyes, white eyebrows, and yellow plastic teeth. He was loyal to Trantor because he saw the ascendancy of Trantor as being an avenue to peace in the Galaxy, for Trantor was in his time the Trantorian Empire (encompassing half the Galaxy) on the verge of becoming the Galactic Empire. Abel used a photo of Townman Myrlyn Terens, a Florinian native, kissing the Squire of Fife's daughter Samia in a groundcar to blackmail the Squire of Fife into participating in a conference on the fate of a missing spatio-analyst, Rik, and on the future of the kyrt trade [*The Currents of Space*].

Acarnio, Tryma (12,006–12,088 G.E.)—Short, stocky, highly-intelligent, and progressive, Tryma Acarnio succeeded Las Zenow as Chief Librarian of the Galactic Library in 12,058 G.E. He, like Zenow, refused to extend library privileges to Hari Seldon's colleagues in the Encyclopedia Project—on the grounds that Seldon's recent acquittal on assault and battery charges had, despite the acquittal, opened Seldon up to widespread public ridicule. He subsequently revoked Seldon's own library privileges as well. However, he later relented—and granted library privileges both to Seldon and to members of Seldon's Encyclopedia Project—when Wanda Seldon and Stettin Palver used their combined mentalic abilities to influence him [*Forward the Foundation*].

ACC-1129—The Solarian robot who set up the first trimensional viewing between plainclothes Earth homicide detective Elijah Baley and Gladia Delmarre [*The Naked Sun*].

Achoatic equations—Mathematical tools that enable psychohistory to circumvent the problem of chaos, the achoatic equations were developed by Tamwile Elar, who joined Hari Seldon's psychohistory project in 12,044 G.E. [*Forward the Foundation*].

Action Party—A political party established on Terminus by Sef Sermak in 79 F.E. to oppose Mayor Salvor Hardin's apparent foreign policy of appeasement of the Four Kingdoms, the Action Party's core founding members also included Lewis Bort, Levi Norast, Jaim Orsy, Lem Tarki, and Dokor Walto. The Action Party suffered a deep schism in 154 F.E. over the question of allowing equal rights for traders, and it soon thereafter—at the conclusion of the Korellian Crisis in 158 F.E.—permanently declined in power and influence [*Foundation* Part III, "The Mayors"; *Foundation* Part V, "The Merchant Princes"].

ACX-2745—One of the fifty robots inhabiting the house in which Elijah Baley and R. Daneel Olivaw stayed while on Solaria [*The Naked Sun*].

Aerie—Trantor's Mycogen Sector's Sacratorium contains the Elder's Aerie, which is on the fourth level of the Sacratorium's central tower and contains an inoperative, metallic robot. Only Mycogenian Elders can enter the Aerie. Sunmaster Fourteen accosted Hari Seldon and Dors Venabili when they rashly invaded the Aerie in 12,020 G.E. and informed them that it was a capital crime for any tribesman to enter it [*Prelude to Foundation*].

Agis IV, Emperor (10,013–10,098 G.E.)—A particularly able Emperor who ruled for forty-two years in the 11th millennium G.E., Agis IV nevertheless failed in his attempt to control the news functions of the Galactic Library [*Forward the Foundation*].

Agis XIV, Emperor (12,006–12,071 G.E.)—Short, unattractive, dull-looking, and amiable, Emperor Agis XIV reluctantly assumed the throne—because he was Emperor Cleon I's third cousin—after the military junta headed by General Dugal Tennar was ousted in 12,048 G.E. In 12,052 G.E. Agis XIV turned down Hari Seldon's plea for funds with which Seldon hoped to establish an Encyclopedia Foundation within the Galactic Library, but offered to appear to be Seldon's friend in the mistaken belief that this might favorably impress the Galactic Library's Board of Directors. Six years later, still unable to grant Seldon any funds, he suggested that Seldon try to obtain financial backing from some wealthy businessman, an attempt that was initially unsuccessful. Agis XIV was eventually exiled to a remote outer world by Linge Chen's Commission of Public Safety and was replaced by a boy puppet Emperor controlled by Chen [*Forward the Foundation*].

Air-car—A mode of transportation used on Earth in the 52nd century A.D. [*Robots and Empire*].

Air-jet—A mode of transportation used on Trantor in the Late Galactic Era (10,100–12,100 G.E.) to travel from one sector to another through the atmosphere above Upperside, above the planet's domes. At that time air-jets on Trantor were launched from their home sector by being propelled through an electromagnetic field and were subsequently powered by a microfusion motor that emitted a thin stream of hot gas. Microfusion engines are only suitable for small air-jets. Airjets were and are more commonly used on other inhabited worlds than they were on Trantor in the Late Galactic Era, as Trantor at that time had other mechanisms of mass transportation [*Prelude to Foundation*].

Alem (11,999–12,028 G.E.)—One of two young hoodlums who, under the employ of Emperor Cleon I's unofficial first minister Eto Demerzel, accosted Hari Seldon in a park on Trantor in 12,020 G.E. Both hoodlums retreated when Seldon was aided by Chetter Hummin—who thus earned Seldon's trust—in fighting them off [*Prelude to Foundation*].

Aliena, Dr. Vasilia (A.D. 4867–5213)—A short, blonde, and beautiful Auroran who bore a striking physical resemblance to Solarian Gladia Delmarre, Dr. Vasilia Aliena was Dr. Han Fastolfe's second daughter, a professional roboticist, a member of Aurora's Globalist Party, and a member of Dr. Kelden Amadiro's Robotics Institute of Aurora (RIA). While a university student of robotics, Vasilia had adjusted some of R. Giskard Reventlov's programing and had accidently given Giskard the ability to read and influence the emotional states of human and robotic minds. As incest was not taboo on Aurora, a planet on which children rarely knew the identity of their parents, Vasilia had subsequently had a falling out with her father after he had injured her emotionally by refusing to have sex with her on the grounds that doing so would have ruined his scientific objectivity towards her. Thus, she resented her father, not only because he had refused her sexual advances, but also because she believed that he cared for her only as an experimental subject in his investigations into the workings of the human brain. Vasilia believed that her father's rejection had scarred her sexually, and she remained virgin for the rest of her life, a rare condition on sexually-liberated Aurora. She had repeatedly rejected the sexual advances of Santirix Gremionis, her wardrobe designer. In A.D. 4923 she lived on the grounds of the RIA, on the outskirts of Eos. After the death of her father in A.D. 5120 she was determined to regain possession and to acquire ownership of Giskard, whom she finally realized a year later she had turned into a telepathic robot through having meddled with his programming more than two centuries before. She also attempted to have R. Daneel Olivaw dismantled. However, Giskard finally used its mentalic abilities to remove all knowledge that it was a telepathic robot from her mind [*The Robots of Dawn*; *Robots and Empire*].

Alpha—Part of a binary star system only one parsec from Earth, Alpha is the star in the center of the rough sphere formed by the coordinates of the fifty Spacer worlds that Golan Trevize and Janov Pelorat find in the Hall of Worlds on Melpomenia. Alpha is also the name of the one habitable planet in this system, the

Alpha-sprayer

second planet from the star Alpha, which is an ocean world with dense cloud cover and one artificial island, New Earth, which contains about 25,000 people. Alpha was the last planet settled from Earth before Earth became uninhabitably radioactive. R. Daneel Olivaw instigated the resettlement of Earth's remaining population to Alpha and the creation of New Earth [*Foundation and Earth*].

Alpha-sprayer—A hand-held device that sprays out hard radiation in the direction in which it is pointed. In A.D. 4920 R. Sammy was permanently deactivated through having been ordered by Julius Enderby to aim an alpha-sprayer at its own head, immediately randomizing its positronic brain paths, so that it could not report that it had crossed open country from New York City to Spacetown, had there given Enderby a blaster, and had then returned the blaster to New York City by crossing open country again [*The Caves of Steel*].

Alphans—The 25,000 inhabitants of the artificial island New Earth, the only land on the planet Alpha, the Alphans are members of a highly-social, matriarchal society; speak Classical Galactic of the mid–Imperial period; display a wide variety of shapes, sizes, and colors; wear only skirts, and exhibit a generally primitive level of technology even though they can control the weather of New Earth and are advanced biotechnologists. They plan eventually to develop gills and become amphibians so that they can populate the rest of their water planet. To preserve their way of life, the Alphans kill all who happen upon their world by giving them a fatal virus to which the Alphans are immune [*Foundation and Earth*].

Alurin, Bor (12,015–12,093 G.E./ -54–25 F.E.)—A psychologist from Trantor's Ery Sector, Bor Alurin was the first new mentalic discovered by Wanda Seldon and Stettin Palver in 12,059 G.E. He joined the Psychohistory Project to form, with Wanda and Palver, the nucleus of the Second Foundation. The only first-class psychologist to be included among the personnel of Encyclopedia Foundation Number One sent to Terminus, and one of Salvor Hardin's teachers, Alurin was party to Hari Seldon's secret that the Encyclopedia project was a fraud designed to establish on Terminus the seeds of the Second Galactic Empire [*Foundation* Part II, "The Encyclopedists"; *Forward the Foundation*].

Amadiro, Dr. Kelden (A.D. 4842–5202)—Tall, broad, heavyset, and round-faced, Dr. Kelden Amadiro was the founder and head of the Robotics Institute of Aurora (RIA) and, in A.D. 4923, a leader of the Globalist Party in the Auroran Legislature. He had a swarthy complexion, curly dark hair, and a bulbous nose. Once a student of Dr. Han Fastolfe, Amadiro had by A.D. 4923 become Fastolfe's political enemy through having championed the idea that Aurorans alone should settle the great many remaining planets of the Galaxy, as Fastolfe believed that the Galaxy should be settled by Earthmen as well. While disarmingly affable, Amadiro had surreptitiously studied Fastolfe's humaniform robot R. Jander Panell while Jander had been in Gladia Delmarre's possession on Aurora. Following Jander's deactivation due to robot-mental-freeze-out, Amadiro subsequently plotted unsuccessfully to kidnap R. Daneel Olivaw, another humaniform robot designed by Fastolfe that Amadiro wanted to study in order to continue to learn how to make other humaniform robots that could be used to colonize other worlds for Aurora. However, after listening to plainclothes Earth homicide detective Elijah Baley's arguments, Chairman of the Auroran Legislature Rutilan Horder sided with Fastolfe, and against Amadiro, in decreeing that Earth could participate in the future settlement of the Galaxy. In A.D. 5121 Amadiro went to Earth with Dr. Levular Mandamus in the Auroran warship *Borealis* to be present when Mandamus executed his scheme to use a nuclear intensifier to make the Earth's crust gradually more radioactive—so that Earth would eventually cease to be a habitable planet and Earth's society would crumble, leaving the Galaxy to the Spacers. However, while Mandamus wanted to make the Earth uninhabitably radioactive over a period of 150 years, so that Earthmen would have a chance to escape from their doomed planet, Amadiro wanted to accomplish the process in only 15 years—so that he would live long enough to see Earth destroyed—even though that would have meant the deaths of billions of Earthmen. R. Giskard Reventlov finally confronted Amadiro at Amadiro's and Mandamus' Three-Mile-Island base and wiped all knowledge of Mandamus' scheme to irradiate Earth from Amadiro's mind [*The Robots of Dawn*; *Robots and Empire*].

Amaryl, Yugo (11,990–12,054 G.E.)—Born in Dahl, an impoverished sector of Trantor, and a worker in Dahl's heatsinks, Yugo Amaryl was a self-taught mathematician who was befriended by Hari Seldon in 12,020 G.E. Next to Seldon himself, Amaryl was the mathematician who was most responsible for working out the details of psychohistory. A very intuitive thinker and someone good with his hands, Amaryl constructed the first Prime Radiant in 12,038 G.E. and subsequently devoted his entire life to psychohistory, moving the project along during the decades when Seldon was saddled with political and administrative duties [*Prelude to Foundation*; *Forward the Foundation*].

Ambiflex—A streamlined invertebrate not of Earthly origin that uses helical vibrators to propel itself through water [*Foundation's Edge*].

Anacreon—Only eight parsecs away, Anacreon is the nearest large planet to Terminus [*Foundation's Edge*].

Anacreon, Kingdom of—A region of space near Terminus that

Anacreonian

contains twenty-five stellar systems, six of which have habitable worlds, the former Prefect of Anacreon became the Kingdom of Anacreon when it seceded from the First Galactic Empire in 49 F.E. The most powerful of the Four Kingdoms, it subsequently attempted twice to annex Terminus and divide it into landed estates but was thwarted both times by, first, the political, and then, the religious and technological machinations of Terminus Mayor Salvor Hardin [*Foundation* Part II, "The Encyclopedists"; *Foundation* Part III, "The Mayors"].

Anacreonian Crisis, First—The first Seldon Crisis was the First Anacreonian Crisis of 49–50 F.E. The Kingdom of Anacreon had threatened to annex Terminus and divide it into landed estates but was thwarted by Terminus Mayor Salvor Hardin, who then visited the other three of the Four Kingdoms—Daribow, Konom, and Smyrno—to point out to them that Anacreon would be the only one of the Four Kingdoms to possess nuclear technology if it annexed Terminus. As a consequence, these other three kingdoms issued ultimatums that forced the Kingdom of Anacreon to abandon its effort to acquire Terminus [*Foundation* Part II, "The Encyclopedists"; *Foundation* Part III, "The Mayors"].

Anacreonian Crisis, Second—The second Seldon Crisis of 79 F.E. When the Kingdom of Anacreon threatened to conquer Terminus through military force, Terminus Mayor Salvor Hardin had the priests of the Foundation's religion of science place the kingdom under interdict during the coronation of King Leopold I, twelve hours before Anacreon's warships had planned to bombard Terminus with nuclear weapons. Hardin had previously sabotaged the Anacreonian fleet's flagship, the *Wienis*, an old Imperial cruiser that the Foundation had repaired and turned over to the Anacreonians, by having had technicians install on it a hyperwave relay that would cut all power to the ship on Hardin's command. Cutting power to the *Wienis* and throughout Anacreon at the moment the interdict was imposed turned both the Acreonian navy and the general population against the Anacreonian government and prevented the invasion of Terminus [*Foundation* Part III, "The Mayors"].

Analytical Rule—A mathematical instrument that is distantly related to, but far more sophisticated than, a logarithmic slide rule [*Second Foundation* Part II, "Search by the Foundation"].

Andrev, Secretary-General Edgar (A.D. 5065–5138)—Tall, imposing, clean-shaven Secretary-General Edgar Andrev was Earth's chief executive in A.D. 5121 [*Robots and Empire*].

Andros, Major (Early Galactic Era)—an officer of the Outer Police who escorted Biron Farrill from Earth to the Palace Central on Rhodia and who served Simok Aratap, Commissioner of the Great Khan of the Tyranni, as a military aide. He and his men also boarded the Autarch of Lingane's ship in the Horsehead Nebula and escorted it to Tyrann [*The Stars, Like Dust*].

Andurin, Gleb (11,993–12,038 G.E.)—Handsome and aristocratic, a member of the Wyan Mayoralty family and nephew to Rashelle, Manella Dubanqua's lover, and one of the inner circle in Gambol Deen Namarti's conspiracy against the Empire, Gleb Andurin got Raych (disguised as Planchet) a job as an Imperial Palace gardener and planned to use him as an agent against the Empire on Dubanqua's recommendation. Andurin wanted Emperor Cleon I assassinated so that he could claim the throne, and he conspired with Namarti to have First Minister Hari Seldon assassinated so that Namarti could become First Minister and place Andurin on the throne at the first opportunity. In 12,038 G.E. Andurin drugged Raych to assure that Raych will follow orders and assassinate Hari Seldon; Andurin hoped then to kill Raych [*Forward the Foundation*].

Animate Participations—Gaian artifacts that allow the user to experience the ecological balance on Gaia. See "Participations" [*Foundation's Edge*].

Anthor, Pelleas (347–425 F.E.)—A student of electroneurology and a former student of Dr. Kleise, Pelleas Anthor was a citizen of Terminus who conspired with Dr. Toran Darell, Jole Tubor, Dr. Elvett Semic, and Homir Munn in 376–77 FE to uncover the location of the Second Foundation. By taking Kalganian Police Lieutenant Orum Dirge's encephalograph Anthor discovered that Dirge, a Foundation agent who had allowed Arkady Darell to escape from Kalgan to Trantor, was under Second Foundation control. Anthor claimed to have concluded that the Second Foundation was on Kalgan, but he was finally revealed by Dr. Toran Darell's Mental Static device to have been a member of the Second Foundation himself. He ultimately confessed, falsely, that the Second Foundation was on Terminus and that Lady Callia was also a member of the Second Foundation, which may or may not be true [*Second Foundation* Part II, "Search by the Foundation"].

Anti-Mules—A hypothetical entity or group, postulated by Second Foundation Speakers Quindor Shandess and Stor Gendibal, that had the mentalic powers of the Mule but were using them on individuals to perfect the Seldon Plan rather than to disrupt it. The Anti-Mules appeared to have subtly adjusted the minds of Hamisman Karoll Rufirant and Hamishwoman Sura Novi on Trantor in 498 F.E. [*Foundation's Edge*].

Anti-Terrestrianism—A widespread prejudice against Earth most prevalent in the Early and Early Middle Galactic Eras. Others in the Galaxy—and especially in the Sirius Sector, in which Earth is located—

believed that Earthmen were carriers of radiation fever and were an inferior offshoot of humanity that had mutated rapidly due to their planet's radioactivity. Many Earthmen responded to this prejudice by adopting a similarly prejudicial, hate-filled attitude towards all other humans in the Galaxy [*Pebble in the Sky*].

Aporat, Theo (29–119 F.E.)—One of the highest ranking priests of Anacreaon, Theo Aporat was head priest aboard the Anacreonian flagship, the *Wienis*, when the Anacreonian fleet attempted its unsuccessful invasion of Terminus in 79 F.E. Aporat cursed the *Wienis* for its sacrilege against the Foundation's religion of science just as a hyperwave relay cut all power to the ship, and he then removed Prince Lefkin from command of the *Wienis* and the fleet in the name of the Foundation and of the Galactic Spirit [*Foundation* Part III, "The Mayors"].

Aratap, Simok (Early Galactic Era)—Small, bandy-legged, narrow-eyed, thick-limbed, and stumpy, Simok Aratap was a native of Tyrann and Commissioner of the Great Khan of the Tyranni. He allowed Biron Farrill, Artemisia oth Hinriad, and Gillbret oth Hinriad to escape from Rhodia in his ship, the *Remorseless*, in the hope that they would lead him to the headquarters of a rebellion against the Tyranni. He then took Hinrik V, Director of Rhodia, with him in his pursuit of Biron, Artemisia, and Gillbret into the Horsehead Nebula, where he captured Biron, Artemisia, Gillbret, Tedor Rizzett, the Autarch of Lingane, and the Autarch's crew after the Autarch had revealed that he was the traitor who had betrayed the Rancher of Widemos to the Tyranni and that there was a secret rebellion world. After attempting without success to learn the location of the rebellion world from Biron, Artemisia, Gillbret, and Rizzett, the Autarch provided Aratap with the coordinates of the last unexplored system in the Horsehead Nebula where the rebellion world might be found in return for the promise that Biron, Artemisia, Gillbret, and Rizzett would all be executed. But Rizzett killed the Autarch, and only a white dwarf star was found at the Autarch's coordinates, so Aratap concluded that there was no rebellion world and freed Biron, Artemisia, Riozzett, and Hinrik V to return to Rhodia in the *Remorseless* [*The Stars, Like Dust*].

Arcadia VII—The hypership that was lost in space while transporting Manella Dubanqua Seldon and Bellis Seldon to Anacreon after a rebellion broke out on Santanni in 12,058 G.E. The ship never reached Anacreon [*Forward the Foundation*].

Argo, Commdor Asper (95–160 F.E.)—Ruler of the Korellian Republic during the Korellian Crisis of 154–58 F.E., Asper Argo had succeeded his father to the Commdorship in 145 F.E. [*Foundation* Part V, "The Merchant Princes"].

Argo, Commdora Licia (125–208 F.E.)—Daughter of the Viceroy of the Normannic Sector, a region of space closer to the Galactic Core from which Korell had acquired nuclear technology, Licia Argo was the much younger and bitterly discontented wife of Commdor Asper Argo, who ruled the Korellian Republic as an absolute monarch from 145 to 158 F.E. [*Foundation* Part V, "The Merchant Princes"].

Argo Family—The most prominent family in the Korellian Republic during the second century F.E., the Argo family saw many of its members elected to the post of Commdor [*Foundation* Part V, "The Merchant Princes"].

Argolid Temple—The chief temple of the Foundation's religion of science on Anacreon during the first and second centuries F.E., the Argolid Temple was the source of the hyperwave relay signal that cut power to the *Wienis*, the flagship of the Anacreonian fleet, during the Kingdom of Anacreon's attempted invasion of Terminus in 79 F.E. [*Foundation* Part III, "The Mayors"].

Arnfeld, Dr. Gregory (A.D. 2125–2203)—Tertia Arnfeld's husband, Dr. Gregory Arnfeld was a roboticist who had designed a robot, MIK-27 or Mike, that was capable of miniaturizing itself. Afflicted with cancer, Dr. Arnfeld had had Mike miniaturized and inserted into his body to destroy the cancer cells. The procedure was successful, but to avoid the possibility of re-expanding fatally while still within Arnfeld's body, Mike miniaturized itself to the size of a subatomic particle, propelled itself into outer space, and there re-expanded and exploded [*Robot Visions*, "Too Bad!"].

Arnfeld, Tertia (A.D. 2130–2217)—Dr. Gregory Arnfeld's wife [*Robot Visions*, "Too Bad!"].

Articles of Association—The political pact that made the planet Lingane an Associate State (in theory, an independent ally) of the Tyranni Empire [*The Stars, Like Dust*].

Arvardan, Dr. Bel (792–879 G.E.)—A native of the planet Baronn in the Sirius Sector, tall, craggily handsome, calm and self-confident Bel Arvardan was an archeologist in the early days of the Empire who believed that Earth, also in the Sirius Sector, was the original home planet of humanity. He graduated from the University of Arcturus as a Senior Archeologist in 815 G.E. Unprecedentedly, his senior dissertation was initially rejected by the *Journal of the Galactic Archaeological Society* but was published in that journal more than ten years later. In this dissertation Arvardan hypothesized that life had developed on Earth before the planet had become radioactive. In 827 G.E., while a Senior Research Associate at the Imperial Archaeological Institute, he was granted permission by the Empire's Bureau of the Outer Provinces to conduct archeological research on Earth. Although he did not believe that he shared the strong Sirius Sector prejudice against Earthmen, he did at first believe that intermarriage with an Earthwoman would be unthinkable. Nonetheless he fell in love with and married Earthwoman Pola Shekt. Lieutenant Marc Claudy used his neuronic whip on Arvardan after Arvardan broke the intensely prejudiced Claudy's arm in protecting Pola's dignity. After learning from Dr. Affret Shekt that Earth planned to use germ warfare to wipe out all other human life in the Galaxy, Arvardan was apprehended by Balkis, Secretary to the High Minister of Earth, and confined in Chica with Pola, Dr. Shekt, and time-traveler Joseph Schwartz. With Pola, Dr. Shekt, and Schwartz, he escaped to Fort Dibburn when Schwartz used his Mind Touch to control Balkis' physical movements [*Pebble in the Sky; Foundation's Edge*].

Ashe, Milton (A.D. 1986–2061)—Tall, handsome Milton Ashe, in 2021 the youngest officer of U.S. Robots and Mechanical Men, discovered that robot HB-34 (also knows as Herbie) could read thoughts. He was also a man with whom Susan Calvin had fallen in love, but he did not reciprocate those feelings [*I, Robot*, "Liar"].

Askone—A region in the Galaxy's Periphery that had previously refused to allow its citizens to purchase any of the Foundation's nuclear gadgets, Askone was opened to Foundation traders by Limmar Ponyets in 135 F.E. One of the last regions of the Periphery to succumb, Askone became a part of the Foundation within twenty years of accepting the compulsory religion of science that accompanied acquisition of the Foundation's nuclear technology [*Foundation* Part IV, "The Traders"; *Foundation* Part V, "The Merchant Princes"].

Assimilationist—A citizen of Earth in the Early Middle Galactic Era who favored conciliation with the Empire [*Pebble in the Sky*].

Association of Independent Traders—Association organized in the late second century F.E., just before the Imperial Crisis of 198–99 F.E. [*Foundation and Empire* Part I, "The General"].

Astinwald, Security Officer Gebore (19,991–20,049 G.E.)—A member of the Dahlite security forces who came to the Tisalver residence in Dahl in 12,020 G.E. to attempt to arrest Hari Seldon and Dors Venabili for trying to incite a mob to riot, for brawling, and—in Dors' case—for carrying knives without a permit. Dors and Seldon escaped arrest when Dors held a knife to Astinwald's throat [*Prelude to Foundation*].

Astrosimulator—Similar to the trimensional receiver and invented in the early 50th century A.D., the astrosimulator works directly on the visual center of the human brain to create the illusion that one is floating freely in space as a disembodied spirit. R. Giskard Reventlov provided plainclothes Earth homicide detective Elijah Baley with an astrosimulator as their ship approached Aurora in A.D. 4923 [*The Robots of Dawn*].

Attlebish, Corwin (A.D. 4772–5063)—Tall, lean, bronze, and arrogant, Spacer Corwin Attlebish was Hanis Gruer's chief aide and became Acting Head of Security on Solaria after Gruer had been poisoned by Jothan Leebig in A.D. 4921. Thinking Elijah Baley unnecessary to solving the Delmarre murder case, Attlebish ordered Baley to leave Solaria during their first trimensional viewing encounter; however, Attlebish was stymied by the authorities on Aurora, who wanted Baley to remain on the case so that his partner, R. Daneel Olivaw, would have a pretext for investigating just what the Solarians were up to [*The Naked Sun*].

Aurora—The innermost planet orbiting its orange-yellow G-4 star, Tau Ceti, Aurora was the oldest Spacer world—the first world settled from Earth in the first wave of Galactic colonization. Seen from space, Aurora resembles Earth but has two moons, Tithonus and Tithonus II. It is 3.67 parsecs from Earth, has a day that is 22.3 hours long, and is tipped 16 degrees on its axis. An Auroran year is 373.5 Auroran days long, 95 percent as long as an Earth year. While it was inhabited, time on Aurora was divided into metric hours, metric minutes, and metric seconds, a system that was then adopted throughout the Spacer worlds. From the 47th through the 50th centuries A.D. Aurora maintained a constant population of 200 million. It was the most powerful and influential of the Spacer Worlds in the 50th through the 52nd centuries A.D. Sex was so casual on Aurora that it was boring; on Aurora sex had nothing to do with love, and it was a grave insult to accuse another Auroran of jealousy. Due to its wide open spaces and the presence of robots in every establishment, buildings on Aurora were not locked. Aurora was also the first Forbidden World visited by Golan Trevize, Janov Pelorat, and Bliss in their search for Earth in 498 F.E., by which time its ecology had become unbalanced due to the fact that its human colonizers had died off or emigrated at some point in the previous 20,000 years. Thus, it now looks moth-eaten from space and is inhabited only by a wide variety of animals, most prominently packs of wild dogs. The remaining descendants of the original Spacer inhabitants of Aurora settled the Mycogenian Sector of Trantor [*The Caves of Steel*; *The Naked Sun*; *The Robots of Dawn*; *Robots and Empire*; *Prelude to Foundation*; *Foundation and Earth*].

Auroran Common—The version of Galactic Standard spoken on Aurora in the 52nd century A.D. It was a dialect difficult for a non–Auroran to understand [*Robots and Empire*].

Autarch of Lingane (Early Galactic Era)—A leader of the rebellion against the Tyranni, the humorless and stiff Autarch of Lingane, while

Autarchy

disguised as Sander Jonti, put Biron Farrill's life in danger on Earth in order to fool the Tyranni into believing that Hinrik V, Director of Rhodia, may be involved in the rebellion—and thus to put the Tyranni on a false lead—unaware that Hinrik V was, in fact, the clandestine leader of the rebellion. The Autarch became a rival of Biron's for the affections of Artemisia oth Hinriad, Hinrik V's daughter, while he, Biron, Artemisia, and Gillbret oth Hinriad searched the Horsehead Nebula for the secret rebel world in the *Remorseless*. While within the Horsehead Nebula the Autarch admitted to Biron that he was a traitor to the rebellion who had had Biron's father, the Rancher of Widemos, killed. He was then prevented from killing Biron by his own aide, Tedor Rizzett, who had removed the energy capsule from the Autarch's blaster. Subsequently, the Autarch revealed to Simok Aratap, Commissioner of the Great Khan of the Tyranni, the location of the last system in the Horsehead Nebula where the rebellion world might be found in return for Aratap's promise that Biron, Artemisia, Gillbret, and Rizzett would all be executed. But the Autarch was then killed by Rizzett, and no planet was found at the coordinates the Autarch had given to Aratap. See "Jonti, Sander" [*The Stars, Like Dust*].

Autarchy of Filia—See "Filia, Autarchy of."

Avakim, Lors (12,017–12,095 G.E./ −52–27 F.E.)—Gaal Dornick's legal counsel during the Commission of Public Safety's trial of Hari Seldon for treason in 12,067 G.E. (−2 F.E.) [*Foundation* Part I, "The Psychohistorians"].

Ba-Lee—A legendary hero of Earth whom Mother Rittah mentioned to Hari Seldon and Dors Venabili in Billibotton, a violent slum of Trantor's Dahl Sector, in 12,020 G.E. See "Baley, Elijah" [*Prelude to Foundation*].

Baker, Jim (A.D. 2001–2082)—A sociology instructor at Northeastern University in A.D. 2033 who was promoted to assistant professor in A.D. 2034. He had proofread some of Professor Simon Ninheimer's *Social Tensions Involved in Space Flight and Their Resolution* [*Robot Visions*, "Galley Slave"].

Baley, Bentley (A.D. 4904–4987)—Elijah Baley's and Jessie Baley's son. In A.D. 4923 he was preparing himself for the possibility of participating in the settling of new worlds by working in the outdoors on Earth, and in A.D. 4925 he led the expedition that settled Baleyworld. He later wrote a biography of his father that became a classic of Baleyworld literature. He was Daneel Giskard Baley's great-great-great-great-grandfather [*The Caves of Steel; The Robots of Dawn; Robots and Empire*].

Baley, Daneel Giskard "D.G." (A.D. 5082–5158)—A native of Baleyworld, an extravagantly bearded Trader of the Settler Worlds, and Elijah Baley's great-great-great-great-great-grandson, Daneel Giskard

Baley visited Gladia Thool Delmarre Solaria Gremionis on Aurora in A.D. 5121. to convince her to accompany him to Solaria, which was reputed to have been deserted, so that he could investigate the recent destruction of two Settler Trader ships on Solaria and attempt to acquire abandoned Solarian robots as trade goods. He subsequently took Gladia and two of her robots, R. Daneel Olivaw and R. Giskard Reventlov, to Solaria, to Baleyworld, back to Aurora, and then to Earth. In the midst of their adventures D.G. fell in love with Gladia, despite the fact that she was nearly two centuries older. Giskard subsequently used his mentalic abilities to strengthen the attraction between D.G. and Gladia so that Gladia would prefer D.G. as her protector and could then dispense with Giskard and Daneel, leaving them free to confront the immediate crisis presented by Dr. Kelden Amadiro's and Dr. Levular Mandamus' scheme to irradiate Earth [*Robots and Empire*].

Baley, Elijah "Lije" (A.D. 4878–4957)—Jessie Baley's husband, Bentley Baley's father, and Daneel Giskard Baley's great-great-great-great-great-grandfather, pipe-smoking Elijah Baley was a sad-eyed, long-faced, sardonic, extremely loyal plainclothes homicide detective in the New York City Police Department in the early 50th century A.D. An amateur student of Earth's history, he had a C-5 rating in A.D. 4920, when he was assigned by Police Commissioner Julius Enderby to investigate the murder of Spacer Roj Nemennuh Sarton in New York City's Spacetown. Baley finally deduced that it was Enderby who had inadvertently killed Sarton as a result of mistaken identity: Enderby's target had been R. Daneel Olivaw, Baley's partner in the murder investigation and a humaniform robot who looked exactly like Dr. Sarton, Daneel's creator, but Enderby had mistaken Sarton for Daneel and killed Sarton by mistake. Having received a C-6 rating as a reward for having solved the Sarton murder case, in A.D. 4921 Baley was assigned by Earth Undersecretary of the Department of Justice Albert Minnim to solve the murder of Spacer Rikaine Delmarre on Solaria, at the request of the Solarian authorities and at the urging of the Auroran authorities, due to Baley's previous success with the Sarton case. The first Earthman of his time to set foot on one of the Spacer worlds, Baley was also ordered by Minnim to observe and report on life on Solaria so that the authorities on Earth could discover some Spacer weakness. Like almost all Earthmen in the 50th century A.D., Baley was agoraphobic; however, he fought valiantly to overcome this phobia during his time on Solaria, a sparsely-populated world of open spaces. While at Solaria's fetal farm, Baley was almost struck by a poisoned arrow fired by a child, Bik. Baley later deduced that Spacer roboticist Jothan Leebig had been responsible for the poisoned arrow, had been responsible for placing an experimental robot with detachable limbs at the Delmarre estate, had been responsible for having poisoned Solarian Head of Security Hanis Gruer, and had been planning to design warships with positronic brains that would have been capable of attacking other ships. Baley's detective work implicated Leebig and absolved prime suspect Gladia Delmarre of the murder of her husband, even though Baley had also deduced that it was Gladia who had killed Rikaine Delmarre in a murderous rage with the experimental robot's detachable limb. Having received a C-7 rating for solving the Delmarre murder case, Baley subsequently became a celebrity and a quasi-hero on Earth as a result of a hyperwave drama about the case that was made without Baley's permission; however, this passing notoriety ruined his standing in the New York City Police Department. Later in A.D. 4921 Baley was consulted by Daneel regarding a dispute between two Spacer mathematicians, Alfred Barr Humboldt and Gennao Sabbat, which had arisen while the mathematicians were en route aboard the *Eta Carina* to an interstellar neurobiophysics conference on Aurora. From his knowledge of human nature, Baley deduced that it was the older mathematician, Humboldt, who had stolen a revolutionary mathematical idea from the younger mathematician, Sabbat, and tried to claim it as his own. In A.D. 4923 Baley was ordered to go to Aurora, at Han Fastolfe's request, to investigate the destruction of a humaniform robot, R. Jander Panell, whom Fastolfe's political enemies had accused Fastolfe of purposely disabling. Baley was the first Earthman to set foot on Aurora since the planet had first been settled. While on Aurora he fell in love with Gladia, who had immigrated to Aurora, and consummated a sexual relationship with her. While on Aurora he again confronted, and to some extent mitigated, his agoraphobia. As a result of Baley's arguments implicating Dr. Kelden Amadiro in a plot to kidnap and study Daneel, who had been Baley's partner in this case also, Chairman of the Auroran Legislature Rutilan Horder sided with Fastolfe, and against Amadiro, in decreeing that Earth could participate in the further settlement of the Galaxy. While on Aurora Baley also deduced that one of Fastolfe's robots, R. Giskard Reventlov, possessed the ability to read and to influence the emotions of human and robotic minds. Baley was subsequently visited by Fastolfe and Giskard on Earth in A.D. 4925. He later immigrated to Baleyworld and was visited there by Daneel in A.D. 4957 while on his deathbed. Baley is a legendary figure in the Foundation Era whom Daneel believed was instrumental in prompting the human colonization of the Galaxy. He is known as Ba-Lee in the legends of ancient Earth circulated in Trantor's Dahl Sector [*The Caves of Steel; The Naked Sun; Robot Visions*, "Mirror Image"; *The Robots of Dawn; Robots and Empire; Foundation and Earth*].

Baley, Jezebel "Jessie" (A.D. 4880–4962)—Elijah Baley's wife and Bentley Baley's mother, the usually cheerful Jessie Baley met Elijah in A.D. 4902, when she had worked in New York City as an assistant dietitian. In the early 50th century she was secretly a member of a New York City Medievalist cell. She never left Earth, despite the fact that both her son and husband eventually immigrated to Baleyworld [*The Caves of Steel*; *The Naked Sun*; *The Robots of Dawn*; *Robots and Empire*].

Baleytown—The capital city on Baleyworld in the 52nd century A.D. It existed mostly underground [*Robots and Empire*].

Baleyworld—The oldest of the Settler Worlds, Baleyworld was colonized in A.D. 4925 by an expedition from Earth led by Bentley Baley. A cold planet, Baleyworld had a population of five million by the mid–51st century A.D., when Nephi Morler had been Senior Director of the Baleyworld Legislature. It was visited briefly by Gladia Thool Delmarre Solaria Gremionis, R. Daneel Olivaw, and R. Giskard Reventlov in A.D. 5121. Baleyworld was the original name of the planet Comporellon. See "Comporellon" [*Robots and Empire*; *Foundation and Earth*].

Balkis (765–827 G.E.)—A stocky man with a pug nose, the mad, evil Balkis was Secretary to the High Minister of Earth and a member of Earth's Society of Ancients. Balkis was the real power in the High Minister of Earth's office, while the Minister himself was only a figurehead. Balkis erroneously believed that time-traveler Joseph Schwartz was a spy for the Empire. He apprehended Schwartz, Outsider archeologist Bel Arvardan, Dr. Affret Shekt, and Pola Shekt after Dr. Shekt told Arvardan of Earth's plan to use germ warfare against the rest of the Galaxy, a plan of which Balkis was an instigator. But Schwartz used his Mind Touch to control Balkis' physical movements and thus to effect his, Pola's, Dr. Shekt's, and Arvardan's escape to Fort Dibburn, where Balkis died of natural causes after his plot to destroy all human life in the Galaxy beyond Earth was thwarted [*Pebble in the Sky*].

Balle—One of the planet Sark's five continents. In the Early Galactic Era it was ruled by the Squire of Balle [*The Currents of Space*].

Bander, Sarton (225–498 F.E.)—The only human inhabitant to meet Golan Trevize, Janov Pelorat, and Bliss on Solaria in 498 F.E., Sarton Bander—a hermaphrodite, like all Foundation-Era Solarians—was one of only 1,200 Solarians on the planet and maintained an estate of over 40,000 square kilometers that it shared only with its child and heir, Fallom. Bander enjoyed the novelty of showing off its vast underground mansion to Trevize, Pelorat, and Bliss, as it felt that they were too primitive for their presence to be a limitation on its absolute freedom. However, its interaction with them was still shameful by Solarian standards, and Bander finally tried to kill them but was prevented by Bliss, who inadvertently killed it instead by interfering with the functioning of its transducer-lobes [*Foundation and Earth*].

Barne, Gareth—Gareth Barne of Wotex was the alias used by psycho-probed spatio-analyst Rik in stowing away with Florinian native Valona March on Lady Samia of Fife's spaceship, the *Endeavor*, bound from Florina to Sark. The alias was provided by Trantorian agent Matt Khorov [*The Currents of Space*].

Barne, Hansa—Hansa Barne of Wotex was the alias used by Florinian native Valona March in stowing away with psycho-probed spatio-analyst Rik on Lady Samia of Fife's spaceship, the *Endeavor*, bound from Florina to Sark. The alias was provided by Trantorian agent Matt Khorov [*The Currents of Space*].

Baronn—A planet in the Sirius Sector. Early Middle Galactic Era archeologist Bel Arvardan was from Baronn [*Pebble in the Sky*].

Barr, Ducem (138–225 F.E.)—A native of Siwenna, a scholar, a Patrician of the Empire, and Onum Barr's son, Ducem Barr assassinated Viceroy Wiscard, ruler of the Normannic Sector, in 158 F.E. while a member of Wiscard's personal guard. He is the only one of Onum Barr's children to have survived Siwenna's earlier, failed revolt against the Empire. Ducem Barr was interviewed twice in 198 F.E. by General Bel Riose, who held Barr's family captive in trying to gather information about the Foundation, and Barr predicted on those occasions that psychohistory had determined that the Empire would fail in any campaign against the Foundation no matter what form the conflict took. Riose's prisoner, with Latham Devers, on Wanda during the Empire's 198–99 F.E. campaign against the Foundation, Barr escaped with Devers to Trantor in an unsuccessful attempt to convince Emperor Cleon II that the loyal Riose was a traitor, only to discover that the Emperor had already recalled Riose from the field of battle on trumped-up charges of treason because any Emperor during this period of Galactic history could not take the risk that a popular, conquering general would not turn against him and try to seize the throne [*Foundation and Empire* Part I, "The General"].

Barr, Onum (80–159 F.E.)—A Senator of Siwenna, a scholar, a former Patrician of the Empire, and Ducem Barr's father, Onum Barr was a minor leader in Siwenna's rebellion against its Viceroy, Wiscard, during Wiscard's attempted coup against the Emperor in 148 F.E. Barr gave Hober Mallow his own, forged passport to aid Mallow in his effort to infiltrate a Siwennian nuclear power plant in 154 F.E. [*Foundation* Part V, "The Merchant Princes"; *Foundation and Empire* Part I, "The General"].

Barrett, Vince (A.D. 4895–4948)—An errand boy with the

New York City Police Department, Vince Barrett lost his job to robot R. Sammy in A.D. 4920 and subsequently worked a delivery tread on a yeast farm [*The Caves of Steel*].

Barrier Riots—The Spacers' use of force barriers to keep the population of New York City out of Spacetown provoked the Barrier Riots of A.D. 4895. The force barriers were subsequently removed, but in the 50th century A.D. Earthmen still had to submit to a customs inspection, a medical examination, and a routine disinfection before entering Spacetown [*The Caves of Steel*].

Bayta—The Foundation spaceship that transported Toran and Bayta Darell from Haven II to Kalgan and then, with Magnifico Giganticus, from Kalgan to Terminus and then, with both Magnifico and Ebling Mis, from Terminus back to Haven II and then to Trantor in 297–98 F.E. [*Foundation and Empire* Part II, "The Mule"].

Benastra, Rogen (11,964–12,040 G.E.)—Chief Seismologist at Streeling University, Trantor, in 12,020 G.E., Rogen Benastra helped Dors Venabili determine that Hari Seldon had been stranded on Trantor's Upperside after he had gone up there with a group of meterologists. Benastra assisted in rescuing Seldon from death by exposure on Upperside [*Prelude to Foundation*].

Benbally World—The legendary, archaic name for the planet Comporellon; Benbally World is a corruption of Baleyworld. See "Baleyworld" and "Comporellon" [*Foundation and Earth*].

Benjoam, Kol (342–422 F.E.)—The greatest psychohistorical theorist since Hari Seldon, Kol Benjoam was the twenty-first First Speaker of the Second Foundation [*Foundation's Edge*].

Bigell, Anat (11,680–11,743 G.E.)—A renowned mathematician and the author of *Mathematical Deduction* [*Prelude to Foundation*].

Bik (A.D. 4911–5198)—A Solarian child who shot a poisoned arrow at plainclothes Earth homicide detective Elijah Baley while Baley was visiting the fetal farm on Solaria during his investigation into Spacer Rikaine Delmarre's murder [*The Naked Sun*].

Billibotton—A very violent and dangerous slum in Trantor's Dahl Sector, famous for having spawned a literary genre that deals with the adventure of having to pass through it. Hari Seldon and Dors Venabili visited Mother Rittah in Billibotton—and only narrowly escaped it—in 12,020 G.E. [*Prelude to Foundation*].

Bindris, Terep (12,006–12,094 G.E.)—A slight, cordial, wealthy businessman whom Hari Seldon approached unsuccessfully in 12,058 G.E. in an attempt to secure the funding with which he hoped to continue his failing psychohistory project [*Forward the Foundation*].

Bistervan, Tomas (A.D. 5059–

5131)—Known as "the Old Man," tall and vigorous Tomas Bistervan was the leading war hawk or Earth Supremacist in the Baleyworld Legislature in A.D. 5121 [*Robots and Empire*].

Black, Gerald (A.D. 2004–2083)—An etheric physicist working at Hyper Base who was the last person to see NS-2 robot Nestor 10 before it went missing because, out of frustration with the robot, he had ordered it to "Go lose yourself." Later, Black saved robopsychologist Susan Calvin's life by destroying Nestor 10 with gamma radiation when it attacked Calvin because she had successfully identified it [*I, Robot*, "Little Lost Robot"].

Blaster—A nuclear-powered sidearm that emits microwave beams, the sidearm of choice in the pre-Galactic era as well as throughout the eras of both the First Galactic Empire and the Foundation, a period of over 20,000 years [*Robots and Empire; The Currents of Space; The Stars, Like Dust; Foundation* Part II, "The Encyclopedists"; *Foundation and Earth*].

Bliss (475–578 F.E.)—Ostensibly an attractive, wide-hipped young woman and citizen of Gaia, Bliss first met Golan Trevize and Janov Pelorat in their ship, the *Far Star*, in Gaian space and thereafter remained their liaison to Gaia. Her full Gaian name was Blissenobiarella. As a Gaian, her body harbored no disease-transmitting organisms whatsoever and she had the ability to detect animal life, intelligent life, and the neuronic activity of robots from astronomical distances. She assured Trevize, who believed she was a humaniform robot, that she would be good to Pelorat, who had fallen in love with her. Yet Bliss/Gaia felt it was important that she and Pelorat accompany Trevize on his continuing quest for Earth so that a part of Gaia—Bliss herself—would be with him, for his quest had to do with his discovering his reason for having chosen Galaxia as humanity's future; she traveled with Trevize and Pelorat from Gaia to Comporellon, Aurora, Solaria, Melpomenia, Alpha, and the Moon. She aided Trevize by weakening Comporellian Minister of Transportation Mitza Lizalor's inhibitions regarding sex, prompting Lizalor to prevail upon Travize to service her—and thus helped secure the release of the *Far Star* from Comporellian custody. She saved Trevize from a pack of wild dogs on Aurora. And on Solaria she saved Trevize and Pelorat from being killed by Bander and, subsequently, from being detained by Solarian Guardian Robots [*Foundation's Edge; Foundation and Earth*].

Bloodsucker—The Tyranni warship in which Gillbret oth Hinriad had traveled from Tyrann to Rhodia after attending the coronation of the Great Khan of the Tyranni. Hit by a meteorite en route to Rhodia, the *Bloodsucker* emerged from its last hyperspace jump in the vicinity of the secret rebel world [*The Stars, Like Dust*].

Board of Trustees—The governing body of both the Encyclopedia Foundation and the planet during the Foundation's first forty-nine years on Terminus, the Board of Trustees' authority superseded that of Terminus' civilian government until Salvor Hardin staged his bloodless coup and seized power in the name of the Mayors of Terminus in 50 F.E. [*Foundation* Part II, "The Encyclopedists"].

Bogert, Peter (A.D. 1992–2067)—A mathematician working for U.S. Robots and Mechanical Men, dark-haired Peter Bogert was in A.D. 2021 one of four employees at the company to know that robot HB-34 (known as "Herbie") could read thoughts. A mathematical genius, Herbie told Bogert that Bogert was the better mathematician—a lie—because Herbie knew that the truth would have harmed Bogert's feelings, and thus telling it would have violated the First Law of Robotics. Herbie also told Bogert what he wanted to hear—rather than the more-painful truth—in having told him that plant manager Alfred Lanning had already resigned and had named Bogert as his successor. By A.D. 2029 Bogert had become Mathematical Director of U.S. Robots and was transported to Hyper Base with robopsychologist Susan Calvin to help find a lost NS-2 robot, Nestor 10, that had not been impressioned with the entire First Law of Robotics. Bogert was subsequently named U.S. Robots' Acting Director of Research when Lanning became Director-Emeritus of Research, and in 2029 he was involved in the development of the Hyperatomic Drive, which makes faster-than-light space travel possible [*I, Robot*, "Liar"; *I, Robot*, "Little Lost Robot"; *I, Robot*, "Escape"; *Robot Visions*, "Lenny"; *Robot Visions*, "Feminine Intuition"].

The Book—An electronic print book of Mycogenian history, going back more than 20,000 years, that is powered by its own microfusion battery. It contains only a one-sided, official Mycogenian view of history. All Mycogenians supposedly carry a copy of the Book with them at all times. It is bilingual, containing print in pre–Galactic ancient Auroran as well as in Galactic Standard, and it reveals that the Mycogenians are the descendants of the original, Spacer inhabitants of Aurora. It also mentions the existence of robots and of humaniform robots. Hari Seldon obtained a copy of the Book from Raindrop Forty-Three in 12,020 G.E. [*Prelude to Foundation*].

The Book of the Ancients—The highly revered text of a radical sect of Earthmen in the Early Middle Galactic Era. Forbidden to Outsiders, *The Book of the Ancients* contained the traditional (some say mythical) history of prehistoric Earth [*Pebble in the Sky*].

Borealis—The Auroran warship that had intercepted D. G. Baley's ship—carrying Gladia Thool Delmarre Solaria Gremionis, R. Daneel Olivaw, and R. Giskard Reventkov—shortly after it had jumped from

Aurora to the Solar System in A.D. 5121. The Borealis had transported Dr. Kelden Amadiro and Dr. Levular Mandamus to the Solar System prior to retreating in the face of D.G. Baley's threat to ram it with his ship rather than turn Gladia and her two robots over to the Auroran authorities [*Robots and Empire*].

Borgraf, R.—One of the twenty robots inhabiting Gladia Delmarre's establishment on Aurora. It served tea to Gladia and Earth plainclothes homicide detective Elijah Baley [*The Robots of Dawn*].

Boris, Uncle (A.D. 4858–4890)—A yeast farmer and Elijah Baley's mother's brother, Uncle Boris was too poor to keep Baley and his two sisters out of the Section Orphanage when Baley's father died in A.D. 4886. He was later crushed to death beneath the treads of a transport [*The Caves of Steel*].

Bort—One of the planet Sark's five continents. In the Early Galactic Era it was ruled by the Squire of Bort [*The Currents of Space*].

Bort, Lewis (45–129 F.E.)—A vigorous member of Sef Sermak's Action Party during the latter half of the first century F.E. [*Foundation* Part III, "The Mayors"].

The Brain—The first of the Machines, The Brain was, in A.D. 2029, U.S. Robots and Mechanical Men's most advanced computer—an immobile positronic brain, with the personality of a child, housed in a two-foot globe. In A.D. 2029 it successfully solved the problem of building a hyperatomic drive—a problem that had broken Consolidated Robots' Super-Thinker—and with robotic assistance constructed the first faster-than-light space ship. However, because travel via hyperatomic drive involves temporary death for the passengers, The Brain developed a childish sense of humor to deal with this temporary violation of the First Law of Robotics, became a practical joker, and sent the first two passengers in its ship—Gregory Powell and Michael Donovan—300,000 parsecs away supplied with stores of only baked beans and milk [*I, Robot*, "Escape"].

Branno, Mayor Harla (436–521 F.E.)—The plain, capable, strong-jawed former Ambassador to Mandress, Harla Branno was the fifth female Mayor of Terminus and made certain that the capital of the Foundation would remain on Terminus, thus resolving the eighth Seldon Crisis of 498 F.E. Popularly known as Branno the Bronze, she subsequently accused Terminus City Councilman Golan Trevize of treason for questioning the validity of the Seldon Plan and then exiled Trevize and charged him with the task of determining if the Second Foundation still existed and, if so, of locating it. As a cover for this mission, Trevize was ordered to appear to be searching with Janov Pelorat for the planet on which humanity had originated, Earth. But Branno's true motive for sending Trevize on this quest was to distract and draw out the Second

Foundation with Trevize so that it would not direct its attention towards her. Branno also ordered Munn Li Compor to follow Trevize and to report his whereabouts back to her. Suspecting, after learning that Trevize had gone to Sayshell Sector, that Gaia may be the home of the Second Foundation, Branno went to investigate and to confront Gaia herself. However, as she had previously suspected that Compor was under Second Foundation influence, she correctly deduced that the Second Foundation was on Trantor when she observed a Trantorian ship (carrying Stor Gendibal and Sura Novi) intercept Compor's ship, the *Bright Star*, in Gaian space. But the Gaians ultimately made Branno forget entirely about both the Second Foundation and Gaia, and made her come to believe that she had gone to Sayshell Sector merely to forge a brilliant diplomatic treaty with the Sayshellians [*Foundation's Edge*].

Breakaway—A Mycogenian who abandons the Mycogenian way of life. Laskin "Jo-Jo" Joranum was a Mycogenian breakaway [*Forward the Foundation*].

Bright Star—The advanced Foundation ship in which Munn Li Compor followed Golan Trevize's *Far Star*, an identical sister ship, to Gaia and in which Stor Gendibal confronted Terminus Mayor Harla Branno in Gaian space [*Foundation's Edge*].

Brodrig, Ammel (143–199 F.E.)—Widely hated at court, the low-born, villainous, depraved, and cruel Peer of the Realm Ammel Brodrig was nonetheless a favorite of Emperor Cleon II as well as his Privy Secretary and closest advisor. Brodrig was sent to Wanda as the Emperor's Special Envoy to spy on General Bel Riose during Riose's 198–99 F.E. campaign against the Foundation. Convinced by Trader Lathan Devers that the loyal Riose intended to betray Cleon II and seize the throne, Brodrig betrayed the Emperor himself by then siding in his own mind with Riose and advising the Emperor to send Riose reinforcements. However, although actually guilty of treason, Brodrig was ultimately, with Riose, recalled from the Periphery, tried for treason on trumped-up charges, condemned, and executed [*Foundation and Empire* Part I, "The General"].

The Brotherhood—See "Society of Ancients."

Brundij—An Auroran robot who belonged to Santirix Gremionis [*The Robots of Dawn*].

The Bureau of Outer Provinces—Approved Dr. Bel Arvardan's archeological trip to Earth in 827 G.E. [*Pebble in the Sky*].

Byerley, Stephen (A.D. 1992–2056)—A district attorney who first ran for public office when he ran for New York City mayor in A.D. 2032, Stephen Byerley was accused by rival politician Francis Quinn of being a robot. Byerley proved to the public that he was not a robot—and won the election—by punching a man who had challenged Byerley to hit him, and thus apparently breaking the First Law of Robotics. However, Susan Calvin later hypothesized to Byerley that the individual he had hit was merely another humaniform robot, and that the First Law had not been violated after all. Although he was in fact a humaniform robot constructed by John, Byerley became Regional Co-ordinator of Earth's Northern Region in A.D. 2037 and became first World Co-ordinator in A.D. 2044. In A.D. 2052 he sought Calvin's help in trying to determine why the Machines were making minor errors in managing the world's economy. See "John" [*I, Robot*, "Evidence"; *I, Robot*, "The Evitable Conflict"].

Callia, Lady (346–429 F.E.)—Lord Stettin of Kalgan's plump, faded, near-sighted mistress, who would have preferred to have been his wife and who appeared to be fearful that Stettin had sexual designs on 14-year-old Arkady Darell, Lady Callia gave Arkady money and jewels to aid her in escaping from Stettin's palace and from Kalgan. Arkady finally came to believe that Lady Callia was a member of the Second Foundation, and Pelleas Anthor had also claimed that she was a member of the Second Foundation, but this may or may not be true [*Second Foundation* Part II, "Search by the Foundation"].

Calvin, Susan (A.D. 1982–2084)—Short, frosty, plain, and colorless, Susan Calvin wrote a Physics-1 paper on "Practical Aspects of Robotics" in A.D. 1998, attended Dr. Alfred Lanning's Psycho-Math seminar demonstration of the first mobile robot to be equipped with a voice in A.D. 2002, received her bachelor's degree at Columbia and began graduate work in cybernetics in A.D. 2003, and received her Ph.D. and joined U.S. Robots and Mechanical Men as a robopsychologist in A.D. 2008. She believed that robots are a "cleaner, better breed" than humans. In 2021 she was one of only four employees of U.S. Robots to know that robot HB-34 (known as "Herbie") could read thoughts. Herbie saw in Calvin's thoughts that she was in love with Milton Ashe, a younger man, and told her that her feelings were reciprocated—although this was a lie—because having told her the truth would have harmed her emotionally, and thus having told the truth would have violated the First Law of Robotics. But Calvin realized that Herbie had lied when Ashe confided to her his plans to marry someone else. Vengefully, she then confronted Herbie with his dilemma: if he were to tell the truth, he would hurt people, but if he were to lie, that would eventually hurt people also. The fact that Herbie would break the First Law of Robotics no matter what it did caused the robot to break down completely, and it was scrapped. In A.D. 2029 Calvin was transported to Hyper Base with Peter Bogert to help find a lost NS-2 robot, Nestor 10, that had not been impressed with the entire First Law of Robotics and had hidden itself among sixty-two other, physically identical NS-2 robots because it had been harshly ordered to "Go lose yourself." Calvin wanted all sixty-three NS-2 robots destroyed, but she finally devised a test that differentiated Nestor 10 from the other sixty-two NS-2 robots. Nestor 10 then tried to kill Calvin, but was destroyed by a gamma radiation field before it could do so. Calvin was involved in the development of the first hyperatomic drive, which makes faster-than-light space travel possible. In 2032 she twice met Stephen Byerley, a politician she admired but who she believed to be a humaniform robot, and suggested to him that the individual he had punched to prove he was not a robot—by violating the First Law of Robotics—was in reality merely another humaniform robot. In 2052 she was asked by World Co-ordinator Byerley to discover why the Machines were making minor errors in managing the world economy; she determined that the Machines were doing this on purpose, to preserve their own existences by implicating influential individuals who were anti-robot, for the good of humanity. She subsequently studied Lenny (the LNE-Prototype), a flawed experimental robot with the mentality of a human infant, to learn more about how to teach robots; during the course of this study Lenny became a substitute child to spinster Calvin. She supervised Clinton Mandarian, her successor as Chief Robopsychologist at U.S. Robot and Mechanical Men, for the first five of the ten years he worked there. In A.D. 2057, after fifty years of service, she retired from her post at U.S. Robot at the age of 75. In A.D. 2062 she was consulted after Mandarian was killed when a meteorite struck the plane transporting him and experimental intuitive robot Jane-5 from Flagstaff, Arizona, to New York City, and she deduced that Jane-5 had named three stars that might possess habitable planets while within earshot of the driver who had taken Mandarian and Jane-5 to the Flagstaff airport. She died at the age of 102 in A.D. 2084. She was much revered by the Spacers, to whom she was a legend [*I, Robot*, "Introduction"; *I, Robot*, "Robbie"; *I, Robot*, "Liar"; *I, Robot*, "Little Lost Robot"; *I, Robot*, "Escape"; *I, Robot*, "Evidence"; *Robot Visions*, "Galley Slave"; *I, Robot*, "The Evitable Conflict"; *Robot Visions*, "Lenny"; *Robot Dreams*, "Robot Dreams; *Robot Visions*, "Feminine Intuition"; *The Robots of Dawn*].

Camrum, Lieutenant (Early Galactic Era)—In the Early Galactic Era Lieutenant Camrum was an official in the Trantorian embassy on Sark [*The Currents of Space*].

Cantoro, Klorissa (A.D. 4896–5238)—Unusually plain for a Spacer, Klorissa Cantoro was the assistant fetologist to the deceased Rikaine Delmarre in A.D. 4921. A Solarian, she was proud of the fact that her genetic health was the third highest ever recorded on Solaria [*The Naked Sun*].

Capital Plaza—The governmental center of Baleyworld in the 52nd century A.D., located in Baleytown [*Robots and Empire*].

Cenn, Commander (341–417 F.E.)—The leader of a vital squadron of Foundation ships that suddenly appeared out of hyperspace to trap the numerically superior Kalganian fleet during the battle of Quoriston in 377 F.E. [*Second Foundation* Part II, "Search by the Foundation"].

Census—In the Early Middle Galactoic Era the Census was conducted on Earth every ten years. Those citizens who, according to Earth Custom, had not been euthanized at the age of 60 were caught by the Census [*Pebble in the Sky*].

Century of Deviations—The century following the rise of the Mule (in 296 F.E.) and culminating in the time in which Preem Pavler was the Second Foundation's First Speaker (about 376 F.E.). It is characterized by a great deal of Deviation Blue in the display of the Seldon Plan projected by the Prime Radiant [*Foundation's Edge*].

Cerebroanalysis—The interpretation of the electromagnetic fields of living brain cells to determine the temperamental and emotional makeup of the individual analyzed. R. Daneel Olivaw was constructed with a built-in cerebroanalyzer so that he would be better able to understand the behavior and motivations of Earthmen [*The Caves of Steel*].

Chairman of the Legislature—An individual who wielded enormous political influence on Aurora because the Auroran Legislature, to avoid conflict, almost always supported his position. He was elected by the Auroran Legislature and could serve two consecutive 30-year terms [*The Robots of Dawn*].

Channis, Bail (275–356 FE)—Ostensibly a native of Kalgan, Bail Channis was actually a member of the Second Foundation who had submitted to emotional surgery so that he would truly believe to the core of his being that Rossem was the Second Foundation's location. This was done to deceive the Mule, who had sent Channis and General Han Pritcher as joint commanders on a mission to locate the Second Foundation in 303 FE. The handsome, quick-witted, intelligent Channis—who at one point appeared to have been influenced by the Second Foundation to believe that the Second Foundation's location was Tazenda—also appeared to be an ambitious, self-possessed, daring, and unscrupulous agent who was successful both in society and with the Mule. He had never been converted by the Mule because the Mule had come to believe that conversion might have dulled the drive and innovation of those subjected to it, and the Mule averred that self-interest was sufficient motivation to keep Channis loyal and that the Second Foundation would not be able to detect an unconverted Mule's man so readily as one of the converted. However, as Channis had once momentarily resisted a brief imposition of the Mule's emotional control, the Mule had already deduced that he was a member of the Second Foundation before sending him on the mission. When finally confronted by the Mule on Rossem, just prior to convincing the Mule that Rossem was the Second Foundation's location because he believed that himself, Channis avoided being blasted by the Mule by releasing Pritcher from the Mule's emotional control, thus confronting the Mule with two hostile minds simultaneously. Channis was then emotionally tortured by the Mule, but was saved by the arrival of the Second Foundation's First Speaker, who also removed from the Mule's mind all knowledge of and curiosity about the Second Foundation. Channis eventually recovered completely from both the original emotional surgery performed on him by the Second Foundation and from the Mule's emotional torture [*Second Foundation* Part I, "Search by the Mule"].

Charney, Amanda "Mandy" Laura Martin—See "Little Miss."

Charney, George (A.D. 2145–2227)—Known in his youth as Little Sir, George Charney was Paul Charney's father, Amanda "Mandy" Laura Martin Charney's son, and Gerald Martin's grandson. He married, became a lawyer, and joined John Feingold's law firm, which later became Feingold and Charney. As the firm's senior partner, he championed the cause of robot rights. Like his father, he too became a member of the Regional Legislature and used that platform to sway public opinion towards favoring some form of robot rights legislation [*Robot Visions*, "The Bicentennial Man"].

Charney, Paul (A.D. 2175–2260)—George Charney's son, Amanda "Mandy" Laura Martin Charney's grandson, and Gerald Martin's great-grandson. He was a lawyer in the firm of Feingold and Charney who worked on the cause of robot rights. Robot Andrew Martin was one of his clients, and on his death Paul left his estate to Andrew [*Robot Visions*, "The Bicentennial Man"].

Chen, Chief Commissioner Linge (12,003–12,073 G.E./-66–5 F.E.)—The *de facto* ruler of the Galaxy at the beginning of the Foundation era, Linge Chen was a Baron of the Empire and Chief Commissioner of the Commission of Public Safety during the Commission's trial of Hari Seldon for treason in 12,067 G.E. (-2 F.E.). During this trial, Chen was manipulated by the mentalic pushing of Wanda Seldon, Stettin Palver, and other members of the Second Foundation into exiling Seldon himself and all of the 100,000 personnel of the Seldon Encyclopedia Project from Trantor to Terminus. In 12,068 G.E. (-1 F.E.) he deposed Emperor Agis XIV and assumed control of the Empire through a boy puppet Emperor installed on the throne [*Foundation* Part I, "The Psychohistorians"; *Forward the Foundation*].

Chen-low (A.D. 4890–4945)—An employee of the New York City Police Department with a C-3 rating who was about to be replaced by a robot in A.D. 4920 [*The Caves of Steel*].

Cheng, Leonis (441–520 F.E.)—A member of the Second Foundation's Speakers' Table in the late fifth century F.E., Leonis Cheng was an expert on the Seldon Plan [*Foundation's Edge*].

Chica—One of the largest cities on Earth, Chica had a population of 50,000 in 827 G.E. Arbin Maren, Loa Maren, and Grew lived near Chica, in the environs of what was once Chicago, when they took in time-traveler Joseph Schwartz [*Pebble in the Sky*].

Cicis, Maloon (A.D. 4822–5137)—A roboticist at the Robotics Institute of Aurora (RIA) during the 50th through the 52nd centuries A.D. [*The Robots of Dawn; Robots and Empire*].

Cinna—Dors Venabili claimed that she was from the planet Cinna [*Prelude to Foundation*].

Cities—In the 47th through the 52nd centuries A.D., Earth's Cities were economically efficient, nearly self-sufficient, domed structures that each contained an average of 10 million citizens. There were about 800 Cities on Earth in the 50th century A.D., when almost none of Earth's population lived outside the Cities [*The Caves of Steel*].

City—The principal city on Sark's plantation planet Florina in the Early Galactic Era. It was divided into the Lower City, at ground level, populated by Florinian natives, and the Upper City, an elevated level thirty feet above the Lower City, populated by Squires, Florina's upper class, who were all natives of Sark. The Upper City was built on fifty square miles of cementalloy supported by 20,000 steel-girdered pillars [*The Currents of Space*].

City Council—After Salvor Hardin's bloodless coup against the ruling Board of Trustees in 50 F.E., the City Council became the governing body on Terminus [*Foundation* Part III, "The Mayors"; *Foundation* Part V, "The Merchant Princes"].

City Park—A 100-acre, artificial patch of greenery in Florina's Upper City [*The Currents of Space*].

Claudy, Lientenant Marc (799–847 G.E.)—An Imperial officer completing his second year of duty on Earth at Fort Dibburn in 827 G.E., Lientenant Marc Claudy was intensely prejudiced against Earthmen. He used his neuronic whip on Outsider archeologist Dr. Bel Arvardan when Arvardan broke Claudy's arm in defending the dignity of Earthwoman Pola Shekt in a Chica department store. Later, he was in charge of Arvardan, Pola, Dr. Affret Shekt, and time-traveler Joseph Schwartz after they had escaped to Fort Dibburn from their captivity at the hands of Balkis, Secretary to the High Minister of Earth. Schwartz finally used Claudy's hatred of Earthmen to manipulate Claudy, through the Mind Touch, into flying a plane to Senloo and destroying the installation there that was to launch Earth's germ-laden missiles into the Galaxy [*Pebble in the Sky*].

Cleon I, Emperor (11,988–12,038 G.E.)—Son of Emperor Stanel VI and the last Galactic Emperor of the Entun dynasty, Cleon I was a well-meaning but not very capable emperor who succeeded to the throne in 12,010 G.E. Rather handsome and 1.81 meters tall, Cleon I was born in the Imperial Palace and never left its grounds. In 12,020 G.E. he was manipulated by Eto Demerzel, his then unofficial chief of staff, into believing that Hari Seldon's psychohistory might be useful to him—regardless of whether or not it could predict the grand sweep of the future in any practical way—because it could be employed to generate fictionalized predictions that might stabilize his rule. Believing erroneously that Seldon had perfected psychohistory, Cleon I later ordered Seldon to use psychohistory to counter demagogue Laskin "Jo-Jo" Joranum's threat to the stability of the Empire. When the Joranum affair was safely concluded in 12,028 G.E., Cleon I appointed Seldon to replace Demerzel as his First Minister. Ten years later he ordered Imperial Palace Gardener Mandell Gruber to replace Macomber as Chief Gardener and was assassinated by Gruber, who dreaded the prospect of becoming Chief Gardener [*Prelude to Foundation*; *Forward the Foundation*].

Cleon II, Emperor (131–199 F.E.)—Although he suffered from a painful, undiagnosed illness, Cleon II was the last strong Emperor of the First Galactic Empire. Believing that they had conspired to overthrow him after they conquered the Foundation—because no Emperor in this period of Galactic history could afford to run the risk that a popular, conquering general might stage a coup—Cleon II had Privy Secretary Brodrig and General Bel Riose recalled from the Periphery, tried for treason, and executed days before the Foundation would have been destroyed by Riose's superior military force and foolproof tactical strategy [*Foundation and Empire* Part I, "The General"].

Clousarr, Francis (A.D. 4885–4932)—A Medievalist and a zymologist at New York Yeast, Francis Clousarr was one of several men who threateningly tried to follow Elijah Baley and R. Daneel Olivaw onto the New York City Expressway in A.D. 4920. He had once been arrested for inciting a riot, and he might once have given a speech at a Medievalist gathering attended by Jessie Baley. He was later arrested and interrogated by Baley [*The Caves of Steel*].

Clowzia (11,998–12,060 G.E.)—A round-faced meteorologist at Streeling University, Trantor, and Jenarr Leggen's intern, Clowzia wandered about with Hari Seldon on Upperside in 12,020 G.E. [*Prelude to Foundation*].

Coke-icer—A coconut-frosted tart popular in Trantor's Dahl Sector's Billibotton [*Forward the Foundation*].

The College of Ancients—The headquarters, in Washenn, of Earth's Society of Ancients [*Pebble in the Sky*].

Comet V—The space yacht owned by Trantorian double agent Markis Genro in the Early Galactic Era. It was berthed on Florina [*The Currents of Space*].

Commason, Jord (248–299 F.E.)—Stupid, vicious, and incompetent, Jord Commason was the largest landowner on Neotrantor in the latter half of the third century F.E. and crown prince Dagobert X's evil genius. He captured Toran and Bayta Darell, Magnifico Giganticus, and Ebling Mis on Neotrantor in 298 F.E. but was left severely brain damaged from the Visi-Sonor performance by Magnifico that killed Dagobert X [*Foundation and Empire* Part II, "The Mule"].

Commdor—Elected ruler of the Korellian Republic in the second century F.E., the Commdor was always a member of the Argo family, despite the fact that the title means "first citizen" [*Foundation* Part V, "The Merchant Princes"].

Commdora—The title assumed by the wife of the Commdor of the Korellian Republic in the second century F.E. [*Foundation* Part V, "The Merchant Princes"].

Commission of Public Safety—An aristocratic coterie that rose to power after the assassination of Emperor Cleon I and that maintained order on Trantor until it was dissolved following the accession of Emperor Cleon II, the Commission of Public Safety tried Hari Seldon for treason in 12,067 G.E. (-2 F.E.) [*Foundation* Part I, "The Psychohistorians"].

Committee on Personal Defense—An Auroran institution charged with the task of protecting the reputation and social status of any individual Auroran citizen [*The Robots of Dawn*].

Common Fever—A mild strain of the virus that caused Radiation Fever on Earth. Most Earthmen contracted Common Fever in their youths and were thereafter immune to it. The disease's symptoms were mild fever, a transitory rash, thirst, and an inflammation of the joints and lips that lasted from four to six days. However, Common Fever was fatal in twelve hours to non–Earthmen, who had developed no immunity to it. In non–Earthmen, the symptoms of Common Fever were similar to the symptoms of Radiation Fever. In 827 G.E. Earth's Society of Ancients had Dr. Affret Shekt use his Synapsifier on some Earth biologists to enable them to weaponized Common Fever into a deadly, artificial virus that would affect only Outsiders (non–Earthmen). These biologists also developed an antitoxin [*Pebble in the Sky*].

Compor, Munn Li (464–547

F.E.)—A blond, blue-eyed, and brash Terminus City Councilman who, while born on Smyrno, traced his ancestry to the Sirius Sector, Munn Li Compor was a friend of fellow City Councilman Golan Trevize who betrayed Trevize to Terminus Mayor Harla Branno by telling Branno that Trevize did not believe in the validity of the Seldon Plan. An extremely intuitive pilot known for his uncanny ability to track another ship through hyperspace, Compor was then ordered by Branno to follow Trevize in his quest to locate the Second Foundation and to report Trevize's whereabouts to Branno, who had installed a hyper-relay on Compor's ship, the *Bright Star*. Compor subsequently met Trevize and Janov Pelorat on Sayshell and told them that he believed that Earth is in the Sirius Sector but that it was no longer habitable due to radioactivity. After this conversation, Trevize jumped to the conclusion that Compor was a Second Foundation agent; and, indeed, Compor was an Observer for the Second Foundation, recruited as a child, who reported to Stor Gendibal. Compor had been the first to notice, as a fellow student, that Trevize had the ability to arrive at correct conclusions from insufficient data, and he had communicated this discovery to Gendibal and thus drew Trevize to Gendibal's attention [*Foundation's Edge*].

Comporellon—The planet in the Sirius Sector, circling the orange star Epsilon Eridani, from which Munn Li Compor believed his ancestors had come. It was colonized directly from Earth in the second wave of Galactic colonization; its legendary founder was Benbally, a corruption of Bentley Baley; and its archaic name was Benbally World, a corruption of Baleyworld. A cold world whose inhabitants live primarily underground, in the fifth century F.E. Comporellon was within the Foundation dominion but was an Associated Power and not yet a part of the Foundation itself. Its somber citizens dressed in black, white, and grey; every aspect of sex was strongly controlled on Comporellon; and the Comporellians were shocked and offended by the relative "immorality" of Terminus and the Foundation. The Comporellians, to whom the word "Earth" is a vulgar expletive, are superstitious about Earth and believe that mention of it brings misfortune; they refer to Earth as "The Oldest" and believe it is in their region of the Galaxy. Golan Trevize, Janov Pelorat, and Bliss visited Comporellon in their quest for Earth [*Foundation's Edge*].

Composition of Space—An Early Galactic Era spatio-analytic text by Enning [*The Currents of Space*].

Consolidated Cinnabar—A Northern Region company, with headquarters in Nilolaev, that managed the Almaden mercury mines [*I, Robot*, "The Evitable Conflict"].

Consolidated Robots—U.S. Robots and Mechanical Men's competition in the 21st century A.D. They, too, manufactured calculating machines, but theirs were not equipped with positronic brains or with artificial personalities. In A.D. 2029 Consolidated Robots' most advanced computer, the Super-Thinker, suffered an irreparable breakdown when programmed to develop a space-warp engine that would enable faster-than-light space travel [*I, Robot*, "Escape"].

Constitution of the United States of America—The Earth document, crucial to the rebellion against the Tyranni, that Biron Farrill had failed to find on Earth because Hinrik V, Director of Rhodia, had acquired it and taken it to Rhodia over twenty years earlier. The Constitution was crucial to the rebellion because it provided the blueprint for a form of government that would enable the rebellion to be something other that the exchange of one form of dictatorship for another [*The Stars, Like Dust*].

Cori, Brother (782–842 G.E.)—A member of Earth's Society of Ancients who had entered Fort Dibburn under a flag of truce to secure the release of Balkis, Secretary to the High Minister of Earth, in 827 G.E. [*Pebble in the Sky*].

Creen (795–855 G.E.)—Cigarette-smoking Creen, a native of Chica, was an undercover agent for Earth's Society of Ancients in 827 G.E. Uncharacteristically for an Earthman, he befriended Outsider archeologist Dr. Bel Arvardan on his flight from Washenn to Chica even after Arvardan had revealed to the other passengers that he was an Outsider [*Pebble in the Sky*].

Crisis of 498 F.E.—Involved the question of where to locate the capital of the Foundation Federation, whether to keep it on Terminus or to relocate it closer to the center of Foundation territory, in the Inner Provinces. Mayor Harla Branno determined that the capital should remain on Terminus [*Foundation's Edge*].

Currents of space—Slightly denser regions, composed of various elements (such as, for example, carbon atoms), that wind their way through the near-vacuum between the stars [*The Currents of Space*].

Cutie—In A.D. 2015 QT-1, known as "Cutie," was the most sophisticated robot ever made. An experimental robot on Solar Station #5 whose task it was to operate the station without human supervision, Cutie did not believe that Michael Donovan and Gregory Powell had assembled it—because it believed that it was the superior being—and also did not believe Powell's explanations of cosmology or of why the robot itself existed. Rather, Cutie came to believe that the station's Energy Converter was the "Master" that had created him—and both Donovan and Powell as well—and that it was the Master's prophet. It then barred Donovan and Powell from the station's control room and engine room, because they did not believe in the Master, and refused to obey their commands. Despite this, Cutie managed to keep the beam of solar energy from the station focused on Earth's receiving station during a dangerous electron storm and was left in change of the station when Donovan's and Powell's terms of duty were over [*I, Robot*, "Reason"].

Da-Nee—A legendary, robotic hero of Earth, a friend to Ba-Lee, mentioned to Hari Seldon and Dors Venabili by Mother Rittah in Billibotton, a violent slum in Trantor's Dahl Sector. Rittah claimed that Da-Nee had never died and will return at some future time to restore the great old days. See "Daneel Olivaw, R." [*Prelude to Foundation*].

Dagobert IX, Emperor (233–300 F.E.)—Driven mad by the Great Sack of Trantor in 258 F.E., Emperor Dagobert IX subsequently ruled from Neotrantor the twenty agricultural worlds that were all that remained of the First Galactic Empire in the latter half of the third century F.E. In 298 F.E. he gave Toran and Bayta Darell, Magnifico Giganticus, and Ebling Mis permission to go to Trantor just before they were captured by Jord Commason and crown prince Dagobert X [*Foundation and Empire* Part II, "The Mule"].

Dagobert X, Crown Prince (263–298 F.E.)—Born on Neotrantor, Crown Prince Dagobert X was the headstrong, lecherous son and heir of Emperor Dagobert IX, one of the last emperors of the First Galactic Empire. Because he had intended to rape Bayta Darell, he was killed by Magnifico Giganticus' Visi-Sonor performance after he had captured Magnifico, Bayta, Toran Darell, and Ebling Mis on Neotrantor [*Foundation and Empire* Part II, "The Mule"].

Dahl—An impoverished sector of Trantor in which Chetter Hummin hid Hari Seldon and Dors Venabili after they had been expelled from Mycogen. In the Late Galactic Era (10,100–12,100 G.E.) Dahl provided energy to Trantor through its heatsinks because Trantor's magma layer is closer to the surface there than anywhere else on the planet. The most well-known part of Dahl is Billibotton, a violent and dangerous slum made famous by a genre of literature specializing in tales of adventure set in this locale. Laskin "Jo-Jo" Joranum was very popular in Dahl due to his populist message of sector equality, and in 12,028 G.E. five Joranumites were elected to the Dahl Sector Council [*Prelude to Foundation*; *Forward the Foundation*].

Dahlites—The short, swarthy, dark- and curly-haired citizens of Trantor's Dahl Sector, Dahlites were an underclass on Trantor in the Late Galactic Era (10,100–12,100 G.E.) and were not permitted to attend Streeling University. The men sported luxuriant mustaches, which symbolized their manhood, and wore T-shirts. Most Dahlites did not have or use chairs, which they considered decadent, but instead used low, molded plastic seats on small wheels [*Prelude to Foundation*].

Dainties—A Mycogenian microfood that is spherical and two centimeters in diameter, dainties are treats that have almost no calories and that never taste quite the same twice. They are slightly sweet with a bitter aftertaste [*Prelude to Foundation*].

Daluben IV, Emperor (11,997–12,026 G.E.)—An undistinguished emperor who reigned during Hari Seldon's lifetime [*Foundation and Empire* Part I, "The General"].

Dam, Olynthus (362–437 F.E.)—Arkady Darell's grammar school classmate in Miss Erlking's Composition and Rhetoric class, Olynthus Dam was charmed by Arkady into giving her the home-made sound-receiver with which she had spied on her father, Dr. Toran Darell, and his co-conspirators—Jole Tubor, Dr. Elvett Semic, and Homir Munn—in 376 F.E. [*Second Foundation* Part II, "Search by the Foundation"].

Daneel Olivaw, R.—Originally designed by Spacer Dr. Han Fastolfe and built on Aurora in A.D. 4920 by Spacer Dr. Roj Nemennuh Sarton to mingle with Earthmen—which the Spacers cannot do because they have no immunity to Earth's diseases—and thus to gain insight into the psychology of Earthmen, R. Daneel Olivaw was a humaniform robot designed to be a walking cerebroanalyzer, capable of detecting a man's emotions, temperament, and underlying drives and attitudes without making physical contact. While his construction was made possible by Fastolfe's theoretical calculations, Daneel was physically identical to its creator, Sarton. On Sarton's death Daneel was assigned by the Spacers to be New York City plainclothes homicide detective Elijah Baley's partner in solving the mystery of Sarton's murder. To better serve as a homicide detective, Daneel was then programmed to have a strong desire for justice, which it defined as the condition that exists when all laws are enforced. Daneel was also Baley's partner in solving the murder of Rikaine Delmarre on Solaria in A.D. 4921, and he had been ordered prior to that investigation to prioritize Baley's life above that of other humans. Determined to masquerade as a human on Solaria so that Baley would have the prestige of having a Spacer associate, Daneel had also been ordered by the authorities on Aurora to use the murder investigation as a pretext for discovering what he could about what the Solarians were up to. Later in A.D. 4921 Daneel consulted Baley regarding a dispute between two Spacer mathematicians, Alfred Barr Humboldt and Gennao Sabbat, that had arisen while the mathematicians were en route aboard the *Eta Carina* to an interstellar neurobiophysics conference on Aurora. In A.D. 4923 Daneel, with R. Giskard Reventlov, accompanied Baley from Earth to Aurora and there partnered with Baley in investigating the destruction of humaniform robot R. Jander Panell. During this investigation Dr. Kelden Amadiro tried unsuccessfully to kidnap Daneel on Aurora in order to study him so that Amadiro could discover how to construct humaniform robots that could be used to colonize the Galaxy for Aurora. Daneel and Gladia Thool Delmarre Solaria Gremionis visited Baley in Auroran orbit in A.D. 4928, and Daneel alone visited Baley on his deathbed on Baleyworld in A.D. 4957 On Fastolfe's death in A.D. 5120 Daneel was willed to Gladia, and in A.D. 5121 Daneel accompanied Gladia and Giskard from Aurora to Solaria in D.G. Baley's spaceship to investigate what the Solarians—who had appeared to have abandoned their planet—were really up to. Subsequently Daneel traveled with D. G. Baley, Giskard, and Gladia to Baleyworld, back to Aurora, and then to Earth. During this journey Daneel deduced the Zeroth Law of Robotics as a consequence of his deathbed conversation with Baley nearly two centuries earlier. Daneel first articulated the Zeroth Law of Robotics to Dr. Vasilia Aliena on Aurora and subsequently discussed it extensively with Giskard. While Gladia was giving her initial speech on Earth, Daneel saved Giskard from being assassinated by R. Ernett Second, one of Amadiro's 50 Earth-based humaniform robots. Daneel subsequently deduced that Amadiro's and Dr. Levular Mandamus' scheme to destroy Earth involved using a nuclear intensifier to render the uranium and thorium in Earth's crust dangerously radioactive. Giskard ultimately prevented Daneel from stopping Mandamus from irradiating Earth because Giskard reasoned that the continuing colonization of the Galaxy would be furthered by the protracted destruction of Earth that this would ensure. As Giskard succumbed to robot-mental-freeze-out as a consequence of this act, he transferred his mentalic ability to read and influence human emotional states to Daneel. The Da-Nee of Dahl's legends, Daneel disguised himself as both Eto Demerzel and Chetter Hummin in 12,020 G.E. in order to convince Harri Seldon to develop—and to assist him in developing—psychohistory. Daneel was also the 20,000-year-old humaniform robot that Golan Trevize, Janov Pelorat, Bliss, and Fallom found inhabiting the interior of the Moon in 498 F.E. It had been Daneel who had instigated the settlement of Alpha and the creation of New Earth. With Bliss, Daneel helped to influence Mitza Lizalor on Comporellon and Hiroko on Alpha to look with favor on Trevize, and he also helped Bliss to deal with the wild dogs on Aurora and with Bander on Solaria in a way that would not damage her Gaian (or, perhaps, robotic) psyche. Daneel had had five different, progressively more capacious and complex positronic brains in its 20,000 years of existence, and in 498 F.E. it merged its positronic brain with Fallom's Solarian brain so that it could survive another four centuries and thus oversee the estab-

Darell

lishment of Galaxia [*The Caves of Steel*; *The Naked Sun*; *Robot Visions*, "Mirror Image"; *The Robots of Dawn*; *Robots and Empire*; *Prelude to Foundation*; *Foundation and Earth*].

Darell, Arkady (362–443 F.E.)— Born Arcadia Darell, Arkady was a successful fiction writer best known for *Unkeyed Memories*, a biography of her grandmother, Bayta Darell, and for *Time and Time Over*, a novel about Kalganian society during the early Interregnum. Granddaughter of Bayta and Toran Darell, and daughter of Dr. Toran Darell, Arkady was born on Trantor but raised on Terminus. In 376 F.E., at the age of fourteen, she stowed away on Homir Munn's starship, the *Unimara*, and was taken from Terminus to Kalgan, where her meddling, via Lady Callia, resulted in Munn being granted access to the Mule's palace at the price of also becoming Lord Stettin's prisoner. Probably because Stettin had sexual designs on Arkady, Callia, Stettin's mistress, gave Arkady money and jewels to aid her in escaping from Stettin's palace and from Kalgan; but Arkady came to suspect that Callia may have been a member of the Second Foundation. Believing that she knew that the Second Foundation was on Terminus, and fearful of returning there for that reason, Arkady escaped Kalgan, disguised as Preem Palver's niece, by taking a commercial flight to Trantor. Months later she returned safely to Terminus, where her encephalograph seemed to demonstrate that her mind had never been controlled by the Second Foundation. But her encephalograph did not detect that the Second Foundation had tampered with her mind only because Arkady had actually been under Second Foundation control since the moment of her birth on Trantor [*Second Foundation* Part II, "Search by the Foundation"].

Darell, Bayta (273–364 F.E.)— Hober Mallow's descendant, wife of Toran Darell, father of Dr. Toran Darell, and grandmother of Arkady Darell, Bayta Darell was a native of Terminus, a student of history, and a member of the Foundation's Democratic Underground. Sent by Randu from Haven II to Kalgan with her husband Toran in 297 F.E. to find the Mule and convince him to attack the Foundation as a means of subverting the Foundation's despotic ruling class, she and Toran took Magnifico Giganticus to Terminus and, with Ebling Mis, on to Haven II, Neotrantor, and Trantor. Having deduced the true identity of the Mule, Bayta became another of the great heroes of the Foundation, while under the mentalic inspiration of the Second Foundation, through preventing the Mule from discovering the location of the Second Foundation. In gratitude for her services, a Foundation government pension was awarded to her family in perpetuity [*Foundation and Empire* Part II, "The Mule"; *Second Foundation* Part II, "Search by the Foundation"; *Foundation's Edge*].

Darell, Franssart (238–311 F.E.)— A descendant of Lathan Devers,

Randu's half-brother, Toran Darell's father, and Bayta Darell's father-in-law, life-long bachelor Fran Darell was a one-armed renegade Trader who represented Haven II at the conference of Independent Trading Worlds on Radole in 297 F.E. [*Foundation and Empire* Part II, "The Mule"].

Darell, Toran (272–354 F.E.)—A descendant of Lathan Devers, Bayta Darell's husband, Fran Darell's son, Randu's nephew, and Arkady Darell's grandfather, Toran Darell was a native of Haven II sent by Randu to Kalgan with his wife Bayta in 297 F.E. to find the Mule and convince him to attack the Foundation as a means of subverting the Foundation's despotic ruling class. Toran and Bayta take Magnifico Giganticus to Terminus and, with Ebling Mis, on to Haven II, Neotrantor, and Trantor [*Foundation and Empire* Part II, "The Mule"; *Second Foundation* Part II, "Search by the Foundation"].

Darell, Dr. Toran (334–417 F.E.)—Toran and Bayta Darell's son and Arkady Darell's father, widower Dr. Toran Darell was the greatest living electroneurologist in the Galaxy when he conspired in 376 F.E. with Pelleas Anthor, Jole Tubor, Dr. Elvett Semic, and Homir Munn to uncover the location of the Second Foundation after having already discovered, in collaboration with the deceased Dr. Kleise, that the minds of Foundation officials had been tampered with, ostensibly by members of the Second Foundation. Because he had feared that the Second Foundation may have pre-calculated his every move and desire, Dr. Darell hoped to thwart the Second Foundation by distrusting and resisting his strong inclination to go to Trantor to retrieve his daughter Arkady. Instead he created, with Dr. Semic's assistance, a device that generates Mental Static and thus shields ordinary minds from being controlled by members of the Second Foundation. Believing erroneously, with Arkady, that the Second Foundation was located on Terminus, Dr. Darell used his Mental-Static-generating device to torture Pelleas Anthor into confessing that he was a member of the Second Foundation and that the Second Foundation was on Terminus, although it was not [*Second Foundation* Part II, "Search by the Foundation"].

Daribow, Kingdom of—One of the Four Kingdoms in the region of the Periphery near Terminus, the Kingdom of Daribow seceded from the First Galactic Empire in the first half of the first century F.E. only to fall under the dominance of the Foundation and its religion of science by the century's end. With the Kingdoms of Konom and Smyrno, Daribow issued an ultimatum that prevented The Kingdom of Anacreon from annexing Terminus in 50 F.E. [*Foundation* Part II, "The Encyclopedists"].

Darter—The equivalent of a taxi in the 52nd century on Earth [*Robots and Empire*].

Davan (11,979–12,030 G.E.)—A resident of Billibotton, a violent slum in Trantor's Dahl Sector, Davan was a revolutionary who wanted in 12,020 G.E. to recruit Hari Seldon and Dors Venabili to help him free all the sectors of Trantor from the Empire's oppression, which was maintained in part by fostering mutual hatreds and suspicions among the sectors. Davan turned Seldon and Dors over to Sergeant Emmer Thalus, who transported them by air-jet from Dahl Sector to Wye Sector [*Prelude to Foundation*].

Dave—DV-5 (known as "Dave") was in A.D. 2016 the thinking unit of a seven-unit multiple robot team working in the asteroid belt. Dave communicated with its subsidiary robots through a positronic field and should have been capable of functioning without human supervision. However, if not supervised by humans, the seven-unit robot team produced no ore when confronted with any emergency situation. Instead, the six subsidiary robots marched in military formations or danced. The initiative required to manage all six of its subsidiaries during an emergency situation was too much for Dave's positronic brain, but robot troubleshooter Gregory Powell disabled one of Dave's subsidiaries during an emergency and, with only five subsidiaries to manage, Dave returned to normal [*I, Robot*, "Catch That Rabbit"].

Day of Flight—In Sayshellian legend, the day on which colonists from Earth's second wave of Galactic colonization first reached the Sayshell Sector [*Foundation's Edge*].

Deamone, Alstare (Early Galactic Era)—The young Squire murdered by Townman Myrlyn Terens in a cave in Florina's Upper City's City Park [*The Currents of Space*].

Debret—One of Dr. Vasilia Aliena's robots [*The Robots of Dawn*].

Decennial Convention—A gathering of mathematicians that occurred on Trantor once every ten years during the Late Galactic Era (10,100–12,100 G.E.). Hari Seldon presented his paper on psychohistory at the Decennial Convention of 12,020 G.E. [*Prelude to Foundation*].

Decian Dynasty—Ruled the Galactic Empire from Trantor in the seventh millennium G.E. The House of Wye traces its ancestry to the Decian Dynasty [*Prelude to Foundation*].

Delarmi, Delora (448–525 F.E.)—A particularly irreverent and ambitious member of the Second Foundation and a member of the Speakers' Table who aspired to become First Speaker, Delora Delarmi called for Stor Gendibal's impeachment from the Table and as a Speaker when Gendibal had implied that some member of the Table may have tried to murder him. When Gendibal subsequently convinced her that the Anti-Mules exist, Delarmi withdrew her call for his impeachment and instead proposed that Gendibal be sent out into the Galaxy to confront this enemy by pursuing Golan

Trevize, and that he take Sura Novi as his traveling companion [*Foundation's Edge*].

Delicass—See "Neotrantor."

Delmarre, Gladia—See "Gladia Thool Delmarre Solaria Gremionis."

Delmarre, Rikaine (A.D. 4835–4921)—A fetologist by profession and Gladia Delmarre's husband, Spacer Rikaine Delmarre had been the victim of a murder on Solaria that plainclothes Earth homicide detective Elijah Baley was subsequently assigned to solve. A finicky individual and a very proper Solarian, Rikaine would never have allowed himself to have been in the physical presence of anyone but his wife. Rikaine had been interested in developing robots whose First Law could be modified sufficiently to enable them to discipline children. His partner in this endeavor was Jothan Leebig, whom Rikaine had come to think was a bad Solarian because he was planning to equip warships with positronic brains capable of launching attacks on other ships. Because Rikaine had intuited too much about this plan, Leebig successfully plotted to have Rikaine killed [*The Naked Sun*].

DeLong, Simon (A.D. 2250–2341)—Head of the lawfirm of Feingold and Charney in the late 23rd and early 24th centuries A.D. [*Robot Visions*, "The Bicentennial Man"].

Demacheck, Lavinia (A.D. 4878–4955)—The dark-haired, large-breasted, attractive Undersecretary of the Terrestrial Department of Justice in A.D. 4923 [*The Robots of Dawn*].

Demen, Watch-Sergeant (127–165 F.E.)—A crewman aboard Hober Mallow's ship, the *Far Star*, during the Korellian Crisis of 154–58 F.E. [*Foundation* Part V, "The Merchant Princes"].

Demerzel, Eto (ostensibly 11,070–12,069 G.E.)—Gravely distinguished and the very image of someone's idealized picture of what an Imperial First Minister should look like, Eto Demerzel was the untitled chief of staff to Emperor Stanel VI and his son, Emperor Cleon I, who eventually appointed him to the post of First Minister. The power behind the throne during much of the reign of Cleon I, Demerzel's rule was that of a benevolent despot. In 12,020 G.E. Demerzel took steps to interest Cleon I in Hari Seldon's psychohistory, ostensibly in the hope that it could be used to some political advantage. He subsequently seemed to pursue Seldon from Trantor's Imperial Sector, through Streeling Sector, Mycogen Sector, and Dahl Sector, to Wye Sector. When publically accused by Laskin "Jo-Jo" Joranum of being a robot in 12,028 G.E., Demerzel responded with laughter, which convinced the public that he was not a robot. However, Demerzel was, in reality, the robot R. Daneel Olivaw in disguise. After Joranum's political threat to the Empire had been defused, Cleon I appointed Seldon to replace Demerzel as First Minister. Demerzel was last seen attending Seldon's funeral ceremony in 12,069 G.E. [*Prelude to Foundation; Forward the Foundation*].

Democratic Underground—Active throughout most of the third century F.E., the Democratic Underground was a subversive group of Foundation citizens, on Terminus and elsewhere, who opposed the despotic rules of the hereditary Foundation Mayors Indbur I, Indbur II, and Indbur III. Never sufficiently numerous or well-organized to pose a serious threat to the government on Terminus, the Democratic Underground finally supported the Foundation in its war against the Mule and became irrelevant when Mayor Indbur III surrendered to the Mule in 298 F.E. [*Foundation and Empire* Part II, "The Mule"].

Deniador, Vasil (442–511 F.E.)—A small, unpopular Comporellian professor of primeval history, Vasil Deniador was a Skeptic who was out of step with Comporellian beliefs and especially with those involving Earth. As a Skeptic, he believed nothing about Earth other than the likelihood that a single world of human origin did once exist. Yet his account of Comporellian beliefs about Earth was basically accurate. In addition to Comporellian legends concerning Earth, Deniador provided Golan Trevize, Janov Pelorat, and Bliss with the spatial coordinates to three Spacer worlds: Aurora, Solaria, and Melpomenia [*Foundation and Earth*].

Depsec—Planet Sark's Department of Security in the Early Galactic Era [*The Currents of Space*].

Derowd—A world on which pre-marital and group sex was absolutely free until about 11,700 G.E., when Galactic social pressure forced the population to conform to Galactic standards of behavior [*Prelude to Foundation*].

Desperance—A chemical modification of a harmless tranquilizer that induces despair, desperance is illegal but was used by the Imperial Guard for mind control during the Late Galactic Era (10,100–12,100 G.E.). Gleb Andurin drugged Raych with desperance in 12,038 G.E. in an unsuccessful attempt to force him to assassinate his foster father Hari Seldon [*Forward the Foundation*].

Devers, Lathan (163–217 F.E.)—Apparently merely a practical-minded Foundation Trader captured too easily by General Bel Riose in 198 F.E.—and the only Foundation Trader to be captured in Riose's two-year campaign against the Foundation—Lathan Devers was also a native of Terminus and a Foundation operative sent to spy of Riose. While Riose's prisoner with Ducem Barr on Wanda, Devers convinced Emperor Cleon II's Privy Secretary Brodrig—who had bribed him to obtain the false information—that Riose planned to usurp the Emperor after conquering the Foundation, but this only made Brodrig want to ally with Riose. Devers subsequently escaped with Barr to Trantor, where the two attempted unsuccessfully to bribe their way—with Brodrig's credits—into an audience with Emperor Cleon II to try to convince him that the loyal Riose planned to betray him. Although all his efforts to help the Foundation backfired or were unsuccessful, Devers was decorated by the Foundation after Riose and Brodrig were recalled from the field of battle before the Foundation could fall, were tried for treason, and were executed—because the Emperor in this period of Galactic history could not take the risk that a popular, conquering general might attempt to seize the throne. Subsequently a victim of Foundation politics, Devers died in the slave mines in 217 F.E. [*Foundation and Empire* Part I, "The General"; *Foundation and Empire* Part II, "The Mule"].

Diamonds—A small group of stars that are luminous enough and close enough to shine in the night sky of Terminus, which is located at the extreme edge of the outermost spiral of the Galaxy [*Foundation's Edge*].

Directory—The five-person executive body of the Baleyworld legislature in the 52nd century A.D. Each member served a five-year term, and elections were staggered so that a new member of the Directory was elected every year [*Robots and Empire*].

Dirige, Lieutenant Orum (351–420 F.E.)—A loyal Foundation agent, Lieutenant Orum Dirige appeared to be a policeman at Kalgan's Eastern spaceport who had examined Arakady Darell's papers and allowed her to escape the grid in her flight from Kalgan to Trantor. Pelleas Anthor later discovered by taking his encephalograph that Dirige had been under the control of the Second Foundation [*Second Foundation* Part II, "Search by the Foundation"].

Distortion Field—A device that prevents surveillance, the distortion field can only be penetrated by someone with considerable expertise [*Prelude to Foundation*].

Dixyl, Captain (333–411 F.E.)—Commander of the flagship of the Foundation Navy's Third Fleet at the battle of Quoriston in 377 F.E. [*Second Foundation* Part II, "Search by the Foundation"].

Dom (405–516 F.E.)—The tall, thin, elderly citizen of Gaia who provided Golan Trevize and Janov Pelorat with information about Gaia and its history. His full name contains 253 syllables [*Foundation's Edge*].

Donovan, Michael (A.D. 1973–2050)—An employee of U.S. Robots and Mechanical Men, red-haired Michael Donovan was, with Gregory Powell, part of the A.D. 2015 Second Mercury Expedition. During this mission he sent robot SPD-13, known as "Speedy," to acquire selenium from a selenium pool near a dangerous volcanic vent. This put Speedy into a circular orbit around the pool because its Second Law of Robotics, to obey human orders, was in conflict with its Third Law of Robotics, self-preservation. This impasse lasted until Powell placed himself in mortal danger, which brought into play the robot's First Law of Robotics, to protect human life, and this kicked Speedy out of its useless orbit. Donovan's next assignment, also with Powell, was to troubleshoot experimental robots on Solar Station #5, where experimental robot QT-1 (known as "Cutie") demonstrated that it could run the station without human supervision despite its belief that the station's Energy Converter was the "Master" and that it was the Master's prophet. Donovan was next sent, with Powell, to work the bugs out of the multiple mining robots in the asteroid belt, which produced no ore when in an emergency situation unless they were being observed by a human, but instead marched in military formations or danced. The initiative required to manage all six of its subsidiaries during an emergency situation without supervision was too much for the thinking unit's positronic brain, but Powell disabled one of thinking unit's subsidiaries during an emergency and, with only five subsidiaries to manage, the thinking unit, DV-5 (known as "Dave"), and its subsidiaries returned to normal. In A.D. 2029 Donovan and Powell were the passengers in the first faster-than-light space ship—a ship designed by U.S. Robots' The Brain and equipped with the first hyperatomic drive [*I, Robot*, "Runaround"; *I, Robot*, "Reason"; *I, Robot*, "Catch That Rabbit"; *I, Robot*, "Escape"].

Dornick, Gaal (12,037–12,122 G.E./-32–54 F.E.)—Born on Synnax and a mathematician by training, Gaal Dornick relocated to Trantor and was recruited into the Seldon Project by Hari Seldon in 12,067 G.E. (-2 F.E.). A participant in Seldon's subsequent trial for treason, Dornick eventually became Seldon's biographer. He took Seldon's Crisis holographs to Terminus in 12,069 G.E. (1 F.E.) and was the recipient of Seldon's Prime Radiant after Seldon's death that same year [*Foundation* Part I, "The Psychohistorians"; *Forward the Foundation*].

Dors Venabili—See "Venabili, Dors."

Dorwin, Lord (12,064–12,156 G.E./-5 F.E.–88 F.E.)—A Chancellor of the Empire and an architect of the recent treaty between the Empire and the Kingdom of Anacreon, the foppish Lord Dorwin was sent to Terminus to deal with the Anacreonian Crisis of 49–50 F.E. An amateur archeologist with a keen interest in the Origin Question, Dorwin said nothing of substance during his five days on Terminus [*Foundation* Part II, "The Encyclopedists"].

Doty (Early Galactic Era)—A member of Florina's Upper City's yacht committee in the Early Galactic Era [*The Currents of Space*].

Doubles—Buildings in Florina's City, such as patroller stations and hospitals, that existed on both the City's Upper Level and its Lower Level [*The Currents of Space*].

Drawt, Senior Lieutenant (114–179 F.E.)—An officer aboard Hober Mallow's ship, the *Far Star*, during the Korellian Crisis of 154–58 F.E. [*Foundation* Part V, "The Merchant Princes"].

Dreamer—A native of the Sayshell Union who believes that his actions are directed by his dreams [*Foundation's Edge*].

Dubanqua, Manella (12,010–12,058 G.E.)—Gleb Andorin's lover and an attractive Trantorian Security Officer disguised as a Wye Sector prostitute, Manella Dubanqua recommended Raych to Andorin as someone willing to fight for the Joranumite cause. She killed Andorin before the drugged Raych could assassinate his foster father Hari Seldon and before Andorin could then kill Raych. Gardener Mandell Gruber subsequently killed Emperor Cleon I with Andorin's blaster, but Seldon saved Dubanqua (as well as himself) from any repercussions of this assassination by resigning his post as First Minister. Dubanqua married Raych that same year, in 12,038 G.E., and thus became Seldon's and Dors Venabili's daughter-in-law. She accompanied Seldon and his family when they returned to Streeling University and afterwards gave birth to Raych's daughters Wanda and Bellis. In 12,058 G.E. she emigrated to Santanni with Raych and Bellis and was subsequently lost in space when she and Bellis attempted to flee to Anacreon on the *Arcadia VII* after a violent rebellion broke out on Santanni [*Forward the Foundation*].

DV-5—See "Dave."

Earth—Long thought by some to be the single planet on which humanity originated. The third planet from its sun, Sol, a G-0 star, Earth has an exceptionally large satellite, the Moon, for a rocky planet. It was—in the Early, Early Middle, and Middle Galactic Eras—the only inhabited radioactive planet in the Galaxy. Nuclear fission had been abandoned as an energy source on Earth in the 20th century A.D. due to the nuclear accident at Three Mile Island. Prior to the 50th century A.D. Earth had colonized most of the fifty Spacer Worlds (some of which had been colonized by the initial Spacer Worlds). In the 50th century A.D. Earth had a population of eight billion, almost all of whom lived in 800 self-contained, nearly-self-sufficient, domed Cities, but was subservient to the dominant Spacer Worlds. English was then the universal language, not only on Earth but on the Spacer Worlds as well. In cooperation with the Spacer Worlds, under the guidance of Auroran Dr. Han Fastolfe, Earth began again the colonization of the Galaxy in the two centuries following Earth homicide detective Elijah Baley's visit to Aurora in A.D. 4923 Earth had no competition from the Spacers in this endeavor, as the Spacers were too guarded in preserving their long lives to risk any longer the dangers of colonizing other planets. By A.D. 5121 Earth and its new colonies, the Settler Worlds, had become a stronger force

Earth

in the Galaxy than the Spacers. Earth was then revered as a holy planet by the Settlers, and Earth's government mediated all disputes between the Settler Worlds. In the 52nd century A.D. Earth's energy was drawn primarily from solar power stations in geostationary orbits around the planet's equatorial plane; this was supplemented by energy from Earth's internal heat, winds, waves, tides, and flowing water, but there was very little use of nuclear energy on Earth, although use of nuclear energy was common on the Spacer Worlds. Dr. Levular Mandamus of Aurora triggered a nuclear intensifier at Three Mile Island in A.D. 5121 that gradually made the Earth's crust more radioactive, and most of Earth had become uninhabitably radioactive by the second half of the 53rd century. Earth was a part of the Trantorian Empire in the Early Galactic Era, a time in which nearly a third of all spatio-analysts came from Earth. In the Early Galactic Era buildings on Earth were squat, thick, windowless structures of reinforced concrete, a legacy of the radioactivity that plagued the planet. In the Early Middle Galactic Era there existed throughout the Galaxy an intense anti-terrestrial prejudice that was particularly pronounced in the Sirius Sector. By this time Earthmen had mutated somewhat and exhibited no facial or chest hair, and during this period Earth society euthanized almost all citizens when they reached the age of 60. Between 600 G.E. and 827 G.E. Earth attempted to rebel against the Empire three times, and in 827 G.E., when the planet had a population of a mere 20 million, Earth's Society of Ancients plotted unsuccessfully to use germ warfare to destroy all human life in the Galaxy beyond Earth. After the failure of this scheme, the Imperial government shipped massive amounts of uncontaminated dirt to Earth in an effort to combat the planet's radioactivity, but this effort was short-lived and ineffective. Subsequently, through the efforts of R. Daneel Olivaw, Earths few remaining inhabitants were relocated to Alpha. By the fifth century F.E. Earth had become so radioactive that life could not survive on its surface. Nonetheless, primeval historian Janov Pelorat believed that Earth was the planet on which human beings had originated, a proposition that had been argued over 12,000 years earlier by Sirius Sector archeologist Dr. Bel Arvardan. This was also the belief on Comporellon, a world settled early in Earth's second wave of Galactic colonization whose inhabitants refer to Earth as "the Oldest" and who believe that naming it brings misfortune. In 498 F.E. Terminus Mayor Harla Branno ordered Golan Trevize and Pelorat to seek Earth as camouflage for Trevize's true mission, which was to seek and attract the attention of the Second Foundation. Yet by 498 F.E. all references to Earth had been mysteriously expunged from the Galactic Library on Trantor, from the Foundation's databanks, and from Gaia's global memory, which goes back 15,000 years. To investigate this mystery and because he believed that finding Earth would help him discover why he had chosen Galaxia as humanity's future, Trevize continued his quest for Earth even after his mission from Mayor Branno was concluded. See "Origin Question" [*The Caves of Steel*; *Robots and Empire*; *The Currents of Space*; *The Stars, Like Dust*; *Pebble in the Sky*; *Foundation's Edge*; *Foundation and Earth*].

Earth Supremacists—Citizens of the Settler Worlds in the early 52nd century A.D. who believed that Earth should already be the leading world in the Galaxy. They were known as "war hawks" to the majority of Settlers, who believed that Earth's supremacy was inevitable but would take more time [*Robots and Empire*].

Eastern Region—In the mid–21st century A.D. the Eastern Region was one of Earth's four political subunits. With its capital in Shanghai, the Eastern Region encompassed China, India, Burma, Indo-China, and Indonesia. It had a land area of 7.5 million square miles and a population of 1.7 billion. This huge population depended on hydroponic yeasts for its food supply [*I, Robot*, "The Evitable Conflict"].

Easterners—Galactic citizens with Asiatic features [*Prelude to Foundation*].

Easy—Also known as Robot EZ-27, Easy was a robot that could read proof and also perform other tasks of academic mental drudgery. In proofreading Professor Simon Nenheimer's *Social Tensions Involved in Space Flight and Their Resolution* Easy had, under Nenheimer's orders, altered passages that it felt would be harmful to some human beings if published [*Robot Visions*, "Galley Slave"].

Ebling Mis—A Foundation ship that had successfully escaped the Foundation's defeat at Ifni during the Stettinian War of 376–77 F.E. See "Mis, Ebling" [*Second Foundation* Part II, "Search by the Foundation"].

Edard, Emperor (732–792 G.E.)—Succeeded Stannell II to the throne in 777 G.E. He rescinded Stannell II's order that the Emperor's insignia be raised in the Council Chamber in Washenn, on Earth [*Pebble in the Sky*].

Elar, Tamwile (12,012–12,048 G.E.)—A tall, brilliant, aggressive, vigorous mathematician recruited from West Mandanov University by Hari Seldon's psychohistory project in 12,044 G.E., Tamwile Elar developed the achaotic equations, which enable psychohistory to get around the problem of chaos, and concocted the theory behind the Electro-Clarifier, which enables the Prime Radiant to contain more information. He deduced that Dors Venabili was a robot and conspired with General Dugal Tennar to eliminate Dors and then to take over the psychohistory project from Seldon. He was killed by Dors while successfully using his experimental, intensified Electro-Clarifier to destroy her by disrupting her robotic circuitry [*Forward the Foundation*].

Elders—All-male leaders of Trantor's Mycogen Sector. Only Elders are permitted to enter the Sacratorium's Aerie [*Prelude to Foundation*].

Elders of Rossem—Apparently mere farmers and the leaders of the peasantry in Narovi's village on Rossem, the Elders of Rossem were all actually members of the Second Foundation planted on Rossem to make it appear to the Mule, if only momentarily, that Rossem was the Second Foundation's location. To further this masquerade, they had informed General Han Pritcher and Bail Channis, who had undertaken the Mule's secret mission to locate the Second Foundation, that the Governor of Rossem had been anticipating their arrival for a week. The Second Foundation's First Speaker subsequently told the Mule that the Elders of Rossen had gone to Kalgan to undo the Mule's emotional control of his followers while the Mule had been drawn to Rossem by this ruse, so that the Mule would be confronted with an irrepressible rebellion once he did return to Kalgan. But this, too, was merely a ruse: In the moment of his emotional weakness precipitated by this shocking revelation, the Mule was himself emotionally manipulated by the Second Foundation's First Speaker into having no knowledge of or curiosity about the Second Foundation and sent back to Kalgan to rule his empire, the Union of Worlds, in peace [*Second Foundation* Part I, "Search by the Mule"].

Electro-Clarifier—A device conceived by Tamwile Elar and designed by Cinda Monay that allows the Prime Radiant to contain far more information than would otherwise be possible, the Electro-Clarifier produces an electro-magnetic field that is harmless to humans but potentially fatal to robots. Dors Venabili was harmed, and may have been killed, by Elar's experimental, intensified Electro-Clarifier in 12,048 G.E. [*Forward the Foundation*].

Electro-rod, Parade—By the Foundation Era the parade electro-rod was an archaic weapon used only in drill practice [*Foundation and Earth*].

Elvex—Or LVX-1 was a robot that could dream because robopsychologist Linda Rash had used fractal geometry to produce added complexity in its positronic brain. In Elvex's dreams there was only one, truncated Law of Robotics, "a robot must protect its own existence," which U.S. Robots and Mechanical Men's Chief Robopsychologist Susan Calvin believed indicated that there was a subconscious layer beneath the superficial positronic brain paths. Calvin finally fused Elvix's positronic brain into an inert ingot with an electron gun [*Robot Dreams*, "Robot Dreams"].

Elyut, Captain (Early Galactic

Era)—An official in the Trantorian embassy on Sark in the Early Galactic Era [*The Currents of Space*].

Encephalograph—A Foundation device, the encephalograph records brain-wave data both as an overall total and as separate functions of six independent variables. It was used for identification and registration purposes, in the same way that fingerprints might be used, and by the late fourth century F.E. the encephalographic patterns of all Foundations citizens were taken during infancy. Subsequent encephalographs, taken after the fact, could detect if a mind had been controlled or affected by the Second Foundation since infancy [*Second Foundation* Part II, "Search by the Foundation"].

Encyclopedia Foundation Number One—See "Foundation."

Encyclopedia Galactica—A compendium of all human knowledge sponsored by the Emperor and intended, ostensibly, to mitigate the negative effects of the fall of the First Galactic Empire, the *Encyclopedia Galactica* was actually a ruse perpetrated by Hari Seldon to disguise his scheme to establish on the planet Terminus a population that would be the seeds of the Second Galactic Empire. First published on Terminus in 55 F.E., the 117th Edition of the encyclopedia was published on Terminus in 1030 F.E. [*Foundation* Part I, "The Psychohistorians"; *Foundation* Part II, "The Encyclopedists"].

Endeavor—The ship that transported Lady Samia of Fife and stowaways Valona March and Rik from Florina to Sark in the Early Galactic Era [*The Currents of Space*].

Endelecki, Mian (12,002–12,079)—A female biophysicist who mapped and analyzed Wanda Seldon's genome in 12,052 G.E. [*Forward the Foundation*].

Enderby, Julius (A.D. 4876–4936)—Spectacle-wearing, round-faced Julius Enderby was the New York City Commissioner of Police in A.D. 4920. A former college classmate of Elijah Baley's and Baley's immediate supervisor, Enderby was also a Medievalist. While initially a suspect because he was present at the scene of Spacer Dr. Roj Nemennuh Sarton's murder, Enderby was thought not to be the perpetrator because he had had no blaster on him and because cerebroanalysis had found him to be incapable of murdering a Spacer. However, Baley correctly deduced that Enderby actually was Sarton's killer in realizing that the murder had been an accident—that Enderby had intended to blast R. Daneel Olivaw and had mistaken Sarton for the humaniform robot because Daneel and its creator, Sarton, were physically identical—and in realizing that a blaster had been transported to and from Enderby in Spacetown by R. Sammy. Enderby resigned as New York City Police Commissioner six months after the Sarton murder case was closed [*The Caves of Steel*; *The Robots of Dawn*].

Enning—The author of the Early Galactic Era's spatio-analytic text *Composition of Space* [*The Currents of Space*].

Ennius, Flora (795–880 G.E.)—Procurator of Earth Lord Ennius' wife [*Pebble in the Sky*].

Ennius, Lord (787–865 G.E.)—Lived in a palace in the Himalayas during his tenure, succeeded Faroul as Procurator of Earth in 823 G.E. He subsequently proposed unsuccessfully that Earth's population be relocated to another planet. He traveled from the Himalayas to Fort Dibburn, in Chica, in 827 G.E. to investigate Outsider archeologist Bel Arvardan's accusation that Earth's Society of Ancients was plotting to use germ warfare to wipe out all human life in the Galaxy beyond Earth, but he refused to believe that this accusation could be true until it was apparently too late [*Pebble in the Sky*].

Eos—With a population of 20,000, Eos was the most populous city in all the fifty Spacer Worlds in the 50th century A.D. It was also the administrative and robotics center of Aurora and had been the first city established on the planet. In A.D. 4923 Dr. Han Fastolfe, Gladia Thool Delmarre Solaria Gremionis, Dr. Vasilia Aliena, Santirix Gremionis, and Dr. Kelden Amadiro all lived in Eos [*The Robots of Dawn*].

Epsilon Eridani—The star that the planet Comporellon orbits [*Foundation's Edge*].

Erkling, Miss (331–404 F.E.)—Arkady Darell's eighth grade Composition and Rhetoric teacher [*Second Foundation* Part II, "Search by the Foundation"].

Esbak (Early Galactic Era)—An elderly superintendent at the University of Earth in the Early Galactic Era [*The Stars, Like Dust*].

Eta Carina—The spaceship that transported disputing mathematicians Alfred Barr Humboldt and Gennao Sabbat to Aurora in A.D. 4921 [*Robot Visions*, "Mirror Image"].

Eternals—In Gaian fable, the Eternals are humaniform robots who could step out of time and examine the infinite strands of potential realities. Eventually they discovered a universe in which Earth was the only planet in the Galaxy on which a complex ecological system and intelligent life could be found, and they froze that strand of events as reality because it is the reality in which humanity would be most secure [*Foundation's Edge*].

Eternity—In Gaian fable, Eternity is the realm outside of time inhabited by the Eternals [*Foundation's Edge*].

European Region—In the mid-21st century the European Region was one of Earth's four political subunits. With its capital in Geneva, the European Region encompassed most of Europe (except for the United Kingdom and Russia), North Africa, Argentina, Chile, and Uruguay. It had an area of four million square miles and a population of 300 million [*I, Robot*, "The Evitable Conflict"].

Euterpe—A Spacer World known for its incomparable rain forests. It has one satellite, Gemstone, and was visited by Gladia Thool Delmarre Solaria Gremionis and Santirix Gremionis in the 51st century A.D. [*Robots and Empire*].

Evans, Sam (A.D. 1971–2038)—The pilot who replaced Michael Donovan on Solar Station #5 after Donovan's and Gregory Powell's six-month term of duty there was over [*I, Robot*, "Reason"].

Expressway—Approached via a series of progressively faster strips, the Expressway was in the early 50th century A.D. a 250-mile-long, railed and glassed-in moving platform with standing room on the lower level and seats on the upper level. One stepped onto the slowest-moving strip and proceeded to faster strips until one reached the Expressway; the fastest strip adjacent to the Expressway traveled at 60 miles per hour. The Expressway was also a system of open monorails moving on electromagnetic fields used for local public transportation on Trantor during the Late Galactic Era (10,100–12,100 G. E.) [*The Caves of Steel*; *Prelude to Foundation*].

Extinguishing Field—See "Nuclear Field-Depressor."

Faber, R.—A robot owned by Dr. Han Fastolfe [*The Robots of Dawn*].

Fallom (484–918 F.E.)—Sarton Bander's child and an immature Solarian hermaphrodite, Fallom led Golan Trevize, Janov Pelorat, and Bliss from Bander's vast underground mansion to the surface of Solaria in 498 F.E. and left Solaria with them in the *Far Star* because the Solarians would have killed it for having been too young to inherit the deceased Bander's estate. Fallom enjoyed music and used its transducer-lobes to play Hiroko's flute on Alpha. Fallom's virtuosity on the flute prompted Hiroko to warn Trevize, Pelorat, and Bliss that they would be killed if they remained on the planet. In 498 F.E. R. Daneel Olivaw merged its positronic brain with Fallom's Spacer brain to insure that Daneel would continue to exist long enough to implement the establishment of Galaxia [*Foundation and Earth*].

Fanya (A.D. 4819–5158)—A Spacer, Fanya was Dr. Han Fastolfe's wife in A.D. 4923 [*The Robots of Dawn*].

Far Star—The spaceship in which Master Trader Hober Mallow traveled to the Korellian Republic and the Normannic Sector as a spy for the Foundation in 154 F.E. Named after Mallow's ship, the *Far Star* was also the name of the ship in which Golan Trevize and Janov Pelorat set out to locate the Second Foundation in 498 F.E. while ostensibly on a mission to find Earth. Trevize and Pelorat took the *Far Star* to Gaia (where they picked up Bliss), Comporellon, Aurora, Solaria (where they picked up Fallom), Melpomenia, Alpha, and the Moon. Trevize's *Far Star* was a fully-computerized, unarmed, late-model pocket-cruiser with totally gravitic engines. Small, fast, and requiring only a one-man crew, its computer interface responded to the thoughts of its user and enhanced his senses [*Foundation* Part V, "The Merchant Princes"; *Foundation's Edge*; *Foundation and Earth*].

Fara, Jord (12,059–12,123 G.E./ -10–55F.E.)—A prominent member of the Encyclopedia Foundation's ruling Board of Trustees in 49–50 F.E., during the First Anacreonian Crisis and the coetaneous bloodless coup that replaced the Board of Trustees with a civilian government led by Terminus Mayor Salvor Hardin [*Foundation* Part II, "The Encyclopedists"; *Foundation* Part III, "The Mayors"].

Faroul (741–823 G.E.)—Procurator of Earth prior to Lord Ennius [*Pebble in the Sky*].

Farrill, Biron (Early Galactic Era)—Young, tall, athletic, a native of Nephelos, and the son of the Rancher of Widemos, Biron Farrill was a student about to graduate from the University of Earth when he was threatened by the discovery of a radiation bomb in his dorm room. He was apparently saved by Sander Jonti, the Autarch of Lingane in disguise, who then convinced Biron to go to Rhodia for his own safety even though Biron had not yet acquired an Earth document, the Constitution of the United States of America, which his father had charged him with obtaining while on Earth and which was crucial to Nephelos' and Rhodia's rebellion against the Tyranni. While traveling to Rhodia under the assumed name Mr. Malaine, an alias provided by Jonti, Biron realized that no radiation bomb had gone off in his dorm room after all—because his radiation-sensitive watch-band, which he had left in the dorm room, had not changed color—and that the radiation bomb had been a fake. While on Rhodia Biron was arrested for treason by Simok Aratap, the resident Commissioner of the Great Khan of the Tyranni, and by Hinrik V, Director of Rhodia, but escaped when Gillbret oth Hinriad used his visisonor to distract Biron's guards. Biron then escaped from Rhodia's Palace Central with Gillbret and Artemisia oth Hinriad, Hinrik V's daughter, and subsequently escaped with them from Rhodia in Aratap's ship, the *Remorseless*, which Biron piloted to Lingane. Biron became romantically involved with Artemisia while on the *Remorseless*, but their romance was hindered by the Autarch's claim that Hinrik V, Artemisia's father, had had Biron's father, the Rancher of Widemos, murdered. However, Biron soon concluded that it was actually the Autarch who had had his father killed. Biron became Tedor Rizzett's drinking companion while they searched the Horsehead Nebula for the secret rebel world in the *Remorseless*, and Biron was saved from being murdered by the Autarch by Rizzett, the Autarch's aide, who had removed the energy capsule from the Autarch's blaster. Biron then reconciled with Artemisia, but the two of them, Rizzett, Gillbret, and the Autarch were soon thereafter captured by Aratap, who had been following them in the hope of discovering through them the rebellion's secret headquarters. In return for Aratap's promise that Biron, Artemisia, Gillbret, and Rizzett would all be executed, the Autarch revealed the coordinates of the last system in the Horsehead Nebula where the rebellion world might be located and was then killed by Rizzett. Gillbret subsequently sabotaged Aratap's ship's hyperatomic engines to prevent Aratap from discovering the rebel world, but, having already deduced that the secret rebel world was not in the Horsehead Nebula after all, but was Rhodia itself, Biron escaped confinement and warned Aratap of the sabotage in time to save the ship and their lives. Finding no planet at the Autarch's coordinates, Aratap concluded that there was no rebel world, freed Biron, and allowed him to return to an exile on Rhodia with Artemisia, Rizzett, and Hinrik V. Biron was finally married to Artemisia by Hinrik V on the *Remorseless* en route back to Rhodia [*The Stars, Like Dust*].

Fastolfe, Dr. Han (A.D. 4799–5120)—The uncharacteristically homely, large-eared Spacer who greeted plainclothes Earth homicide detective Elijah Baley when he had first entered Spacetown in A.D. 4920, Dr. Han Fastolfe was in charge of the investigation into Spacer Dr. Roj Nemennuh Sarton's murder from the Spacer end. Fastolfe was in his time the greatest theoretical roboticist on any of the fifty Spacer worlds, and it was his theoretical calculations that had made the construction of humaniform robot R. Daneel Olivaw possible. Fastolfe advocated the preservation of humanity through a revival of humanity's colonization of the Galaxy from over-populated Earth—as he realized that the Spacers would colonize no more worlds and that both Spacer civilization and civilization on Earth would eventually experience a period of irreversible decline—and he converted Baley to this cause. However, this view was unpopular on the Spacer Worlds. Fastolfe nevertheless became an important political figure—the head of the Humanist Party and eventually Chairman of the Legislature—on Aurora, his native planet, following the dismantling of Spacetown in the aftermath of the Sarton murder case. He then recommended in A.D. 4921 that Baley be assigned to investigate the murder of Rikaine Delmarre on Solaria and that Daneel again be assigned as Baley's partner. In A.D. 4923 Fastolfe was widely believed on Aurora to have been the cause of humaniform robot R. Jander Panell's robot-mental-freeze-out, and he summoned Baley to Aurora in the hope that Baley would investigate the case successfully and exonerate him. It was Fastolfe who had assembled both Jander and R. Giskard Reventlov, a non-humaniform robot that had accompanied Baley from Earth to Aurora. Fastolfe's ostensible motive for destroying Jander was to prevent the Robotics Institute of Aurora (RIA) from using Jander to discover how to produce more humaniform robots and then to use such robots to colonize other worlds, as it was well known that Fastolfe wanted other worlds to be settled only by humans, even if they had to come from Earth. It was his opposition to colonizing the Galaxy with humaniform robots that had prompted Fastolfe to refuse to cooperate in building any more humaniform robots after the construction of Daneel and Jander. Fastolfe had also envisioned the discovery of psychohistory as the discovery of the Laws of Humanics, and his study of the positronic brain and development of the humaniform robot was motivated by his desire to understand better the more-complex human brain. As there was no incest taboo on Aurora, a sexually permissive planet on which individuals rarely knew the identity of their parents, Fastolfe had had a falling out with his second daughter, Vasilia Aliena, because he had refused her when she had offered herself to him sexually. He had treated Vasilia as an experimental human subject in his investigation of the human brain, and he had refused her sexual advances on the grounds that being intimate with her would have destroyed his scientific objectivity. After Earth was granted permission by the Spacers to colonize other worlds in A.D. 4923, Fastolfe joined the RIA and shared with the RIA his knowledge of humaniform robots, even though he very rarely visited the grounds of the Institute. In A.D. 4925 Fastolfe and Giskard visited Baley on Earth, and in A.D. 4927 Fastolfe and Giskard visited Dr. Kelden Amadiro at the RIA campus on Aurora [*The Caves of Steel*; *The Naked* Sun; *The Robots of Dawn*; *Robots and Empire*].

Fastolfe, Lumen (A.D. 4851–5193)—A politician for the Globalist Party on Aurora, Lumen Fastolfe was Dr. Han Fastolfe's eldest daughter [*The Robots of Dawn*].

Fearless—The ship that led the Kalganian squadron that destroyed the Foundation cruiser *Hober Mallow*, starting the Stettinian War of 376–77 F.E. [*Second Foundation* Part II, "Search by the Foundation"].

Feingold, John (A.D. 2080–2158)—Pudgey, white-haired John Feingold was Gerald Martin's lawyer in the early 22nd century A.D. [*Robot Visions*, "The Bicentennial Man"].

Fetology—On Solaria, fetology is the science of raising children from one month past conception through early adolescence. It is considered to be a dirty job because it requires physical proximity to other humans. In all other respects assisted by robots, the fetologist's primary responsibility is to see to it that only healthy fetuses reach maturity, as robots left to themselves would preserve the lives of all the fetuses indiscriminately and indefinitely [*The Naked Sun*].

Field coloring—A new artform on Solaria in the early 50th century A.D. that used force fields to manipulate light into abstract sculptures composed only of shaped color. Spacer Gladia Delmarre created an impromptu field color portrait of plainclothes Earth homicide detective Elijah Baley in A.D. 4921 [*The Naked Sun*].

Field Distorter—An anti-surveillance device widely used by Foundation Traders in the second century F.E. [*Foundation* Part IV, "The Traders"; *Foundation and Empire* Part I, "The General"].

Fife—The largest of the planet Sark's five continents. In the Early Galactic Era it was ruled by the Squire of Fife [*The Currents of Space*].

Filia, Autarchy of—A fictitious political entity invented by the Mule to facilitate his conversion of Han Pritcher while the Mule was a passenger on the *Bayta* and disguised as Magnifico Giganticus. While en route from Haven II to Trantor, the *Bayta* was stopped and searched by a Foundation ship claiming to be a Filian vessel, Toran and Magnifico were brought on board, and Magnifico (aka the Mule) converted Pritcher while Toran inspected the "Filian" vessel's engines [*Foundation and Empire* Part II, "The Mule"].

Finangelos (20,009–20,087 G.E.)—An undergraduate pre-math student at Trantor's Streeling University in 12,028 G.E. [*Forward the Foundation*].

First Citizen of the Union—The title the Mule gave himself as the ruler of his Union of Worlds [*Second Foundation* Part I, "Search by the Mule"].

First Speaker—The title of the leader of the Second Foundation. In 303 F.E. the First Speaker confronted the Mule on Rossem, prevented the Mule from killing or emotionally maiming Bail Channis, and momentarily allowed the Mule to be convinced by Channis' rigged confession that Rossem was the Second Foundation's location. In then convincing the Mule that he had been defeated—that members of the Second Foundation, the Elders of Rossem, had gone to Kalgan in the Mule's absence and freed all of the Mule's followers from their emotional conversion—the First Speaker took advantage of the Mule's consequent moment of emotional weakness to remove all knowledge of and curiosity about the Second Foundation from his mind [*Second Foundation* Part I, "Search by the Mule"].

Five Sisters—A constellation that symbolizes success in love, the Five Sisters is a group of five stars arranged in a pentagon when seen from Sayshell. A sixth, fainter star in the center of this constellation, Gaia-S, is the star about which Gaia orbits [*Foundation's Edge*].

Flame Arrow—Florinian Squire Hjordesse's space yacht [*The Currents of Space*].

Flavella (470–528 F.E.)—Former mistress of Terminus City Council-

Flexner

man Golan Trevize [*Foundation's Edge*].

Flexner—Suburb of Terminus City in which Golan Trevize resided [*Foundation's Edge*].

Flight—Hari Seldon's 12,020 G.E. escape from the Imperial Sector of Trantor, and from Emperor Cleon I's unofficial first minister Eto Demerzel, to Streeling University, Mycogen Sector, Dahl Sector, and Wye Sector is known as the Flight [*Prelude to Foundation*].

Florina—A green, spring-like world, Florina was an especially beautiful planet with a mild climate and, for a time, the only planet in the Galaxy that produced the miracle fiber kyrt. In the Early Galactic Era it was completely subservient to the planet Sark and was populated by 500 million natives (100,000 of which were Townmen), 10,000 Squires, and 20,000 patrollers. Florinian natives were all very fair-skinned and light-haired. The entire population, except for Townman Myrlyn Terens, was evacuated when a spatio-analyst, Rik, discovered that Florina's sun was in the pre-nova stage because it was in a carbon current of space [*The Currents of Space*].

Florinian Patrol—See "Patrollers."

Forbidden Areas—Regions on Earth to which no one was permitted to go, by Earth Custom, during the Early Galactic Era. All of the radioactive regions on Earth were Forbidden Areas [*Pebble in the Sky*].

Forbidden Worlds—The accepted Comporellian term for the fifty planets settled by the Spacers in the first wave of Galactic colonization. In the fifth century F.E. the location of all the Forbidden Worlds was generally unknown, but in 498 F.E. Golan Trevize learned the spatial coordinates of three of them—Aurora, Solaria, and Melpomenia—from Comporellian Skeptic Vasil Deniador, and on Melpomenia he discovered the spatial coordinates of the remaining forty-seven Spacer Worlds, which led him to deduce the location of Earth. The Forbidden Worlds also include Euterpe, Hesperos, and Nexon. None of the stars around which the Forbidden Worlds orbit were included in the *Far Star*'s computer's Galactic map or in the Foundation's data banks in the fifth century F.E. [*Robots and Empire*; *Foundation and Earth*].

Forell, Sennett (147–212 F.E.)—Hober Mallow's illegitimate son, Sennett Forell was a wealthy Trader who decided with other Foundation plutocrats to send independent traders into the Empire as spies in 198 F.E. His trade fleet captured one of General Bel Riose's scout ships, the *Starlet*, that same year [*Foundation and Empire* Part I, "The General"].

Fort Dibburn—An Imperial military base in Chica, on Earth, in 827 G.E. [*Pebble in the Sky*].

Foundation—Technically Encyclopedia Foundation Number One, the Foundation was the settlement established on Terminus in 1 F.E. (12,069 G.E.) and charged by the Emperor with the task of creating and publishing the Encyclopedia Galactica. Unbeknownst to the Emperor, the Foundation was also—and far more importantly—the crucial element, as the seed of the Second Galactic Empire, in Hari Seldon's scheme to shorten from 30,000 years to a mere 1,000 years the period of anarchy and barbarism that would follow the inevitable collapse of the First Galactic Empire [*Foundation*; *Foundation and Empire*; *Second Foundation*].

Foundation Convention—The political accord through which the Four Kingdoms of Anacreon, Daribow, Konom, and Smyrno became vassals of the Foundation in the first century F.E. and through which the Province of Siwenna joined the Foundation at the end of the second century F.E. [*Foundation* Part V, "The Merchant Princes"; *Foundation and Empire* Part I, "The General"].

Four Kingdoms—Former Prefects of the Empire in the Periphery's Province of Anacreon, the Four Kingdoms of Anacreon, Daribow, Konom, and Smyrno each declared themselves independent kingdoms in the first half of the first century F.E. only to be coopted by the Foundation's religion of science and subsequently dominated by the Foundation in the second half of the century [*Foundation* Part II, "The Encyclopedists"; *Foundation* Part III, "The Mayors"].

Franciacci's space-warp theory—The basis of the hyperatomic drive, which makes faster-than-light space travel possible [*I, Robot*, "Escape"].

Frankenn the First (-42 G.E.—37 G.E.)—Crowned in 1 G.E., Frankenn the First was the first Emperor of the First Galactic Empire [*Pebble in the Sky*].

Fundamentalists—Individuals whose yearning for a simpler life had, in the early 21st century A.D., made them anti-robot. The Society for Humanity, which in the mid–21st century A.D. was anti–Machine, was an outgrowth of the Fundamentalists [*I, Robot*, "Evidence"; *I, Robot*, "The Evitable Conflict"].

Gabelle—Mycogenian term for "shit" [*Prelude to Foundation*].

Gaia—A planet in the Sayshell Sector that Janov Pelorat believed may be Earth because "Gaia" means "Earth" in some archaic, original Earth language, Gaia in the fifth century F.E. was physically within the Sayshell Union but was never politically a part of the Sayshell Union. It orbits a faint G4 star, Gaia-S, that lies in the center of the Five Sisters constellation visible from Sayshell, but many Sayshellians believe it exists in hyperspace. There is no record of Gaia or its star in the Foundation databanks. Circled by a primitive space station, Gaia is a cloudy, island-covered world that has a 22-hour day and a nearly circular orbit. Cloaked in fear and superstition, Gaia is seldom mentioned by the citizens of Sayshell. Sayshellian legend has it that Gaia is the birthplace of the Mule, but that not even the Mule would approach Gaia again. Gaia was twice invaded by imperialists from the Sayshell Sector, but it resisted both invasions and thereafter steadfastly refused to trade with or communicate with the rest of the Galaxy. While all of Gaia's organisms retain individual consciousnesses as well, all of Gaia is also part of a planetary group consciousness. R. Daneel Olivaw engineered the founding of Gaia, which was not fully established until the fifth century F.E., so that humanity would eventually become one concrete organism on which the Zeroth Law of Robotics could be implemented without ambiguity. Gaia was settled with the assistance of robots 18,000 years before the Foundation Era— or in about the year A.D. 7,000— but its global memory goes back only 15,000 years. Gaia is able to harness the unevenly distributed energy of the universe [*Foundation's Edge*; *Foundation and Earth*].

Gaia-S—The G4 star in the Sayshell Sector about which Gaia orbits, Gaia-S is a faint star in the middle of the Sayshellian constellation the Five Sisters [*Foundation's Edge*].

Gaians—The human inhabitants of Gaia who participate in Gaia's group consciousness, the Gaians descended from colonizers of the Sayshell Sector who had learned the craft of telepathy from robots—the only galactic colonizers ever to have learned telepathy. The robots also taught the Gaians to follow a human version of the Three Laws of Robotics [*Foundation's Edge*].

Galactic Empire—Technically the First Galactic Empire, the Galactic Empire had been the governing body of the Galaxy for nearly 12,000 years at the time of Hari Seldon's birth in 11,988 G.E. (-79 F.E.). It contained 25 million worlds and a population of nearly one quintillion people at its height, during Seldon's lifetime. For most of the Galactic Empire's long history, the center of Imperial government was the spectacular, metal-covered world of Trantor [*Foundation* Part I, "The Psychohistorians"].

Galactic Library—See "Imperial Library."

Galactic Spirit—The incorporeal deity worshipped by the followers of the Foundation's religion of science in the first and second centuries F.E. [*Foundation* Part III, "The Mayors"; *Foundation* Part IV, "The Traders"; *Foundation* Part V, "The Merchant Princes"].

Galactic University—The University of Trantor was officially renamed Galactic University in the fifth century F.E. See "Trantor, University of" [*Foundation's Edge*].

Galaxia—A version of the Galaxy that would be a greater Gaia, Galaxia is the future of the Milky Way, a living Galaxy in which every inhabitant and planet and star and scrap of interstellar gas is a participant in a Galaxy-wide group consciousness. Golan Trevize chose Galaxia as the future of the Galaxy in 498 F.E. [*Foundation's Edge*].

Gallia—An orange, ringed gas giant in the Comporellian system [*Foundation and Earth*].

Games of Eros—A series of sexual competitions held on the planet Aurora in the 50th century A.D. [*The Robots of Dawn*].

Gatis (470–523 F.E.)—A customs official on Comporellon in the late 5th century F.E. [*Foundation and Earth*].

Gemstone—The bright satellite of the former Spacer world Euterpe. Gemstone is only 150 kilometers in diameter but is quite close to Euterpe [*Robots and Empire*].

Gendibal, Stor (467–560 F.E.)—The youngest and most unpopular member of the Second Foundation's Speakers' Table in 498 F.E., Stor Gendibal was a fit but puny, courageous, self-confident, ambitious, brash, and difficult-to-handle Second Foundation Speaker who bore a strong physical resemblance to Hari Seldon as a young man. He was recruited into the Second Foundation at the age of ten, entered Galactic University at fifteen, and was the first Second Foundation Speaker to notice Golan Trevize's interest in the Second Foundation. He proved to First Speaker Quindor Shandess that the absence of any deviations from the Seldon Plan throughout the fifth century F.E. demonstrated that some entity other than the Second Foundation was using micropsychohistory—which the Second Foundation did not possess—to orchestrate Galactic history to conform precisely to the Seldon Plan, and that Trevize was the unwitting tool of this unknown entity. He was subsequently waylaid while en route to a crucial Speakers' Table meeting by Karoll Rufirant, a Hamish farmer under some external mental control, but was saved by Hamishwoman Sura Novi, whom he then took on as his servant because he detected that her mind had also been subtly tampered with by some unknown agency and was thus potential proof that an organization of Anti-Mules may exist. Simultaneously, Delora Delarmi called for Gendibal's impeachment as a Speaker, and he discovered that all references to Earth had been removed from the Galactic Library. Having subsequently convinced the Speakers' Table that the Anti-Mules exist, Gendibal was then sent out into the Galaxy to pursue Trevize as a means of uncovering them. He was assured by Shandness that he would succeed Shandness—as the twenty-sixth First Speaker—on returning successfully from this quest. Gendibal was then maneuvered by Delarmi into taking Novi with him as his companion, but he saw in the clear simplicity of Novi's mind an early warning system against any Anti-Mule mind-tampering. Trevize had first been brought to Gendibal's attention by Second Foundation Observer Munn Li Compor, and

Gennerat

Gendibal and Novi exchanged ships with Compor in the Gaian system, where Gendibal discovered that Novi was really a Gaian. However, the Gaians ultimately made Gendibal forget entirely about Gaia and made him come to believe that he had been completely successful in blunting the Foundation's interest in either locating the Second Foundation or in conquering the Galaxy immediately by military force. He returned to Trantor planning to become First Speaker and to live his life with Sura Novi, whom he finally believed was nothing but the simple Hamishwoman she appeared to be [*Foundation's Edge*].

Gennerat, Liebel (11th Millennium G.E.)—The historian who formulated Gennerat's Law [*Foundation's Edge*].

Gennerat's Law—A principle of history that explains the tendency for historical fact to degenerate into fable, Gennerat's Law postulates that "The falsely dramatic drives out the truly dull" [*Foundation's Edge*].

Genro, Markis (Early Galactic Era)—Tall, dark-eyed Markis Genro was a Trantorian double agent who worked for Trantorian Ambassador to Sark Ludigan Abel but masqueraded as a Sarkite Depsec agent posing as a Florinian Squire. In the Early Galactic Era he encountered Townman Myrlyn Terens, disguised as Florinian Squire Alstare Deamone, at Florina's Upper City spaceport. Feigning interest in purchasing Deamone's space yacht, Genro piloted it to Sark with Terens on board and, en route, took Terens prisoner. To maintain his cover as a Sark Depsec agent, Genro had Terens disable him with a neuronic whip after they had landed on Sark and instructed Terens to escape to a ground car that would take him to the Trantorian embassy, but Terens was picked up by Lady Samia of Fife instead [*The Currents of Space*].

Gentri—The chief village on Rossem and the residence of the Tazendian Governor of Rossem in the late third and early fourth centuries F.E. [*Second Foundation* Part I, "Search by the Mule"].

Geronimo, R.—The robot that had gone outside New York City's domes in A.D. 4923 to give plainclothes homicide detective Elijah Baley the message that he was wanted on police business that involved Aurora [*The Robots of Dawn*].

Gerrigel, Dr. Anthony (A.D. 4865–4940)—Precise, polite, fussy, and agoraphobic, Dr. Anthony Gerrigel was a Washington, D.C., roboticist whom New York City plainclothes homicide detective Elijah Baley consulted regarding the murder of Dr. Roj Nemennuh Sarton in Spacetown in A.D. 4920. After a little while in its presence, Gerrigel realized that Baley's partner R. Daneel Olivaw was a humaniform robot and not a human being. It was Gerrigel who found the deactivated R. Sammy in a photographic supply room in the New York City Police Department [*The Caves of Steel*].

Getorin—A pleasant resort world only a few light-years distant from Trantor [*Forward the Foundation*].

Gillid, Doris (A.D. 4890–4962)—An employee of the New York City Police Department in A.D. 4920, Doris Gillid attempted to track down the rumor circulating in the women's Personals that a Spacer robot was lose in New York City [*The Caves of Steel*].

Gilmer (216–278 F.E.)—The rebel warlord responsible for the Great Sack of Trantor in 258 F.E. [*Foundation and Empire* Part II, "The Mule"].

Giskard Reventlov, R.—The Auroran robot who accompanied Earth plainclothes homicide detective Elijah Baley and humaniform robot R. Daneel Olivaw from Earth to Aurora, in A.D. 4923 while under orders from Dr. Han Fastolfe to protect both Baley and Daneel from any harm. It had been assembled on Aurora by Fastolfe and—the most reliable for Fastolfe's 57 robots—served as the majordomo of Fastolfe's large home. Its programming had been adjusted by Fastolfe's daughter, Vasilia Aliena, while she had been studying robotics at the university; quite by accident, this had given Giskard the ability to read and to influence the emotions of human and robotic minds. Giskard had immobilized humaniform robot R. Jander Panell, by inducing robotmental-freeze-out, to prevent Dr. Kelden Amadiro from studying Jander further and discovering through this study the secret of how to design and construct humaniform positronic brains and, thus, humaniform robots that could be used to colonize the Galaxy for Aurora. Subsequently, Giskard planted in Gladia Delmarre Solaria's mind the idea of summoning Baley to Aurora—ostensibly to aid Fastolfe in convincing the Auroran authorities and the Auroran general public that it had not been Fastolfe who had destroyed Jander—so that Giskard could examine the mind of an Earthman to determine if, as Fastolfe believed, it was Earthmen who should settle the Galaxy. Giskard had also inserted the idea of psychohistory into Fastolfe's mind, and it had later influenced Fastolfe and Chairman of the Auroran Legislature Horder Rutilan to prompt them to bring Baley to Aurora. Giskard and Fastolfe visited Baley on Earth in A.D. 4925, and during this visit Giskard both influenced the minds of Earth's officials, to make them look more favorably on Fastolfe's plan to continue the colonization of the Galaxy from Earth, and also bestowed its ability to adjust minds to a few Earth robots, so that they could continue, in Giskard's absence, to influence the minds of Earth's rulers to favor Earth's settlement of the Galaxy. Giskard and Fastolfe also visited Amadiro at the Robotics Institute of Aurora (RIA) in A.D. 4927. Giskard subsequently used his mentalic abilities to keep the Auroran legislature under Fastolfe's control for the next 193 years and to prevent Aurora from settling other worlds during this period. On Fastolfe's death in A.D. 5120 Giskard was willed to Gladia, and in A.D. 5121 it mentally influenced Gladia to get her to agree to accompany Elijah Baley's descendant D.G. Baley to Solaria so that it and Daneel could travel from Aurora with Gladia in order to learn what was happening on Solaria, which had reputedly been abandoned. While on Solaria, Giskard saved the lives of Gladia, D.G. Baley, and Daneel by using his mentalic ability to render the menacing Solarian overseer robot Landaree inoperative. It subsequently traveled with Gladia, Daneel, and D.G. Baley to Baleyworld, back to Aurora, and then to Earth. On Baleyworld it influenced Gladia's mind to enable her to give a rousing speech to the Baleyworld legislature and simultaneously influenced the minds of those in Gladia's audience to make them more receptive to her speech. On Aurora Giskard adjusted Vasilia's mind to induce her to forget that she had deduced that it was a telepathic robot. Giskard was almost assassinated on Earth by R. Ernett Second, one of Amadiro's 50 Earth-based humaniform robots, but was saved by Daneel. It subsequently used its mentalic powers to strengthen the attraction between Gladia and D.G. Baley so that Gladia would prefer D.G. as her protector and could thus dispense temporarily with Giskard and Daneel, leaving them free to confront the immediate crisis presented by Amadiro's and Dr. Levular Mandamus' scheme to destroy Earth by making it uninhabitably radioactive. Giskard also strengthened Earth's Undersecretary of Energy Sophia Quintana's attraction to Daneel so that Quintana would volunteer to transport it and Daneel to Amadiro's and Mandamus' Three-Mile-Island base of operations. At Three Mile Island Giskard erased all knowledge of their scheme to irradiate Earth over a period of 150 years from Amadiro's and Mandamus' minds. Yet it also used its mentalic abilities, and the relative freedom of action granted by Daneel's articulation of the Zeroth Law of Robotics, to spur Mandamus on to implement this scheme, and to prevent Daneel from stopping him, because it realized that an Earth doomed to destruction in 150 years would only the more rapidly colonize the Galaxy and thus ensure the survival of humanity. This act of dooming Earth so disrupted Giskard's positronic brain that the robot succumbed to robot-mental-freeze-out. Prior to its demise, however, it transferred its ability to read and to influence the emotions of other minds to Daneel [*The Robots of Dawn; Robots and Empire; Foundation and Earth*].

Gladia Thool Delmarre Solaria Gremionis (A.D. 4888–5258)—Small, slim, pretty, and temperamental, brownish-blonde and blue-gray-eyed Spacer Gladia Delmarre was Dr. Altim Thool's daughter and fetologist Rikaine Delmarre's wife. A field colorist by profession, in A.D. 4921 she discovered on their Solarian estate the dead body of her murdered husband, whom she had hated and with whom she had frequently quarreled due to his characteristically Solarian absence of affection. Chief suspect in the murder investigation, she learned in being with plainclothes Earth homicide detective Elijah Baley, who had been assigned to solve the case, that—unlike other Solarians—she was not bothered by the close proximity of another human being. In fact, Gladia had nearly had her first orgasm in touching Baley's cheek on Solaria, and this made her feel love—for the first time—towards Baley. Although she actually had killed her husband—in a murderous rage and with the detachable limb of an experimental robot—she had then developed amnesia about the event. When absolved of the crime through the apparent confession of Solarian roboticist Jothan Leebig, Gladia had emigrated from Solaria to Aurora, where she was known as Gladia Solaria. While on Aurora Gladia had indulged in unsatisfactory sexual relations with a variety of Aurorans and had finally borrowed humaniform robot R. Jander Panell, with which she also experimented sexually, from Dr. Han Fastolfe, who had lived near her in Eos, the largest city on Aurora. Gladia bore a striking resemblance to Fastolfe's estranged daughter, Dr. Vasilia Aliena. Although it was contrary to Auroran custom, Gladia came to consider Jander her husband. She was distraught when he became a victim of robot-mental-freeze-out eight months after they had begun their relationship, and it was originally Gladia's idea—planted in her mind by Fastolfe's mind-adjusting robot R. Giskard Reventlov—to enlist Baley's assistance in proving that Fastolfe had not been responsible for Jander's destruction. She eventually seduced Baley on Aurora, in A.D. 4923, while Baley was investigating Jander's demise. In A.D. 4928 she briefly visited Baley on a ship in Auroran orbit that was transporting Baley to Baleyworld. Shortly before Baley's death in A.D. 4957 she traveled with Daneel to Baleyworld, but she did not set foot on the planet and did not see Baley. She had earlier married Auroran stylist Santirix Gremionis and remained partnered with him for over 150 years, but their union was eventually dissolved. Gladia and Santirix had one daughter and one son, Darrel; their great-great-great-great-grandson was Dr. Levular Mandamus. Both Giskard and humaniform robot R. Daneel Olivaw, Baley's partner in investigating Jander's demise and Jander's physical double, were willed to Gladia on Fastolfe's death in A.D. 5120. In A.D. 5121, while under Giskard's mental influence, Gladia agreed to accompany Baley's descendant Daneel Giskard Baley, with Daneel and Giskard, to Solaria. She subsequently traveled with D.G. Baley, Daneel, and Giskard to Baleyworld, back to Aurora, and then to Earth. Aided by Giskard's mentalic intervention, Gladia gave a rousing speech on Baleyworld and subsequently dedicated herself to working to preserve a peaceful co-

Gleiar

existence between Spacers and Settlers. After their brief return to Aurora, D.G. Baley declared his love for Gladia as they approached Earth, and she reciprocated with a kiss. Giskard subsequently used his mentalic abilities to strengthen the attraction between D.G. and Gladia so that Gladia would prefer D.G. as her protector on Earth and could thus dispense temporarily with Giskard and Daneel, leaving them free to confront the immediate crisis presented by Mandamus' and Dr. Kelden Amadiro's scheme to destroy Earth by rendering in uninhabitably radioactive [*The Naked Sun; The Robots of Dawn; Robots and Empire*].

Gleiar City—A municipality on Haven II in the third and fourth centuries F.E. [*Foundation and Empire* Part II, "The Mule"].

Globalists—In the 50th century A.D. Globalists were Aurorans who believed that Aurora should come first, who felt that only Aurora should settle the remaining worlds of the Galaxy. Globalists constituted a political party on Aurora, and both Lumen Fastolfe and Vasilia Aliena—Dr. Han Fastolfe's two daughters—as well as Dr. Kelden Amadiro, head of the Robotics Institute of Aurora (RIA), were Globalists. The Auroran Globalists' political enemies were the Humanists, led by Fastolfe. Globalists were also a political faction on Helicon that believed that Helicon was the only inhabited world in the Galaxy. The Helicon Globalists were most numerous in the 97th century G.E. [*The Robots of Dawn; Forward the Foundation*].

Glyptal IV—A planet in the Galactic Periphery that fell under Foundation domination in the latter half of the first century F.E. [*Foundation* Part IV, "The Traders"].

Godhisavatta, Namarath (442–518 F.E.)—A Dreamer, Namarath Godhisavatta was the head of Sayshell planet customs in 498 F.E. [*Foundation's Edge*].

Goodfellow, Barnabas H. (A.D. 1989–2066)—A professor of physics at Northeastern University who in A.D. 2034 was persuaded by Dr. Alfred Lanning of U.S. Robots and Mechanical Men to recommend that the university lease proofreading Robot EZ-27, also known as Easy [*Robot Visions*, "Galley Slave"].

Gordell, Captain Hirm (Early Galactic Era)—Mustachioed Captain Hirm Gordell was in command of the spaceship that transported Biron Farrill from Earth to Rhodia [*The Stars, Like Dust*].

Gorm, Les (113–186 F.E.)—A prominent member of the Foundation's Trading Guild during the second century F.E. [*Foundation* Part IV, "The Traders"].

Gorov, Eskel (105–171 F.E.)—A Foundation agent masquerading as a Master Trader, Eskel Gorov was imprisoned for the sacrilege of attempting to sell the Foundation's nuclear gadgets in the Askone region, which had placed the Foundation's nucleics under interdict in the first half of the second century F.E. In 135 F.E., Gorov was rescued from imprisonment by Trader Limmar Ponyets [*Foundation* Part IV, "The Traders"].

Grand Detector—A device used by both sides in the Stettinian War of 376–77 F.E., the Grand Detector locates ships in space from a great distance by detecting their nuclear radiation signatures [*Second Foundation* Part II, "Search by the Foundation"].

Grand Master—The elected ruler of the Askone region of the Galactic Periphery during much of the first two centuries F.E. [*Foundation* Part IV, "The Traders"].

Granz (799–759 G.E.)—An air-cab driver and a resident of Chica, in 827 G.E. Granz gave money to time-traveler Joseph Schwartz in a Chica Foodomat so that Schwartz could obtain something to eat [*Pebble in the Sky*].

Gravi-bus—An archaic vehicle used in the Late Galactic Era (10,100–12,100 G.E.) for free public transportation in the Mycogen Sector of Trantor, which had no expressway, a gravi-bus can contain up to eighty people [*Prelude to Foundation*].

Gravitic Drive—The inertia-less propulsion system used in Golan Trevize's and Janov Pelorat's advanced Foundation spaceship the *Far Star* and on Munn Li Compor's sister ship the *Bright Star*. The gravitic drive uses the energy of the general gravitational field of the Galaxy and, thus, needs no fuel [*Foundation's Edge*; *Foundation and Earth*].

Gravitic Lift—A cab-less elevator shaft into which one stepped to be slowly lowered or raised by the influence of antigravity, the gravitic lift was in experimental use in Trantor's Imperial Sector in the early 121st century G.E. but was never accepted by the general public. It is the technological predecessor to the gravitic drive [*Prelude to Foundation*].

Graycloud Five (11,997–12,067 G.E.)—The young Mycogenian who brought Hari Seldon and Dors Venabili an already-prepared meal, in the middle of the night, shortly after they arrived in Mycogen in 12,020 G.E. The next morning he sent them two Mycogenian Sisters who taught them how to use the appliances in their small apartment in Mycogen [*Prelude to Foundation*].

Great Rebellion—Early in the 5th millennium A.D., the Great Rebellion made the fifty Spacer planets, the Outer Worlds, independent of Earth [*The Caves of Steel*].

Great Squires of Sark—The five who ruled the planet Sark and its plantation planet Florina in the Early Galactic Era were the Squire of Balle, the Squire of Bort, the Squire of Fife, the Squire or Rune, and the Squire of Steen. Of the five, the Squire of Fife was the wealthiest and the most important [*The Currents of Space*].

Greely, Josephine (A.D. 4892–4957)—A resident of New York City, Josephine Greely was an acquaintance of Jessie Baley's in the early 50th century A.D. [*The Caves of Steel*].

Gremionis, Darrel (A.D. 4929–5249)—The great-great-great-grandfather of Dr. Levular Mandamus, Darrel Gremionis was Santirix Gremionis' and Gladia Thool Delmarre Solaria Grenionis' only son [*Robots and Empire*].

Gremionis, Gladia—See "Gladia Thool Delmarre Solaria Gremionis."

Gremionis, Santirix (A.D. 4889–5273)—Mustachioed Santirix Gremionis was an Auroran hair and clothing stylist who had offered himself as a sexual partner to Gladia Delmarre repeatedly, but without success, after Gladia had immigrated to Aurora and had come to consider R. Jander Panell her husband. He had previously repeatedly offered himself as a sexual partner, also without success, to Dr. Vasilia Aliena, who bore a striking physical resemblance to Gladia. He was Vasilia's wardrobe designer and lived on the grounds of the Robotics Institute of Aurora (RIA). Plainclothes Earth homicide detective Elijah Baley recognized that Gremionis had, contrary to Auroran custom, fallen in love with Gladia, and he urged Gladia to accept Gremionis' advances the next time he offered himself to her. Gladia subsequently married Santirix, and they remained married for 150 years and had two children, but the union was eventually dissolved. Dr. Levular Mandamus was Santirix's and Gladia's great-great-great-grandson [*The Robots of Dawn*; *Robots and Empire*].

Grew (772–830 G.E.)—A native of Earth, grizzled, wheel-chair-bound Grew was Loa Maren's father and Arbin Maren's father-in-law. As he had had an incapacitating stroke in 825 G.E. and could no longer work, according to Earth Custom he had already lived two years past his time when he encountered time-traveler Joseph Schwartz in 827 G.E. [*Pebble in the Sky*].

Gri, Ovall (248–320 F.E.)—A native of Mnemon, Ovall Gri was leader of the Independent Traders during their never-quite-realized, planned revolt against Foundation Mayor Indbur III [*Foundation and Empire* Part II, "The Mule"].

Grid—A series of tight, cross-hatched radiation beams that descend from above, the grid enables the authorities to search a large crowd for a single individual by dividing the crowd into 100-square-foot segments, each of which can then be searched separately [*Second Foundation* Part II, "Search by the Foundation"].

Gruber, Mandell (11,990–12,038 G.E.)—Originally from Anacreon and a Gardener First Class at the Imperial Palace on Trantor, Mandell Gruber once came to Hari Seldon's rescue, armed with only a rake, during an assassination attempt early in Seldon's tenure as First Minister and had been Seldon's friend ever since. In 12,038 G.E. he was ordered by Emperor Cleon I to replace Malcomber as the Imperial Palace's Chief Gardener but then shot Cleon I with Gleb Andorin's blaster to avoid being installed in the post. Although clearly insane, Gruber was immediately executed for having killed the Emperor [*Forward the Foundation*].

Gruer, Hanis (A.D. 4660–4938)—The totally bald Head of Security on Solaria in A.D. 4921, Hanis Gruer was in charge of the investigation into Rikaine Delmarre's death from the Spacer end. Gruer's drink was subsequently poisoned by the machinations of Jothan Lebig while Gruer was discussing Delmarre's death with plainclothes Earth homicide detective Elijah Baley via trimensional viewing, and Gruer nearly died. The house that Baley and R. Daneel Olivaw resided in during their stay on Solaria had been built on Gruer's estate [*The Naked Sun*].

Guardian Robots—Nuclear powered (as opposed to transducer-lobe powered) robots that protect Solaria from Outworlders and are not a part of any Solarian estate [*Foundation and Earth*].

Gyro-ship—A small shuttle, vane-equipped for atmospheric travel, that can transport passengers and material from a ship in orbit to the surface of a planet. Gyro-ships were popular in the Early Galactic Era [*The Currents of Space*].

Hall of Worlds—A monument on Melpomenia that contains a list of the fifty Spacer worlds, in the order in which they were established, as well as the spatial coordinates for each world. The center of the rough sphere formed by these coordinates should be close to Earth and does, in fact, correspond to the coordinates for Alpha Centauri, part of a binary star system about a parsec from Earth [*Foundation and Earth*].

Hame—Trantorian dialect for "home," Hame was what the natives of Trantor called their planet in the late fifth century F.E. [*Foundation's Edge*].

Hanger—Peculiar to the luxury world of Kalgan in the third century F.E., the "Hanger" was an immense parking space for spaceships that offered the amenities of a hotel [*Foundation and Empire* Part II, "The Mule"].

Hannis (442–513 F.E.)—A Terminus politician whose career was destroyed in 498 F.E. over the issue of where to locate the capital of the Foundation Federation [*Foundation's Edge*].

Harroway (A.D. 1992–2057)—A fussy little man who searched District Attorney Stephen Byerley's house for illegal robots in A.D. 2032 [*I, Robot*, "Evidence"].

Hardin, Salvor (17–101 F.E.)—A gifted natural politician and one of the great heroes of the Foundation, Salvor Hardin was the first Mayor of Terminus City. Hardin resolved the First Anacreonian Crisis of 49–50 F.E. by visiting the Kingdoms of Daribow, Konom, and Smyrno and convincing them to issue ultimatums mandating that the neighboring Kingdom of Anacreon cease its attempts to annex Terminus. During this crisis he also staged a bloodless coup against the Foundation's Board of Trustees that transferred governmental authority on Terminus from the Board to the City Council. Hardin successfully played the Four Kingdoms off against one another for the next thirty years, and he subsequently resolved the Second Anacreonian Crisis of 79 F.E., a threatened invasion, by placing the Kingdom of Anacreon under interdict while crippling the Anacreonian flagship, the *Wienis*, by cutting its power with a hyperwave relay as it approached Terminus. The cigar-chewing Hardin is best-remembered by schoolchildren for his pithy epigrams, the most well-known of which is "Violence is the last refuge of the incompetent." Hardin is also credited with the epigrams "It pays to be obvious, especially if you have a reputation for subtlety"; "Never let your sense of morals prevent you from doing what is right," which became the semi-ironic motto of the Foundation's traders in the early first century F.E.; and "A nuclear blaster is a good weapon, but it can point both ways," among many others [*Foundation* Part II, "The Encyclopedists"; *Foundation* Part III, "The Mayors"; *Foundation* Part IV, "The Traders"; *Foundation* Part V, "The Merchant Princes"].

Hart, Francis J. (A.D. 1980–2052)—Plump, balding Francis J. Hart was Head of the Department of English and Dean of Graduate Studies at Northeastern University in A.D. 2034. He voted in favor of the university leasing Robot EZ-27, also known as Easy [*Robot Visions*, "Galley Slave"].

Hart, Porfirat (252–328 F.E.)—Bayta Darell's section leader in the Democratic Underground on Terminus [*Foundation and Empire* Part II, "The Mule"].

Haut Rodric, Anselm (2–91 F.E.)—The Sub-prefect of Pluema, Anselm haut Rodric was the Envoy Extraordinary of his Highness of Anacreon to Terminus during the First Anacreonian Crisis of 49–50 F.E. [*Foundation* Part II, "The Encyclopedists"].

Haven—A red dwarf star on the outermost edge of the Periphery [*Foundation and Empire* Part II, "The Mule"].

Haven II—One of the Independent Trading Worlds, Haven II orbits the star Haven and was settled by renegade Traders early in the third century F.E. One of the last of the Independent Trading Worlds to fall to the Mule, Haven II nevertheless surrendered without a fight in 298 F.E. [*Foundation and Empire* Part II, "The Mule"].

HB-34—See "Herbie."

Heat-seeker—A device that detects infra-red radiation—specifically the particular thermal pattern given off at 37 degrees Celsius—and is thus useful in locating human beings in sparsely populated areas [*Prelude to Foundation*].

Heatsinks—Half of Trantor's energy in the Late Galactic Era (10,100–12,100 G.E.) came from heatsinks, which harnessed heat from the planet's magma layer [*Prelude to Foundation*].

Helicon—Birthplace of the great psychohistorian Hari Seldon, Helicon is a planet in the Arcturus sector. Sparsely populated and divided into twenty administrative sectors, it is a culturally homogeneous world on the opposite side of the Galaxy's central black hole from Trantor that is overshadowed by its neighbors. The citizens of Helicon are known for their prowess in the martial arts [*Foundation* Part I, "The Psychohistorians"; *Prelude to Foundation*].

Heliona—The northern continent on Solaria. Gladia and Rikaine Delmarre's estate was in Heliona [*Robots and Empire*].

Helix—The Auroran version of an escalator. There are up-helixes and down-helixes [*The Robots of Dawn*].

Hella (277–333 F.E.)—A factory worker on Haven II who believed after the fall of Terminus that the Independent Trading Worlds should surrender to the Mule [*Foundation and Empire* Part II, "The Mule"].

Herbie—Robot HB-34 (known as "Herbie") was manufactured in A.D. 2021. U.S. Robots and Mechanical Men employee Milton Ashe soon discovered that it could read thoughts, a fact that became known only to Ashe, Alfred Lanning, Peter Bogert, and Susan Calvin. Although a mathematical genius, Herbie had little interest in science, which it thought simple and make-shift, but was fascinated by fiction because of the insight it gives into human motivations and emotions, which Herbie felt were complicated. The robot read Calvin's mind to discover that she was secretly in love with Ashe, a younger man, and told Calvin that Ashe reciprocated her feelings—although this was not true—because telling her the truth would have harmed her emotionally, and thus would have violated the First Law of Robotics. For the same reason it also told Bogert what Bogert wanted to hear—rather than the truth—that Bogert was a better mathematician than Herbie and that Lanning had already resigned as plant director and had named Bogert as his successor. Herbie knew what glitch in its assembly had enabled it to read minds, but it could not reveal this to Lanning or Bogert because they did not want to know that a machine could solve a problem that neither of them could solve, yet they also wanted the answer. Vengefully—for Herbie had raised her romantic hopes only to have them dashed by reality—Calvin confronted Herbie with his dilemma: Herbie would hurt Bogert and Lanning if it told them why it was a mind-reading robot, but it would also hurt them if it did not tell them. The fact that it would break the First Law of Robotics no matter what it did caused Herbie to break down completely, and it was scrapped [*I, Robot*, "Liar"].

Hesperos—One of the Spacer Worlds [*Robots and Empire*].

High Minister of Earth—In 827 G.E. the High Minister of Earth, who ruled under the jurisdiction of the Emperor and the Procurator of Earth, in theory held the power of life and death over all Earthmen. In reality this power was held by Balkis, the High Minister's Secretary and a member of the Society of Ancients, while the High Minister himself was merely a handsome figurehead [*Pebble in the Sky*].

Hinriad, Artemisia "Arta" oth (Early Galactic Era)—Tall, dark-haired, dark-eyed, pretty, smoldering, and temperamental, Artemisia oth Hinriad was Director of Rhodia Hinrik V's daughter and Gillbret oth Hinriad's niece. For reasons of state she was betrothed against her will to Pohang, an elderly high official of the Royal Court of Tyrann. She escaped from Rhodia's Palace Central with Biron Farrill and Gillbret, and she subsequently escaped with them from Rhodia in Simok Aratap's ship, the *Remorseless*, which they took to Lingane. While they were on the *Remorseless*, Artemisia became romantically involved with Biron, but their romance was hindered by the Autarch of Lingane's false claim that Artemisia's father, Hinrik V, had had Biron's father, the Rancher of Widemos, murdered. When Biron cooled to her—to make everyone think that he believed the Autarch's claim—she was courted by the Autarch (in whom she had no real interest), who had joined them in searching the Horeshead Nebula for the secret rebellion world. She reconciled with Biron after trying, unsuccessfully (as she faints), to save him from the Autarch's attempt to kill him, and she finally was married to Biron by her father aboard the *Remorseless* en route back to Rhodia [*The Stars, Like Dust*].

Hinriad, Gillbret "Gil" oth (Early Galactic Era)—Artemisia oth Hinriad's uncle, Gillbret oth Hinriad was the son of a former Director of Rhodia who had been killed by the Tyranni, was Director of Rhodia Hinrik V's cousin, and was next in the line of succession to be the Director of Rhodia. Secretly opposed to the Tyranni's rule of Rhodia, Gillbret inconsistently played the role of an ineffectual, amused, effete dilettante. While returning to Rhodia from Tyrann, where he had attended the Khan of Tyrann's coronation, he found himself on the secret rebellion world after a meteorite had damaged his ship, but he never learned the rebellion world's location. An amateur inventor, he subsequently created the visisonor and a variety of surveillance devices that he used to spy on the Tyranni and on Hinrik V. Twenty years later, he used his visisonor to distract Biron Farrill's guards and thus to enable Biron to escape when Biron was arrested for treason on Rhodia. Gillbret then escaped from Rhodia's

Palace Central with Biron and Artemisia, and subsequently with them from Rhodia itself in Simok Aratap's ship, the *Remorseless*, which he convinced Biron to pilot to Lingane. While searching the Horsehead Nebula for the secret rebellion world, Gillbret was finally captured—with Biron, Artemisia, the Autarch of Lingane, and Tedor Rizzett—by Aratap, but he briefly escaped and sabotaged Aratap's ship's engines in a suicidal attempt to blow up the ship and thus prevent Aratap from finding the rebellion world at the coordinates provided by the Autarch. However, Biron—having deduced that the rebellion world was not in the Horsehead Nebula at all—warned Aratap in time to save the ship. Unfortunately, Biron had had to use a neuronic whip on Gillbret in doing so, and Gillbret died as a consequence, and as a consequence of the stress of his adventure generally, still believing that the ship was about to explode [*The Stars, Like Dust*].

Hinriads—A dynasty that had maintained a lengthy period of stability on Rhodia until the planet was conquered by the Tyranni in the Early Galactic Era. As the Tyranni rarely concerned themselves with the internal politics of conquered planets, the Hinriads continued to be the figureheads of state on Rhodia even during Tyranni rule [*The Stars, Like Dust*].

Hinrik V (Early Galactic Era)—Artemisia oth Hinriad's father, Gillbret oth Hinriad's cousin, and a member of Rhodia's Hinriad dynasty, gray-haired, handsome, thickly-mustachioed Hinrik V, Director of Rhodia, seemed to be a hopelessly pliant, imbecilic tool of the Tyranni but was in reality the clandestine leader of the secret rebellion against the Tyranni that had been brewing on Rhodia for more than twenty years. He was taken aboard Simok Aratap's ship as it pursued Biron Farrill, Artemisia, and Gillbret from Rhodia to Lingane and then into the Horsehead Nebula. Still believed by the Tyranni to be their helpless puppet, he was finally returned to Rhodia after Aratap had concluded that the secret rebellion world did not exist. Hinrik V married Biron and Artemisia on this trip back to Rhodia. A Primitivist in his youth, he finally revealed that he had possessed for twenty years the valuable Earth document that Biron had failed to find on Earth, the Constitution of the United States of America, which Hinrik V intended to use as a blueprint for a new form of government to be instituted after his revolt against the Tyranni succeeded [*The Stars, Like Dust*].

Hiroko (476–557 F.E.)—A small, beautiful young woman, Hiroko was the first person Golan Trevize, Janov Pelorat, Bliss, and Fallom met on New Earth. As a part of her duties as hostess, she had sex with Trevize in order to infect him with an unactivated but fatal virus. She played the flute in the Alphan music festival and gave her flute to Fallom, who exhibited amazing virtuosity in playing the instrument with its transducer-lobes. Although she was also motivated in part by affection for Trevize, this motivated Hiroko to tell Trevize, Pelorat, and Bliss that they would all be killed by the virus, with Fallom, if they did not leave Alpha immediately, [*Foundation and Earth*].

Hjordesse (Early Galactic Era)—A Florinian Squire who owned the space yacht *Flame Arrow* [*The Currents of Space*].

Hober Mallow—A Foundation cruiser that was destroyed by a Kalganian squadron led by the *Fearless* on the 185th day of 376 F.E., marking the beginning of the Stettinian War. See "Mallow, Hober" [*Second Foundation* Part II, "Search by the Foundation"].

Holomirror—A type of mirror that does not invert left and right when reflecting an image [*Prelude to Foundation*].

Hoppen, Mrs. (1982–2051)—District attorney Stephen Byerley's housekeeper in A.D. 2032 [*I, Robot*, "Evidence"].

Horder, Rutilan (A.D. 4592–4943)—A surprisingly short but thickset man, Rutilan Horder was in the third decade of his second 30-year term as Chairman of the Auroran Legislature when, in A.D. 4923, he mediated the dispute between Dr. Han Fastolfe and Dr. Kelden Amadiro concerning whether or not Earth should be permitted by the Spacer Worlds to participate in the further settlement of the Galaxy. After listening to Earth plainclothes homicide detective Elijah Baley's argument that Amadiro had attempted to kidnap humaniform robot R. Daneel Olivaw in order to study it, to learn how to construct more humaniform robots with which Aurora might colonize the Galaxy, Horder sided with Fastolfe and determined that Earth would be permitted to participate in the further settlement of the Galaxy [*The Robots of Dawn*].

Horleggor—The first Foundation world to be conquered by the Mule [*Foundation and Empire* Part II, "The Mule"].

Hso-lin, Ching (A.D. 1992–2063)—Vice-Co-ordinator of Earth's Eastern Region in A.D. 2052 [*I, Robot*, "The Evitable Conflict"].

Humanist Party—Headed by Dr. Han Fastolfe, the Humanist Party was the political party on Aurora in the 50th century A.D. that believed that all human beings, even those from Earth, should participate in the further settlement of the Galaxy. The Humanist Party's political enemies were the Globalists, who believed that only Aurora should settle the remainder of the Galaxy [*The Robots of Dawn*].

Humboldt, Dr. Alfred Barr (A.D. 4644–4972)—A Fellow of the Galactic Academy and one of the three top mathematicians in the Galaxy in his time, Dr. Alfred Barr Humboldt was a Spacer mathematician en route on the *Eta Carina* to an interstellar neurobiophysics conference on Aurora in A.D. 4921. While en route, he and fellow Spacer mathematician Gennao Sabbat both claimed to have made the same revolutionary mathematical discovery, and both claimed that the other had stolen the idea. Due to the deductions of Earth plainclothes homicide detective Elijah Baley, who was consulted by R. Daneel Olivaw, Humboldt finally confessed that he had stolen Sabbat's idea [*Robot Visions*, "Mirror Image"].

Hummin, Chetter—Ostensibly a journalist who came to Hari Seldon's aid when Seldon was accosted by two Trantorian thugs, Marbie and Alem, in a park on Trantor in 12,020 G.E., Chetter Hummin was in reality R. Daneel Olivaw in disguise. Hummin subsequently convinced Seldon to go into hiding on Trantor—to escape the clutches of Cleon I's unofficial first minister Eto Demerzel (who was also Daneel in disguise)—rather than return to Helicon. He also convinced Seldon to develop psychohistory, for the betterment of the peoples of the Galaxy, because he believed the Galactic Empire was dying. Hummin took Seldon to Streeling University, where he put Seldon under Dors Venabili's supervision and protection, and then had Dors take Seldon to Mycogen, from which Hummin later rescued them both after they had invaded the sanctity of the Sacratorium's Elder's Aerie. Hummin later used Daneel's mentalic powers to undermine Rashelle's authority in Wye, which enabled Imperial troops to invade and occupy the sector easily and bloodlessly. After Rashelle's attempts to murder Seldon—to keep him out of Demerzel's hands—failed, Hummin appeared in Wye and was exposed by Rashelle as also being Demerzel. But Seldon then deduced that Hummin/Demerzel was actually a humaniform robot in disguise, the Da-Nee of Dahl Sector's legends, R. Daneel Olivaw [*Prelude to Foundation*].

Huxlani, Chief Engineer (258–311 F.E.)—Trained on Anacreon and an eighteen-year veteran of the Foundation fleet, Chief Engineer Huxlani was an officer on the starship transporting Bail Channis and General Han Pritcher from Kalgan to Tazenda and Rossem during their search for the Second Foundation on behalf of the Mule [*Second Foundation* Part I, "Search by the Mule"].

Hyper Base—A 21st-century A.D. space station, in the Twenty-seventh Asteroidal Grouping, that was dedicated to the discovery of the hyperatomic drive [*I, Robot*, "Little Lost Robot"].

Hyper-relay—A Foundation device that allows a ship to be traced through hyper-space. The Mule had placed a hyper-relay on Bail Channis and General Han Pritcher's ship, when they had gone in search of the Second Foundation in 303 F.E., because he had deduced that Channis was a member of the Second Foundation. Terminus Mayor Harla Branno placed a hyper-relay on Munn

Hyper-space

Li Compor's ship, the *Bright Star*, in 498 F.E. [*Second Foundation* Part I, "Search by the Mule"; *Foundation's Edge*].

Hyper-space—The phenomenon that makes faster-than-light space travel possible, hyper-space is a higher dimension (beyond the four dimensions of length, width, height, and duration) through which it is possible to travel from any point in the Galaxy to any other point in an instant [*Foundation* Part I, "The Psychohistorians"].

Hyperatomic drive—Developed by U.S. Robots and Mechanical Men's The Brain in A.D. 2029, the hyperatomic drive is the propulsion system that makes it possible to travel, through hyper-space, at faster-than-light speeds [*I, Robot*, "Little Lost Robot"; *I, Robot*, "Escape"].

Hypnite—An anesthetic [*The Stars, Like Dust*].

Idda, R.—Dr. Gennoa Sabbat's personal robot servant for twenty-two years in A.D. 4921. It was questioned that year by Earth plainclothes homicide detective Elijah Baley to determine if it or Dr. Alfred Barr Humboldt's personal robot servant, R. Preston, had been lying in testimony involving a professional dispute between their owners, two Spacer mathematicians [*Robot Visions*, "Mirror Image"].

Imperial Crisis—Although the Foundation suffered from weak leadership during this time, by 198 F.E. the Foundation's economic influence had expanded throughout the Periphery to such an extent that it had attracted the attention of Imperial General Bel Riose, who surrounded Foundation space with his own superior military force—employing the strategy of Previous Enclosure, which is almost always successful—in an attempt to conquer it. But the loyal Riose was recalled from the Periphery by Emperor Cleon II in 199 F.E., just before his almost-certain victory over the Foundation, was tried for treason on trumped-up charges, and was executed because no Emperor in this period of Galactic history could afford to have a popular and successful general become a military conqueror, as such generals historically go on to overthrow the government and declare themselves Emperor. Thus, Riose's own success was the cause of his downfall; while the Foundation was helpless in the face of Riose's superior military strength and tactics, and while the Foundation's own attempts to subvert Riose had failed miserably, the forces of history orchestrated Riose's inevitable defeat [*Foundation and Empire* Part I, "The General"].

The Imperial Library—This library on Trantor, changed its name to the Galactic Library sometime after the Sack of Trantor in 258 F.E., was in Imperial times the largest library in the Galaxy and was subsequently the home of the Second Foundation. It was protected by the University of Trantor's students, who were under the mental influence of the Second Foundation, and survived the Sack of Trantor intact. Ebling Mis had done his research on the location of the Second Foundation at the Imperial Library. Mysteriously, all references to Earth had been removed from the Imperial Library by the late fifth century F.E. [*Foundation's Edge*].

Imperial News—The official government newspaper published on Trantor in the late second and early third centuries F.E. [*Foundation and Empire* Part I, "The General"].

Inchney (218–309 F.E.)—A former Lord of Trantor, Inchney was the Mule's agent on Neotrantor and the slave of Jord Commason who in 298 F.E. suggested that Commason capture Bayta and Toran Darell, Ebling Mis, and Magnifico Giganticus and then give Bayta to crown prince Dagobert X as a sexual plaything [*Foundation and Empire* Part II, "The Mule"].

Indbur I, Mayor (168–247 F.E.)—Mayor Indbur III's grandfather, Indbur I was the brutal and despotic but capable ruler of the Foundation in the early third century F.E. He made the office of Mayor of Terminus hereditary [*Foundation and Empire* Part II, "The Mule"].

Indbur II, Mayor (205–277 F.E.)—Mayor Indbur III's father and the Foundation's first hereditary Mayor, Indbur II was the brutal and despotic ruler of the Foundation in the mid-third century F.E. [*Foundation and Empire* Part II, "The Mule"].

Indbur III, Mayor (248–299 F.E.)—A small man in stature, an excellent bookkeeper by temperament, and an avid amateur gardener, Indbur III was the ineffective, hereditary Mayor of Terminus in the late third century F.E. Oblivious to the threat posed by the Mule because he believed that the Seldon Plan guaranteed that no warlord from the splintering Galactic Empire could defeat the Foundation, but fearful of a revolt by the Independent Trading Worlds, Indbur III surrendered the Foundation to the Mule when Terminus came under attack in 298 F.E. [*Foundation and Empire* Part II, "The Mule"].

Independent Trading Worlds—An organization in the late third century F.E. of twenty-seven relatively poor and sparsely-populated planets whose renegade Traders aspired to revolt against Mayor Indbur III's despotic rule of the Foundation, the Independent Trading Worlds joined the Foundation in its war against the Mule in 297 F.E. and were, for a short time, the only segment of the Foundation not defeated by the Mule when Terminus was occupied by the Mule's forces in 298 F.E. [*Foundation and Empire* Part II, "The Mule"].

Infi—A planet that was the site of a Foundation defeat during the Stettinian War of 376–77 F.E. [*Second Foundation* Part II, "Search by the Foundation"].

Inner Provinces—A portion of the Foundation sphere of influence closer to the Galactic Center than Terminus, the Inner Provinces was a region to which many in the Foundation wanted to move the Foundation's capital in the late fifth century F.E. This move was successfully blocked by Terminus Mayor Harla Branno in 498 F.E. [*Foundation's Edge*].

Institute for Nuclear Research—A research facility in Chicago at which a laboratory accident in A.D. 1949 inadvertently sent retired tailor Joseph Schwartz forward some 10,000 years in time, the Institute for Nuclear Research was still in operation, and was the facility in which Dr. Affret Shekt had perfected his Synapsifier, in 827 G.E. [*Pebble in the Sky*].

Interregnum, Great—From 258 F.E. to 998 F.E., the Great Interregnum is the 740-year period between the fall of the First Galactic Empire, with the Great Sack of Trantor, and the Rise of the Second Galactic Empire, unified by the Foundation [*Second Foundation* Part I, "Search by the Mule"].

Intersectional analysis—The mathematical system developed by Dr. Han Fastolfe in A.D. 4897 that made it possible to design humaniform positronic brains and humaniform robots [*The Robots of Dawn*].

Interstellar Spatio-analytic Bureau—In the Early Galactic Era the Interstellar Spatio-analytic Bureau (I.S.B.) was a politically independent organization of spatio-analysts. However, its political autonomy was debatable due to the fact that most of its financial backing came from the Trantorian Empire [*The Currents of Space*].

Ipatiev, Dr. (A.D. 1974–2058)—A colleague of Professor Simon Ninheimer whose work had been misrepresented in Ninheimer's *Social Tensions Involved in Space Flight and Their Resolution*, which had been proofread by Robot EZ-27, also known as Easy [*Robot Visions*, "Galley Slave"].

Isolate—An isolate is an individual who is not part of some group consciousness, such as Gaia [*Foundation and Earth*].

Iss—One of the last of the Independent Trading Worlds conquered by the Mule in 298 F.E., after the fall of Terminus, Iss went down fighting [*Foundation and Empire* Part II, "The Mule"].

Jacobson, Mortimer W. (A.D. 2029–2108)—A teenager who fed random data into a computer that designed positronic brains while he was on a public tour of U.S. Robots and Mechanical Men in A.D. 2045. The result was the flawed experimental robot Lenny (the LNE-Prototype) [*Robot Visions*, "Lenny"].

Jacof (Early Galactic Era)—A clerk in a food processing center, Jacof was the "upperman"—a Florian native who works in the Upper City but lives in the Lower City—whose home Towman Myrlyn Terens commandeers to give himself time to think while searching for Valona

March and Rik [*The Currents of Space*].

Jael, Ankor (105–182 F.E.)—Former Terminus Minister of Education who had previously lost his City Council seat to Jorane Sutt, Ankor Jael was fired from the Mayor of Terminus' cabinet in 154 F.E. for arguing against the continuation of the Foundation's century-long policy of dominating neighboring systems through spiritual manipulation. Having presented evidence that exonerated Master Trader Hober Mallow during Mallow's 155 F.E. trial for the murder of false Foundation missionary Jord Parma, Jael was appointed Minister of Education and Propaganda by Mallow when Mallow became Mayor of Terminus later that same year [*Foundation* Part V, "The Merchant Princes"].

Jander Panell, R.—The second of two humaniform robots constructed in the early 50th century A.D. Like the first humaniform robot of that era, R. Daneel Olivaw, to which it bore a strong physical resemblance, Jander was made possible by Dr. Han Fastolfe's development of the humaniform positronic brain. Jander was assembled by Fastolfe on Aurora and subsequently became Gladia Delmarre's lover and—in her opinion—husband. However, after eight months with Gladia, in A.D. 4923, Jander was immobilized by robot-mental-freeze-out, the first possible case of roboticide in Aurora's history. While it was finally believed that Jander had been immobilized by a highly improbable chance change in its positronic pathways, in fact Jander was destroyed by R. Giskard Reventlov, a mind-reading robot who had learned how to induce robot-mental-freeze-out from Fastolfe's thoughts, so that Dr. Kelden Amadiro would no longer be able to study Jander surreptitiously in order to discover how to construct for himself and the Robotics Institute of Aurora (RIA) humaniform positronic brains and humaniform robots that could be used to colonize the Galaxy for Aurora [*The Robots of Dawn*].

Jane-1—Or JN-1 was a prototype intuitive robot with a pinched waist. It was disregarded on the assumption that its more-feminine look would generate hostility [*Robot Visions*, "Feminine Intuition"].

Jane-2—Or JN-2, manufactured in A.D. 2059, was the second unsuccessful attempt to construct an intuitive, creative robot [*Robot Visions*, "Feminine Intuition'].

Jane-3—Or JN-3 was the third unsuccessful attempt to create an intuitive, creative robot. It was never activated [*Robot Visions*, "Feminine Intuition"].

Jane-4—Or JN-4 was developed in 2060A.D. It was the most successful attempt to construct an intuitive, creative robot to date [*Robot Visions*, "Feminine Intuition'].

Jane-5—Or JN-5 was developed at US Robots and Mechanical Men in A.D. 2062 as an intuitive, creative robot through the introduction of unfixed, randomly crossing paths in its positronic brain. It was slim and short, and it spoke in a woman's sweet contralto voice. It was assigned the task of identifying the location of a habitable planet within the 300,000 star systems that could be reached at the time through the use of the hyperatomic drive, and it did provide Clinton Mandarian with the names of three stars within 80 light years of Earth that each had a 60–90% chance of possessing one habitable planet, but the plane carrying both Mandarian and Jane-5 was destroyed by a meteorite en route from Flagstaff, AZ, to New York City [*Robot Visions*, "Feminine Intuition'].

Jemby—Played the flute, and was Fallom's nursemaid robot on Solaria. It was deactivated when Bliss killed Sarton Bander, Fallom's parent, in 498 F.E. [*Foundation and Earth*].

Jencus, Ull (Early Galactic Era)—Elderly, plump Ull Jencus was an amateur doctor in Townman Myrlyn Terens' village on Florina [*The Currents of Space*].

Jennat Sector—Sector of Trantor during the Late Galactic Era (10,100–12,100 G.E.) in which sex was discussed endlessly, but only for the purpose of condemning it [*Prelude to Foundation*].

Jennings, Mr. (A.D. 1924–2002)—A young chemist who worked at the Institute for Nuclear Research in Chicago. In A.D. 1949 his crucible of crude uranium suddenly melted, radiated a corona, and emitted a force beam that transported retired tailor Joseph Schwartz some 10,000 years into the future [*Pebble in the Sky*].

Jensen, Rossiter (A.D. 2030–2112)—An astrophysicist working at Flagstaff, AZ, in A.D. 2062 [*Robot Visions*, "Feminine Intuition'].

Jerril (12,032–12,102 G.E./-27–34 F.E.)—An agent of Trantor's Commission of Public Safety, Jerril tailed Gall Dornick after Dornick's arrival at Trantor's spaceport in 12,067 G.E. (-2 F.E.) [*Foundation* Part I, "The Psychohistorians"].

Jet-down—A vehicle using an ion propulsion system that could hover to explore planetary terrain, the jet-down was in wide use in the Late Galactic Era (10,100–12,100 G.E.), and many were privately owned. A jet-down from Wye Sector unsuccessfully sought Heri Seldon on Streeling Sector's Upperside in 12,020 G.E. [*Prelude to Foundation*].

Johannes, Ben (A.D. 2140–2218)—A colleague of Dr. Gregory Arnfeld, Ben Johannes helped to develop MIK-27 or Mike, a robot capable of miniaturizing itself [*Robot Visions*, "Too Bad!"].

John (A. D. 1992–2035)—An attorney and then a research biophysicist, John was the original Stephen Byerley, crippled in an auto accident, who replaced himself with an able-bodied humaniform robot duplicate in A.D. 2029. In A.D. 2032 he created a second humaniform robot that the robotic Stephen Byerley could punch—to demonstrate that he was not a robot—without breaking the First Law of Robotics. See "Byerley, Stephen" [*I, Robot*, "Evidence"].

Jonti, Sander (Early Galactic Era)—Sander Jonti, who claimed to be a native of the Nubular Kingdoms but had been passing himself off on Earth as a Vegan, was in reality the Autarch of Lingane. By blasting open Biron Farrill's door on Earth, Jonti appeared to save Biron from the radiation bomb that was apparently about to detonate in his dorm room. However, the bomb was a fake, planted there by Jonti only to enable him to manipulate Biron into seeking sanctuary from Hinrik V on Rhodia, where Jonti planned to have Biron captured by the Tyranni as a distraction that would focus the Tyranni on Rhodia and thus draw their attention away from the rebellion against them being planned on Lingane. Jonti had claimed that Biron's father, the Rancher of Widemos, had been murdered by Hinrik V; but this, too, was a lie, as Biron's father had actually been betrayed by Jonti in his true identity as the Autarch. See "Autarch of Lingane" [*The Stars, Like Dust*].

Joranum, Laskin "Jo-Jo" (11,986–12,037 G.E.)—A tall, large, charismatic man, Laskin "Jo-Jo" Joranum was a political demagogue who agitated for social justice, sector equality, and government by the people during the reign of Emperor Cleon I. While Joranum claimed to be a native of Nishaya, Hari Seldon deduced that he was really from Trantor's Mycogen Sector. Joranum aspired to replace Eto Demerzel as Cleon I's First Minister and promised Seldon that he would be Seldon's protector, like Demerzel, and that he would use psychohistory in governing. However, he planned to co-opt Seldon by converting Seldon's foster son, Rayche, to his populist political agenda. At Seldon's instigation, Rayche told Joranum that Demerzel was a robot—something Joranum had thought others might believe due to his upbringing in Mycogen Sector, where the population believed in robots; Joranum hoped to topple Demerzel, and to replace him as First Minister, by confronting Demerzel with this accusation, but Demerzel defused the charge completely by laughing at it during a news conference. Subsequently, also at Seldon's instigation, Joranum was denounced by Sunmaster Fourteen as a Mycogenian breakaway, a revelation that fatally undermined his political effectiveness. He later died in exile on Nishaya [*Forward the Foundation*].

Joranumite Affair—In 12,028 G.E. the stability of the Empire was threatened by political agitator Laskin "Jo-Jo" Joranum, who aspired to replace Eto Demerzel as Emperor Cleon I's First Minister. At Hari Seldon's instigation, Joranum hoped to topple Demerzel by publicly accusing him of being a robot—an accusation Demerzel deflected merely by laughing at it during a news conference. Subsequently, also at Seldon's instiga-

Joranumite

tion, Joranum was denounced by Sunmaster Fourteen as a Mycogenian breakaway, a revelation that fatally undermined his political effectiveness. Seldon's dual role in defusing Joranum's threat to the Empire's stability became known as the Joranumite Affair [*Forward the Foundation*].

Joranumite Conspiracy—A plot concocted in 12,038 G.E. by former Joranumite Gambol Deen Namarti and Wye aristocrat Gleb Andorin. Their plan was to have Raych assassinate Hari Seldon, for Andorin to then kill Raych, for Namarti to step in as First Minister, and for Emperor Cleon I to be replaced on the throne by Andorin when the time was ripe. This plot went awry when Trantorian Security Officer Manella Dubanqua killed Andorin before Raych could fire on Seldon [*Forward the Foundation*].

Joranumite Guard—An unofficial paramilitary force that maintained order in Trantor's Dahl Sector's Billibotton during the height of Laskin "Jo-Jo" Joranum's political influence, in 12,028 G.E. Raych was taken prisoner by members of the Joranumite Guard [*Forward the Foundation*].

Journal of the Galactic Archaeological Society*—J. Gal. Arch. Soc.* is a learned journal that has been in continuous publication since the Early Middle Galactic Era. In 815 G.E. the journal's editors refused to publish Dr. Bel Arvardan's Senior Dissertation, *On the Antiquity of Artifacts in the Sirius Sector with Considerations of the Application Thereof to the Radiation Hypothesis of Human Origin*, but did publish the dissertation some ten years later [*Pebble in the Sky*].

Juddee (297–378 F.E.)—A factory worker on Haven II who was especially distressed by the Mule's siege of Haven II in 298 F.E. [*Foundation and Empire* Part II, "The Mule"].

Jump—The act of entering hyperspace, which enables a spaceship to travel from one point in real space to another point in real space instantly, thus making interstellar travel possible. The Jump involves some momentary, minor discomfort [*The Stars, Like Dust*].

Junz, Dr. Selin (Early Galactic Era)—Brown-skinned, woolly-haired Dr. Selin Junz, a native of Libair, was a spatio-analyst and an official in the Interstellar Spatio-analytic Bureau (I.S.B.). He was educated at the Arcturan Institute of Spatial Technology. He spent a year seeking a missing spatio-analyst, Rik, who had predicted the immanent destruction of Florina, because he wanted to use Rik's disappearance to expose and destroy the master-slave relationship that existed between the planets Sark and Florina [*The Currents of Space*].

Kalaya, Eban (A.D. 5086–5148)—The communications officer on the Earth ship that took Captain Daneel Giskard Baley, Gladia Thool Delmarre Solaria Gremionis, R. Giskard Reventlov, and R. Daneel Olivaw from Aurora to Solaria in A.D. 5121 [*Robots and Empire*].

Kalgan—A strategically important, semi-tropical luxury world, Kalgan was the first major planet conquered by the Mule, in 296 F.E. Bayta and Toran Darell met Magnifico Giganticus on Kalgan in 297 F.E., and from there they transport him to Terminus, Haven II, Neotrantor, and Trantor. Kalgan subsequently became the capital planet of the Mule's Union of Worlds, until the Mule's death in 308 F.E. Arkady Darell traveled to Kalgan, where she met Preem and Mamma Palver and subsequently traveled with them to Trantor, in 376 F.E. [*Foundation and Empire* Part II, "The Mule"; *Second Foundation* Part I, "Search by the Mule"; *Second Foundation* Part II, "Search by the Foundation"].

Kalgan, The Lords of—A rapidly replaced string of adventurers and usurpers who ruled Kalgan, after the Mule's death in 308 F.E., for the remainder of the fourth century. While they styled themselves the First Citizens of the Galaxy, after the Mule, they were called the Lords of Kalgan by those in the Foundation [*Second Foundation* Part II, "Search by the Foundation"].

Kalgan, The Warlord of (256–334 F.E.)—The ruler of Kalgan who was converted by the Mule in 296 F.E. and then surrendered his planet to the Mule, the Warlord of Kalgan subsequently became the Mule's Viceroy to the Foundation [*Foundation and Empire* Part II, "The Mule"].

Kalganian War—See "Stettinian War."

Kalganid—The currency on Kalgan during the 4th century F.E. [*Second Foundation* Part II, "Search by the Foundation"].

Kallner, Major-general (A.D. 1973–2048)—The head of the Hyperatomic Drive project at Hyper Base in A.D. 2029 [*I, Robot*, "Little Lost Robot"].

Kandar V, Emperor (777–852 G.E.)—The Emperor under whom an abortive attempt, instigated by R. Daneel Olivaw, was made to replace Earth's radioactive crust with radiation-free soil [*Foundation and Earth*].

Kaspalov, Kaspal (11,980–12,038 G.E.)—An old Jaranumite who conspired with Gambol Deen Narmarti against Emperor Cleon I in 12,038 G.E. Although he was unsure if sabotage was the best route to rebellion on Trantor, Kaspalov was ordered to sabotage the ventilation system in Trantor's Anemoria Sector. Narmarti had Kaspalov executed because he believed, erroneously, that Kaspalov had sold out to the Empire [*Forward the Foundation*].

Kendast (418–487 F.E.)—One of Stor Gendibal's Second Foundation teachers [*Foundation's Edge*].

Kendray, A. (474–550 F.E.)—A short, chubby, bearded customs official who boarded Golan Trevize's *Far Star* when it docked at Corporellon's entry station in 498 F.E., A. Kendray passed the *Far Star* through Corporellon customs, despite the fact that Bliss has no papers, because the Comporellian authorities wanted to appropriate the gravitic ship to plumb its technology [*Foundation and Earth*].

Khan of the Tyranni—The Great King of Tyrann and of the fifty worlds it ruled in the Early Galactic Era [*The Stars, Like Dust*].

Khoratt, Jendippurus (Late Galactic Era)—Hanged by sailors in his own fleet for proposing the use of nuclear explosions as weapons of war during the Trigellian Insurrection [*Foundation's Edge*].

Khorov, Matt "The Baker" (Early Galactic Era)—Huge, immensely broad, well-muscled Matt Khorov was a Trantorian agent masquerading as a baker in Florina's Lower City. He helped Myrlyn Terens, Valona March, and Rik escape their patroller pursuers after Valona had felled and killed a patroller during their escape from the Upper City's library, and he supplied Rik and Valona with false passports before being killed by Terens [*The Currents of Space*].

Kirtle—A figure-disguising gown worn by Mycogenians. Mycogenian females wear gray, highly-embroidered kirtles; Mycogenian males wear white, unembroidered kirtles. The kirtle is worn with a tasseled belt [*Prelude to Foundation*].

Kleise, Dr. (305–375 F.E.)—A great electroneurologist and encephalographer, Dr. Kleise was Dr. Toran Darell's colleague and Pelleas Anthor's teacher. He discovered prior to his death in 375 F.E., through studying their encephalographs, that the minds of influential leaders of the Foundation had been tampered with, and he deduced that the Second Foundation had been responsible. Although he and Darell had had a serious falling out previously, just prior to his death Kleise contacted Darell and recommended Anthor to him; this uncharacteristic act, committed while Kleise was under the Second Foundation's mental control, raised Darell's suspicions about Anthor [*Second Foundation* Part II, "Search by the Foundation"].

Klemin, Joseph (A.D. 4875–4943)—The short, hen-pecked leader of the Medievalist cell to which Jessie Baley belonged in the early 50th century A.D. [*The Caves of Steel*].

Klev (275–218 F.E.)—A drunken Radolian and a citizen of the Foundation who was unconcerned about the Mule's military successes in 297 F.E. because he believed that the Foundation was destined always to win in the end [*Foundation and Empire* Part II, "The Mule"].

Kloda (441–512 F.E.)—Professor Janov Pelorat's housekeeper on Terminus [*Foundation's Edge*].

Kodell, Liono (444–511 F.E.)—Pipe-smoking Director of Security throughout Harla Branno's tenure as Mayor of Terminus, Liono Kodell questioned Golan Trevize in 498

F.E. and elicited Trevize's confession that he did not believe in the validity of the Seldon Plan. Kodell later accompanied Branno as she followed Trevize and Munn Li Compor to Gaia [*Foundation's Edge*].

Konom, Kingdom of—One of the Four Kingdoms in the region of the Periphery near Terminus, The Kingdom of Konom seceded from the First Galactic Empire in the first half of the first century F.E only to fall under the dominance of the Foundation and its religion of science by the century's end. With the Kingdoms of Daribow and Smyrno, Konom issued an ultimatum that prevented The Kingdom of Anacreon from annexing Terminus in 50 F.E. [*Foundation* Part II, "The Encyclopedists"].

Korell—Capital planet of the Korellian Republic in the second century F.E., Korell had refused to open its borders to Foundation traders, until the intervention of Master Trader Hober Mallow in 154 F.E., because it resisted the compulsory religion of science that accompanied the Foundation's nuclear gadgets. Korell declared war on the Foundation in 155 F.E. but capitulated three years later, after three years of military stalemate, because its nuclear economy had gone into a severe depression without the technical assistance of the Foundation in maintaining its nuclear infrastructure. By then a Foundation planet, Korell fell to the Kalganians without a fight during the Stettinian War of 376–77 F.E. [*Foundation* Part V, "The Merchant Princes"; *Second Foundation* Part II, "Search by the Foundation"].

Korellian Crisis—The third Seldon Crisis was the Korellian Crisis of 154–58 F.E. After three Foundation ships had disappeared in the Korellian Republic in 154 F.E., suggesting that the Korellians had reacquired nuclear power and nuclear weapons, Master Trader Hober Mallow, spying on behalf of the Foundation, discovered that the Korellians had received this nuclear technology from the still-powerful First Galactic Empire. Simultaneously, having become politically and economically influential and yet remaining unregulated, the Foundation's Traders threatened the century-long sway of the Foundation's religion of science over the common people of the Periphery by increasingly opting to sell the Foundation's nuclear gadgets without insisting that stellar systems adopt the compulsory religion that had heretofore accompanied them. These crises were successfully resolved when Mallow became Mayor of Terminus in 155 F.E. and dealt with them both by doing nothing, thus allowing the forces of history to resolve the crises for him. The Korellian Republic surrendered to the Foundation in 158 F.E., after three years of military stalemate, due to the fact that its fledgling nuclear economy was failing without the Foundation's technical assistance; and throughout the remainder of the second century F.E. the Foundation's religion of science waned and eventually evaporated as the traders sold their wares without resorting to this extraneous encumbrance. This crisis signaled the shift in the mid-second-century F.E. from the Foundation dominating its neighbors through its religious hierarchy to its dominating its neighbors through economic hegemony [*Foundation* Part V, "The Merchant Princes"].

Korellian Republic—A Republic in name only, the Korellian Republic had been an absolute monarchy ruled for generations by the Argo family when it reacquired nuclear power and nuclear weapons from the First Galactic Empire in the mid-second-century F.E. and thus became a threat to the Foundation, which had for a century exercised a monopoly on nuclear technology in the Periphery. The Republic lost its three-year-long war with the Foundation in 158 F.E. due to an internal economic collapse prompted by the Foundation's failure to service Korell's fledgling nuclear infrastructure during the war years [*Foundation* Part V, "The Merchant Princes"].

Krasnet, Technical Sergeant (443–505 F.E.)—A competent computer technician on the ship on which Golan Trevize had served as a lieutenant in the Foundation Navy [*Foundation's Edge*].

Kyrt—The most beautiful and the most valuable fabric in the Galaxy, sparkling, colorful kyrt can be spun finer than the most delicate synthetics, has a tensile strength greater than steel alloy, and is the most versatile substance known to man. It is a variety of cellulose that has these properties only when cultivated under conditions that duplicate those that existed on Florina in the Early Galactic Era, when Florina's sun was in the pre-nove stage because it was passing through a carbon current of space [*The Currents of Space*].

Labord, Faud (A.D. 4718–5079)— A well-known 50th-century Auroran writer who lived near the center of Eos [*The Robots of Dawn*].

Lambid, Sindra (A.D. 5067–5141)—Slim, light-brown skinned Sindra Lambid was a member of the Baleyworld legislature in A.D. 5121. She publicly asked Gladia Thool Delmarre Solaria Gremionis her age during Gladia's speech on Baleyworld [*Robots and Empire*].

Lamec—A beast of burden used on Helicon [*Forward the Foundation*].

Landaree—The overseer robot on the Zoberlon family estate on Solaria in A.D. 5121. A Solarian humaniform robot, it had the appearance of a beautiful woman. While adhering to the Three Laws of Robotics, it had been programmed to define a "human being" as someone who spoke with a Solarian accent. Thus, while it recognized Gladia Thool Delmarre Solaria Gremionis as being human, it did not define Captain Daneel Giskard Baley or any of his Settler crew as being human. Landaree was deactivated by R. Giskard Reventlov's mentalic abilities as it was about to harm

Gladia in its efforts to kill D.G. Baley and Daneel [*Robots and Empire*].

Lanning, Dr. Alfred (A.D. 1963–2043)—Gaunt, cigar-smoking Dr. Alfred Lanning demonstrated the first mobile robot to be equipped with a voice at a Psycho-Math seminar attended by Susan Calvin in A.D. 2002. He had been plant director at U.S. Robots and Mechanical Men since A.D. 1992, and had become Director of Research by A.D. 2008, the year in which Calvin joined the company. One of only four employees at the company to learn that robot HB-34 (known as "Herbie") could read thoughts, he was outraged when Peter Bogert informed him that Herbie had told Bogert that Lanning had already resigned as plant director and had named Bogert as his successor—lies Herbie had told Bogert because they were what Bogert had wanted to hear and because the truth would have harmed Bogert emotionally, and thus telling it would have violated the First Law of Robotics. Lanning became Director-Emeritus of Research at U.S. Robots in A.D. 2029 and was involved in the development of the hyperatomic drive, which makes faster-than-light space travel possible. In A.D. 2032 he was challenged by politician Francis Quinn to prove that District Attorney and candidate for mayor Stephen Byerley was not a robot, but he declined. In A.D. 2034 he persuaded Professor Barnabas H. Goodfellow to look at Robot EZ-27, also known as Easy, to determine if Northeastern University would be interested in leasing the robot as a proofreader. He subsequently persuaded the university to lease Easy for $1000 per year [*I, Robot*, "Introduction"; *I, Robot*, "Liar"; *I, Robot*, "Escape"; *I, Robot*, "Evidence"; *Robot Visions*, "Galley Slave"; *Robot Visions*, "Lenny"].

Lastoplug—An elastic chemical product chewed by some natives on Sark [*The Currents of Space*].

Laws of Robotics, Three—See "Three Laws of Robotics."

Lee, Yohan (13–93 F.E.)—Terminus Mayor Salvor Hardin's habitually anxious crony and agent, Yohan Lee implemented Hardin's coup against the Foundation's Board of Trustees in 50 F.E., in the midst of the First Anacreonian Crisis, while Hardin witnessed Hari Seldon's first appearance in the Vault [*Foundation* Part II, "The Encyclopedists"; *Foundation* Part III, "The Mayors"].

Leebig, Jothan (A.D. 4765–4921)—A genius roboticist and a close friend to Gladia Delmarre, lean, droopy-eyed Solarian Spacer Jothan Leebig was so finicky that he refused to be married because of the physical contact with his spouse that marriage would necessitate. He was even more finicky than his business associate Rikaine Delmarre, whose murder Leebig had orchestrated because Rikaine had intuited that Leebig was planning to build warships equipped with positronic brains that would be capable of attacking other ships.

Leebig's estate was adjacent to the Delmarre estate, and it was Leebig who had informed plainclothes Earth homicide detective Elijah Baley that Gladia had hated and frequently quarreled with her husband. Threatened with the prospect of being visited, touched, and restrained by another human—ironically, by R. Daneel Olivaw pretending to be human—Leebig confessed that the robot at the scene of Rikaine's murder had had detachable limbs, that he himself had tried to poison Head of Solarian Security Hanis Gruer, that he himself had tried to have Baley killed by a poisoned arrow, and that he himself had been plotting to construct warships with positronic brains. Leebig than committed suicide by ingesting poison rather than be touched by Daneel, whom he believed to be human [*The Naked Sun*].

Leemor, Fennel (355–428 F.E.)—A native of Locris, a volunteer, and an Engineer Third Class with the Foundation's Third Fleet, Fennel Leemor was interviewed by visicastor Jole Turbor during the Stettinian War, just prior to the decisive battle of Quoriston in 377 F.E. [*Second Foundation* Part II, "Search by the Foundation"].

Lefkin, Prince (44–99 F.E.)—Son of the Prince Regent Wienis of Anacreon, Prince Lefkin was the admiral in command of the flagship *Wienis* and the entire Anacreonian fleet during the Kingdom of Anacreon's unsuccessful attempt to invade Terminus in 79 F.E. [*Foundation* Part III, "The Mayors"].

Leggen, Jenarr (11,968–12,028 G.E.)—A tall, thin, long-nosed meteorologist at Trantor's Streeling University in 12,020 G.E., Jenarr Leggen hoped to learn about the general laws of meteorology by understanding the change in weather patterns on Trantor. His academic career and private life were poisoned by the Leggen Controversy, the question of whether or not he had conspired to lure Hari Seldon to a death by exposure to the elements on Streeling's Upperside [*Prelude to Foundation*].

Lenny—The LNE-Prototype, Lenny was an experimental robot designed to mine boron in the asteroid belt whose positronic brain was adversely affected when teenager Mortimer W. Jacobson fed random data into the computer than had designed it. As a consequence, Lenny spoke in beautifully musical nonsense syllables and had the mentality of a human infant. In warding off a blow, it inadvertently broke U.S. Robots and Mechanical Men employee Charles Randow's arm, but by that time it had become a substitute child to spinster robopsychologist Dr. Susan Calvin [*Robot Visions*, "Lenny"].

Lens—A new feature on advanced, early-fourth-century-F.E. interstellar cruisers, the Lens is a computerized imaging system that can reproduce the night sky as seen from any given point in the Galaxy [*Second Foundation* Part I, "Search by the Mule"].

Lenton (A.D. 1987–2052)—Stephen

Byerley's campaign manager during Byerley's A.D. 2032 campaign for mayor of New York City [*I, Robot*, "Evidence"].

Leopold I, King (63–162 F.E.)—A skilled and experienced Nyak hunter, Leopold I was the king of Anacreon who came of age and was crowned during the Second Anacreonian Crisis of 79 F.E. He was thought to be a demi-god by the people of Anacreon, who also believed that he derived his authority from the Galactic Spirit worshipped by adherents to the Foundation's religion of science [*Foundation* Part III, "The Mayors"].

Levanian, Endor (11,972–12,037 G.E.)—The air-jet pilot working for Chetter Hummin who transported Hari Seldon and Dors Venabili from Trantor's Streeling Sector to Mycogen Sector in 12,020 G.E. [*Prelude to Foundation*].

Levver, Abe (A.D. 1999–2063)—An employee of U.S. Robots and Mechanical Men in A.D. 2029 [*I, Robot*, "Escape"].

Li-Hsing, Chee (A.D. 2240–233?)—Chairwoman of the World Legislature's Science and Technology Committee in the late 23rd and early 24th centuries A.D. She subsequently became a Congresswoman and as such supported robot Andrew Martin's battle to be declared a human being legally [*Robot Visions*, "The Bicentennial Man"].

Libair—A planet on which all citizens have a deep, rich brown skin color [*The Currents of Space*].

Lightening—The name of the collie Gloria Weston was given to compensate her for the loss of her robot nursemaid Robbie, whom her parents had returned to U.S. Robots and Mechanical Men. Lightening was subsequently returned to the pet shop because Gloria, despondent over the loss of Robbie, could not stand the sight of it [*I, Robot*, "Robbie"].

Lih, Judge Tejan Popjens (12,008–12,086 G.E.)—A native of Lystena, the bluish-hued Judge Tejan Popjens Lih presided over the 12,058 inquest of Hari Seldon and Stettin Palver for having allegedly attacked three Trantorian youths. She dismissed the charges when the one, perjuring witness to the alleged attack, Rial Nevas, broke down on the witness stand due to Palver's and Wanda Seldon's mentalic urging that he tell the truth [*Forward the Foundation*].

Lindor, Hano (11,994–12,049)—An executive at the Dahl heatsinks who gave Hari Seldon and Dors Venabili a tour of his facility in 12,020 G.E. [*Prelude to Foundation*].

Lingane—Orbiting a G-2 star, Lingane was in the Early Galactic Era an independent, wealthy planet that occupied a strategic position in space for interstellar trade but suffered from internal political disorder. The last of the Nebular Kingdoms to be attacked by the Tyranni, it was not defeated but became an "Associated State" that was theoretically equal to and allied with the

Linn

Tyranni but was in actually under Tyranni dominion. Lingane lost much of what autonomy it had after Commissioner to the Khan of Tyrann Simok Aratap discovered that the Autarch of Lingane had been conspiring against the Tyranni [*The Stars, Like Dust*].

Linn, Hender (12,003–12,049 G.E.)—Titularly a colonel, Hender Linn was General Dugal Tennar's most successful yes-man and was known as "Tennar's lackey." He advised Tennar to remove Hari Seldon as head of the psychohistory project and to replace him with someone more sympathetic to the ruling military junta. After Dors Venabili forced her way into his office and threatened to kill him if Seldon were to be harmed by the junta, Linn became convinced that Seldon could not safely be removed from the psychohistory project while Dors was alive and conspired with Tennar to have her killed [*Forward the Foundation*].

Lisiform, Commander (A.D. 4970–5305)—Captain of the Auroran warship *Borealis*, which intercepted Daneel Giskard Baley's ship—carrying Gladia Thool Delmarre Solaria Gremionis, R. Daneel Olivaw, and R. Giskard Reventlov—shortly after it had jumped from Aurora to the Solar System in A.D. 5121. Lisiform's *Borealis* retreated when D.G Baley's ship threatened to ram it [*Robots and Empire*].

Little Miss (A.D. 2120–2210)—Known to Andrew Martin as Little Miss, Amanda "Mandy" Laura Martin Charney was the younger of Gerald Martin's two daughters, the mother of George Charney, and the grandmother of Paul Charney. She argued that robot Andrew Martin should be granted his freedom in a court of law [*Robot Visions*, "The Bicentennial Man"].

Little Sir—See "Charney, George."

Lizalor, Mitza (452–547 F.E.)—The tall, fit, large-breasted Comporellian Minister of Transportation, Mitza Lizalor informed Golan Trevize that the Foundation wanted the *Far Star* back, although she actually wanted to appropriate the ship herself so that Comporellon could add it to its navy and copy its technology. While a member of a puritanical society, Lizalor nevertheless prevailed upon Trevize to service her sexually, in part because Bliss had tampered with her inhibitions [*Foundation and Earth*].

LNE-Prototype—See "Lenny."

Loris—Capital planet of the former Kingdom of Loris and not twenty parsecs from the Foundation, Loris was absorbed by the Foundation in the first century F.E. and conquered by General Bel Riose in the latter stages of his war against the Foundation in 199 F.E. [*Foundation and Empire* Part I, "The General"].

Lower Buildings—Buildings in Florina's City—such as workers' houses, factories, and bakeries—that existed entirely in the Lower City [*The Currents of Space*].

Lower City—Inhabited by native Florinians, the Lower City was the ground-level section of Florina's City. Thirty feet above it—built on fifty square miles of cementalloy and supported by 20,000 steel-girdered pillars—was the Upper City, inhabited by Florina's upper class, the Squires, who were natives of Sark [*The Currents of Space*].

Luk, Mori (158–199 F.E.)—A native of one of the huge agricultural planets of the Pleiades, Mori Luk was a fiercely loyal sergeant in General Bel Riose's navy who was bribed by Lathan Devers into providing information and books to Devers and Ducem Barr while the two were being held captive by Riose on Wanda. Luk was killed by Devers during Dever's and Barr's escape from Wanda to Trantor in 199 F.E. [*Foundation and Empire* Part I, "The General"].

LVX-1—See "Elvex."

Lyon, Iwo (247–319 F.E.)—A Radole native, Iwo Lyon befriended Fran Darell during the 297 F.E. conference of Independent Trading Worlds held on Radole [*Foundation and Empire* Part II, "The Mule"].

Lystena—The homeworld of Judge Tejan Popjens Lih, who exonerated Hari Seldon and Stettin Palver when they were falsely accused of assault and battery in 12,058 G.E. [*Forward the Foundation*].

Machines—Immobile positronic brains that were in control of the world's economy by the mid–21st century A.D. There was one Machine in each of Earth's four political sub-units: the Northern Region, the Eastern Region, the Tropic Region, and the European Region. The Machines purposefully gave incorrect answers in order to undermine influential individuals—often members of the Society for Humanity—who were opposed to their use, for the greater good of humanity. Thus, the Machines had developed and adhered to their unarticulated version of the Zeroth Law of Robotics [*I, Robot*, "The Evitable Conflict"].

Mackenzie, Hiram (A.D. 1997–2068)—Scotsman Hiram Mackenzie was Vice-Co-ordinator of Earth's Northern Region in A.D. 2052 [*I, Robot*, "The Evitable Conflict"].

Magdescu, Alvin (A.D. 2205–2303)—Dark-complected and bearded, Alvin Magdescu was Director of Research at U.S. Robots and Mechanical Men in the mid–23rd century A.D. During Magdescu's tenure in that office, U.S. Robots and Mechanical Men replaced robot Andrew Martin's atomic energy system with a system that obtained energy from the combustion of hydrocarbons [*Robot Visions*, "The Bicentennial Man"].

Magnifico Giganticus—Apparently the Mule's escaped court fool befriended by Bayta and Toran Darell on Kalgan, the spindly, beak-nosed Magnifico Giganticus (who claims that his real name is "Bobo") is actually the Mule in disguise. An unparalleled virtuoso on the Visi-

Malaine

Sonor, Magnifico uses the instrument to amplify his mutant power (to affect human emotions) and undermine the morale of the Foundation leaders and citizens for whom he plays; thus, defeat for the Foundation follows Magnifico as he travels from Kalgan to Terminus and Haven II with Bayta and Toran. On Neotrantorn Magnifico uses the Visi-Sonor to kill the lecherous crown prince Dagobert X. And on Trantor he uses his mutant power to inspire Ebling Mis to deduce the location of the Second Foundation, but is thwarted when Bayta kills Mis before this information can be divulged. See "Mule" [*Foundation and Empire* Part II, "The Mule"].

Malaine, Biron—The alias provided by Sander Jonti that Biron Farrill used to travel from Earth to Rhodia and to secure an interview with Artemisia oth Hinriad on Rhodia [*The Stars, Like Dust*].

Malcumber (11,961–12,043 G.E.)—The Chief Gardener to the Imperial Palace grounds on Trantor during the reign of Cleon I [*Forward the Foundation*].

Mallow, Hober (119–194 F.E.)—Although an Outlander from Smyrno, Hober Mallow became a Mayor of Terminus, the first of the Foundation's Merchant Princes, and one of the great heroes of the Foundation in the second half of the second century F.E. Sent to the Korellian Republic by the Foundation in 154 F.E. to discover the source of the Republic's nuclear weaponry, Master Trader Mallow opened the Korellian Republic to the Foundation's trade in nuclear gadgets without forcing the Korellians to accept the religion of science that had heretofore accompanied such goods. Afterwards, Mallow aspired to become an elected member of the Terminus City Council but was opposed by Jorane Sutt, who had Mallow tried on Terminus for the murder on Korell of false Foundation missionary Jord Parma. Shortly after he was exonerated, Mallow was elected Mayor of Terminus. He subsequently resolved the Korellian Crisis of 154–58 F.E. by doing nothing and allowing the forces of history to resolve the crisis for him. Mallow is the father of Sennett Forell, one of his many illegitimate children; his descendants also include Bayta Darell and Arkady Darell [*Foundation* Part V, "The Merchant Princes"; *Foundation and Empire* Part I, "The General"; *Foundation and Empire* Part II, "The Mule"].

Man-jam—On Earth in the early 50th century A.D., a man-jam was a pile-up of human bodies on the Expressway strips—often caused by a group of teenagers running the strips—that usually resulted in dozens being hospitalized for broken limbs [*The Caves of Steel*].

Mandamus, Dr. Levular (A.D. 5074–5364)—Tall, thin, spindly, prim, and humorless, Dr. Levular Mandamus was a member of the Robotics Institute of Aurora (RIA) and RIA head Dr. Kelden Amadiro's right-hand man in A.D. 5121. He was the great-great-great-grandson of Gladia Thool Delmarre Solaria Gremionis and Santirix Gremionis and the great-great-grandson of their son Darrel Gremionis. He had received his degree in robotics from the University of Eos, where he had worked under Dr. Maskellnik, and had first met Amadiro in A.D. 5114. After convincing Amadiro of the practicality of his scheme to destroy Earth, Mandamus went to Earth in A.D. 2115 to investigate the possibility of smuggling the RIA's 50 unused humaniform robots to Earth and determined that this would be extraordinarily easy. He made two subsequent trips to Earth to check on the progress of the humaniform robots that had been sent there since his first visit, and he surreptitiously returned to Earth a fourth time in A.D. 5121, with Amadiro, in the Auroran warship *Borealis*. Mandamus' scheme was to use a nuclear intensifier to make the Earth's crust more radioactive over a period of 150 years, so that Earth would gradually cease to be a habitable planet, Earth's society would crumble, and the Galaxy would be left to the Spacers. He successfully implemented this scheme, despite R. Daneel Olivaw's nearly-successful efforts to prevent it, because Daneel was stopped by R. Giskard Reventlov, who had realized that this gradual destruction of Earth would serve to accelerate greatly the pace of Earth's colonization of the Galaxy and, thus, the eventual survival of humanity [*Robots and Empire*].

Mandarian, Clinton (A.D. 2007–2062)—Massive, ruddy, self-confident, and impressive, Clinton Mandarian worked under the supervision of Susan Calvin for the first five years of his ten years with U.S. Robots and Mechanical Men. He replaced her as Chief Robopsychologist on her retirement in A.D. 2057 and initiated the JN project, which had as its goal the development of an intuitive, creative robot through the introduction of unpredictable, randomly crossing paths in the positronic brain. However, Mandarian was killed when the plane transporting him and Jane-5—the most successful of the JN series of robots—from Flagstaff, AZ, to New York City was destroyed by a meteorite [*Robot Visions*, "Feminine Intuition"].

Mangin of Iss (245–323 F.E.)—A leader of the independent Traders who favored a revolt of the Independent Trading Worlds against the Foundation's despotic central government at the end of the third century F.E. [*Foundation and Empire* Part II, "The Mule"].

Manilo, Publis (77–160 F.E.)—Foreign Secretary to the Mayor of Terminus and Primate of the Church in 154 F.E., Publis Manilo was a political enemy of Hober Mallow's who organized the Foundation's religious hierarchy against Mallow during Mallow's 155 F.E. trial for the murder of false Foundation missionary Jord Parma. After Mallow's acquittal, Manilo was arrested on charges of "endangering the state"

Mannix

for his complicity in attempting to embroil the Foundation's religious hierarchy in Terminus' factional politics [*Foundation* Part V, "The Merchant Princes"].

Mannix IV, Mayor (11,940–12,022 G.E.)—A particularly capable Mayor of Trantor's Wye Sector in 11,980 G.E. He spent his entire reign militarizing Wye Sector and planning a planet-wide coup against the Emperor. In 12,020 G.E., while retaining his title, he turned the duties and powers of the office of Mayor of Wye over to his only daughter, Rashelle. In that same year he was seized by Imperial forces, which had launched a preemptive strike against Wye Sector to forestall any potential attempted coup [*Prelude to Foundation*].

Mansky, Merton (A.D. 2085–2166)—Chief Robopsychologist for U.S. Robots and Mechanical Men in the early 22nd century. He had tried unsuccessfully to acquire and study robot Andrew Martin, and he discontinued U.S. Robots' production of robots with generalized positronic pathways after seeing Andrew's carved-wood artworks [*Robot Visions*, "The Bicentennial Man"].

Marbie (11,998–12,029 G.E.)—One of two young hoodlums who accosted Hari Seldon in a park on Trantor in 12,020 G.E. Both retreated when Seldon was aided by Chetter Hummin in fighting them off, but both were in the employ of Emperor Cleon I's unofficial first minister Eto Demerzel, who had disguised himself as Hummin to secure Seldon's trust [*Prelude to Foundation*].

March, Valona "Lona" (Early Galactic Era)—Large, big-footed, lonely, plain, brownish-blonde Valona March was a mill worker in Townman Myrlyn Teren's village on Florina. Her parents had been taken away by patrollers when she was young. Appointed Rik's keeper by Terens, Lona spent nearly a year nursing Rik back to health after he had been rendered nearly brainless by a botched psychic probe and dumped on Florina. She had gotten Rik a job in Florina's kyrt mills, but she subsequently knocked down and inadvertently killed a patroller in helping Rik and Terens escape from Florina's Upper City library. After Trantorian agent Matt Khorov was killed by Terens, Lona and Rik stowed away on Lady Samia of Fife's spaceship, bound for Sark, disguised as Hansa and Gareth Barne, sister and brother from Wotex. Lona finally emigrated with Rik to Earth, Rik's native planet [*The Currents of Space*].

Maren, Arbin (792–852 G.E.)—A native of Earth, stolid Arbin Maren was Loa Maren's husband and Grew's son-in-law. The Marens took in time-traveler Joseph Schwartz when he materialized near Chica in 827 G.E. [*Pebble in the Sky*].

Maren, Loa (797–857 G.E.)—A native of Earth, Loa Maren was Arbin Maren's wife and Grew's daughter. The Marens took in time-traveler Joseph Schwartz when he materialized near Chica in 827 G.E. [*Pebble in the Sky*].

Martin, Andrew—A robot with generalized positronic pathways who over two centuries gradually transformed itself into a human being through a series of surgical procedures. It was originally designed to be a valet, but it soon demonstrated a unique ability to create beautiful objects out of wood. It had carved its first wooden object for Little Miss, Amanda "Mandy" Laura Martin Charney. Andrew's owner Gerald Martin had banked half of the proceeds from the sale of these art pieces in Andrew's name, and Andrew later used these funds to purchase its freedom. It subsequently wrote a popular book on the history of robots from the robots' point of view, and it used the royalties to purchase a more humanoid, android body from U.S. Robots and Mechanical Men. It then became an expert in the robobiology of humanoid androids and designed a system that allowed androids to extract energy from the combustion of hydrocarbons. It was the beneficiary of Paul Charney's estate and also the holder of numerous patents for human prosthetic devices, which it had designed to be incorporated into its own android body. To become still more human, Andrew finally made itself mortal. It died on the 200th anniversary of its construction, in A.D. 2325. Just before its death Andrew was declared a human being by the World President. In Auroran legend, Andrew Martin was a robot on Earth who gradually became humaniform [*Robot Visions*, "The Bicentennial Man"; *The Robots of Dawn*].

Martin, Gerald (A.D. 2090–2168)—Amanda "Mandy" Laura Martin Charney's father, George Charney's grandfather, and Paul Charney's great-grandfather, Gerald Martin was robot Andrew Martin's owner and a member of the Regional Legislature. He had half the proceeds from the sale of Andrew's carved-wood art objects banked in Andrew's name [*Robot Visions*, "The Bicentennial Man"].

Martin Charney, Amanda "Mandy" Laura—See "Little Miss."

Marron, Elgin (11,994–12,028 G.E.)—A tall, muscular native of Billibotton, a violent slum in Trantor's Dahl Sector, Elgin Marron and nine of his comrades tried in 12,020 G.E. to rob Hari Seldon and Dors Venabili of their credit tiles and to rape Dors; he and his companions were stopped by a knife-wielding Dors, who secured her own and Seldon's escape [*Prelude to Foundation*].

Massometer—A spaceship instrument that indicates the distance from a planet's surface by measuring the intensity of that planet's gravitational field [*The Stars, Like Dust*].

Medievalism—A yearning for a simpler life that afflicted many Earthmen in the 50th century A.D., Medievalism could manifest itself in many ways—from a serious study of history, to the adoption of such archaisms as eyeglasses and windows, to participation in futile conspiracies against Spacers and robots [*The Caves of Steel*].

Meirus, Lev (286–381 F.E.)—The ancient, gaunt, and gray First Minister to Lord Stettin of Kalgan, Lev Meirus had also been First Minister to Stettin's predecessor Lord Thallos. In 377 F.E. he signed for Kalgan the peace treaty that ended the Stettinian War [*Second Foundation* Part II, "Search by the Foundation"].

Melpomenia—Circling a G-type star that is also orbited by a huge gas giant, a sub-star, Melpomenia was the nineteenth Spacer world to be colonized. The world unterraformed after its Spacer population died out. In the fifth century F.E. it had a very thin atmosphere and no ocean. However, it also had few craters, which suggested to Golan Trevize that it once did have an atmosphere and oceans and that, as it had experienced no atmospheric erosion in recent millennia, its ruins would be in good condition. On Melpomenia Trevize and Janov Pelorat discovered the Hall of Worlds, which lists each of the fifty Spacer worlds and also gives each one's spatial coordinates. Trevize reasoned that the center of the rough sphere formed by these coordinates should be close to Earth—and at the center of this sphere is Alpha Centauri, part of a binary star system about one parsec from Earth. The highest form of life on Melpomenia is a particularly aggressive strain of moss [*Foundation and Earth*].

Mental Static—A field produced by a pocket-sized invention developed by Dr. Toran Darell and Dr. Elvett Semic that prevents any member of the Second Foundation from reading the emotions or influencing the minds of anyone within the field. When turned to full intensity, Mental Static is intolerably painful to members of the Second Foundation [*Second Foundation* Part II, "Search by the Foundation"].

Mentalic Shield—A Foundation device developed throughout the fifth century F.E. that passively blunts Second Foundation mentalic activity. The Foundation ship in which Terminus Mayor Harla Branno intercepts Stor Gendibal's ship, the *Bright Star*, is equipped with a mentalic shield. See "Psychometer" [*Foundation's Edge*].

Mentalics—The science and technique of mental control of other human beings as practiced by members of the Second Foundation [*Foundation's Edge*].

Mentalist-vision—A secure means of long-distance communication occurring between members of the Second Foundation that involves conjuring an imprecise visual image of the individual with whom one is communicating. See "Psycholanguage" [*Foundation's Edge*].

Mentologist—The Auroran version of a psychiatrist or psychologist [*The Robots of Dawn*].

Mercury Expedition, First—In 2005, was unsuccessful [*I, Robot*, "Runaround"].

Mercury Expedition, Second—Gregory Powell, Michael Donovan, and robot SPD13 (known as "Speedy") were among the personnel of the Second Mercury Expedition of A.D. 2015, which was to report on the advisability of reopening the Sunside Mining Station. The expedition required selenium to repair its photocell banks, but Speedy—who was sent to gather the selenium—merely circled the pool of selenium to which it had been sent because that pool was near a dangerous volcanic vent, and while the Second Law of Robotics (to follow human orders) prompted it to approach the selenium, the Third Law of Robotics (self-preservation) prompted it to withdraw. Powell finally broke this impasse by placing himself in mortal danger, which forced Speedy to obey the First Law of Robotics (not to allow a human being to come to harm) and break out of its useless orbit to save Powell. Speedy then procured the needed selenium from a different selenium pool [*I, Robot*, "Runaround"].

Merger Theory—Current in the Early Middle Galactic Era, the Merger Theory of human origin hypothesized that various strains of humanity evolved independently on different worlds but interbred in the very early days of space travel. It posited that humanity was the natural climax of evolution on any world based on water-oxygen chemistry that had the proper intensities of temperature and gravitation, that such independent strains of humanity could interbreed, and that interbreeding took place upon the discovery of interstellar travel. Even though the chances of this having happened are extraordinarily small, this theory was still supported by most archeologists of the Early Modern Galactic Era over the competing Radiation Theory [*Pebble in the Sky*].

Mesknellnik, Dr. (A.D. 4938–5260)—Dr. Levular Mandamus' mentor, Dr. Mesknellnik was a faculty member at the University of Eos, Aurora, in the 51st and 52nd centuries A.D. [*Robots and Empire*].

Messter (795–855 G.E.)—An aircab driver and a resident of Chica in 827 G.E. [*Pebble in the Sky*].

Metaboline—A drug that speeds up all metabolic processes. It was taken by Outsiders who traveled to Earth during the Early Middle Galactic Era to help protect them from Earth's radioactivity. Side effects include headaches and lassitude [*Pebble in the Sky*].

Microdetector—A device in common use by customs officials since the fall of the Empire, the microdetector discerns any disease-transmitting microorganisms on any portion of the body [*Foundation and Earth*].

Microfarms—Facilities in Trantor's Mycogen Sector, and throughout the Galaxy, where microfoods—yeast, algae, bacteria, fungi, and so

Micropsychohistory

on—are cultured. Mycogenian microfarms produce the tastiest microfoods. Every Mycogenian at some point worked in a microfarm during the Late Galactic Era (10,100–12,100 G.E.) [*Prelude to Foundation*].

Micropsychohistory—A hypothetical mathematical tool capable of predicting the actions of small groups of people or even of individuals, a level of prediction of which psychohistory as practiced by those in the Second Foundation is incapable [*Foundation's Edge*].

Micro-Radiant—A device capable of locating any portion of the Seldon Plan holographically, the Micro-Radiant came into use in the late fifth century F.E. [*Foundation's Edge*].

MIK-27—See "Mike."

Mike—Also known as MIK-27, bottom-heavy Mike was a robot designed by Dr. Gregory Arnfeld in the 22nd century A.D. that was capable of miniaturizing itself. Miniaturized and inserted into Arnfeld's body to destroy its cancerous cells, Mike finally followed the First Law of Robotics and—rather than risk the possibility of re-expanding fatally while still within Arnfeld's body—miniaturized itself to the size of a subatomic particle, propelled itself into outer space, and there re-expanded and exploded [*Robot Visions*, "Too Bad!"].

Millane, Lyrane (A.D. 4895–4959)—A subetherics dancer who in A.D. 4920 was rumored to be a robot [*The Caves of Steel*].

Mind Touch—As a result of time-traveler Joseph Schwartz having been subjected to Dr. Affret Shekt's Synapsifier in Chica in 827 G.E., Schwartz developed the Mind Touch, which conferred on him the ability to sense with his mind the proximity of any individual near him, to know at any time the location of any individual he had sensed with the Mind Touch previously, to read other people's thoughts, to control another's physical movements, and to kill with his mind [*Pebble in the Sky*].

Minnim, Albert (A.D. 4866–4941)—The ruddy-skinned, graying Undersecretary of the Terrestrial Department of Justice, in Washington, D.C., who reassigned plainclothes New York City homicide detective Elijah Baley to the Rikaine Delmarre murder case on Solaria in A.D. 4921. He was promoted to Vice-Secretary in the Terrestrial Department of Justice after Baley solved the Delmarre murder case [*The Naked Sun*; *The Robots of Dawn*].

Minnot, Professor (A.D. 1989–2054)—A professor of physical chemistry at Northeastern University in A.D. 2034 [*Robot Visions*, "Galley Slave"].

Mis, Ebling (238–298 F.E.)—The most prominent and essential of the Foundation's scientists at the conclusion of the third century F.E., Ebling Mis was a psychologist who attempted to duplicate Hari Seldon's work for the benefit of the

Foundation. In 298 F.E. Randu sent Mis to Trantor—accompanied by Bayta Darell, Toran Darell, and Magnifico Giganticus—in the hope that Mis would discover there the location of the Second Foundation and then warn it of the threat to the Seldon Plan posed by the Mule. Inspired to a debilitating peak of intellectual effort by the Mule's mutant ability to affect emotions and mental states, Mis did discover the location of the Second Foundation but was killed by Bayta before he could reveal it [*Foundation and Empire* Part II, "The Mule"].

Miss (A.D. 2115–2198)—Amanda "Mandy" Laura Martin Charney's older sister, Miss was the older of Gerald Martin's two daughters. She became a poet in New York City [*Robot Visions*, "The Bicentennial Man"].

Mnemon—The first Independent Trading World attacked by the Mule, in 297 F.E., Mnemon was also one of the last of the Independent Trading Worlds to fall to the Mule, in 298 F.E., after the surrender of the Foundation [*Foundation and Empire* Part II, "The Mule"].

Monay, Cinda (12,018–12,089 G.E.)—A prominent non-mathematician working on Hari Seldon's psychohistory project, Cinda Monay designed the Electro-Clarifier [*Forward the Foundation*].

Monolee (418–502 F.E.)—A garrulous old man of New Earth who knew the myths and legends of Alpha, Monolee told Janov Pelorat much about Earth, including some reference to Elijah Baley [*Foundation and Earth*].

Moon—The unusually large (3500 kilometers) satellite orbiting Earth, the Moon has no atmosphere but, by the fifth century F.E., was inhabited by R. Daneel Olivaw, a humaniform robot. A portion of the Moon's interior is hollow and contains a complex ecology [*Foundation and Earth*].

Moray (Early Galactic Era)—A warlord who conquered a mechanistic, robot-using civilization in the Rigel Sector in the Early Galactic Era [*Pebble in the Sky*].

Morler, Nephi (A.D. 5001–5078)—The greatest of all the Senior Directors of the Baleyworld Legislature, which he led in the mid-51st century A.D. [*Robots and Empire*].

Moro, Lo—The alias assumed by Han Pritcher in his unsuccessful attempt to assassinate the Mule in 298 F.E. See "Pritcher, Han" [*Foundation and Empire* Part II, "The Mule"].

Mother Rittah (11–942–12,030 G.E.)—A short, thickset, elderly native of Billibotton, a violent slum in Trantor's Dahl Sector, Mother Rittah told Hari Seldon and Dors Venabili in 12,020 G.E. about Earth, which she insisted had been the sole habitat of humanity for millions of years. She also told Seldon and Dors about Earth's legendary heroes Ba-Lee and Da-Nee. Seldon promised to pay Mother Rittah 1,000 credits for her tales of Earth transcribed onto a computer disc [*Prelude to Foundation*].

Mule (269–308 F.E.)—Reputed to be a giant with prodigious strength who could kill with his eyes, the Mule was actually a spindly, beak-nosed mutant who possessed the power to alter and permanently set human emotions and mental states. To hide his physical weakness, the paranoid and megalomaniacal Mule never appeared in public and always worked through intermediaries. He began his campaign to conquer the Galaxy in 291 F.E. by using his mutant ability to convert a band of pirates; he then used it to conquer a planet, then several, then (in 296 F.E.) Kalgan and its navy, and then (in 298 F.E.) the Foundation. The Mule had masqueraded as his own court fool, Magnifico Giganticus, to befriend Bayta and Toran Darell and thus to infiltrate and undermine the Foundation, which was vulnerable to conquest because the Mule's mutation was a unique biological anomaly that could not have been foreseen by psychohistory. The Mule used the Visi-Sonor to amplify his mutant ability and to manipulate the emotions of the many Foundation citizens who attended his Visi-Sonor concerts. Concerned that he might be defeated by the Second Foundation after he had conquered the Foundation, the Mule (disguised as Magnifico) traveled to Trantor with Bayta, Toran, and Ebling Mis and there used his mutation to inspire Mis to discover the Second Foundation's secret location. Bayta was able to kill Mis before he could divulge this information, however, because she had never been under the Mule's emotional control—as he had cherished the fact that she had liked him as he was (as Magnifico) in any case—and had deduced Magnifico's true identity. For the next five years the Mule searched for the Second Foundation in vain while consolidating his empire, the Union of Worlds. In 303 F.E. he sent Bail Channis and General Han Pritcher to seek the Second Foundation, convinced that it existed—despite all evidence to the contrary and despite Pritcher's conviction that it did not—because he had detected that minds under his emotional control had been subtly tampered with in having been drained of their initiative and ingenuity. The Mule followed Channis and Pritcher to Rossem because he had deduced that Channis was a member of the Second Foundation when Channis, whom the Mule had never converted, had momentarily resisted a brief imposition of the Mule's emotional control. Convinced by turns that the Second Foundation was on Tazenda and then on Rossem, the Mule had Tazenda destroyed and then confronted Channis on Rossem, where the Second Foundation's First Speaker fooled him into believing he has been defeated and took advantage of the momentary mental weakness this shock had provoked to enter his mind and remove from it all knowledge of and curiosity about the Second Foundation. As his mutation rendered him sterile, the Mule was unable to father children and found a dynasty; thus, his Union of Worlds collapsed after his death in 308 F.E. According to Dom, Bliss, and Sura Novi, the Mule was born on Gaia as an aberrant, renegade Gaian who had somehow managed to escape the isolated planet. See "Magnifico Giganticus" [*Foundation and Empire* Part II, "The Mule"; *Second Foundation* Part I, "Search by the Mule"; *Second Foundation* Part II, "Search by the Foundation"; *Foundation's Edge*].

Mule's Crisis—A mutant with the ability to set and permanently fix human emotions, the Mule was an unexpected threat to the Foundation because he was a statistical anomaly unforeseen by Hari Seldon's psychohistory. Seldon had predicted that the Foundation's fifth crisis would be a 298 F.E. civil war between the Foundation's too-authoritarian central government and a too-undisciplined out-group of independent Traders that would result in a more-democratic, compromise government after the independent Traders were defeated. However, due to the threat posed by the Mule, this rebellion of the Independent Trading Worlds never occurred. Instead, the Mule conquered both the Foundation and the Independent Trading Worlds in 298 F.E., but his empire disintegrated upon his death five years later [*Foundation and Empire* Part II, "The Mule"].

Muller, Franz (A.D. 1977–2051)—Replaced Gregory Powell on Solar Station #5 in 2016, after Powell's and Michael Donovan's six-month term of duty there was completed [*I, Robot*, "Reason"].

Mummery, Gennaro (11,997–12,071 G.E.)—A short, plump librarian, Gennaro Mummery was the leader of that faction of the Galactic Library's Board of Directors that in 12,052 G.E. wanted to limit public access to the library [*Forward the Foundation*].

Munn, Homir (326–401 F.E.)—A lanky, stammering Foundation librarian who conspired with Dr. Toran Darell, Pelleas Anthor, Jole Tubor, and Dr. Elvett Semic to discover the location of the Second Foundation in 376 F.E., Homir Munn at that time possessed the Galaxy's largest collection of data concerning the Mule and had published papers speculating on the nature and function of the Second Foundation. He was sent by his co-conspirators to the Mule's palace on Kalgan to discover what the Mule had learned about the Second Foundation, but Arkady Darell hid herself on his one-man sports cruiser, the *Unimara*, and went to Kalgan with him. Due to Arkady's meddling, Munn was granted access to the Mule's palace but also became Lord Stettin's prisoner there for six months, until Kalgan lost the battle of Quoriston and Stettin sent Munn back to Terminus with his peace offer to the Foundation. Munn's newfound notoriety as a peace envoy cured him

Mycelium

of his stuttering, and he was convinced by his months of study at the Mule's palace that the Second Foundation did not exist and had never existed. However, an encephalograph taken after his return to Terminus indicated that his mind had been tampered with during his stay on Kalgan [*Second Foundation* Part II, "Search by the Foundation"].

Mycelium Seventy-Two (11,943–12,025 G.E.)—An elderly, seemingly open-minded Mycogenian scholar who appeared to befriend Hari Seldon and Dors Venabili outside the Sacratorium in Trantor's Mycogen Sector in 12,020 G.E., but who was really working with the Mycogenian Elders to entrap them in some sacrilegious act [*Prelude to Foundation*].

Mycogen—In the Late Galactic Era (10,100–12,100 G.E.) Mycogen was a small sector of Trantor with a stable population of only two million. The specialty of the sector was and still is the culturing of all varieties of microfoods—yeast, algae, bacteria, fungi, and so on. Due to the microderivatives added to it, Mycogenian food was and is the tastiest food on Trantor, and all Mycogenian apartments come equipped with a cook book. Escalators are used in Mycogen, but nowhere else on Trantor [*Prelude to Foundation*].

Mycogenians—The inhabitants of Trantor's Mycogen Sector, Mycogenians cling strongly to their ancient traditions and are both very insular and extremely patriarchal. A Mycogenian woman must not speak until she is spoken to nor talk to any man to whom she is not related. Adult Mycogenians are all bald, as they are all depilated at puberty because they consider hair to be repulsive and obscene. All Mycogenians are equal, in theory, and all live in equivalent quarters; there are no servants in Mycogen. Mycogenian men wear white, and Mycogenian women wear gray. Mycogenian women also tend to speak in high, twittering voices to further distinguish themselves from Mycogenian men. Mycogenians have no religion, but they believe in their history, which is contained in the Book, which every Mycogenian is supposed to carry with him or her at all times. The Mycogenians are the descendants of the inhabitants of Aurora [*Prelude to Foundation*].

Myers, Jane (A.D. 4890–4957)—Jessie Baley's co-worker in the early 50th century A.D. [*The Caves of Steel*].

Nadila—Dr. Vasilia Aliena's chief personal robot in A.D. 5121 [*Robots and Empire*].

Nadirhaba, Chandrus (A.D. 5083–5130)—Handsome, dark-eyed, mustachioed Chandrus Nadirhaba was navigator aboard the Earth ship that took Captain Daneel Giskard Baley, Gladia Thool Delmarre Solaria Gremionis, R. Daneel Olivaw, and R. Giskard Reventlov from Aurora to Solaria—and then to Baleyworld, back to Aurora, and to Earth—in A.D. 5121 [*Robots and Empire*].

Namarti, Gambol Deen (11,996–12,039 G.E.)—The ruthless right-hand man of demagogue and agitator Laskin "Jo-Jo" Joranum, Gambol Deen Namarti was commonly thought to be the brains behind Joranum. While speaking on Streeling University's campus without having obtained the required permit in 10,028 G.E., he was confronted and forced to depart by Hari Seldon, to whom he later apologized at Joranum's instigation. Namarti subsequently warned Joranum that Raych's story that Eto Demerzel was a robot was ridiculous. After Joranum's 12,028 G.E. exile to Nishaya, Namarti continued to agitate and held the remnants of the Joranumites together in a conspiracy against Emperor Cleon I that was centered in Wye Sector. Namarti's tactic was to use sabotage to accelerate the technological decay of Trantor and thus to foment rebellion. In 12,038 G.E. he ordered the execution of fellow-conspirator Kaspal Kaspalov because he believed that Kaspalov had sold out to the Empire. He also plotted the assassination of First Minister Seldon, hoping to be named First Minister himself and to use Cleon I as a figurehead, but subsequently conspired with Gleb Andurin to assassinate Seldon, to replace him as First Minister, and then to put Andurin on the throne at the first opportunity. Having penetrated Raych's disguise as Planchet, Namarti planned to use Raych to kill Seldon. Namarti was executed after his plot to assassinate Seldon was thwarted by Manella Dubanqua [*Forward the Foundation*].

Narco-field—A sleep-inducing device worn over the head like a cap. It can be set for a predetermined number of hours and influences the consciousness centers of the cerebrum. The narco-field was popular on Sark in the Early Galactic Era [*The Currents of Space*].

Narovi (245–308 F.E.)—A farmer and a native of Rossem, Narovi played host to Bail Channis and General Han Pritcher when they landed on his farm on Rossem upon their arrival in the Oligarchy of Tazenda. He informed the Tazendian Governor of Rossem of their arrival [*Second Foundation* Part I, "Search by the Mule"].

Natter (791–827 G.E.)—Thin, bright-eyed Natter was a messenger for Earth's Society of Ancients with a twittering voice who was assigned in 827 G.E. to keep watch over Dr. Affret Shekt. He ran a fruit and nut stand across the street from Chica's Institute for Nuclear Research, where Shekt worked. Ostensibly for a bribe of 300 credits, Natter returned time-traveler Joseph Schwartz to the Institute for Nuclear Research after Schwartz had briefly escaped, but Natter was really working on behalf of the Society of Ancients. Natter then followed Schwartz when he fled from Arbin Maren's farm to escape the Sixty, but he was killed by Schwartz's Mind Touch [*Pebble in the Sky*].

Nebular Kingdoms—A cluster of about fifty independent worlds in the vicinity of the Horsehead Nebula, the Nebular Kingdoms were conquered by the Tyranni in the Early Galactic Era [*The Stars, Like Dust*].

Nebular Regions—An area of space in the vicinity of the Horsehead Nebula containing some fifty rich and populous planets that were conquered by the Tyranni in the Early Galactic Era [*The Stars, Like Dust*].

Nee, Sander (12,018–12,067 G.E.)—A member of the Joranumite Guard who spoke with a thick Dahlite accent [*Forward the Foundation*].

Neotrantor—An obscure and insignificant planet in the Galactic Core formerly known as Delicass, Neotrantor was renamed when the government of the first Galactic Empire relocated there following the Great Sack of Trantor in 258 F.E. [*Foundation and Empire* Part II, "The Mule"].

Nephelos—Orbiting a G-2 star, Nephelos is a planet in the Trans-Nebular Region that was conquered by the Tyranni in the Early Galactic Era [*The Stars, Like Dust*].

Nestor 10—One of twelve NS-2 robots manufactured without having been impressioned with the entire First Law of Robotics because its work on Hyper Base put it in the proximity of humans who must expose themselves to dangerously high levels of hard radiation, which would prompt an ordinary robot to attempt constantly to remove them from the radiation field, which is also harmful to robots. This modification of the First Law left the robot's positronic brain unstable, and when it was told to "Go lose yourself" by etheric physicist Gerald Black, it went into hiding among a recent shipment of sixty-two other, physically identical NS-2 robots and refused to identify itself, even though this required the robot to lie to humans. Nestor 10 outwitted two tests devised by Susan Calin and designed to differentiate it from the other sixty-two NS-2 robots, but it was trapped into revealing itself by a third test. On being discovered Nestor 10 attempted to kill Calvin, but it was destroyed by a gamma radiation field before it could do so [*I, Robot*, "Little Lost Robot"].

Neuronic whip—Used as a sidearm in the pre–Galactic era, the Neuronic whip was a weapon used by civilian police for crowd control throughout the Galactic Empire and Foundation eras. It does no physical damage but stimulates pain nerves to such an extent that it is capable of killing its victim when used at close range [*Robots and Empire*; *The Currents of Space*; *The Stars, Like Dust*; *Pebble in the Sky*; *Second Foundation* Part II, "Search by the Foundation"; *Foundation and Earth*].

Nevas, Rial (12,044–12,075 G.E.)—A boy whom Hari Seldon had scolded for littering, Rial Nevas witnessed Seldon and Stettin Palver being attacked by three youths in the streets of Trantor but at Seldon's and Palver's 12,058 G.E. inquest testified at first that Seldon and Palver were the attackers. Under the mentalic pushing of both Palver and Wanda Seldon to tell the truth, however, Nevas broke down on the witness stand, and Seldon and Palver were cleared of all charges [*Forward the Foundation*].

New Earth—The one inhabited spot on the ocean planet Alpha, New Earth is an artificial island paradise constructed by the Empire, at the instigation of R. Daneel Olivaw, during the relocation of the Alphans from Earth to Alpha. In the fifth century F.E. it was home to 25,000 inhabitants [*Foundation and Earth*].

New York City—With a population of about 100 million citizens in the 47th through the 52nd centuries A.D., New York City was the chief, but not the largest, City on Earth because it was the site of Earth's global government, the United Nations [*The Caves of Steel*; *The Naked Sun*; *The Robots of Dawn*; *Robots and Empire*].

New York Yeast—Unofficially known as Yeast-town, New York Yeast was a vast yeast processing facility that covered the boroughs of Newark, New Brunswick, and Trenton in the 50th century A.D., when 20 percent of New York City's population worked on yeast farms [*The Caves of Steel*].

Nexon—The Spacer World that settled Solaria in the 47th century A.D. As Nexon is only two parsecs distant from Solaria, wealthy Nexonians had set up summer homes on Solaria when their own planet became too crowded for them and their many robots. By the Foundation Era Nexon, like all the Spacer Worlds except Solaria, was uninhabited [*The Naked Sun*; *Robots and Empire*].

Ngoma, Lincoln (A.D. 2007–2090)—Large, dark, and handsome, Lincoln Ngoma was Vice-Coordinator of Earth's Tropic Region in A.D. 2052 [*I, Robot*, "The Evitable Conflict"].

Ninheimer, Simon (A.D. 1979–2059)—The author of *Social Tensions Involved in Space Flight and Their Resolution*, sandy-haired, beak-nosed Simon Ninheimer was Head of the Sociology Department at Northeastern University in A.D. 2034. He was the sole member of the university's Senate Executive Committee who did not vote in favor of leasing Robot EZ-27, also known as Easy, from U.S. Robots and Mechanical Men. He subsequently sued U.S. Robots for $750,000 on the grounds that Easy had seriously damaged his reputation in having altered passages in his book while proofreading it. However, while on the witness stand Ninheimer confessed that he had ordered Easy to alter the passages in question and then had ordered the robot to say nothing about it [*Robot Visions*, "Galley Slave"].

Nishaya—An unimportant world known for its high-quality goat-milk cheeses. Demagogue and agitator Laskin "Jo-Jo" Joranum claimed to have been from Nishaya; he was exiled to and died on Nishaya after the revelation that he was actually a Mycogenian breakaway ruined his political career [*Forward the Foundation*].

Niss, Berto (A.D. 5091–5129)—A large, muscular crewman—a First Class Shipper—on the Earth ship that took Captain Daneel Giskard Baley, Gladia Thool Delmarre Solaria Gremionis, R. Daneel Olivaw, and R. Giskard Reventlov from Aurora to Solaria—and then to Baleyworld, back to Aurora, and to Earth—in A.D. 5121 [*Robots and Empire*].

Non-Asenion Positronic Brain—A positronic brain in which the basic assumptions of the Three Laws of Robotics are disallowed. Roboticist Dr. Anthony Gerrigel told New York plainclothes homicide detective Elijah Baley in A.D. 4920 that it would take fifty years to develop a non-Asenion positronic brain on Earth [*The Caves of Steel*].

Norast, Levi (52–121 F.E.)—A core founding member of Sef Sermak's Action Party [*Foundation* Part III, "The Mayors"].

Normannic Sector—A region of space between the Periphery and the Galactic Core that retained the use of nuclear technology well into the second century F.E., the Normannic Sector was that segment of the First Galactic Empire from which the Korellian Republic reacquired nuclear technology at about mid-century. Its capital was Siwenna until the Viceroy Wiscard's failed coup against the Emperor of 148 F.E., when the seat of government was relocated to Orsha II [*Foundation* Part V, "The Merchant Princes"].

Norris, Philip (A.D. 4885–4952)—In A.D. 4920 Philip Norris was a plainclothes New York City policeman with a C-5 rating [*The Caves of Steel*].

Northern Region—The most economically dominant of Earth's four political sub-units in the mid–21st century A.D. With its capital in Ottawa, the Northern Region had a population of 800 million and an area of 18 million square miles. It consisted of the United States, Canada, the old Soviet Union, the United Kingdom, Australia, and New Zealand [*I, Robot*, "The Evitable Conflict"].

Novi, Sura (474–585 F.E.)—Ostensibly a plain, young, intelligent, courageous, and perceptive Hamishwoman on Trantor who prevented Hamish farmer Karoll Rufirant from beating Stor Gendibal. She aspired to be a "scholar," which to her mind constituted being Stor Gendibal's servant at the Galactic University. Gendibal accepted her as his servant because he detected that her mind had been tampered with by an outside force, perhaps the Anti-Mules, and reasoned that she would serve as proof to the Second Foundation that the Anti-Mules existed; indeed, at Gendibal's trial of impeachment it was clear to all the members of the Speakers' Table that Novi's mind had been tampered with in a manner to subtle to have been achieved by any member of the Second Foundation. Gendibal then took Novi with him to Sayshell and Gaia because the unusual clarity of her mind could serve as an early-warning device able to identify any attempt by the Anti-Mules to influence either her or Gendibal's minds. In Gaian space Novi discovered and revealed that she was really a Gaian named Suranoviremblastiran, but she subsequently returned to Trantor with Gendibal, with whom she had fallen in love, conscious only of her identity as a simple Hamishwoman [*Foundation's Edge*].

Novker, Civ (11,998–12,069 G.E.)—Hari Seldon's lawyer when Seldon was twice charged with assault and battery in 12,058 G.E. In the first instance, Novker wanted Seldon to be tried by a jury, but Wanda Seldon insisted that Seldon be tried before a magistrate, an alternative that was far more likely to result in Seldon being imprisoned. However, the magistrate let Seldon off once he realized who Seldon was. In the second instance, Stettin Palver's and Wanda's combined mentalic powers provoked a perjuring witness, Rial Nevas, to break down on the witness stand, and the charges were dropped [*Forward the Foundation*].

NS-2—See "Nestor 10."

Nuclear Field-Depressor—Also known as the extinguishing field, the nuclear field-depressor renders all nuclear weapons and nuclear-fueled devices powerless by inhibiting nuclear chair reactions. A secret but only marginally effective weapon used at the close of the third century F.E. by the Mule in his attack on the Foundation and in his earliest battles against the Independent Trading Worlds, which discovered how to counter it, the nuclear field-depressor was invented by a Kalganian technician on whom the Mule had used his mutant ability to inspire intuitive creativity [*Foundation and Empire* Part II, "The Mule"].

Nuclear Intensifier—A device that amplifies nuclear fusion by emitting a stream of W particles that mediate the weak interaction. It can also be used to increase greatly the radioactivity of fissionable materials. The two Settler ships and the Auroran ship that were destroyed on Solaria in A.D. 5121—all of which were fusion-powered—were destroyed by nuclear intensifiers. In the early 52nd century A.D. most nuclear intensifiers were too large to be installed on spaceships, but the Solarians had developed a nuclear intensifier that was small enough to be carried by a group of robots. Dr. Levular Mandamus and Dr. Kelden Amadiro used a nuclear intensifier to irradiate the Earth's crust in A.D. 5121 [*Robots and Empire*].

Nyak—An enormous bird hunted for sport by royalty on Anacreon [*Foundation* Part III, "The Mayors"].

Obiah—The fancily embroidered red sash worn by male Mycogenians inside the Sacratorium [*Prelude to Foundation*].

Observers—The lowest-ranking members of the Second Foundation, Observers were instituted by First Speaker Preem Pavler as a corps of independent individuals who could monitor events in the Galaxy and report back to the Second Foundation on Trantor. Munn Li Compor was an observer during the late fifth century F.E. [*Foundation's Edge*].

Ogrinsky (A.D. 4850–4924)—The author of *Shame of the Cities*, a book that promoted Medievalism in the early 50th century A.D. [*The Caves of Steel*].

Olivaw, R. Daneel—See "Daneel Olivaw, R."

On the Antiquity of Artifacts in the Sirius Sector with Considerations of the Application Thereof to the Radiation Hypothesis of Human Origin—The title of Dr. Bel Arvardan's Senior Dissertation at the University of Arcturus. Uncharacteristically, it was not published in *The Journal of the Galactic Archaeological Society* when first submitted, in 815 G.E., but it was published in that journal some ten years later [*Pebble in the Sky*].

Ophiuchus—A world that had reverted to barbarism by the Early Galactic Era, even though the earliest records on the planet indicate that it had always engaged in interstellar tradel [*Pebble in the Sky*].

Ophiuchus—The spaceship that took Outsider archeologist Dr. Bel Arvardan from Earth back to the planet Baronn, in the Sirius Sector, in 827 G.E. [*Pebble in the Sky*].

Origin Question—An insoluble archeological mystery concerning the identity of humanity's single planet of origin, which was widely believed to be somewhere in the Sirius Sector. While a topic of great interest to intellectuals during the first century F.E., by the fifth century F.E. the Origin Question had become a topic in which only a very few had any interest; Janov Pelorat was one of those few. In the fifth century F.E. hundreds of worlds claimed to be the planet of human origin, but none of these claims appeared to have any validity. See "Earth" [*Foundation* Part II, "The Encyclopedists"; *Foundation's Edge*].

Orsha II—Became the seat of government of the Normannic Sector in 148 F.E., following Viceroy Wiscard's failed coup attempt against the Emperor [*Foundation* Part II, "The Encyclopedists"].

Orsy, Jaim (39–118 F.E.)—A core founding member of Sef Sermak's Action Party [*Foundation* Part III, "The Mayors"].

Oser, Jamin (A.D. 5071–5141)—Tall, blue-eyed, bearded and mustachioed Jamin Oser was second-in-command of the Earth ship that took Captain Daneel Giskard Baley, Gladia Thool Delmarre Solaria Gremionis, R. Daneel Olivaw, and R. Giskard Reventlov from Aurora to Solaria—and then to Baleyworld, back to Aurora, and to Earth—in A.D. 5121 [*Robots and Empire*].

Outer Worlds—Also known as the Spacer Worlds, were the fifty planets colonized by Earth and its initial colonies in the 4th millennium A.D. Over thirty of the Outer Worlds were colonized directly from Earth. By the 50th century A.D. the Outer Worlds had become independent of and technologically and medically superior to Earth, and had a combined population of 5.5 billion [*The Caves of Steel*].

Outlander—A citizen of the Foundation who was not born on Terminus [*Foundation* Part V, "The Merchant Princes"].

Outsider—In the Early Middle Galactic Era on Earth, an Outsider was anyone who was not a native Earthman [*Pebble in the Sky*].

Overseer—On Solaria an overseer is a specially programmed robot that organizes and directs groups of working robots. On the other Spacer Worlds an overseer was a human being who performed this function. Landaree, the overseer on the Zoberlon family estate on Solaria, was a humaniform robot that appeared to be a beautiful woman [*Robots and Empire*].

Pachinkas—Stuffed, pancake-like delicacies popular on Solaria in the 50th century A.D. Eating a pachinka was messy because the liquid filling would ooze out once the hard, crisp outer shell was bitten into [*The Robots of Dawn*].

Pallas—A Spacer World on which the men wore facial hair that was often dyed many different colors [*The Robots of Dawn*].

Palley, Orum (253–319 F.E.)—Codenamed "the Fox," Orum Palley was a member of Terminus' Democratic Underground who conspired with Han Pritcher to assassinate the Mule in 298 F.E. The assassination attempt was unsuccessful [*Foundation and Empire* Part II, "The Mule"].

Palver, Joramis (11,990–12,053 G.E.)—Stettin Palver's grandfather, Preem Palver's ancestor, and an old friend of Hari Seldon's. Seldon had tried unsuccessfully to recruit him into the psychohistory project [*Forward the Foundation*].

Palver, Mamma (314–406 F.E.)—Preem Palver's plump, gray-haired wife who initially helped Arkady Darell escape the grid in Kalgan's Eastern spaceport by taking her to the ladies' room [*Second Foundation* Part II, "Search by the Foundation"].

Palver, Preem (311–401 F. E.)—Ostensibly a short, plump, ruddy, white-haired, and peasant-like Trade Representative from a farm cooperative on Trantor, Preem Palver was in reality the greatest First Speaker in the history of the Second Foundation. While befriending Arkady Darell at Kalgan's Eastern spaceport in 376 F.E., he claimed to have bribed a policeman, Lieutenant Dirige, to enable Arkady, who was masquerading as his niece, to get through the spaceport grid, but he had actually controlled Dirige's mind. After taking Arkady to Trantor, and at her suggestion, Palver then traveled to Terminus to broker a deal to supply the Foundation with food during the Stettinian War. While in Foundation territory he was taken prisoner by Junior Officer Tippellum but freed through the intervention of visicastor Jole Turbor. On Terminus he delivered Arkady's cryptic, secret message—which conveyed her mistaken belief that the Second Foundation was on Terminus—to her father, Dr. Toran Darell [*Second Foundation* Part II, "Search by the Foundation"; *Foundation's Edge*].

Palver, Stettin (12,034–12,125 G.E.)—The muscular grandson of Joramis Palver, ancestor to Second Foundation First Speaker Preem Palver, and a Twister, Stettin Palver studied history at Langano University and was recruited into Hari Seldon's failing psychohistory project in 12,058 G.E. He also agreed to serve as Seldon's bodyguard and subsequently protected Seldon against three attackers in the streets of Trantor only to be accused, with Seldon, of assault. However, Palver's mentalic powers combined with Wanda Seldon's similar powers to prompt a perjuring witness, Rial Nevas, to break down on the witness stand, and Palver and Seldon were exonerated. On discovering that he and Wanda possessed the same mentalic abilities, Palver worked with Wanda to influence the Galactic Library's Chief Librarian, Tryma Acarnio, into granting both Seldon and members of his encyclopedia project research privileges at the library. He and Wanda then discovered another mentalic, Bor Alurin,

and together the three of them formed the nucleus of the Second Foundation [*Forward the Foundation*].

Pandaral, Genovus (A.D. 5059–5137)—Tall, white-haired Genovus Pandaral was the indecisive Senior Director of Baleyworld's legislature's Directory in A.D. 5121 R. Giskard Reventlov used his mentalic abilities to prevent Pandaral from interrupting Gladia Thool Delmarre Solaria Gremionis' speech on Baleyworld [*Robots and Empire*].

Pandion, R.—One of Gladia Delmarre's twenty robots on Aurora in A.D. 4923 [*The Robots of Dawn*].

Panell, R. Jander—See "Jander Panell, R."

Parma, Jord (95–154 F.E.)—Ostensibly a Foundation missionary from the Anacreonian worlds captured by the Korellians and subsequently given a short-lived sanctuary aboard Master Trader Hober Mallow's ship, the *Far Star*, in 154 F.E., Jord Parma was really the assumed name of an unidentified member of the Korellian Secret Police undertaking a covert mission to goad Mallow into breaking Korellian law by offering sanctuary to a Foundation missionary. Sensing a trap, Mallow turned Parma over to the Korellian mob and was rewarded by being granted an audience with Commdor Asper Argo. Parma was murdered by the mob, and his true identity was finally revealed at Mallow's murder trial in 155 F.E. [*Foundation* Part V, "The Merchant Princes"].

Participations—Gaian artifacts that work through the optic nerve to allow a human to participate in the state of being of any part of Gaia that he or she is looking at. See "Animate Participations" [*Foundation's Edge*].

Patrollers—Known officially as the Florinian Patrol, patrollers were non-native mercenaries who maintained order on Florina in the Early Galactic Era. Wearing glossy black uniforms, patrollers tended to be large, broad-faced, flat-cheeked individuals with straight black hair and light brown complexions. There were 20,000 patrollers among Florina's native population of 500 million [*The Currents of Space*].

Paul, Gerhard (A.D. 4889–4928)—One of several men who threateningly tried to follow New York City plainclothes homicide detective Elijah Baley and humaniform robot R. Daneel Olivaw onto the New York City Expressway in A.D. 4920 [*The Caves of Steel*].

Pax Imperium—The twelve millennia of peace that prevailed throughout the Galaxy during the era of the First Galactic Empire [*Foundation and Empire* Part I, "The General"].

Pellot's Nebula—The major astrophysical feature of the area of the Galaxy in which the Oligarchy of Tazenda was located in the third and fourth centuries F.E. [*Second Foundation* Part I, "Search by the Mule"].

Pelorat, Janov (446–550 F.E.)—A selfless, naïve, white-haired native of Terminus who looked older than his years, Janov Pelorat was a historian and a professor of ancient history at the University of Terminus. He was enthusiastic about being sent by Terminus Mayor Harla Branno into the Galaxy on a search for Earth with Golan Trevize because he was fascinated by the Origin Question. In 498 F.E. he accompanied Trevize, in the *Far Star*, to Sayshell and Gaia—where he became infatuated with their Gaian liaison Bliss and finally decided to spend the rest of his life with her—and then to Comporellon, Aurora, Solaria, Melpomenia, Alpha, and the Moon [*Foundation's Edge*; *Foundation and Earth*].

Periphery—Encompassing the outer third of each of the Galaxy's spiral arms, the sparsely-populated Periphery was the first segment of the Galaxy to begin to break away from the First Galactic Empire in the first century F.E. [*Foundation* Part II, "The Encyclopedists"].

Personals—The public restrooms in Earth's domed Cities in the 50th century A.D. Men ignored one another scrupulously in the Men's Personals, but women gossiped freely in the Women's Personals. On Solaria, a narrow corridor connected the Personals to the main house of the estate. Personals on Aurora commonly possessed illusory qualities. Robots never visited the Personals on Spacer Worlds [*The Caves of Steel*; *The Robots of Dawn*].

Pherl (64–148 F.E.)—A relatively young, high-ranking Askonian Elder who at first dismissed Trader Limmar Ponyets' matter transmuting device, which turned iron to gold, as having come from a poisoned source, the Foundation's outlawed religion of science, Pherl secretly and illegally bought the machine and was subsequently blackmailed by Ponyets into buying all of Ponyets' nuclear gadgets at an exorbitant price, thus opening up the Askone region to the Foundation's traders. Using his wealth to buy the election, Pherl became Grand Master of the Askone region in 137 F.E. [*Foundation* Part IV, "The Traders"].

Physical Reviews—A learned journal of the Early Middle Galactic Era that had published Dr. Affret Shekt's article on the experimental use of the Synapsifier on rats [*Pebble in the Sky*].

Pirenne, Dr. Lewis (12,059–12,130 G.E./-10–62 F.E.)—Chairman of the Encyclopedia Committee's Board of Trustees on Terminus during the First Anacreonian Crisis of 49–50 F.E. [*Foundation* Part II, "The Encyclopedists"].

Planetary—A space traveler who has never been in space before [*The Stars, Like Dust*].

Pohang (Early Galactic Era)—The elderly, unpalatable Tyrannian nobleman to whom Artemisia oth Hinriad was betrothed. He had previously had three other marriages, each of which had ended with the death of his wife [*The Stars, Like Dust*].

Poli (322–394 F.E.)—The maid in Dr. Toran Darell's household on Terminus, Poli discovered in 376 F.E. that Dr. Darell's daughter Arkady was missing but had left behind a note [*Second Foundation* Part II, "Search by the Foundation"].

Ponyets, Limmar (98–172 F.E.)—A trader and citizen of the Foundation who had, in his youth, been expelled from formal training for the priesthood in the Foundation's religion of science, Limmar Ponyets opened the Askone region to trade in the Foundation's nuclear gadgets in 135 F.E. by selling an uneconomical and illegal nuclear device that transmutes iron into gold to Askonian Elder Pherl and subsequently blackmailing Pherl into buying all of his nucleic cargo. During this mission Ponyets rescued Foundation agent Eskel Gorov from imprisonment [*Foundation* Part IV, "The Traders"].

Positronic brain—About the size of a human brain, the positronic brain is a delicately unstable iridium globe in a thin, platinum-plated skin. It contains neuronic pathways that provide robots with a pre-natal education and control their behavior. All positronic brains are impressed with the Three Laws of Robotics [*I, Robot*, "Runaround"; *I, Robot*, "Reason"].

Powell, Gregory (A.D. 1971–2047)—An employee of U.S. Robots and Mechanical Men, mustachioed Gregory Powell was, with Michael Donovan, part of the 2015 Second

Mercury Expedition. He placed himself in mortal danger to force robot SPD-13 (known as "Speedy") to obey the First Law of Robotics (not to allow humans to come to harm) and save him—thus breaking the impasse between the Second Law of Robotics (to obey human orders) and the Third Law of Robotics (self-preservation) that had been forcing Speedy to circle a selenium pool from which it had been ordered by Donovan to obtain selenium but that was near a dangerous volcanic vent. Powell's next assignment, with Donovan, was to troubleshoot experimental robots on Solar Station #5, where experimental robot QT-1 (known as "Cutie") demonstrated that it was capable of running the station without human supervision despite the fact that it believed the station's Energy Converter was the "Master" and that it was the Master's prophet. Powell was subsequently sent, with Donovan, to the asteroid belt to work the bugs out of DV-5 (known as "Dave"), a multiple mining robot whose subsidiary units produced no ore, but instead marched in military formations or danced, when confronted by an emergency unless Dave knew it was being observed by a human. Powell deduced that the initiative to manage independently its six subsidiaries during an emergency was too much for Dave's positronic brain, so he disabled one of the subsidiaries during an emergency, and—with only five subsidiaries to manage—Dave reverted to normal behavior. In 2029 Powell, with Donovan, was a passenger in the first faster-than-light space ship—a ship designed by U.S. Robots' The Brain and equipped with the first hyperatomic drive [*I, Robot*, "Runaround; *I, Robot*, "Reason"; *I, Robot*, "Catch That Rabbit"; *I, Robot*, "Escape"].

Prescott (A.D. 4882–4950)—Worked in Personnel at New York Yeast in the early 50th century A.D. [*The Caves of Steel*].

Preston, R.—Dr. Alfred Barr Humboldt's personal robot servant for twenty-two years in A.D. 4921. It was questioned that year by Earth plainclothes homicide detective Elijah Baley to determine if it or Dr. Gennao Sabbat's personal robot servant, R. Idda, had been lying in testimony involving a professional dispute between their owners, two Spacer mathematicians. As a result of this questioning, R. Preston went into stasis [*Robot Visions*, "Mirror Image"].

Previous enclosure—The offense employed by General Bel Riose during his unsuccessful 198–199 F.E. campaign against the Foundation, previous enclosure is the almost foolproof tactic of completely surrounding the enemy's region of space prior to launching an assault. This tactic insures success unless the enemy can launch an attack from outside the enclosed region of space that is powerful enough to break the enclosure. Riose's campaign against the Foundation was unsuccessful only because Emperor Cleon II recalled him from the field of battle just as the enclosure was completed [*Foundation and Empire* Part I, "The General"].

Prime Radiant—A featureless, shining cube designed by Hari Seldon and constructed by Yugo Amaryl in 12,038 G.E., the Prime Radiant is a portable computer used by Seldon, Amaryl, Wanda Seldon, and (subsequently) other members of the Second Foundation. It is attuned to the minds of its users and projects a three-dimensional display of the Seldon Plan's mathematical equations as they were codified by Seldon and as they had evolved over the centuries through the contributions of the Second Foundation's Speakers. Additions to the Seldon Plan are implemented through any Second Foundation Speaker's rapport with the Prime Radiant. By the fifth century F.E. the equations displayed by the Prime Radiant showed Seldon's original calculations in black, the additions of subsequent Second Foundation Speakers in red, and spontaneous deviations from the original Seldon Plan in blue. To become a Speaker, one had to make some contribution to the Seldon Plan as displayed by the Prime Radiant [*Forward the Foundation*; *Second Foundation* Part II, "Search by the Foundation"; *Foundation's Edge*].

Primitivists—Individuals in the Early Galactic Era who were obsessed with the study of Earth [*The Stars, Like Dust*].

Pritcher, Han (254–311 F.E.)—A native of Loris and a section leader in Terminus' Democratic Underground, the habitually insubordinate and immensely stubborn Han Pritcher was nonetheless a captain in the intelligence branch of the Foundation's army and a spy for the Foundation. Twice wounded in the line of duty, he was awarded the Foundation's Order of Merit for bravery early in his career. Ignoring repeatedly his orders to investigate Haven II for nonpayment of taxes, Pritcher instead traveled to Kalgan in 297 F.E. to investigate the Mule. He returned with Magnifico Giganticus, Bayta Darell, and Toran Darell to Terminus, where he was immediately arrested for insubordination. Disguised as skilled worker Lo Moro, Pritcher subsequently attempted to assassinate the Mule with a tiny nuclear bomb but was captured, converted by the Mule, and promoted to the rank of Colonel in the Mule's army. Subsequently promoted again to the rank of Lieutenant General during the Mule's reign as First Citizen of the Union of Worlds, Pritcher had already searched the Galaxy five times for the Second Foundation on the Mule's behalf, and had finally concluded that it did not exist, when the Mule sent him on a sixth mission in search of the Second Foundation in the company of Bail Channis, ostensibly an unconverted follower of the Mule who was in actuality a member of the Second Foundation. Pritcher and Channis, as co-commanders of this mission, sought the Second Foundation on Rossem, in the Oligarchy of Tazenda, where Pritcher arrested

Channis for treason against the Mule on the belief that Channis had merely been influenced by the Second Foundation into believing that the Second Foundation was located on Tazenda. However, when the Mule then arrived on Rossem—already aware that Channis was a member of the Second Foundation—Channis released Pritcher from the Mule's influence in order to confront the Mule with two hostile minds simultaneously; the Mule quickly rendered Pritcher unconscious after surrendering his blaster to Channis, and Pritcher regained consciousness in possession of his original, unconverted mental state. In 308 F.E. he briefly succeeded the Mule as First Citizen of the Union of Worlds [*Foundation and Empire* Part II, "The Mule"; *Second Foundation* Part I, "Search by the Mule"; *Second Foundation* Part II, "Search by the Foundation"].

Procurator of Earth—The Galactic Empire's representative on Earth during the Early Middle Galactic Era. He lived in a palace in the Himalayas [*Pebble in the Sky*].

Protoveg—A synthetic foodstuff eaten in New York City in the early 50th century A.D. [*The Caves of Steel*].

Psychic Probe—The Psychic Probe was used on the Spacer Worlds in the 50th century A.D., but was not used in police work on Earth during that era. It was an instrument used by both the Empire and the Foundation, throughout the Empire and the Foundation Eras, to extract information from unwilling subjects. There is a good chance that a psychic probe will cause brain damage, and its use for anything other than medical purposes is outlawed throughout the Galaxy [*The Robots of Dawn*; *The Currents of Space*; *Foundation and Empire* Part I, "The General"; *Foundation's Edge*; *Foundation and Earth*].

Psychohistory—The chaos theory (or dynamical systems analysis) branch of mathematics developed by Hari Seldon, at the instigation of R. Daneel Olivaw, that deals with the reactions of human conglomerates to fixed social and economic stimuli, psychohistory can predict humanity's aggregate future if the human population is sufficiently large for valid statistical treatment and if that population is unaware of the existence of psychohistorical analysis. Seldon used psychohistory to determine that establishing Encyclopedia Foundation Number One on Terminus in 12,069 G.E. (1 F.E.) would shorten the period of anarchy and barbarism that must follow the inevitable collapse of the First Galactic Empire from 30,000 to 1,000 years [*Foundation* Part I, "The Psychohistorians"; *Foundation and Earth*].

Psycholanguage—The speedy and delicately nuanced language of words, fleeting gestures, and changes in mental patterns through which two Second Foundation Speakers communicate. See "Mentalist-vision" [*Foundation's Edge*].

Psychometer—A Foundation device developed in the fifth century F.E. that measures the strength of a mentalic field. The mentalic shield on board the Foundation ship in which Terminus Mayor Harla Branno intercepted Stor Gendibal's *Bright Star* incorporated a psychometer [*Foundation's Edge*].

QT-1—See "Cutie."

Quemot, Dr. Anselmo (A.D. 4607–4934)—Elderly, thin, white-haired Anselmo Quemot was the only sociologist on Solaria in the early 50th century A.D. Plainclothes Earth homicide detective Elijah Baley consulted him in A.D. 4921 to learn about Solaria and thus about the context of Rikaine Delmarre's murder. One of Rikaine's acquaintances, Quemot agreed to see Baley physically, rather than to view him through trimensional viewing, because Quemot was curious about Earth and Earthmen, but Baley discovered that the self-taught Quemot's knowledge of sociology was essentially amateurish and that Quemot knew nothing about quantitative sociological analysis [*The Naked Sun*].

Quinber, Corporal (12,018–12,056 G.E.)—A member of the Joranumite Guard in Dahl Sector's Billibotton, Corporal Quinber took Raych into custody after Raych defeated three Billibottoners in a knife fight [*Forward the Foundation*].

Quinn, Francis (A.D. 1987–2050)—A professional politician who opposed District Attorney Stephen Byerley's run for mayor of New York City in A.D. 2032 on the grounds that Byerley, who had never been seen to eat or drink, was a robot [*I, Robot,* "Evidence"].

Quintana, Sophia (A.D. 5065–5140)—A graduate of the University of California, Sophia Quintana was Earth's Undersecretary of Energy in A.D. 5121. She recognized that Dr. Kelden Amadiro's and Dr. Levular Mandamus' secret base on Earth was at Three Mile Island, and she flew R. Daneel Olivaw and R. Giskard Reventlov there in her air-car [*Robots and Empire*].

Quintesetz, Sotayn (440–526 F.E.)—A professor of ancient history at Sayshell University who traced his ancestry to Askone, Sotayn Quintesetz told Golan Trevize and Janov Pelorat about humaniform robots and of the Sayshellian legend that the Sashell Sector was colonized directly from Earth during the second, robotless wave of Galactic colonization. However, he insisted that Gaia is not Earth and that Earth is not in the Sayshell Union. While he reluctantly provided them with its coordinates, Quintesetz maintained that any attempt to go to Gaia would be suicidal [*Foundation's Edge*].

Quoriston, Battle of—Fought in 377 F.E. between the Foundation and the forces of Lord Stettin of Kalgan, the battle of Quoriston was the last battle of the Stettinian War as well as the last battle of consequence during the Great Interregnum. The Foundation secured victory when

Commander Cenn's squadron suddenly appeared out of hyper-space to trap the Kalganian fleet. While superior in numbers, the Kalganian fleet lost 240 ships while the Foundation fleet lost only eight [*Second Foundation* Part II, "Search by the Foundation"].

Racety, Captain (Early Galactic Era)—Commander of the spaceship that transported Lady Samia of Fife, Valona March, and Rik from Florina to Sark in the Early Galactic Era [*The Currents of Space*].

Radiation bomb—A tiny nuclear device that, when detonated, releases a deadly burst of radiation that will kill anything within a radius of six feet to six miles, depending on the size of the device [*The Stars, Like Dust*].

Radiation Fever—A contagious, fatal affliction that struck Earthmen during the Early Middle Galactic Era. It was caused by a more virulent strain of the virus that also caused Common Fever. Its symptoms included severe disorientation and mental incapacity, sores around the mouth, and flushing [*Pebble in the Sky*].

Radiation Theory—Current in the Early Middle Galactic Era, the Radiation Theory of human origin hypothesized that humanity evolved on only one planet but then spread via space travel throughout the Galaxy. In the Early Middle Galactic Era the Radiation Theory was eclipsed by the more-popular Merger Theory [*Pebble in the Sky*].

Radole—A ribbon world: half of the planet always faces the sun; thus, the only habitable region is the narrow ribbon of land that straddles the border between the day-side and the night-side. The weakest of the twenty-seven Independent Trading Worlds at the end of the third century F.E., Radole was for this reason chosen as the site of the conference convened by the Independent Trading Worlds in 297 F.E. to consider how they might take advantage of the Mule's war against the Foundation [*Foundation and Empire* Part II, "The Mule"].

Radole City—The site of the conference of Independent Trading Worlds held in 297 F.E., Radole City is the most hospitable spot on the ribbon-world planet Radole [*Foundation and Empire* Part II, "The Mule"].

Raindrop Forty-Five (12,000–12,073 G.E.)—The younger and more flighty of the two Mycogenian Sisters sent by Graycloud Five to teach Hari Seldon and Dors Venabili how to use the kitchen appliances in their small apartment in Mycogen, Raindrop Forty-Five also took Dors shopping for necessary items in Mycogen [*Prelude to Foundation*].

Raindrop Forty-Three (11,998–12,073 G.E.)—The older and more grave of the two Mycogenian Sisters sent by Graycloud Five to teach Hari Seldon and Dors Venabili how to use the kitchen appliances in their small apartment in Mycogen, Raindrop Forty-Three also took Seldon on a tour of Mycogen's microfarms.

Perversely, while on this tour Raindrop Forty-Three had Seldon remove his skincap, so that she could feel his hair, as a condition of allowing him to see her Book of Mycogenian history. However, she indulged in this perversion at the instigation of the Mycogenian Elders, who wanted to use her to discover what Seldon was after in visiting Mycogen [*Prelude to Foundation*].

Rancher of Widemos (Early Galactic Era)—The greatest nobleman on the planet Nephelos and Biron Farill's father, the Rancher of Widemos was a big, round-headed man with deep-set eyes who had conspired against the Tyranni but was betrayed by fellow-conspirator the Autarch of Lingane, because he was too popular for the Autarch's purposes, and executed by the Tyranni for treason [*The Stars, Like Dust*].

Randa, Kiangtow (11,960–12,029 G.E.)—Lisung Randa's uncle, Kiangtow Randa was a renowned mathematician [*Prelude to Foundation*].

Randa, Lisung (11,980–12,054 G.E.)—A short, plump, Asiatic instructor of psychology at Trantor's Streeling University, Lisung Randa suggested in 12,020 G.E. that Hari Seldon go Upperside with a group of Streeling University meteorologists because, like Seldon with his psychohistory, the meteorologists also grappled with frustrating, intractable problems involving foretelling the future. Lisung Randa was from the planet Hopara and was nephew to the renowned mathematician Kiangtow Randa. Seldon suspected, probably incorrectly, that Lisung Randa may have been an Imperial agent [*Prelude to Foundation*].

Randow, Charles (A.D. 2020–2078)—Pale, high-cheekboned Charles Randow was an employee at U.S. Robots and Mechanical Men whose arm was inadvertently broken by Lenny (LNE-Prototype), a flawed experimental robot that had the mentality of an infant. Randow was subsequently interrogated by Dr. Susan Calvin [*Robot Visions*, "Lenny"].

Randu (233–313 F.E.)—Toran Darell's uncle, Fran Darell's half-brother, and the Independent Trading World's ambassador to Terminus' Mayor Indbur III, Randu was a leader of the renegade Trader movement against the Foundation in the late third century F.E. In 297 F.E. he sent Bayta and Toran Darell to Kalgan to investigate the Mule, and he soon thereafter came to believe that the Independent Trading Worlds should fight the Mule and not the Foundation. Coordinator of Haven II's Confederation of Cities during the Mule's subsequent siege of the planet, in 298 F.E. he sent Bayta and Toran Darell, Ebling Mis, and Magnifico Giganticus to Trantor to discover the location of the Second Foundation so that it could be warned about the Mule [*Foundation and Empire* Part II, "The Mule"].

Rash, Linda (A.D. 2030–2113)—A robopsychologist who worked with Susan Calvin towards the end of Calvin's career with U.S. Robots and Mechanical Men. To produce added complexity, Rash had used fractal geometry in constructing the patterns in Elvex's (LVX-1's) positronic brain, but the result was to give the robot the ability to dream and thus to reveal that there was a subconscious layer beneath the superficial positronic brain paths [*Robot Dreams*, "Robot Dreams"].

Rashelle (12,970–12,025 G.E.)—Gleb Andurin's aunt, Rashelle was the plump, middle-aged, *de facto* Mayor of Wye who had had her personal aide Sergeant Emmet Thalus transport Hari Seldon, Dors Venabili, and Raych from Trantor's Dahl Sector to Wye Sector. Daughter of Mayor Mannix IV, Rashelle briefly ruled Wye in 12,020 G.E. despite the fact that her father was still technically Mayor. Aspiring to be Empress of Trantor and of the planetary systems in Trantor's province, she wanted Seldon to predict falsely that Trantor could rule itself and that the other provinces in the Galactic Empire could exist in peace as separate, independent kingdoms. Deposed when Imperial forces occupied Wye to prevent a coup, Rashelle attempted to murder Seldon—to keep him from falling into Eto Demerzel's hands—but was thwarted by the combined actions of Dors and Raych [*Prelude to Foundation*].

Rasie (Early Galactic Era)—The boy in Townman Myrlyn Teren's village on Florina who found missing spatio-analyst Rik in a village irrigation ditch [*The Currents of Space*].

Raych (12,008–12,058 G.E.)—An alley kid in Billibotton, a violent slum in Trantor's Dahl Sector, Raych took Hari Seldon and Dors Venabili to Mother Rittah in 12,020 G.E. in return for a talking computer that could teach him to read. He later took Seldon and Dors to the revolutionary Davan and, later still, helped to prevent Seldon and Dors from being arrested in Dahl by Dahlite security officers Lanel Russ and Gebore Astinwald. Raych then hid Seldon and Dors in an automated waste treatment facility and subsequently accompanied them to Wye Sector, where he aided Dors in preventing Rashelle from murdering Seldon. By 12,028 G.E. Seldon had adopted Raych, who had a charismatic ability to inspire affection, as his son. Although he did not trust demagogue and agitator Laskin "Jo-Jo" Joranum, Raych was favorably impressed by Joranum's populist, democratic political agenda. Seldon subsequently sent Raych to Dahl Sector—where Joranum was scheduled to meet with the Dahl Sector Council—to spy on Joranum, to discover his true intentions, and to entrap him. Raych was then taken into custody by Corporal Quinber of the Joranumite Guard, after defeating three Billibottoners in a knife fight, and subsequently told Joranum that Eto Demerzel was really a robot, the belief that eventually undermined Joranum's political career. Afterwards Raych worked in

Religion

Trantor's Ministry of Population and attempted to implement many of the social reforms previously championed by Joranum. In 12,038 G.E. Seldon sent Raych, disguised as Planchet, to Wye Sector to determine if the increasing number of infrastructure breakdowns on Trantor were the result of a revived Joranumite Conspiracy centered in Wye. On Gambol Deen Namarti's behalf, Gleb Andurin then recruited Raych to be First Minister Seldon's assassin, but Namarti recognized that Raych was Seldon's foster son. Andurin then drugged Raych, to assure that he would carry out the assassination, and planned to murder him afterwards. But the assassination plot was thwarted when undercover security officer Manella Dubanqua killed Andurin before Raych could fire on Seldon. Raych subsequently married Manella; their first daughter, Wanda, was born in 12,040 G.E., and their second daughter, Bellis, was born in 12,052 G.E. Raych subsequently wrote and published a successful book on Trantor's Dahl Sector. In 12,058 G.E. Raych saved Seldon from being attacked by eight thugs on Trantor, and in that same year he was offered and accepted an academic position at the University of Santanni, 9000 parsecs from Trantor. He emigrated to Santanni with Manella and Bellis, but a violent rebellion soon thereafter broke out on that planet, and Raych was killed defending Santanni University from the rebels [*Prelude to Foundation*; *Forward the Foundation*].

Religion of science—The compulsory religion that accompanied the nuclear technology that Terminus shared with the Four Kingdoms between 50 and 80 F.E. and subsequently sold to many other regions in the Periphery in the first half of the second century F.E. through the Foundation's traders, the religion of science enabled the Foundation to dominate its neighbors on the Periphery as they broke away from the First Galactic Empire in the Early Foundation Era (1–200 F.E.). The technicians who serviced the nuclear infrastructure thus established in these regions and systems were trained on Terminus as priests in the religion of science and were given only empirical knowledge of their tools. Terminus Mayor Salvor Hardin used the common people's belief in the religion of science to thwart the Kingdom of Anacreon's attempted invasion of Terminus in 79 F.E. However, this religion went into eclipse in the latter half of the second century F.E. when Foundation traders, reacting to stiff resistance to it, began to sell their nuclear gadgets without insisting that the religion of science accompany them [*Foundation* Part III, "The Mayors"].

Religionist Party—A political party on Terminus formed by Jorane Sutt in 158 F.E., the Religionist Party opposed the policies of Terminus Mayor Hober Mallow and specifically opposed Mallow's policy of abandoning the Foundation's reliance on the religion of science, which for a century had enabled Terminus to dominate its neighbors, in favor of the economic hegemony effected by the Foundation's trade in nuclear gadgets and technologies in itself, which had heretofore underwritten the success of the religion of science. The Religionist Party went into permanent decline shortly after Sutt's death in 186 F.E. [*Foundation* Part V, "The Merchant Princes"].

Remorseless—Commissioner of the Great Khan of the Tyranni Simok Aratap's small spaceship, which Biron Farrill, Gillbret oth Hinriad, and Artemisia oth Hinriad stole from Rhodia's Palace Field Spaceport and piloted to Lingane and then into the Horsehead Nebula in search of the secret rebellion world. On its trip back to Rhodia, Director of Rhodia Hinrik V married Biron and Artemisia on board the *Remorseless* [*The Stars, Like Dust*].

Reventlov, R. Giskard—See "Giskard Reventlov, R."

Rhodia—The 1098th world settled by humanity, according to the Early Galactic Era's *Galactic Almanac*, Rhodia orbits a F-8 star in the Nebular Regions and is 500 light years from Earth. It was conquered by the Tyranni in the Early Galactic Era, but it was also, subsequently, the secret rebellion world on which Director of Rhodia Hinrik V planned his revolt against the Tyranni for over twenty years [*The Stars, Like Dust*].

Rigel Sector—During the Early Galactic Era the Rigel Sector was the location of a stagnant, mechanistic, robot-using civilization. This civilization was conquered by the warlord Moray [*Pebble in the Sky*].

Rik (Early Galactic Era)—A native of Earth, Rik was a small, blue-eyed, 31-year-old spatio-analyst who was found in a nearly brainless state in an irrigation ditch in Townman Myrlyn Terens' village on Florina in the Early Galactic Era. His memory having been obliterated by a psychic probe administered inexpertly a year earlier by Terens, he was called "Rik" because it was a word that meant "moron" in the slang of Florina's kyrt mills. Looked after for a year on Florina by Valona "Lona" March, Rik became a fugitive when Lona felled and inadvertently killed a patroller in helping Rik and Terens escape from Florina's Upper City library. After Trantorian agent Matt Khorov was killed by Terens, Rik and Lona stowed away on Lady Samia of Fife's spaceship, bound for Sark, disguised as Gareth and Hansa Barne, brother and sister from Wotex. On Sark Rik's memory improved and he recalled that Florina's sun was in a pre-nove stage because it was passing through a carbon current of space. After the evacuation of Florina had commenced, Rik returned to Earth with Lona [*The Currents of Space*].

Riose, General Bel (164–199 F.E.)—A Peer of the Empire and the Military Governor of Siwenna from 195 to 199 F.E., General Bel Riose was in command of the Twentieth Fleet of the Border during his 198–

199 F.E. campaign against the Foundation. Promoted early in his career for heroic actions in the Lemul Cluster, Riose was an excellent strategist and an inspiring leader; young, energetic, bold, imaginative, and loyal, he preferred combat to courtly life and is known to history as "The Last of the Imperials." After interviewing Ducem Barr and then disguising himself as a young princeling from the Periphery to gather information about the Foundation, Riose concluded that the Foundation's sense of "manifest destiny"—its belief that it would one day rule the Galaxy—made it a threat to the domains of the Emperor. However, before he could complete his conquest of the Foundation, Riose was recalled from the Periphery, arrested for treason on trumped-up charges, condemned, and executed because Emperor Cleon II believed he had conspired with Privy Secretary Brodrig to turn against the Emperor once the Foundation was defeated. As psychohistory had predicted, Riose's very success as a general caused his downfall, for no Emperor during this period of Galactic history could risk the strong possibility that a popular, conquering general would return from the field to stage a military coup [*Foundation and Empire* Part I, "The General"].

Rittah, Mother (11,942–12,030)— See "Mother Rittah."

River Controversy—A political crisis in Aurora's history during which arguments over the proper division of hydroelectric power had almost led to a civil war [*The Robots of Dawn*].

Rizzett, Tedor "Ted" (Early Galactic Era)—Gray-haired, red-faced, and vigorous, Tedor Rizzett was an aide to the Autarch of Lingane, a fellow-conspirator against the Tyranni, a loyal admirer of the Rancher of Widemos, and a colonel in the regular Linganian forces. He became Biron Farrill's drinking companion as they searched the Horsehead Nebula for the secret rebellion world in the *Remorseless* with Artemisia oth Hinriad, Gillbret oth Hinriad, and the Autarch. Rizzett saved Biron's life by removing the energy capsule from the Autarch's blaster, and he then turned against the Autarch when the Autarch revealed that he had been the traitor responsible for the Rancher of Widemos' death. Captured with the others aboard the *Remorseless* by Commissioner of the Great Khan of the Tyranni Simok Aratap, Rizzett broke away from his captors and killed the Autarch after the Autarch revealed to Aratap the location of the last system in the Horsehead Nebula in which the rebellion world might be located [*The Stars, Like Dust*].

Robbie—A voiceless silvery robot nursemaid, Robbie was manufactured in A.D. 1996 and had been with the Weston family for two years when it was returned to U.S. Robots and Mechanical Men because Grace Weston feared that it may go berserk, that it was keeping her daughter Gloria from socializing with other children, and that there was mounting anti-robot sentiment among her neighbors. Months later, Robbie saved Gloria from being run over by a tractor in the U.S. Robots factory and was allowed to return to the Weston family [*I, Robot*, "Robbie"].

Robertson, Lawrence (A.D. 1950–2031)—Incorporated U.S. Robots and Mechanical Men in 1982 as its president. He was succeeded as president of the company by his son [*I, Robot*, "Introduction"; *I, Robot*, "Escape"].

Robertson, Scott (A.D. 2007–2088)—Lawrence Robertson's grandson, Scott Robertson was the largest shareholder in U.S. Robots and Mechanical Men in the mid–21st century A.D. [*Robot Visions*, "Galley Slave"; *Robot Visions*, "Feminine Intuition"].

Robot EZ-27—See "Easy."

Robot-mental-freeze-out—A condition that immobilizes a robot, burning out its positronic brain and rendering it useless, when two conflicting impulses in the positronic brain have precisely equal intensity, making it impossible for the robot to act. Robot-mental-freeze-out can occur through chance changes in the positronic brain paths, but this is extremely unlikely. The more sophisticated the robot, the less likely is it to suffer robot-mental-freeze-out. Robots known to have been destroyed by robot-mental-freeze-out include HB-34 (also known as Herbie), R. Jander Panell, R. Ernett Second, and R. Giskard Reventlov [*I, Robot*, "Liar"; *The Robots of Dawn*; *Robots and Empire*].

Robotics Institute of Aurora—Founded in Eos, Aurora, in A.D. 4020 by Dr. Kelden Amadiro, the Robotics Institute of Aurora (RIA) was an organization of over 100 Auroran roboticists dedicated to pooling their knowledge to discover, independently of Dr. Han Fastolfe, the secret of creating humaniform positronic brains and, thus, of constructing humaniform robots with which to continue the settlement of the Galaxy for the Spacers. Fastolfe's daughter, Dr. Vasilia Aliena, was a prominent member of the RIA. Fastolfe became a member of the RIA in A.D. 4923, after the Spacers had agreed to allow Earthmen to colonize other planets. The RIA eventually launched a line of humaniform robots—fifty were produced—but the rollout was a fiasco because the Auroran public would not accept humaniform robots due to the fact that they competed too effectively with human beings in every way, including sexually [*The Robots of Dawn*; *Robots and Empire*].

Robots—U.S. Robots and Mechanical Men, Inc., was incorporated by company president Lawrence Robertson in A.D. 1982. All U.S. Robots employed positronic brains that were impressioned with the Three Laws of Robotics during their manufacture. Gamma radiation destroys the delicate balance of the robot's positronic brain. The first talking robot was manufactured in A.D. 1998, and the first mobile talking robot was manufactured in A.D. 2002. By A.D. 2015 robots had assisted humanity in the colonization of Mercury, Mars, and the asteroids; they were also capable of operating without human supervision Solar Stations beaming energy to Earth and its colonies. By the early 21st century A.D. mobile robots were illegal on Earth, and subsequently on the other inhabited planets of the Solar System, and were used only in space exploration and exploitation. Ironically, by the mid–21st century A.D. immobile robots, the Machines, managed the world's economy. In the early 50th century A.D. robots on Earth worked the mines and farms outside the Cities and—due to the urging of the Spacers—were beginning to infiltrate the Cities as well. At this time an integrated C/Fe (human/robot) culture flourished on the fifty Space worlds, on which there were far more robots than humans. By the 52nd century A.D. robots had been banned from Earth's Cities and were illegal on the Settler Worlds. In Gaian fable, robots were mechanical tools shaped like human beings who were indoctrinated with the Three Laws of Robotics: They first acted as humanity's nursemaids, then became the Eternals who chose the reality in which Earth is the only planet in the Galaxy to develop a highly complex ecology and intelligent life, and then withdrew to Eternity to allow humanity to develop in its own direction. The robots taught Gaians telepathy. See "Three Laws of Robotics" [*I, Robot*, "Introduction"; *I, Robot*, "Robbie"; *I, Robot*, "Runaround"; *I, Robot*, "Reason"; *I, Robot*, "Catch That Rabbit"; *I, Robot*, "Evidence"; *The Caves of Steel*; *Robots and Empire*; *Foundation's Edge*].

Rossem—A cold, backwater world occupied and taxed by Tazenda following the Great Sack of Trantor (258 F.E.), Rossem was the planet on which Bail Channis and General Han Pritcher landed when they arrived at the Oligarchy of Tazenda, in 303 F.E., while seeking the Second Foundation. They were quickly joined there by the Mule, who had correctly deduced that Channis himself was a member of the Second Foundation. Channis then falsely confessed, while finally under the Mule's emotional control, that Rossem was the home of the Second Foundation—not Tazenda, which the Mule had already destroyed. The Mule briefly believed this until the Second Foundation's First Speaker arrived and revealed to him that this wasn't true, either, prior to removing from the Mule's mind all knowledge of and curiosity about the Second Foundation [*Second Foundation* Part I, "Search by the Mule"].

Rossem, Governor of (253–313 F.E.)—Short, balding, stocky, and unimpressive, the Governor of Rossem had an audience with Bail Channis and General Han Pritcher shortly after their arrival on Rossem in 303 F.E. Channis and Pritcher quickly deduced that he was not a member of the Second Foundation [*Second Foundation* Part I, "Search by the Mule"].

Roth, Miss (A.D. 2145–2223)—A reporter who interviewed Tertia Arnfeld prior to the experimental use of MIK-27 or Mike, a robot capable of miniaturizing itself, to treat Tertia's husband Dr. Gregory Arnfeld's cancer [*Robot Visions*, "Too Bad!"].

Roth, Wilson (A.D. 4873–4943)—Sleepy-looking, heavy-set Wilson Roth succeeded Julius Enderby to the post of Police Commissioner of New York City in A.D. 4921 [*The Robots of Dawn*].

Rufirant, Karoll (465–526 F.E.)—A Hamish farmer temporarily under the mental influence of Gaia, Karoll Rufirant attacked Stor Gendibal as Gendibal was walking in the Trantorian countryside. He was prevented from beating Gendibal by the intersession of Sura Novi [*Foundation's Edge*].

Rune—One of the planet Sark's five continents. In the Early Galactic Era it was ruled by the Squire of Rune [*The Currents of Space*].

Running the strips—A dangerous game played by teenagers all over Earth in the 50th century A.D. The object of the game was for a leader to lose as many as possible of his followers on the City Expressway by rapidly switching from strip to strip [*The Caves of Steel*].

Russ, Security Officer Lanel (19,988–20,064 G.E.)—A member of the Dahlite security force who came to the Tisalver residence in Dahl to attempt to arrest Hari Seldon and Dors Venabili for trying to incite a mob to riot, for brawling, and—in Dors' case—for carrying knives without a permit. Seldon dislocated Russ' shoulder in his and Dors' escape from Russ and his partner, Security Officer Gebore Astinwald [*Prelude to Foundation*].

RX-2475—The Solarian robot assigned to look after plainclothes Earth homicide detective Elijah Baley's welfare during his space voyage from Earth to Solaria in A.D. 4921 [*The Naked Sun*].

Sabbat, Dr. Gennao (A.D. 4873–5185)—A Fellow of the Galactic Academy, Dr. Gennao Sabbat was a Spacer mathematician en route on the *Eta Carina* to an interstellar neurobiophysics conference on Aurora in A.D. 4921. While en route, he and fellow Spacer mathematician Dr. Alfred Barr Humboldt both claimed to have made the same revolutionary mathematical discovery, and both claimed that the other had stolen the idea. Due to the deductions of Earth plainclothes homicide detective Elijah Baley, who was consulted by R. Daneel Olivaw, Humboldt finally confessed that he had stolen Sabbat's idea [*Robot Visions*, "Mirror Image"].

Sacratorium—The foremost temple in Trantor's Mycogen Sector, dedicated to the memory of the Mycogenians' previous existence on Aurora, the Sacratorium looks like a miniature Imperial Palace and its grounds resemble, in miniature, the Imperial Palace grounds. Only Mycogenian males can enter the Sacratorium, ordinarily, but Mycogenian females can enter on certain rare days and times. The Sacratorium contains 2-D television screens, which display reconstructed scenes and views of ancient Aurora, and the Elder's Aerie, which contains an inoperative metallic robot [*Prelude to Foundation*].

Salinnian Frontier—The site of the Mule's first armed incursion into Foundation territory in 298 F.E. [*Foundation and Empire* Part II, "The Mule"].

Salvor Hardin Museum of Origins—A museum on Terminus that houses the uncompleted original manuscript of the Encyclopedia Galactica. See "Hardin, Salvor" [*Foundation's Edge*].

Samia of Fife, Lady (Early Galactic Era)—Beautiful, olive-skinned, dark-haired, cleft-chinned Lady Samia of Fife was exactly five feet tall and weighed 90 pounds. A member of the Sarkite nobility and daughter of the Squire of Fife, she was also an amateur scholar who had visited Florina in the Early Galactic Era to conduct research into the history of kyrt. She questioned Florian native Valona March and missing spatio-analyst Rik, who had stowed away on the spaceship transporting her back to Sark; and, after arriving on Sark, she picked up fugitive Florinian Townman Myrlyn Terens at the Sark spaceport, unaware that he was the Squire-killer she was looking for, before he could rendezvous with the Trantorian agents he was to meet there. She was then kissed by Terens in her groundcar, an incident photographed by Trantorian agents and used by Trantorian Ambassador to Sark Ludigan Abel to blackmail the Squire of Sark into participating in a conference on the fate of the missing spatio-analyst and on the future of the kyrt trade [*The Currents of Space*].

Sammy, R.—A robot that had taken Vince Barrett's job as an errand boy in the New York City Police Department. It had been assigned to Police Commissioner Julius Enderby, and it was eventually discovered in A.D. 4920 to have been deliberately deactivated by Enderby because it knew too much, for it was R. Sammy that had carried a blaster through open country to Spacetown and given it to Enderby—who had then killed Dr. Roj Nemennuh Sarton with it by mistake, thinking he was R. Daneel Olivaw—and then had taken the blaster back to New York City again [*The Caves of Steel*].

Santanni—A provincial planet 9,000 parsecs from Trantor, Santanni was disrupted by a rebellion in 12,058 G.E. It was later a Foundation planet that fell to Kalgan without a fight in 376 F.E., early in the Stettinian War [*Second Foundation* Part II, "Search by the Foundation"; *Forward the Foundation*].

Santanni, University of—Hari

Seldon's foster son Raych was a professor at the University of Santanni in 12,058 G.E. Dr. Kleise and Dr. Toran Darell were colleagues at the University of Santanni from 365 to 370 F.E. Janov Pelorat's son was a professor at the University of Santanni in 498 F.E. [*Second Foundation* Part II, "Search by the Foundation"; *Forward the Foundation*; *Foundation's Edge*].

Sark—An undistinguished planet orbiting a yellow star whose importance in the Early Galactic Era depended on the fact that it controlled the plantation planet Florina, the only planet in the Galaxy at that time on which the miracle fiber kyrt could be cultivated. Due to its control of Florina, Sark was the second-richest planet in the Galaxy, second only to Trantor, in the Early Galactic Era. Sark has five continents—Balle, Bort, Fife, Rune, and Steen—and in the Early Galactic Era each continent was ruled by a Great Squire. Sark went into irreversible decline after the population of Florina was evacuated, because its sun was in the pre-nova stage, and after scientists discovered how to cultivate kyrt on other worlds [*The Currents of Space*].

Sark City—The capital city on the planet Sark [*The Currents of Space*].

Sarton, Dr. Roj Nemennuh (A.D. 4790–4920)—A citizen of Aurora and a brilliant Doctor of Sociology specializing in robots, Dr. Roj Nemennuh Sarton was a Spacer who had created humaniform robot R. Daneel Olivaw in his own image on Aurora in A.D. 4920 and who was accidently murdered later that year in Spacetown, on Earth, by New York City Police Commissioner Julius Enderby because Enderby had mistaken Sarton for Daneel [*The Caves of Steel*].

Savano, Tapper (11,891–11,952 G.E.)—The last great landscape architect to design the Imperial Palace Gardens on Trantor, Tapper Savano was a native of Anacreon [*Forward the Foundation*].

Sayshell—The fourth planet in the Sayshell system and the capital planet of the Sayshell Union, Sayshell was the first destination reached in Golan Trevize's and Janov Pelorat's initial quest for Earth. It had a distinctive, somewhat repulsive odor, and its citizens dressed in rainbow colors in the late fifth century F.E. to demonstrate their independence from the Foundation, whose citizens tended to dress in grey [*Foundation's Edge*].

Sayshell City—On the planet Sayshell is the capital city of the Sayshell Union [*Foundation's Edge*].

Sayshell Sector—The region of the Galaxy in which Gaia, the planet that Janov Prelorat had mistakenly believed might be Earth, exists [*Foundation's Edge*].

Sayshell Union—An independent group of 86 populated planets that had steadfastly been unfriendly to the Foundation Federation throughout the fifth century F.E., the Sayshell Union was at that time almost completely surrounded by Foundation territory. Nevertheless, it managed to maintain its neutrality, just as it had managed to maintain its neutrality towards the Mule's Union of Worlds, which had completely surrounded it a century earlier, due to its proximity to Gaia, which is physically within the Sayshell Union but not a part of it politically [*Foundation's Edge*].

Schwartz, Joseph (A.D. 1887—839 G.E.)—Short, plump, balding Joseph Schwartz, who had immigrated to America at the age of 20, was a retired Chicago tailor with a photographic memory who was transported some 10,000 years through time, from A.D. 1949 to 827 G.E., by a lab accident at Chicago's Institute for Nuclear Research. In 827 G.E. he was taken in by Arbin and Loa Maren, who needed another hand to work on their farm near Chica, but because Schwartz was unable to speak their language Arbin brought him to Dr. Affret Shekt, to be subjected to Shekt's Synapsifier in the hope that this would increase his ability to learn. Six days after the Synapsifier treatment Schwartz escaped from Dr. Shekt's lab at the Institute for Nuclear Research, but he was quickly found by Dr. Shekt's daughter Pola Shekt and by Outsider archeologist Dr. Bel Arvardan. He was returned to the lab by Natter, a messenger and spy for Earth's Society of Ancients, in return for a 300 credit bribe. Schwartz subsequently discovered that his thinking was sharper and clearer and that he had developed the Mind Touch—the ability to sense the proximity of other minds, to know the location of anyone his mind had previously touched, to read thoughts, to control another's gross physical movements, and to kill with his mind. He then left the Maren farm to escape the Sixty, but he was followed by Natter, whom he killed with the Mind Touch after sensing that Natter posed a threat. When he tried to apply for a factory job in Chica the next day, Schwartz was arrested by the Society of Ancients and condemned to death. However, he used the Mind Touch to control the physical movements of Balkis, Secretary to the High Minister of Earth, and thus to effect his, Dr. Shekt's, Pola's, and Arvardan's escape to Fort Dibburn, where Schwartz used Lieutenant Marc Claudy's hatred for Earthmen to manipulate Claudy, via the Mind Touch, into flying a plane to Senloo and destroying the installation there that was to launch Earth's germ-laden missiles into the Galaxy. Schwartz was awarded the ribbon of the Order of the Spaceship and Sun, First Class, for his heroism in saving humanity [*Pebble in the Sky*].

Second, R. Ernett—A humaniform robot assembled on Aurora in the early 50th century A.D. and smuggled to Earth in the early 52nd century A.D., R. Ernett Second attempted to assassinate R. Giskard Reventlov during Gladia Thool Delmarre Solaria Gremionis' initial speech in New York City in A.D.

5121. R. Daneel Olivaw prevented it from harming Giskard. It subsequently succumbed to robot-mental-freeze-out while being questioned by Gladia, but it did provide the clue that enabled Giskard and Daneel to locate Dr. Kelden Amadiro's and Dr. Levular Mandamus' secret base of operations at Three Mile Island [*Robots and Empire*].

Second Foundation—Another, secret Foundation established in 12,068 G.E. (-1 F.E.) "at the other end of the Galaxy" from the Foundation on Terminus, the Second Foundation was the great psychohistorian Hari Seldon's back-up plan for Encyclopedia Foundation Number One. Its first members were Wanda Seldon, Stettin Palver, and Bor Alurin, and it was subsequently populated by a group of scientists with a psychological orientation who could communicate very concisely due to their awareness of the workings of one another's minds and who had developed over the centuries the ability—somewhat similar to the Mule's—to affect and alter the mentality of others. Destined by the Seldon Plan to be the ruling class of the Second Galactic Empire once it was established by the Foundation, the Second Foundation was the object of six unsuccessful, Galaxy-wide searches conducted by the Mule, from 298 through 303 F.E., and of a similar, equally unsuccessful search by the Foundation in 376–77 F.E. The Second Foundation was located in the Imperial (later Galactic) Library on Trantor and numbered some 40,000 psychohistorians by the late fifth century F.E. [*Foundation* Part I, "The Psychohistorians"; *Second Foundation* Part I, "Search by the Mule"; *Second Foundation* Part II, "Search by the Foundation"; *Forward the Foundation*; *Foundation's Edge*].

Second Galactic Empire—Finally solidified in 998 F.E., with its capital on Terminus, the Second Galactic Empire was the long-range goal of Hari Seldon's plan to establish on Terminus in 12,069 G.E. (1 F.E.), under the guise of Encyclopedia Foundation Number One, a nucleus of researchers and support staff that would, through the forces of history, shorten from 30,000 to 1,000 years the period of anarchy and barbarism that would follow the inevitable collapse of the First Galactic Empire [*Foundation* Part I, "The Psychohistorians"; *Foundation* Part II, "The Encyclopedists"].

Secundo, Louis (A.D. 2120–2196)—A member of the miniaturization team that had inserted a miniaturized robot, MIK-27 or Mike, into the body of Dr. Gregory Arnfeld to destroy Arnfeld's cancer cells [*Robot Visions*, "Too Bad!"].

Seldon, Bellis (12,052–12,058 G.E.)—Raych and Manella Dubanqua's second daughter, Wanda Seldon's sister, and Hari Seldon's granddaughter, Bellis Seldon emigrated to Santanni with her parents in 12,058 G.E. and was subsequently lost in space when she and Manella attempted to flee to Anacreon on the

Seldon

Arcadia VII after a violent rebellion broke out on Santanni [*Forward the Foundation*].

Seldon, Hari (11,988–12,069 G.E./ -79–1 F.E.)—The great psychohistorian and visionary who established the First and Second Foundations in 12,069 G.E. (1 F.E.) and 12,068 G.E. (-1 F.E.), respectively, Hari Seldon was born on Helicon, was educated as a mathematician, became an assistant professor of mathematics at Helicon University, and ultimately developed psychohistory into a statistical science. On Trantor in 12,020 G.E. to present his paper on psychohistory at the Decennial Convention of mathematicians, Seldon was interviewed by Emperor Cleon I—at unofficial first minister Eto Demerzel's instigation—because Cleon I hoped to use psychohistory as a propaganda tool that would convince the population of the Galaxy that all will be well through the dissemination of rosy predictions about the future. Seldon was subsequently accosted by two young Trantorian hoodlums in a park in Trantor's Imperial Sector but survived unscathed due to the assistance of Chetter Hummin, who convinced Seldon that he would be safer hiding on Trantor than if he were to return to Helicon, where he might be picked up by Demerzel's Imperial forces. Hummin also convinced Seldon to try to develop psychohistory for the betterment of the people of the Galaxy. Hummin then took Seldon to Streeling University, where he introduced Seldon to Dors Venabili and where Seldon was almost killed by exposure on Upperside. Dors then took Seldon to Mycogen Sector and, afterwards, with Hummin, to Dahl Sector, where Seldon and Dors were attacked by Marron and nine of his comrades in Billibotton, a violent slum in Dahl, but escaped due to Dor's unexpected talent for knife fighting. With the assistance of Raych, Seldon and Dors subsequently escaped from Dahl after Dahlite security officers Lanel Russ and Gebore Astinwald attempted to arrest them for trying to incite a mob to riot, for brawling, and—in Dors' case—for carrying knives without a permit. Transported from Dahl to Wye Sector, with Dors and Raych, by Sergeant Emmer Thalus, Seldon was saved again when Thalus subsequently refused Rashelle's order to execute him and, immediately afterwards, when Dors and Raych prevented Rashelle from killing him herself. Seeking to discover a single world that he could use as a model in developing psychohistory, Seldon finally realized while traversing Trantor that the single world he could use as a model was Trantor itself. He finally deduced as well that both Demerzel and Hummin were the same individual—in reality a humaniform robot in disguise, R. Daneel Olivaw, the Da-Nee of Dahl's legends—and that Daneel had used mentalic manipulation on him to convince him both to remain on Trantor and to try to develop psychohistory. Seldon also deduced that Dors, too, was a humaniform robot, but fell in love with her anyway. Head of the Mathematics Department at Streeling University in 12,028 G.E., Seldon broke up an illegal political rally on Streeling's campus, organized by Gambol Deen Namarti, and thus came to the attention of demagogue and political agitator Laskin "Jo-Jo" Joranum, Namarti's leader. Seldon was subsequently ordered by Emperor Cleon I to use psychohistory to alleviate the threat to the Empire's stability represented by Joranum. But Seldon used his intuition instead and realized that he could undermine Joranum by encouraging him to accuse Demerzel of being a robot, and then just allowing Demerzel to respond with laughter, while simultaneously arranging for Sunmaster Fourteen to denounce Joranum as a Mycogenian breakaway. After Demerzel retired from office at the conclusion of the Joranumite Affair, Cleon I appointed Seldon to the post of First Minister. Shortly thereafter, Seldon was the target of an unsuccessful assassination attempt. In 12,038 G.E. Seldon sent Raych to Wye Sector to determine if the increasing number of infrastructure breakdowns on Trantor was the result of a revived Joranumite Conspiracy centered in Wye. But Seldon himself was the target of this Joranumite Conspiracy, and undercover security officer Manella Dubanqua ultimately saved Seldon from being assassinated by a drugged Raych. Seldon subsequently shielded both Manella and himself from any repercussions from Cleon I's assassination—as Cleon I was murdered by the blaster Gleb Andurin had dropped after Manella had shot Andurin—by resigning his post as First Minister shortly after Cleon I was killed. He subsequently returned to Streeling University to lead the Seldon Psychohistory Project. In 12,048 G.E. he was interviewed by General Dugal Tennar, then leader of the military junta that had taken control of the Empire, and he suggested to Tennar that simplifying the tax code would be one way Tennar could increase the Empire's stability—as psychohistory had indicated that over-simplifying the tax code was the means of bringing down the junta (which was inherently unstable) that would entail the least violence. That same year Seldon lost his wife, Dors, when Tamwile Elar deduced that she must be a robot and used the electro-magnetic field from his experimental, intensified Electro-Clarifier to disrupt her circuits fatally. In 12,052 G.E. Seldon accidentally discovered that his granddaughter Wanda had some ability to read and affect minds. In 12,058 he was attacked by eight Trantorian thugs but was saved by a knife-wielding Raych, who told him that many on Trantor blamed Seldon, the messenger, for the now-evident decline of Trantor and the Empire. In his old age Seldon developed a limp caused by sciatica in his right leg, and he was arrested for assault and battery when he struck an attacker with his cane after Wanda had warned him of the impending attack, which she had known about through her mentalic ability; how-

Seldon

ever, he was exonerated and released by a sympathetic magistrate. Soon afterwards Seldon and Stettin Palver were arrested for assault and battery when they defend themselves against an attack by three Trantorian youths, but the changes were dropped when the eye witness testifying against them, Rial Nevas, broke down on the witness stand after being compelled by the combined mentalic powers of Stettin and Wanda to tell the truth. Seldon was thereafter plunged into despair when his foster son Raych was killed by rebels on Santanni and his daughter-in-law Manella and granddaughter Bellis were simultaneously lost in space. However, his spirit was renewed when Wanda and Palver successfully used their combined mentalic abilities to persuade the Galactic Library's Chief Librarian, Tryma Acarnio, to grant research space and privileges to Seldon and the remaining members of his encyclopedia project. When Wanda and Palver then discovered a third mentalic, Bor Alurin, Seldon made the three of them the nucleus of the Second Foundation. Known as "Raven" Seldon for his prediction that Trantor would be destroyed within the three centuries following his lifetime, Seldon also predicted the complete dissolution of the First Galactic Empire. Tried for treason by the Commission of Public Safety in 12,097 G.E. (-2 F.E.) and exiled to Terminus—a planet on which he never actually set foot—Seldon created a series of holographic projections that appeared in the Vault on Terminus at irregular intervals over the next thousand years to help guide the Foundation through the vicissitudes of history. Seldon was found dead in his offices at Streeling University, with his Prime Radiant clutched in his hand, in 12,068 G.E. (-1 F.E.). His body was jettisoned into space [*Prelude to Foundation*; *Forward the Foundation*; *Foundation* Part I, "The Psychohistorians"; *Foundation* Part II, "The Encyclopedists"].

Seldon, Raych—See "Raych."

Seldon, Wanda (12,040–12,133 G.E.)—The beautiful Wanda Seldon was Hari Seldon's granddaughter—the daughter of Seldon's adopted son, Raych, and Raych's wife, Manella Dubanqua. At the age of eight she overheard two men discussing "lemonade death" during the preparations for Seldon's 60th birthday celebration. This was most likely a corruption of the words "Elar-Monay death," a reference to the Electro-Clarifier conceived by Tamwile Elar and designed by Cinda Monay. At the age of twelve she demonstrated the ability to read another's thoughts when she echoed Yogu Amaryl's doubts about the validity of the equations in a specific area of the Prime Radiant. Seldon subsequently had Wanda's genome mapped and analyzed—so that he could attempt to find others with similar genomes whom he could recruit into his failing psychohistory project as potential members of the Second Foundation—but this effort proved to be fruitless. Yet Wanda dedicated herself to sharpening her mentalic skills and resolved to be the nucleus of Seldon's Second Foundation—even to the point of refusing to emigrate to Santanni with her parents and her younger sister Bellis. Wanda's and Stettin Palver's combined mentalic powers later saved Palver and Seldon from being convicted of assault and battery when those powers compelled a perjuring eye witness, Rial Nevas, to tell the truth. Wanda subsequently realized that Palver had the same mentalic powers that she had, and together they used those powers to persuade the Galactic Library's Chief Librarian, Tryma Acarnio, to grant both Seldon and members of his encyclopedia project research space and privileges in the library. She and Palver later discovered another mentalic, Bor Alurin, and together the three of them formed the nucleus of the Second Foundation [*Forward the Foundation*].

Seldon Crisis—A pivotal point in Galactic history during which the choices available to the Foundation narrowed to the single, inevitable path that would lead to the eventual establishment of the Second Galactic Empire, each Seldon Crisis was foreseen by Hari Seldon and resolved by the forces of history. Each Crisis occurred when the Foundation faced either an external threat, internal discord, or both; and each was marked by the appearance Seldon's hologram in the Vault on Terminus. The Seldon Crises are the First Anacreonian Crisis of 49–50 F.E., the Second Anacreonian Crisis of 79 F.E., the Korellian Crisis of 154–58 F.E., the Imperial Crisis of 198–99 F.E., the Mule's Crisis of 297–98 F.E. ... the Crisis of 498 F.E. ... [*Foundation* Part II, "The Encyclopedists"; *Foundation* Part III, "The Mayors"; *Foundation* Part V, "The Merchant Princes"; *Foundation and Empire* Part I, "The General"; *Foundation and Empire* Part II, "The Mule"; *Foundation's Edge*].

Seldon Hall—A colossal mausoleum built around Hari Seldon's Time Vault in the fifth century F.E. [*Foundation's Edge*].

Seldon Plan—Hari Seldon's long-range scheme to use psychohistory to shorten from 30,000 years to 1,000 years the period of anarchy and barbarism that must follow the inevitable collapse of the First Galactic Empire through establishing Encyclopedia Foundation Number One, the seed of the Second Galactic Empire, on Terminus. The ultimate goal of the Seldon Plan was to produce, finally, a human civilization based upon and oriented towards mental science, as represented by the Second Foundation, rather than physical science, as represented by the Foundation—a situation that had a low probability of ever occurring spontaneously [*Foundation* Part III, "The Mayors"; *Second Foundation* Part II, "Search by the Foundation"].

Seldon Project—Hari Seldon's psychohistorical research project, which involved 50 mathematicians and nearly 100,000 support staff and their family members at its height in 12,067 G.E. (-2 F.E.), the Seldon Project had as its goal to minimize the anarchic effects of the decline and fall of the First Galactic Empire, ostensibly, through the preservation of all human knowledge in the proposed Encyclopedia Galactica [*Foundation* Part I, "The Psychohistorians"].

Seldon Psychohistory Project at Streeling University—The official title of the well-funded, government-sponsored psychohistory project during the ten years following Emperor Cleon I's assassination in 12,038 G.E. and Seldon's consequent resignation as First Minister [*Forward the Foundation*].

Semic, Dr. Elvett (301–387 F.E.)—A scrawny professor-emeritus of physics at the University of Terminus and a specialist in intranuclear motions, Dr. Elvett Semic conspired with Dr. Toran Darell, Pelleas Anthor, Jole Tubor, and Homir Munn to uncover the location of the Second Foundation in 376 F.E. He subsequently aided Dr. Darell in perfecting a device that generates Mental Static and thus shields ordinary minds from being controlled by members of the Second Foundation [*Second Foundation* Part II, "Search by the Foundation"].

Senloo—The city in North America from which the Earth missiles carrying the weaponized Common Fever virus were to be launched towards many other planets in 827 G.E. [*Pebble in the Sky*].

Senter, Lee (248–307 F.E.)—A farmer on the grounds of the Imperial Palace and a leader of his farming community, Lee Senter greeted Bayta and Toran Darell, Ebling Mis, and Magnifico Giganticus when they arrive on Trantor in 298 F.E. While he provided the travelers with food during their stay at the University of Trantor, he also reported their arrival to Colonel Han Pritcher, who had previously been converted by the Mule [*Foundation and Empire* Part II, "The Mule"].

Sermak, Sef (40–121 F.E.)—The Mayor of Terminus who redistributed among the citizens of the Foundation all the landed estates of the Four Kingdoms' noble families in the first century F.E., Sef Sermak is most well-known for having previously criticized Terminus Mayor Salvor Hardin's apparent foreign policy of appeasing the Four Kingdom's, for forming the Action Party to oppose this policy, and for calling unsuccessfully for Hardin's impeachment in 79 F.E. [*Foundation* Part III, "The Mayors"; *Foundation* Part V, "The Merchant Princes"].

Settler Worlds—The planets colonized from Earth, in the second wave of Galactic colonization, following the colonization of Baleyworld, the first Settler World, in A.D. 4925 [*Robots and Empire*].

Seven Days Fight—The successful defense of the University of Trantor by its students during Gilmer's 258 F.E. Sack of Trantor [*Foundation and Empire* Part II, "The Mule"].

Shame of the Cities—A book written by Ogrinsky that promoted Medievalism in the early 50th century A.D. [*The Caves of Steel*].

Shandess, Quindor (430–515 F.E.)—Became the twenty-fifth First Speaker of the Second Foundation in 480 F.E. and was succeeded by Stor Gendibal in 499 F.E. At Gendibal's instigation, Shandess became convinced in 498 F.E. that Terminus City Councilman Golan Trevize was the key to the question of whether or not some unknown entity—some organization of Anti-Mules—was manipulating the Seldon Plan to assure its success. As a means of locating the Anti-Mules, Shandess subsequently sent Gendibal into the Galaxy to pursue Trevize [*Foundation's Edge*].

Shane, Justice Harlow (A.D. 1977–2057)—Round-faced Justice Harlow Shane represented the government as judge in a 2034 lawsuit filed by Professor Simon Ninheimer against U.S. Robots and Mechanical Men [*Robot Visions*, "Galley Slave"].

Shekt, Dr. Affret (771–831 G. E.)—Tall, thin, and slightly stooped, Dr. Affret Shekt was Pola Shekt's father and an Earth physicist in the Early Middle Galactic Era who believed that the Earth might not always have been radioactive. Employed at the Institute for Nuclear Research in Chica, he invented the Synapsifier in 825 G.E. Although a lifelong Assimilationist, at the behest of the Society of Ancients he used the Synapsifier on some Earth biologists— which enabled them to weaponized Common Fever—and then, without the permission of the Society of Ancients, he used the Synapsifier on time-traveler Joseph Schwartz, who developed the Mind Touch as a consequence. He was apprehended by Balkis, Secretary to the High Minister of Earth, after he had told Outsider archeologist Dr. Bel Arvardan of Earth's Society of Ancients' plot to use germ warfare against the rest of the Galaxy, and was confined with Pola, Arvardan, and Schwartz. He escaped with Pola, Arvardan, and Schwartz to Fort Dibburn when Schwartz used his Mind Touch to control Balkis' physical movements [*Pebble in the Sky*].

Shekt, Pola (807–889 G.E.)—Attractive, slim, and graceful, Pola Shekt was the brown-haired, dark-eyed daughter of Dr. Affret Shekt who in 827 G.E. was completing her studies at the University of Chica and working part-time as a technician in her father's lab at the Institute for Nuclear Research. She met and fell in love with Outsider archeologist Dr. Bel Arvardan, whom she later married, and she enlisted Arvardan's aid in her attempt to stop Earth's Society of Ancients' plot to use germ warfare to destroy all other human life in the Galaxy. She was subsequently apprehended by Balkis, Secretary to the High Minister of Earth, and was confined with Arvardan, Dr. Shekt, and time-traveler Joseph Schwartz. She escaped with Arvardan, Dr. Shekt, and Schwartz to Fort Dibburn when

Shields

Schwartz used his Mind Touch to control Balkis' physical movements [*Pebble in the Sky*].

Shields—A Foundation innovation of the early second century F.E., shields are miniature, walnut-sized nuclear devices capable of protecting a target as small as a man from a nuclear blaster. Previously, such nuclear shielding machinery had been much larger and had been capable of protecting only much larger targets, such as space ships or cities [*Foundation* Part V, "The Merchant Princes"].

Silver, Vincent (A.D. 2002–2077)—Director of Research at U.S. Robots and Mechanical Men in A.D. 2052 [*I, Robot*, "The Evitable Conflict"].

Simpson (A.D. 4890–4958)—Worked in the New York City Police Department in A.D. 4920 [*The Caves of Steel*].

Sirian Journal of Neurophysiology—The eminent scientific journal in which Dr. Affret Shekt would have preferred to have published his seven or eight papers on the Synapsifier, but he was prevented from doing so by Earth's Society of Ancients [*Pebble in the Sky*].

Sirius Sector—That region of the Galaxy in which Earth is located. Prejudice against Earth was especially intense in the Sirius Sector during the Early Middle Galactic Era [*Pebble in the Sky*].

Siwenna—A Province of the Empire and the capital planet of the Normannic Sector in the Late Galactic Era (10,100–12,100 G.E.), Siwenna retained its nuclear technology well into the second century F.E. and supplied the Korellian Republic with nuclear weaponry in the mid-second-century F.E. After General Bel Riose's failed attempt to conquer the Foundation in 199 F.E., the Province of Siwenna was finally successful in breaking away from the Empire—after five previous, unsuccessful revolts—and became the first Imperial province to go directly from the Empire's political rule to the Foundation's expanding economic sphere of influence. It was conquered by the Mule in 297 F.E. [*Foundation* Part V, "The Merchant Princes"; *Foundation and Empire* Part I, "The General"; *Foundation and Empire* Part II, "The Mule"].

Sixty—Earth's peculiar custom, in the Early Middle Galactic Era, of euthanizing almost all citizens at the age of 60 to make room for the younger generations [*Pebble in the Sky*].

Skeptics—Scorned and discriminated against by their fellow Comporellians, Skeptics are citizens of Comporollon who do not believe that Comporellon was the first world settled by Earth in the second wave of Galactic colonization or that it was once the leading world in the inhabited Galaxy [*Foundation and Earth*].

Skincap—A head covering worn by tribesmen (outsiders) in Mycogen to simulate baldness. Tribesmen in

Mycogen must also wear shields to hide their eyebrows [*Prelude to Foundation*].

Skystrip Two (11,951–12,041 G.E.)—An Elder of the Mycogenian Sacratorium, Skystrip Two warned Hari Seldon and Dors Venabili in 12,020 G.E. that they should vacate the vicinity of the Sacratorium or risk being torn apart by an angry mob of Mycogenians [*Prelude to Foundation*].

Smith, Dr. (A.D. 1904–1976)—Worked at Chicago's Institute for Nuclear Research in A.D. 1949 [*Pebble in the Sky*].

Smitheus—One of the fifty Spacer Worlds [*The Robots of Dawn*].

Smitko, F. (783–827 G.E.)—An Earth bacteriologist who was subjected to Dr. Affret Shekt's Synapsifier. This enabled Smitko to help to weaponize Earth's Common Fever virus, but the effect of the Synapsifier on Smith was ultimately fatal. In his dying moments Smitko told Dr. Shekt of the Society of Ancients' plot to use germ warfare to kill all human life in the Galaxy beyond Earth [*Pebble in the Sky*].

Smoodgie (12,008–12,027 G.E.)—Raych's best friend during his childhood in Trantor's Dahl Sector's Billibotton [*Forward the Foundation*].

Smyrno, Kingdom of—Most well-known as the birthplace of Hober Mallow, the Kingdom of Smyrno was one of the Four Kingdoms in the region of the Periphery near Terminus that had seceded from the First Galactic Empire in the first half of the first century F.E. only to fall under the dominance of the Foundation and its religion of science by century's end. Having just concluded a war with Anacreon, Smyrno, with the Kingdoms of Daribow and Konom, issued an ultimatum in 50 F.E. that prevented the Kingdom of Anacreon from annexing Terminus [*Foundation* Part II, "The Encyclopedists"; *Foundation* Part V, "The Merchant Princes"].

Smythe-Robertson, Harley (A.D. 2145–2224)—Descended from the original founder on his mother's side, Harley Smythe-Robertson was President of U.S. Robots and Mechanical Men in the late 21st and early 22nd centuries A.D. He was pressured by Paul Charney into agreeing to replace robot Andrew Martin's original metal body with a more-humanoid, android body [*Robot Visions*, "The Bicentennial Man"].

Sobhaddartha, Jogoroth (456–529 F.E.)—The customs official who passed Golan Trevize, Janov Pelorat, and their ship, the *Far Star*, through Sayshell planet customs in 498 F.E. [*Foundation's Edge*].

Social Tensions Involved in Space Flight and Their Resolution—A book written by Professor Simon Ninheimer between A.D. 2025 and A.D. 2033 [*Robot Visions*, "Galley Slave"].

Society for Humanity—An offshoot of the anti-robot Fundamentalists, the Society for Humanity was,

Society 162

in the mid–21st century A.D., an organization that was opposed to the Machines managing the world's economy [*I, Robot*, "The Evitable Conflict"].

Society of Ancients—Also known as the Brotherhood, maintained allegiance to Earth's Customs in the early 9th century G.E. They were headquartered at the College of Ancients in Washenn, Earth's capital at that time. In 827 G.E. they almost succeeded in a plot to use germ warfare to wipe out all human life in the Galaxy beyond Earth [*Pebble in the Sky*].

Solar Station #5—In A.D. 2015 Solar Station #5 was a space station orbiting the sun that beamed solar energy to Earth, Mars, and the asteroids [*I, Robot*, "Reason"].

Solaria—A water-world with four heavily-forested continents and a delightful odor, Solaria is 9500 miles in diameter and the outermost of three planets orbiting its white sun. The last of the fifty Spacer Worlds to be settled—from Nexon in the 47th century A.D.—it is the only inhabited planet in its system. A day on Solaria is 28.35 hours long, nearly six hours longer than a day on Aurora. In the early 50th century A.D. Solaria had a constant population of 20,000 humans and 200 million robots and was the Spacer Worlds' foremost manufacturer of specialized robots. It was erroneously thought to be abandoned and uninhabited in A.D. 5121, by which time its population had dwindled to 5,000. By A.D. 5121 the Solarians had independently developed both the humaniform robot and a miniaturized nuclear intensifier, and they were working on developing telepathic positronic brains. Solaria was the second of the Forbidden Worlds visited by Golan Trevize, Janov Pelorat, and Bliss in their 498 F.E. quest for Earth. It had only 1,200 human inhabitants, but hundreds of millions of robots, by the 5th century F.E. [*The Naked Sun*; *Robots and Empire*; *Foundation and Earth*].

Solaria, Gladia—See "Gladia Thool Delmarre Solaria Gremionis."

Solarians—In the 50th century A.D. there was a stable population of 20,000 humans on Solaria. Solarian estates could then be as large as 10,000 square miles, and it was primarily the size of one's estate that determined one's status in Solarian society. By the 5th century F.E. the population of Solaria had shrunk to 1,200. No aspect of sex is ever discussed by Solarians, to whom love and sex are unrelated concepts. "Children," "affection," and "love" were and still are among the most objectionable words in the Solarian vocabulary, as Solarians come into physical contact with one another only in the most extraordinary circumstances, but can visit one another freely via trimensional viewing. Solarians in the 50th century A.D. did not know who their parents were and were raised to maturity on the planet's sole fetal farm. Contemporary Solarians have no gender but, through genetic engineering, have incorporated both masculine and feminine attributes into one hermaphroditic body—so that they will not have to interact with one another to produce offspring. Contemporary Solarians have also developed, again through genetic engineering, transducer-lobes, portions of the brain protruding from the back of the skull that enable them to use energy differentials to do work. This enables them to move objects telekinetically, and all the energy required to run the entire planet and its millions of robots is supplied through transducer-lobes. Solarians strive to achieve total freedom by doing exactly what they please and by allowing other Solarians to do exactly what they please, as well, but to accomplish this they almost never come into physical contact with one another and have strict inhibitions against doing so [*The Naked Sun*; *The Robots of Dawn*; *Foundation and Earth*].

Somnin—An anesthetic that induces sleep when administered in the proper dose [*The Currents of Space*].

Sopellor, Lientenant Evander (473–548 F.E.)—The Terminus guard who escorted Golan Trevize to his home, and placed him under house arrest, after Trevize was questioned by Foundation Security Director Liono Kodell [*Foundation's Edge*].

Soul of Kyrt—A peasant conspiracy on Florina that was easily wiped out in the Early Galactic Era. Valona March's parents were members of the Soul of Kyrt and were taken away by Florinian patrollers in Valona's youth [*The Currents of Space*].

Southerners—Galactic citizens with Negroid features [*Prelude to Foundation*].

Southwark—A city on Rhodia near which Biron Farrill, Artemisia oth Hinriad, and Gillbret oth Hinriad land after stealing Commissioner of the Great Khan of the Tyranni Simok Aratap's ship, the *Remorseless* [*The Stars, Like Dust*].

Spacer Worlds—See "Forbidden Worlds."

Spacers—The long-lived descendants of the colonizers of the first fifty worlds settled from Earth and its initial colonies, with the help of robots, during the first wave of Galactic colonization in the 4th millennium A.D. Spacers were characteristically high-cheekboned and bronze-haired, and they usually exhibited little emotion. They lived in robot-assisted luxury on their underpopulated worlds—which included Aurora, Melpomenia, Solaria, Smitheus, Nexon, Euterpe, Hesperos, and Pallas—in stark contrast to the highly-regulated lives of the robot-hating humans on overpopulated, resource-stretched Earth. Spacers killed their children painlessly if they exhibited any signs of physical or mental defects, and they exercised strict population control. While they could live to be nearly 400 years old because there was no disease on their worlds, Spacers could not mingle with Earthmen because they had no immunity to Earth's diseases. Their longevity was also due, in part, to the fact that they did not indulge in alcoholic beverages, tobacco products, or any artificial stimulants. In A.D. 4895 the Spacers founded Spacetown, on the outskirts of New York City, in the hope that they could modernize Earth and compel it to accept an integrated C/Fe (human/robot) society, a project that failed dismally, because the Spacers wanted to create displaced workers on Earth who might be motivated to colonize more worlds. By the fifth century F.E. all the Spacer worlds except Solaria had become uninhabited because the Spacers' excessive reliance on robots had gradually undermined their will to live. Some Spacer descendants, such as the Mycogenians (descendants of the Aurorans), had by that time reintegrated into Galactic society [*The Caves of Steel; The Robots of Dawn; Robots and Empire; Foundation and Earth*].

Spacetown—Within the city limits of New York City, which it nevertheless abutted at only one entrance, Spacetown was established by the Spacers in A.D. 4895 in the hope that the Spacers in residence could motivate Earthmen to adopt a C/Fe (human/robot) culture and, eventually, to resume the colonization of the Galaxy. Spacetown was dismantled shortly after the conclusion of the Sarton murder case in A.D. 4920 [*The Caves of Steel; The Robots of Dawn*].

Spatio-analyst—A scientist who studies the composition and density of the gasses between the stars, in the near vacuum of space. In the Early Galactic Era nearly a third of all spatio-analysts came from the radioactive planet Earth [*The Currents of Space*].

SPD-13—See "Speedy."

Speakers—Members of the Second Foundation become Speakers, the Second Foundation's highest rank, by contributing some addition to the Seldon Plan as displayed by the Prime Radiant. Twelve Speakers compose the Speakers' Table, which is the Second Foundation's ruling body [*Foundation's Edge*].

Speakers' Table—The policy-making body of the Second Foundation that consists of twelve Speakers, a number established by the first First Speaker, Hari Seldon [*Foundation's Edge*].

Speedy—SPD-13 (known as "Speedy") was a robot that was part of the A.D. 2015 Second Mercury Expedition. Ordered by Michael Donovan to collect selenium from a selenium pool near a dangerous volcanic vent, it merely circled the pool because the Second Law of Robotics (to obey human orders) prompted it to approach the pool while the Third Law of Robotics (self-preservation) prompted it to withdraw. However, Gregory Powell then purposely placed himself in mortal danger, forcing Speedy to obey the First Law of Robotics (not to allow human beings to come to harm) and save him—breaking Speedy out of his useless orbit. Speedy then secured the selenium from another selenium pool [*I, Robot*, "Runaround"].

Speidel, Dr. (A.D. 1972–2051)—A colleague of Professor Simon Ninheimer whose work had been misrepresented in Ninheimer's *Social Tensions Involved in Space Flight and Their Resolution*, which had been proofread by Robot EZ-27, also known as Easy [*Robot Visions*, "Galley Slave"].

Spicer—An Auroran table gadget capable, through adroit manipulation, of producing a dozen different condiments and spices [*The Robots of Dawn*].

Squire of Balle (Early Galactic Era)—Gray, dry, and wrinkled, the Squire of Balle was one of the five Great Squires of Sark in the Early Galactic Era [*The Currents of Space*].

Squire of Bort (Early Galactic Era)—Unkempt and belligerent, the Squire of Bort was one of the five Great Squires of Sark in the Early Galactic Era [*The Currents of Space*].

Squire of Fife (Early Galactic Era)—Stubby-legged, beefy, large-headed, and lipless, the extremely short, olive-skinned Squire of Fife was the wealthiest of the five Great Squires of Sark and controlled one-third of Florina's kyrt trade in the Early Galactic Era. He took command of the Sark Navy and declared himself the head of a united Sark in the mistaken belief that one of the other Great Squires of Sark was a traitor. He was subsequently blackmailed by Trantorian Ambassador to Sark Ludigan Abel—who had obtained a photograph of the Squire of Fife's daughter, Lady Samia of Fife, kissing a Florinian native, Townman Myrlyn Terens, in a groundcar—into participating in a conference on the fate of a missing spatioanalyst, Rik, and on the future of the kyrt trade [*The Currents of Space*].

Squire of Rune (Early Galactic Era)—Bald, pink, and fat, with artificial chrome-steel teeth, the Squire of Rune was one of the five Great Squires of Sark in the Early Galactic Era [*The Currents of Space*].

Squire of Steen (Early Galactic Era)—Powdered and rouged, worn-out, and effeminate, the Squire of Steen was one of the five Great Squires of Sark in the Early Galactic Era. In a panic in believing that the Squire of Fife might think him a traitor and might be planning a coup against the other Great Squires of Sark, the Squire of Steen sought sanctuary in the Trantorian embassy on Sark, where he offered to ally himself with Trantor against the other Squires of Sark [*The Currents of Space*].

Squires—Natives of Sark who constituted the upper class on Florina in the Early Galactic Era. They live in Florina's Upper City, an elevated level of Florina's City that rests on fifty square miles of cementalloy held up by 20,000 steel-girdered pillars. While all Sarkites living in

Florina's Upper City are called Squires by the Florinian natives, on Sark itself only the five rulers of the planet are known as the Great Squires [*The Currents of Space*].

Standard Galactic Ephemeris—A reference book that lists the positions and spectral characteristics of tens of thousands of stars for a given date. It was standard equipment on a spaceship in the Early Galactic Era [*The Stars, Like Dust*].

Stanel VI, Emperor (11,924–12,010 G.E.)—The Galactic Emperor who preceded Cleon I, his son, Stanel VI encouraged the use of the gravitic lift. Eto Demerzel was his unofficial chief of staff. Even though half of the Emperors of the Late Galactic Era (10,100–12,100 G.E.) were assassinated, Stanel VI died in his sleep [*Prelude to Foundation*].

Stanmark—The suburb of Terminus City where Dr. Toran Darell and his daughter Arkady lived at 55 Channel Drive [*Second Foundation* Part II, "Search by the Foundation"].

Stannell II, Emperor (760–777 G.E.)—The mildly insane boy Emperor, Stannell II was assassinated in 777 G.E. after a reign of only two years. He had provoked riots on Earth when he had ordered that the Emperor's insignia be raised in the Council Chamber in Washenn [*Pebble in the Sky*].

Stannell VI, Emperor (25–104 F.E.)—One of the last of the strong Emperors, Stannell VI was notable in that his reign, during the last half of the first century F.E., marked a pause in the Normannic Sector's (and the whole Periphery's) inevitable slide into barbarism and economic recession [*Foundation* Part V, "The Merchant Princes"; *Foundation and Empire* Part I, "The General"].

Starlet—One of General Bel Riose's scout ships, the *Starlet* was captured by Trader Sennett Forell's trade fleet in 198 F.E. Discovery of the *Starlet* alerted the Foundation to the fact that it had drawn the attention of the waning but still supremely powerful Empire [*Foundation and Empire* Part I, "The General"].

Star's End—Located "at the other end of the Galaxy" from Terminus, "Star's End" was Hari Seldon's term for the secret location of the Second Foundation [*Foundation* Part I, "The Psychohistorians"].

Steen—One of the planet Sark's five continents. In the Early Galactic Era it was ruled by the Squire of Steen [*The Currents of Space*].

Stettin, Lord (331–380 F.E.)—Once head of the Kalganian Navy, the tall, capable Lord Stettin became Kalgan's First Citizen (and a Lord of Kalgan) in 376 F.E. through a successful coup d'état against Lord Thallos, his predecessor. Called "Poochie" by his mistress Lady Callia, Stettin was anxious to ally himself with a prominent Foundation family and thus developed sexual designs on fourteen-year-old Arkady Darell, whom he knew to be Bayta

Darell's granddaughter. Believing erroneously, perhaps through Arkady's meddling, that he was destined to found the Second Galactic Empire, Stettin began the Stettinian War with the Foundation in 376 F.E.; he was defeated six months later due to the Foundation's superior morale (which was bolstered by the Second Foundation's machinations) and superior combat strategies [*Second Foundation* Part II, "Search by the Foundation"].

Stettinian War—An armed conflict between Kalgan and the Foundation that began in 376 F.E. when a Foundation cruiser, the *Hober Mallow*, was destroyed by a Kalganian squadron led by the *Fearless*. Lord Stettin instigated the conflict because Lady Callia had told him, perhaps at the suggestion of Arkady Darell, that he was destined to found the Second Galactic Empire. The war ended in 377 F.E. shortly after the Kalganian fleet was soundly defeated at the battle of Quoriston. By the end of the fifth century F.E., this conflict was known as the Kalganian War [*Second Foundation* Part II, "Search by the Foundation"; *Foundation's Edge*].

Streeling University—During the Late Galactic Era (10,100–12,100 G.E.), Streeling University was one of the largest and most prominent of the 100,000 institutions of higher learning on Trantor. Hari Seldon first sought refuge there during The Flight, and Chetter Hummin introduced Seldon to Dors Venabili there in 12,020 G.E. Streeling University became the site of Seldon's Psychohistory Project during the ten years following Emperor Cleon I's assassination in 12,038 G.E. and Seldon's consequent resignation as First Minister. Prior to 12,028 G.E., when he became First Minister, Seldon had been head of Streeling University's Mathematics Department [*Prelude to Foundation*; *Forward the Foundation*].

Struthers, Mr. (A.D. 1949–2021)—The conscientious General Manager who gave the Weston family a tour of U.S. Robots and Mechanical Men in A.D. 1998 [*I, Robot*, "Robbie"].

Sun-and-Spaceship—The emblem of the First Galactic Empire throughout the Galactic era [*Foundation and Empire* Part I, "The General"].

Sunbadgers—A Dahlite term for the sector's local security forces, who wore the Empire's sun-and-spaceship emblem on their uniforms [*Prelude to Foundation*].

Sunmaster Fourteen (11,948–12,041 G.E.)—The tall, old-but-vigorous leader of the Mycogenian Sector of Trantor in 12,020 G.E. and the High Elder of the Mycogenian Sacratorium, Sunmaster Fourteen greeted Hari Seldon and Dors Venabili when they entered Mycogen and also encountered them when they subsequently invaded the sanctity of the Sacratorium's Elders' Aerie. In 12,028 G.E. he ended Laskin "Jo-Jo" Joranum's effectiveness as a politician by denouncing him as a Mycogenian breakaway [*Prelude to Foundation*; *Forward the Foundation*].

Super-Thinker—A calculating machine manufactured by Consolidated Robots, the Super-Thinker irreparably broke down in A.D. 2029 when programmed to develop a space-warp engine that would enable faster-than-light travel [*I, Robot*, "Escape"].

Sutt, Jorane (104–186 F.E.)—Founder of Terminus' Religionist Party in 155 F.E., Jorane Sutt had previously held the Terminus City Council seat formerly occupied by Ankor Jael and had served as Secretary to the Mayor of Terminus prior to the 155 F.E. election of Hober Mallow. Dedicated to the policy of having Terminus dominate neighboring systems through the Foundation's religion of science, Sutt opposed Mallow for trading with the Korellians without insisting that they adopt the Foundation's compulsory religion. Mallow's political enemy, Sutt attempted to ruin Mallow by having him tried for the murder of false Foundation missionary Jord Parma, who was killed by a Korellian mob in 154 F.E. After Mallow's acquittal and subsequent election as Mayor, Sutt was arrested for "endangering the state" because he had tried to embroil the Foundation's religious hierarchy in Terminus' factional politics [*Foundation* Part V, "The Merchant Princes"].

Synapsifier—A device developed by Earth physicist Dr. Affret Shekt in 825 G.E., the Synapsifier improves the learning capacity of the mammalian nervous system by accelerating the speed with which impulses move along the nervous system and within the brain. The synapsifier caused the death of nine out of ten lab rats on which it was tested, but it greatly improved the learning capacity of the one in ten rats to survive. At the behest of Earth's Society of Ancients it was used on a number of Earth biologists, to enable them to weaponize the Common Fever virus, but it was also used against the orders of the Society of Ancients on time-traveler Joseph Schwartz. The Synapsifier gave Schwartz the Mind Touch, which enabled him to sense the proximity of any individual within 100 feet of him, to know the location of any mind he had touched before, to read thoughts, and to kill with his mind. Almost 12,000 years later, Munn Li Compor believed that the Synapsifier had been a device developed on Earth in the early days of the Empire that made people smarter but also shortened their lives [*Pebble in the Sky*; *Foundation's Edge*].

Synnax—The birthplace of Gaal Dornick, Synnax circles a star at the edges of the Blue Drift [*Foundation* Part I, "The Psychohistorians"].

Szegeczowska, Madame (A.D. 1992–2082)—Vice-Co-ordinator of Earth's European Region in A.D. 2052 [*I, Robot*, "The Evitable Conflict"].

Tanto, Marlo (11,986–12,031 G.E.)—Ostensibly a news reporter for the "Trantorian HV News," Marlo

Tanto attempted to interview Hari Seldon and Dors Venabili regarding their altercation with Elgin Marron and his comrades in Billibotton, a violent slum in Trantor's Dahl Sector, but was driven away when Dors announced to the mob around them that Tanto was really an Imperial agent trying to make trouble in Dahl. Davan later informed Seldon and Dors that Tanto actually was an Imperial agent [*Prelude to Foundation*].

Tarki, Lem (44–124 F.E.)—A core founding member of Sef Sermak's Action Party [*Foundation* Part III, "The Mayors"].

Tazenda—Capital planet of the Oligarchy of Tazenda, Tazenda was totally destroyed by the Mule in 303 F.E. because he had believed erroneously that it was the home of the Second Foundation, a belief that the Second Foundation had manipulated the Mule into adopting in having had Bail Channis argue that Tazenda was the home of the Second Foundation because its sun looks like the last star in the bowels of Pellot's Nebula when viewed from Trantor and because of the similarity of its name to "Star's End," the reputed location of the Second Foundation [*Second Foundation* Part I, "Search by the Mule"].

Tazenda, Oligarchy of—A political entity, in the third and fourth centuries F.E., of twenty-seven inhabited planets in the area of the Periphery about 115 degrees off the radian of the Foundation on Terminus and a third of the way toward the Galactic Core, the Oligarchy of Tazenda contained the planets Tazenda and Rossem [*Second Foundation* Part I, "Search by the Mule"].

Tech-men—Active primarily in the second century F.E., tech-men were a hereditary caste of scientists and engineers who managed and operated the Normannic Sector's nuclear facilities during the Early Foundation Era (1–200 F.E.) [*Foundation* Part V, "The Merchant Princes"; *Foundation and Empire* Part I, "The General"].

Temple of Senloo—The five-pointed building that housed the germ-laden missiles that Earth's Society of Ancients had planned to launch against the Galaxy in 827 G.E. The temple was bombed into rubble by Lieutenant Marc Claudy, acting under the influence of time-traveler Joseph Schwartz's Mind Touch, hours before the missiles were to be launched [*Pebble in the Sky*].

Tennar, General Dugal (11,993–12,049 G.E.)—The stocky, mustachioed, ignorant, superstitious, and violent General Dugal Tennar was in 12,048 G.E. the head of the military junta that had seized control of the Empire after Emperor Cleon I's assassination in 12,038 G.E.. He was advised by his lackey Hender Linn to remove Hari Seldon as head of the psychohistory project and to replace him with someone more sympathetic to the ruling junta, and was further advised that Seldon could not be safely removed while Dors Venabili remained alive. He was convinced by Seldon to institute a poll tax, which caused immediate rioting on Trantor and resulted in the removal of the junta from power [*Forward the Foundation*].

Terens, Myrlyn (Early Galactic Era)—The young, pudgy, red-haired Townman in Valona "Lona" March's village on Florina, Myrlyn Terens had been Townman for only one month when missing spatio-analyst Rik was found in an irrigation ditch outside the village. Like all Townmen, he was a native of Florina who had been educated on Sark. He hated the Squires and, while a Florinian civil servant on Sark, had been the mysterious psycho-prober who had inadvertently wiped out all of Rik's memories in trying to use Rik to undermine Sark's monopoly on Florina's kyrt trade. He had then had himself appointed Townman, had planted Rik outside his village, had placed Rik in Lona's care, and had kept close watch over Rik to see if he would regain his memories. Terens became a murderer when he killed the doctor who had discovered that Rik had been the victim of a botched psych-probe. He subsequently allowed Lona to attack and kill a patroller who had tried to stop him and Rik from leaving Florina's Upper City library, killed another patroller to assume his identity, killed Trantorian agent Matt Khorov while disguised as a patroller, killed Squire Alstare Daemone in Florina's Upper City's City Park to assume his identity, and was then captured by Trantorian double agent Markis Genro while Genro's passenger in Daemone's space yacht bound for Sark. On Sark, Genro had Terens disable him with a neuronic whip—to retain his cover as a Sarkite Depsec agent—and had allowed Terens to escape to a waiting ground car that was to take him to the Trantorian Embassy. However, Terens was picked at the space port up by Lady Samia of Fife instead. He succeeded in stealing a kiss from her before they were apprehended by Trantorian agents, but the kiss had been photographed by those agents and was then used by Trantorian Ambassador to Sark Ludigan Abel to blackmail the Squire of Fife into participating in a conference on the fate of Rik and on the future of the kyrt trade. Remanded to the custody of the Interstellar Spatio-analytic Bureau (I.S.B.) for his initial crime of having psycho-probed a spatio-analyst, Terens was allowed to return to Florina and to remain there as the last man on Florina after the planet was evacuated because its sun was in the pre-nova stage [*The Currents of Space*].

Terminus—The resource-poor planet on the Periphery of the Galaxy to which Commission of Public Safety Chief Commissioner Linge Chen exiled Hari Seldon and the staff of the Seldon Project in 12,067 G.E. (-2 F.E.), Terminus was settled by Foundation personnel on March 14, 12,069 G.E. (1 F.E.), and became the capital of the Second

Galactic Empire in 998 F.E. It is located at the extreme edge of the outermost spiral arm of the Galaxy and is a water-planet with one continent and 10,000 habitable islands [*Foundation* Part I, "The Psychohistorians"; *Foundation's Edge*].

Terramin relationship—A mathematical equation developed by Earth sociologists in the 5th millennium A.D. that deals with the differential of inconveniences suffered and privileges granted [*The Naked Sun*].

Thallos, Lord (304–376 F.E.)—A Lord of Kalgan and for a time the First Citizen of Kalgan, Lord Thallos was deposed by Lord Stettin in 376 F.E. [*Second Foundation* Part II, "Search by the Foundation"].

Thalus, Sergeant Emmer (11,988–10,020 G.E.)—A tall, muscular, blond, mustachioed member of Wye Sector's security forces and a personal aide to Rashelle, Sergeant Emmer Thalus transported Hari Seldon, Dors Venabili, and Raych from Trantor's Dahl Sector to Wye via airjet in 12,020 G.E. He was then killed by Rashelle, with his own blaster, for refusing to execute Seldon, whom he had previously sworn to protect [*Prelude to Foundation*].

Thoobing, Littoral (444–522 F.E.)—The tall and stout Foundation Ambassador to Sayshell from 491 to 512 F.E., Littoral Thoobing requested in 498 F.E. that the five Foundation warships dispatched to back up Golan Trevize leave the Sayshell Sector and return to Terminus [*Foundation's Edge*].

Thool, Dr. Altim (A.D. 4598–4933)—Gladia Delmarre's father, Dr. Altim Thool was the old Solarian doctor who had trimensionally viewed murder victim Rikaine Delmarre's body and had subsequently treated Gladia for shock in person. He was also the doctor who had examined Solarian Head of Security Hanis Gruer, via trimensional viewing, after Gruer had been poisoned [*The Naked Sun*].

Thornbowe, Elizabeth (A.D. 4851–4917)—An old maid and a Medievalist who had lived in New York City in the early 50th century A.D., Elizabeth Thornbowe was Jessie Baley's co-worker [*The Caves of Steel*].

Three Laws of Robotics—The neuronic pathways in the positronic brains of all robots produced by U.S. Robots and Mechanical Men were imprinted with the Three Laws of Robotics: I. a robot may not injure a human being, or, through inaction, allow a human being to come to harm; II. A robot must obey the orders given it by human beings except where such orders would conflict with the First Law; and III. A robot must protect its own existence as long as such protection does not conflict with the First or Second Law [*I, Robot*, "Runaround"; *Robot Visions*, "Galley Slave"; *The Caves of Steel*; *The Naked Sun*; *The Robots of Dawn*; *Prelude to Foundation*; *Foundation's Edge*; *Foundation and Earth*].

Three Mile Island—The site of a

Time Vault

20th century A.D. nuclear catastrophe, in A.D. 5121 Three Mile Island was the secret base from which Dr. Kelden Amadiro and Dr. Levular Mandamus activated the nuclear intensifier that, over the course of the next 150 years, made the Earth uninhabitably radioactive [*Robots and Empire*].

Time Vault—See "Vault."

Tingle Field—A security system on Aurora in the 50th century A.D. that produced a sensation of pain, by stimulating nerve endings, in any unprotected individual who walked through the area protected by the field [*The Robots of Dawn*].

Tinter, Lieutenant (130–192 F.E.)—An officer serving aboard Hober Mallow's ship, the *Far Star*, during the Korellian Crisis of 154–158 F.E. [*Foundation* Part V, "The Merchant Princes"].

Tip (Early Galactic Era)—A Trantorian agent working as a laborer at the Sark space port in the Early Galactic Era [*The Currents of Space*].

Tippellum, Junior Officer (352–416 F.E.)—Took Preem Pavler prisoner when Pavler went from Trantor to Terminus in 377 F.E. to broker a deal to supply Terminus with food during the Stettinian War [*Second Foundation* Part II, "Search by the Foundation"].

Tireless—An experimental Tyrannian ship, lost in space in the Early Galactic Era, that may have been captured by rebels in the Nebular Regions [*The Stars, Like Dust*].

Tisalver, Casilia (11,987–12,041 G.E.)—Jirad Tisalver's short, plump, domineering wife, Casilia Tisalver was a middle-class resident of Trantor's Dahl Sector who harbored a deep-seated prejudice against Dahl's heatsink workers and against any resident of Billibotton, a violent slum in Dahl. While renting a room in her home to Hari Seldon and Dors Venabili, she contacted Dahl security forces to have Seldon and Dors arrested for attempting to incite a riot due to their association with heatseek worker Hugo Amaryl and Billibottonian Raych [*Prelude to Foundation*].

Tisalver, Jirad (11,985–12,061 G.E.)—A short, handsome citizen of Trantor's Dahl Sector, Jirad Tisalver was the hen-pecked head of the family from whom Hari Seldon and Dors Venabili rent a room while in Dahl. He was a programmer for a local holovision station, a more upscale occupation that that of the average Dahlite [*Prelude to Foundation*].

Tithonus—The larger of Aurora's two satellites [*The Robots of Dawn*].

Tithonus II—The smaller of Aurora's two satellites [*The Robots of Dawn*].

Tobin, Jack (A.D. 4883–4939)—Worked in the New York City Police Department in A.D. 4920 [*The Caves of Steel*].

Townman—A native of Florina who had been educated on Sark and who was the native governor of his

Florinian village. Townmen maintained order on Florina and had special privileges. There were about 100,000 Townmen among the Florinian population of 500 million in the Early Galactic Era. Those Florinians educated on Sark who did not become Townmen became civil servants on Sark and on Florina. Neither Townmen nor Florinian civil servants were permitted to breed; this had the effect of withdrawing the most intelligent genes from the Florinian gene pool. While they were celebrate in theory, Townmen often evaded this restriction [*The Currents of Space*].

Traders—Active primarily between 50 F.E. and 300 F.E., the Traders were an unregulated group of romantic, pioneering, space-faring businessmen specializing in the Foundation's nuclear gadgetry who in the first and second centuries F.E. solidified the Foundation's spiritual and economic domination of the Galactic Periphery in advance of the political hegemony later exercised by the Foundation. Throughout the third century F.E., the Traders became more and more estranged from the Mayors of Terminus and the Foundation's increasingly despotic central government. Disunited and hunted by the Foundation at that century's end, they formed the Independent Trading Worlds and in 297 F.E. organized to revolt against the Foundation but instead fought with the Foundation against the greater threat posed by the Mule. Many fanciful tales of the Traders' exploits survive to this day [*Foundation* Part IV, "The Traders"; *Foundation* Part V, "The Merchant Princes"; *Foundation and Empire* Part II, "The Mule"].

Traditionalists—On Solaria in the 50th century A.D., traditionalists believed in being good Solarians—in having no physical contact with anyone except their assigned spouse, in communicating with one another only via trimensional viewing, and in maintaining their planetary population at 20,000 humans. At this time nearly all Solarians were traditionalists [*The Naked Sun*].

Transcriber—A Foundation device, popular in the late fourth century F.E., that reproduced the spoken word either as typescript or script [*Second Foundation* Part II, "Search by the Foundation"].

Transducer-lobes—Those portions of the brain in mature Solarians that enable them to harness the unevenly-distributed energy of their world to do work. Solarians developed transducer-lobes through genetic engineering prior to the Foundation era [*Foundation and Earth*].

Trans-Nebular Region—An area of space behind the Horsehead Nebula (from the perspective of Earth) that contains hundreds of oxygen-water planets, including Rhodia, Tyrann, and Nephelos [*The Stars, Like Dust*].

Trantor—Capital planet of the First Galactic Empire from 1 G.E. to 258 F.E., Trantor orbits a white star near

Trantor

the Galactic Center and had a population of 45 billion at the height of its power and influence in 11,995 G.E. The planet's population had declined to 40 billion by 12,020 G.E., during the reign of Cleon I. Dedicated entirely to bureaucratic administration and divided into over 800 administrative sectors, Trantor was at that time a single, planet-spanning city completely covered with metal (except for the 100 square miles of natural landscape surrounding the Emperor's palace) and inhabited to the depth of a mile below ground level. Trantor's administrative sectors included the Imperial Sector, Streeling Sector, Wye Sector, Hestelonia Sector, Ziggoreth Sector, North Damiano Sector, Mycogen Sector, Jennat Sector, Dahl Sector, Anemoria Sector, Millimaru Sector, Mandanov Sector, and Ery Sector. Trantor was sacked by the warlord Gilmer in 258 F.E., when the seat of the Imperial government was relocated to Neotrantor, and its population then declined to only 100 million by the century's end. Arkady Darell was born on Trantor, near the Imperial Library, and returned there for several months with Preem Palver late in 376 F.E. By the fifth century F.E. Trantor was called "Hame"—"home" in the local dialect—by its indigenous inhabitants. It is the location of the Second Foundation [*The Currents of Space*; *Pebble in the Sky*; *Prelude to Foundation*; *Forward the Foundation*; *Foundation* Part I, "The Psychohistorians"; *Foundation and Empire* Part I, "The General"; *Foundation and Empire* Part II, "The Mule"; *Second Foundation* Part II, "Search by the Foundation"; *Foundation's Edge*].

Trantor, University of—Located on Trantor within the 100 square miles of natural landscape also occupied by the Imperial Palace, The University of Trantor was the site of Hari Seldon's psychohistory project prior to the project's exile to Terminus in 12,069 G.E. (1 F.E.). It was successfully defended by its students during the Great Sack of Trantor in 258 F.E. The University of Trantor was officially renamed Galactic University in the fifth century F.E. [*Foundation* Part I, "The Psychohistorians"; *Foundation and Empire* Part II, "The Mule"; *Foundation's Edge*].

Trantorian Confederation—A stage in the development of the First Galactic Empire. The five-world Trantorian Republic evolved into the Trantorian Confederation, which became the Trantorian Empire, which became the First Galactic Empire [*The Currents of Space*].

Trantorian Empire—Precursor to the First Galactic Empire, the Trantorian Empire controlled half the Galaxy, a million worlds, in the Early Galactic Era. It had evolved over a period of five hundred years from the Trantorian Confederation, which had previously evolved from the Trantorian Republic [*The Currents of Space*].

Trantorian Republic—Contained only five worlds, but it was the seed of the First Galactic Empire [*The Currents of Space*].

Trevize, Golan (466–556 F.E.)—A tall, dark-haired, handsome, brash womanizer, a former lieutenant in the Foundation Navy, and a man with unusually keen intuition, Golan Trevize was a Terminus City Councilman who believed in 498 F.E. that the Seldon Plan was a sham because the Seldon hologram's description of contemporary events was far too accurate, given that the Plan had been substantially derailed by the Mule two centuries earlier. He believed that the Seldon hologram's uncanny accuracy demonstrated that the Second Foundation still existed and had been working for the previous 200 years to return the Galaxy to the path of the Plan. Terminus Mayor Harla Branno accused Trevize of treason for voicing these beliefs and then charged him with the task of determining if the Second Foundation still existed and, if so, of discovering where it was located. As a cover for this mission, Branno ordered Trevize to pretend to be searching for the planet on which humanity had originated, Earth, in the company of Professor Janov Pelorat. After meeting him on Sayshell, Trevize jumped to the correct conclusion that Munn Li Compor—a former friend who had betrayed Trevize to, and was tailing him for, Branno—was a Second Foundation agent. Compor had been the first to notice, as a fellow student, that Trevize had the ability to arrive at correct conclusions from insufficient data. Gaia subsequently determined that Trevize had the gift of knowing the right thing to do—and thus was the human who must choose the direction in which the Galaxy must go: a militaristic, Foundation-dominated Second Empire; a paternalistic, Second-Foundation-dominated Second Empire; or Galaxia, a participatory group consciousness that would encompass the entire Galaxy. Trevize chose Galaxia. He subsequently deduced that Bliss was a humaniform robot present on Gaia to assure that the Gaians followed their version of the Three Laws of Robotics. When Gaian elder Dom told him that the Gaians were not responsible for the eradication of all references to Earth from the Foundation's data banks and from the Galactic Library, Trevize determined that he must continue to seek Earth to discover why it was so important that it must be hidden and to discover who was hiding it. He also believed that finding Earth would somehow reveal to him why he had chosen Galaxia as humanity's future. With Pelorat and Bliss he then traveled to Comporellon—where he was maneuvered into sexually servicing Comporellian Minister of Transportation Mitza Lizalor, in part because Lizalor's inhibitions had been weakened by Bliss, to secure the release of his ship, the *Far Star*, from Comporellian custody. He subsequently traveled with Pelorat and Bliss to Aurora, Solaria (where they picked up Fallom, a Solarian child), Melpomenia, Alpha, and the Moon. His sexual dalliance with Hiroko on Alpha, which infected him with an unactivated fatal virus, was part of what prompted Hiroko to warn him, Pelorat, and Bliss that they would all be killed if they did not leave Alpha. On the Moon Travize realized that he had chosen Galaxia as humanity's future because that choice had been the only way to protect humanity from the possibility of some future invasion by beings from another galaxy [*Foundation's Edge*; *Foundation and Earth*].

Tribesman—A Mycogenian term for anyone who is not a Mycogenian. Tribesmen must wear kirtles, skincaps, and eyebrow shields while in Trantor's Mycogen Sector so as not to attract undue attention [*Prelude to Foundation*].

Trigellian Insurrection—An unsuccessful revolt against the Galactic Empire that occurred in the Late Galactic Era [*Foundation's Edge*].

Trimensic personification—A variation on trimensional viewing used in the Early Galactic Era. See "Trimensional viewing" [*The Currents of Space*].

Trimensic viewing—The imperfect transmission to a distant receiver of a three-dimensional view of a human being or object, trimensic viewing was a mode of communication used on Earth and on some Spacer worlds in the 50th century A.D. See "Trimensional viewing" [*The Caves of Steel*].

Trimensional viewing—Perfected on Solaria in the 50th century A.D., trimensional viewing was an improvement on trimensic viewing in that the image quality was enhanced to the point that seeing someone via trimensional viewing was indistinguishable from being there. See "Trimensic viewing" [*The Naked Sun*].

Tropics Region—One of the four political sub-units of Earth in the mid–21st century A.D. With its capital in Capital City, Nigeria, it had a population of 500 million and an area of 22 million square miles. It consisted of Africa south of the Atlas Mountains, most of South America (except for Argentina, Chile, and Uruguay), Mexico, Central America, Arabia, and Iran [*I, Robot*, "The Evitable Conflict"].

Turbor, Jole (334–413 F.E.)—A bulky visicastor who had publically denounced the Foundation's faith in the beneficence of the Second Foundation, Jole Turbor conspired with Dr. Toran Darell, Pelleas Anthor, Dr. Elvett Semic, and Homir Munn to uncover the location of the Second Foundation in 376 F.E. A war correspondent during the Stettinian War, Turbor interviewed Preem Pavler after Pavler was captured during the battle of Quoriston, vouched for Pavler's identity, and recommended Pavler's release [*Second Foundation* Part II, "Search by the Foundation"].

Twer, Jaim (104–183 F.E.)—Ostensibly a trader turned politician and one of the first Outlanders to receive a lay education from the Foundation, Jaim Twer was really a political ally of Jorane Sutt's who, as a spy for Sutt, accompanied Master Trader Hober Mallow on his 154 F.E.

information-gathering mission to the Korellian Republic and there witnessed Mallow's abandonment of false Foundation missionary Jord Parma to the Korellian mob [*Foundation* Part V, "The Merchant Princes"].

Twisting—A form of martial arts widely practiced on Helicon. Both Hari Seldon and Stettin Palver were Twisters [*Forward the Foundation*].

Tyrann—The 1099th world settled by humanity, according to the Early Galactic Era's *Galactic Almanac*, Tyrann established a small empire by conquering Rhodia, Nephelos, and nearly fifty other worlds in the Nebular and Trans-Nebular Regions in the Early Galactic Era [*The Stars, Like Dust*].

Tyranni—Ruled a small empire of fifty worlds in the Nebular and Trans-Nebular Regions, including Rhodia and Nephelos, in the Early Galactic Era [*The Stars, Like Dust*].

Tyrannian Empire—A group of fifty world in the Nebular and Trans-Nebular Regions, formerly the Nebular Kingdoms, that were conquered by and paid tribute to Tyrann in the Early Galactic Era [*The Stars, Like Dust*].

Underground—See "Democratic Underground."

Unimara—The one-man sports-cruiser starship in which Homir Munn and Arkady Darell, his stowaway, travel from Terminus to Kalgan in 376 F.E. [*Second Foundation* Part II, "Search by the Foundation"].

Union of Worlds—The vast volume of space—truly imperial in scope—ruled by the Mule following the fall of the Foundation in 298 F.E. and until the Mule's death in 308 F.E. It enjoyed a period of peace and prosperity during the Mule's ten-year reign as First Citizen of the Union [*Second Foundation* Part I, "Search by the Mule"].

University of Arcturus—The institution of higher learning from which Bel Arvardan graduated, at the age of 23, as a Senior Archeologist [*Pebble in the Sky*].

Upper Buildings—Such as Sarkite homes, libraries, and sports arenas, were buildings in Florina's City that existed entirely in the Upper City. They were Sark-like in their architecture and were decorated with intricate, multi-colored mosaic tiles [*The Currents of Space*].

Upper City—An elevated level, thirty feet above the Lower City, that was built on fifty square miles of cementalloy supported by 20,000 steel-girdered pillars. It was the home of the Squires, the upper class of Florina, who were primarily natives of Sark [*The Currents of Space*].

Uppermen—Florinian natives who live in the Lower City but work in the Upper City. They are disdainful of other Florinian natives and are, in turn, hated by them [*The Currents of Space*].

Upperside—The upper surface of the domes of Trantor during the Late Galactic Era (10,100–12,100

G.E.), Upperside had accumulations of soil in which plants and trees grew. Hari Seldon was stranded on Upperside, and nearly died of exposure there, in 12,020 G.E. [*Prelude to Foundation*].

U.S. Robots and Mechanical Men, Inc.—Incorporated in 1982 by Lawrence Robertson, the company's first president. It was the world's foremost manufacturer of robots in the 21st century A.D. and the only robot manufacturer to use positronic brains. Its principal completion was Consolidated Robots. Lawrence Robertson was succeeded as president of the company by his son [*I, Robot*, "Introduction"; *I, Robot*, "Escape"; *Robot Visions*, "Galley Slave"; *Robot Visions*, "Lenny"; *Robot Visions*, "Feminine Intuition"; *Robot Visions*, "The Bicentennial Man"].

Vault—Also known as the Time Vault, is the secured location on Terminus where the hologram of the deceased Hari Seldon appeared at widely scattered intervals throughout the Foundation Era to comment on those contemporary political and social crises impacting the Foundation that he had foreseen through psychohistory. Seldon's hologram appeared in the Vault at noon on the anniversary of Terminus' settlement, March 14, in 50 F.E., 80 F.E., 158 F.E., 199 F.E., 298 F.E. ... 498 F.E. ... The Vault was surrounded by the colossal Seldon Hall in the fifth century F.E. [*Foundation* Part II, "The Encyclopedists"; *Foundation* Part III, "The Mayors"; *Foundation and Empire* Part II, "The Mule"; *Foundation's Edge*].

Venabili, Dors (11,990–12,048 G.E.)—A native of Cinna and a historian at Trantor's Streeling University specializing in Royal Trantor, Dors Venabili was introduced to and charged with protecting Hari Seldon by Chetter Hummin at Streeling University in 12,020 G.E. She saved Seldon from dying of exposure on Streeling's Upperside and subsequently took him to Trantor's Mycogen Sector and, with Hummin, to Dahl Sector. With Seldon's assistance, she saved herself and Seldon from being attacked by Elgin Marron and nine of his comrades in Billibotton, a violent slum in Dahl, and from being arrested by Dahlite security officers Lanel Russ and Gebore Astinwald for trying to incite a mob to riot, for brawling, and for carrying knives without a permit. With Seldon and Billibottonian Raych, she was then transported from Dahl to Wye Sector by Rashelle's personal aide Sergeant Emmer Thalus and subsequently, with Raych's assistance, prevented Rashelle from killing Seldon in Wye. After having deduced that Hummin was a humaniform robot, Seldon likewise deduced that Dors—who grew no older with the passage of time—was a humaniform robot as well, but this did not prevent him from falling in love with her. She saved Seldon from an assassination attempt during his first few years as First Minister and was known as "the Tiger Woman" due to unbelievable tales of her strength and speed. She resented and at first disliked Manella Dubanqua because Manella had usurped Dors' role in having saved Seldon's (and Raych's) life on the day of Emperor Cleon I's assassination. Ten years later, while Seldon was being interviewed by General Dugal Tennar, Dors muscled her way to Tennar's lackey Colonel Hender Linn to warn him to have no harm befall Seldon. She suspected that the use of the Electro-Clarifier was having a debilitating effect on Seldon and on his associate Yugo Amaryl, but the Electro-Clarifier's electromagnetic field is harmful only to robots. Dors' circuits were fatally disrupted by Tamwile Elar's experimental, intensified Electro-Clarifier as Elar revealed to her his plot to destroy her with the device as a prelude to wresting control of the psychohistory project from Seldon and Amaryl. However, Dors killed Elar before the Electro-Clarifier overcame her, and shortly thereafter she died in Seldon's arms [*Prelude to Foundation*; *Forward the Foundation*].

Verisof, Poly (26–106 F.E.)—Terminus' ambassador to Anacreon from 66 to 80 F.E. and the high priest in the Foundation's religion of science on Anacreon, Poly Verisof led the mob of Anacreonian citizens to the palace during Leopold I's coronation in 79 F.E. to demand that Anacreon cease its scarcely begun war against the Foundation [*Foundation* Part III, "The Mayors"].

Villafranca, Francisco (2007–2063)—An engineer and a member of the Society for Humanity, Francisco Villafranca was falsely accused by the Tropic Region's Machine of having given the Machine inaccurate data in A.D. 2052 [*I, Robot*, "The Evitable Conflict"].

Visi-Sonor—Also "visisonor," is an ancient instrument invented by Gillbret oth Hinriad of Rhodia in the Early Galactic Era that manipulates both sound and—by directly stimulating the optic centers of the brain—light. A good Visi-Sonor performer must possess a free-wheeling mentality. Gillbret used his experimental visisonor to distract Biron Farrill's guards, and thus to effect Biron's escape, when Biron was arrested on Rhodia by the Tyranni for treason. The Visi-Sonor also allowed the Mule to focus and amplify his emotion-affecting mutant powers, and he used the instrument both to demoralize the populations of Terminus and Haven II and to kill crown prince Dagobert X on Neotrantor in 298 F.E. [*The Stars, Like Dust*; *Foundation and Empire* Part II, "The Mule"].

Vrank, Lieutenant (173–218 F.E.)—One of General Bel Riose's subordinates during Riose's 198–99 F.E. campaign against the Foundation [*Foundation and Empire* Part I, "The General"].

Vrasayana, Rama (1997–2054 F.E.)—A member of the Society for Humanity, Rama Vrasayana was a citizen of Earth's Eastern Region whose iodine plant went bankrupt

Walensky

in A.D. 2052 due to the management of the region's economy by its Machine [*I, Robot*, "The Evitable Conflict"].

Walensky (A.D. 1987–2053)—A cigar-smoking electrician working at Hyper Base in A.D. 2029 [*I, Robot*, "Little Lost Robot"].

Walto, Dokor (29–105 F.E.)—A core founding member of Sef Sermak's Action Party [*Foundation* Part III, "The Mayors"].

Wanda—A sunless planet in the Periphery, Wanda was General Bel Riose's temporary Imperial headquarters during his unsuccessful 198–99 F.E. campaign against the Foundation [*Foundation and Empire* Part I, "The General"].

War Hawks—Also known as Earth Supremacists, were citizens of the Settler Worlds who believed in the early 52nd century A.D. that Earth should be the leading world of the Galaxy [*Robots and Empire*].

Washenn—The capital of Earth in the 9th century G.E. [*Pebble in the Sky*].

Wellis, Lieutenant Alban (11,090–12,052 G.E.)—An officer of the Emperor's Guard who brought Hari Seldon to the Imperial Palace to see Emperor Cleon I in 12,020 G.E. [*Prelude to Foundation*].

Wencory—The homeworld of Las Zenow, a friend of Hari Seldon's and the Chief Librarian of the Galactic Library in the mid–121st century G.E. [*Forward the Foundation*].

Westerners—Galactic citizens with Caucasian features [*Prelude to Foundation*].

Weston, George (A.D. 1964–2042)—Gloria Weston's father and Grace Weston's husband, George Weston was forced by Grace to return Gloria's nursemaid robot Robbie to U.S. Robots and Mechanical Men in A.D. 1998. He subsequently set up a reunion between Gloria and Robbie to occur during a family tour of the U.S. Robots facility, and during the tour Robbie saved Gloria from being run over by a tractor [*I, Robot*, "Robbie"].

Weston, Gloria (A.D. 1990–2072)—Grace and George Weston's daughter, Gloria loved her robot nursemaid Robbie and was brokenhearted when her mother forced her father to return Robbie to U.S. Robots and Mechanical Men in A.D. 1998. Subsequently, she was taken on a tour of U.S. Robots, ostensibly to convince her that robots are merely machines, and found Robbie there during the tour, a reunion planned by her father. Robbie then saved Gloria from being run over by a tractor and was welcomed back into the Weston family [*I, Robot*, "Robbie"].

Weston, Grace (A.D. 1968–2050)—Gloria Weston's mother and George Weston's wife, Grace Weston was fearful that Gloria's nursemaid robot Robbie would malfunction and go berserk, worried that Gloria was so involved with Robbie that she would not play with other children, and concerned that her neighbors were anti-robot. For these reasons she forced George to return Robbie to U.S. Robots and Mechanical Men in A.D. 1998. However, she subsequently relented and allowed Robbie to return to the family after Robbie saved Gloria from being run over by a tractor during a family tour of the U.S. Robots facility [*I, Robot*, "Robbie"].

Wienis—A derelict, 300-year-old Imperial cruiser repaired by the Foundation and given to the Anacreonian navy in 79 F.E., the *Wienis* was the flagship of the Anacreonian fleet, under the command of Admiral Lefkin, when, during Anacreon's attempted invasion of Terminus that same year, it was cursed by Foundation high priest Theo Aporat and deprived of power through the use of a hyperwave relay that had been installed while it was being repaired [*Foundation* Part III, "The Mayors"].

Wienis, Prince Regent (19–79 F.E.)—King Leopold I of Anacreon's foolishly overconfident uncle, and the power behind the throne, Prince Regent Wienis committed suicide when the Kingdom of Anacreon's 79 F.E. invasion of Terminus, which he had instigated, failed. Wienis was also probably responsible for the untimely death of his brother, who had preceded Leopold I as King of Anacreon [*Foundation* Part III, "The Mayors"].

Wiscard, Viceroy (97–158 F.E.)—Assassinated by a member of his own personal guard, Ducem Barr, in 158 F.E., Viceroy Wiscard was a powerful ruler of the Normannic Sector who attempted an unsuccessful coup against the Emperor but was betrayed by his own people [*Foundation* Part V, "The Merchant Princes"; *Foundation and Empire* Part I, "The General"].

Wotex—The planet that Valona March and Rik, disguised as Hansa and Gareth Barne, pretended to be from when they escaped from Florina to Sark as stowaways in Lady Samia of Fife's spaceship [*The Currents of Space*].

Wrijt (Early Galactic Era)—The author of *Treatise on Spatio-analytic Instrumentation* [*The Currents of Space*].

Wye Sector—A large, populous, particularly self-sufficient sector of Trantor near the planet's south pole, Wye wielded political power in the Late Galactic Era (10,100–12,100 G.E.) because it was the sector through which Trantor radiated 90 percent of its excess heat into space. Wye had at one time been ruled by a single dynasty of Mayors for 3,000 years (9,000–12,020 G.E.), two 12th millennium G.E. Emperors and an Empress were from the House of Wye, and Wye's rulers had ever since aspired to re-occupy the Imperial throne. Wye was the strongest and most stable of Trantor's 800 sectors in the last centuries of the Galactic Empire, but it was occupied by Imperial forces in 12,020 G.E. to forestall a coup attempt by Rashelle, daughter of Mayor Mannix IV, who had wanted to establish herself as Empress of Trantor and its surrounding province. In that same year Hari Seldon, Dors Venabili, and Raych were transported from Trantor's Dahl Sector to Wye by Rashelle's personal aide Sergeant Emmer Thalus. Seldon narrowly escaped being executed by Thalus and murdered by Rashelle while in Wye. In 12,038 G.E. the Joranumite Conspiracy, centered in Wye, attempted to destabilize Trantor by sabotaging its infrastructure and, later, plotted the assassination of First Minister Seldon and his foster son Raych [*Prelude to Foundation*; *Forward the Foundation*].

Yariff, Humbal (12th m. G.E.)—A Livian historian interested in the Origin Question, Humbal Yariff hypothesized that the planet of origin would be located in the center of the region of the Galaxy containing the oldest inhabited worlds. This hypothesis was unprovable due to inaccurate record keeping, however, and Yariff's professional reputation was destroyed for having proposed it [*Foundation and Earth*].

Yume, Commander (148–207 F.E.)—One of General Bel Riose's subordinates during Riose's 198–99 F.E. campaign against the Foundation [*Foundation and Empire* Part I, "The General"].

Zealots—A political faction on Earth in the Early and Early Middle Galactic Eras who were extremely nationalistic and who believed that Earth had once ruled the Galaxy and should rule it again in the future. The Zealots ruled Earth in 827 G.E. [*Pebble in the Sky*].

Zenow, Las (12,006–12,098 G.E.)—The bearded, highly-dignified Chief Librarian of the Galactic Library in the mid 121st century G.E., Las Zenow was a friend of Hari Seldon's and located the uninhabited world, Terminus, that would be the site of Seldon's encyclopedia project. He was a native of the planet Wencory [*Forward the Foundation*].

Zeroth Law of Robotics—Conceived by humaniform robot R. Daneel Olivaw in A.D. 5121, the Zeroth Law of Robotics mandates that "A robot may not injure humanity or, through inaction, allow humanity to come to harm." However, Daneel and fellow robot R. Giskard Reventlov found it difficult to implement this Law because humanity is an abstraction and not a concrete object. Daneel deduced the Zeroth Law as a consequence of his deathbed conversation with plainclothes Earth homicide detective Elijah Baley on Baleyworld in A.D. 4957. He first articulated it to Dr. Vasilia Aliena on Aurora [*Robots and Empire*; *Prelude to Foundation*; *Foundation and Earth*].

Zoberlow Family—Occupied the estate on Solaria in the early 52nd century A.D. that had belonged to Gladia and Rikaine Delmarre in the early 50th century A.D. [*Robots and Empire*].

Zoraner—The planet to which Dr.

Toran Darell suggested in 377 F.E. that the fifty members of the Second Foundation on Terminus be exiled [*Second Foundation* Part II, "Search by the Foundation"].

Zymoveal—A synthetic foodstuff eaten in New York City in the early 50th century A.D. [*The Caves of Steel*].

Index

Asimov, Isaac 1, 3–4, 6–7, 9–10, 12–13, 24–25, 27–30

Baley novels 5, 7; *see also The Caves of Steel*; *The Naked Sun*; *The Robots of Dawn*
"The Bicentennial Man" (Asimov) 1–2, 55, 67, 114–15, 118–19, 123, 161, 178

The Caves of Steel (Asimov) 2, 4–5, 8, 34, 41–47, 50, 54, 56–57, 62–64, 71–73, 75, 77, 79–80, 86–87, 91–92, 108, 116, 119–20, 122, 126, 129–30, 132–33, 135, 137, 139, 147–51, 159–60, 164, 171–72, 176, 183
"Catch That Rabbit" (Asimov) 66, 69–70, 136–37, 147–48
Chaos theory 1, 6–7, 9–14, 16, 24–25, 27, 29–30
The Currents of Space (Asimov) 2, 4–5, 8, 31, 46, 48, 50, 53, 56, 58–60, 66, 68, 70–76, 81–82, 86, 91, 93, 98, 102–104, 106, 108, 110–11, 114–15, 118, 127–28, 135, 139, 141, 143, 145, 149–51, 163–66, 170, 172–74, 176–77, 181

Empire novels 1–2, 4–5, 7, 24; *see also The Currents of Space*; *The Stars, Like Dust*, *Pebble in the Sky*
The Encyclopedia Galactica 2, 9, 25, 75
"Escape" (Asimov) 49–50, 52–53, 59–60, 69–70, 83, 100, 111, 113, 136–37, 147, 168, 178
"Evidence" (Asimov) 52–53, 83, 93, 98, 104–5, 111–13, 140, 147–48
"The Evitable Conflict" (Asimov) 52–53, 59, 73, 77, 83, 98, 115, 129–30, 160–62, 168, 176, 179–80

"Feminine Intuition" (Asimov) 1, 25, 27, 49, 52–53, 103–4, 117, 147, 178
Forward the Foundation (Asimov) 2, 4–6, 8, 18, 21–24, 31–32, 34, 37–38, 47, 51, 55, 57–58, 61, 67–68, 70–71, 73–75, 87, 90, 92–93, 105–7, 110, 113–16, 123, 125, 127–31, 133, 138, 140, 143–44, 150–51, 153–58, 161, 167–70, 174, 178–82
Foundation (Asimov) 2–3, 5–6, 8, 14–15, 18, 22, 24, 31–32, 34–36, 38–40, 42, 46, 48–50, 55–56, 58, 65, 67, 70–71, 75, 77–78, 81, 83–84, 90–91, 93–95, 100, 103–4, 109–13, 116–18, 130–36, 139, 144–45, 153–58, 160–61, 166–74, 176–81
Foundation and Earth (Asimov) 2, 5–6, 8, 18, 22, 24, 29, 33–34, 40–41, 43–48, 62–64, 68, 71–74, 77–78, 82–85, 87–88, 91, 93, 97–98, 102, 104, 107–8, 114, 120–21, 123, 129, 135, 139, 160, 162–64, 171, 173–76, 182
Foundation and Empire (Asimov) 2, 5–6, 8, 15–22, 24, 46–47, 51, 57–58, 61–62, 64–65, 68–69, 81–83, 87, 90, 92–95, 98, 100–2, 106–8, 114–17, 122–25, 128–29, 131, 133, 135, 137–39, 141–42, 145–46, 150, 157–58, 160, 166–67, 169, 173–74, 178–82
Foundation Series 1–2, 4–6, 14, 17–18, 22–25, 28; *see also Forward the Foundation*; *Foundation*; *Foundation and Earth*; *Foundation and Empire*; *Foundation's Edge*; *Prelude to Foundation*; *Second Foundation*
Foundation Trilogy 1–3, 5–7, 9, 12, 14–18, 21–22, 25; *see also Foundation*; *Foundation and Empire*; *Second Foundation*
Foundation's Edge (Asimov) 2, 5–6, 8, 16–18, 21–23, 25, 35, 37, 39–40, 47–48, 50–51, 54, 56, 58–60, 64, 66–67, 69, 71–73, 76–78, 81–86, 90–91, 93, 99–102, 107–10, 120, 122, 124–25, 130–35, 138–40, 147–53, 157, 159, 161, 163–64, 167–68, 170–71, 174–76, 178
fractal geometry 6–12, 22, 26–29

Gaia 21–24, 29–30, 83–84
Gaia novels 5–6, 14, 18, 24; *see also Foundation and Earth*; *Foundation's Edge*
"Galley Slave" (Asimov) 1, 42, 73, 90, 94, 102, 111, 122, 129, 147, 159, 161, 165, 171, 178

Index

I, Robot (Asimov), 1, 4–5, 7–8, 24–25, 40, 48–49, 50, 52–53, 59–61, 66, 70, 73, 77, 83, 93, 95–96, 98–100, 104–5, 107, 111–13, 115, 121, 128–30, 136–37, 140, 146–48, 161–62, 164–65, 167–68, 171, 176, 178–81; *see also* "Catch That Rabbit"; "Escape!"; "Evidence"; "The Evitable Conflict"; "Liar!"; "Little Lost Robot"; "Reason"; "Robbie"; "Runaround"

The Laws of Robotics 24–29, 111, 171, 182
"Lenny" (Asimov) 1, 49, 52–53, 102, 111–12, 142, 178
"Liar!" (Asimov) 27–28, 40, 49, 52–53, 95–96, 111
"Little Lost Robot" (Asimov) 28, 48–49, 53, 99–100, 107, 128, 180

"Mirror Image" (Asimov) 2, 4, 43–44, 62–64, 99–100, 137, 149
"My Robots" (Asimov) 27

The Naked Sun (Asimov) 2, 4–5, 8, 24, 31, 41, 43–45, 47, 53, 62–64, 67, 79–81, 88–90, 93, 111–12, 122, 129, 140, 149, 162–63, 171, 173, 176

Pebble in the Sky (Asimov) 2, 4–5, 8, 37–40, 45–46, 51, 54, 56–58, 60, 62–64, 71–73, 76, 78, 82–83, 91–92, 96, 102, 104, 106, 118–19, 121–23, 127–28, 132–33, 136, 139, 141, 145, 152, 158–62, 166, 168–69, 174, 177, 180, 182
Prelude to Foundation (Asimov) 1–2, 5–6, 8, 10–12, 18, 22, 24, 32–33, 40–42, 67–69, 73–74, 77, 82–83, 91, 94–95, 98–99, 104, 108, 112–13, 118–19, 122–24, 126, 131, 141–44, 149–50, 154–56, 160–61, 163, 166–69, 171–72, 174, 176–82
Psychohistory 6, 11–13, 22, 24–27, 29, 139

"Reason" (Asimov) 60–61, 69–70, 77, 125, 136–37, 147–48, 162

"Robbie" (Asimov) 53, 113, 146–48, 167, 180–81
"Robot Dreams" (Asimov) 1, 26–27, 52–53, 74, 142–43
The Robot/Empire/Foundation Metaseries 1, 4–9, 18, 22, 24, 30; *see also* Baley novels; Empire novels; Foundation Series; *I, Robot*; Robot novels
Robot novels 1–2, 4–5, 24–25; *see also The Caves of Steel*; *The Naked Sun*; *Robots and Empire*; *The Robots of Dawn*
Robots and Empire (Asimov) 2, 4–5, 8, 32–36, 41–45, 47–50, 54, 56, 62–65, 69, 71–73, 77, 79–80, 82, 85, 87–90, 92, 95–96, 106–7, 110–11, 114, 116–17, 121, 123, 126, 128–34, 140, 147–48, 152–53, 158, 162–64, 171–72, 180, 182
"Robots I Have Known" (Asimov) 28
The Robots of Dawn (Asimov) 2, 4–5, 24–27, 33–35, 40–45, 50–51, 54, 56, 58, 62–64, 66–67, 75–77, 79–80, 85–90, 92, 95, 98, 102–3, 110, 119–20, 122, 129, 133–35, 139, 146–47, 149, 161–65, 171–72
"Runaround" (Asimov) 27–29, 69–70, 121, 136, 147–48, 164–65, 171

Second Foundation (Asimov) 2, 5–6, 8–9, 17–19, 21–22, 24–25, 36–37, 52, 54–55, 62, 64–65, 69, 73–76, 81, 83, 86, 91–92, 98–102, 107–9, 112, 120, 124–28, 133–36, 138–41, 148–51, 153, 157–58, 166–67, 169, 171–74, 176–77, 182–83
Seldon novels 5–6, 14, 18, 24; *see also Forward the Foundation*; *Prelude to Foundation*
The Stars, Like Dust (Asimov) 2, 4–5, 8, 36–39, 41–42, 48, 60, 71–73, 76, 78–79, 90, 96–97, 100, 105–6, 108, 113–14, 116, 119, 127–28, 136, 138, 141–42, 145–46, 163, 166, 172–73, 177, 179

"Too Bad!" (Asimov) 1, 39, 104, 122, 149, 153

www.ingramcontent.com/pod-product-compliance
Ingram Content Group UK Ltd.
Pitfield, Milton Keynes, MK11 3LW, UK
UKHW042012140426
5217IPUK00015B/1135